Praise for beloved romance author Betty Neels

"Neels is especially good at painting her scenes with choice words, and this adds to the charm of the story."
—*USATODAY.com's Happy Ever After* blog
on *Tulips for Augusta*

"Betty Neels surpasses herself with an excellent storyline, a hearty conflict and pleasing characters."
—*RT Book Reviews* on *The Right Kind of Girl*

"Once again Betty Neels delights readers with a sweet tale in which love conquers all."
—*RT Book Reviews* on *Fate Takes a Hand*

"One of the first Harlequin authors I remember reading. I was completely enthralled by the exotic locales... Her books will always be some of my favorites to re-read."
—*Goodreads* on *A Valentine for Daisy*

"I just love Betty Neels!... If you like a good old-fashioned romance...you can't go wrong with this author."
—*Goodreads* on *Caroline's Waterloo*

Romance readers around the world were sad to note the passing of **Betty Neels** in June 2001. Her career spanned thirty years, and she continued to write into her ninetieth year. To her millions of fans, Betty epitomized the romance writer, and yet she began writing almost by accident. She had retired from nursing, but her inquiring mind still sought stimulation. Her new career was born when she heard a lady in her local library bemoaning the lack of good romance novels. Betty's first book, *Sister Peters in Amsterdam*, was published in 1969, and she eventually completed 134 books. Her novels offer a reassuring warmth that was very much a part of her own personality. She was a wonderful writer, and she is greatly missed. Her spirit and genuine talent live on in all her stories.

BETTY NEELS

Emma's Wedding
& Marrying Mary

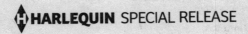

H HARLEQUIN SPECIAL RELEASE

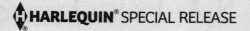 HARLEQUIN® SPECIAL RELEASE

Recycling programs
for this product may
not exist in your area.

ISBN-13: 978-1-335-00842-8

Emma's Wedding & Marrying Mary

Copyright © 2020 by Harlequin Books S.A.

Emma's Wedding
First published in 2001. This edition published in 2020.
Copyright © 2001 by Betty Neels

Marrying Mary
First published in 1995. This edition published in 2020.
Copyright © 1995 by Betty Neels

For questions and comments about the quality of this book,
please contact us at CustomerService@Harlequin.com.

Harlequin Enterprises ULC
22 Adelaide St. West, 40th Floor
Toronto, Ontario M5H 4E3, Canada
www.Harlequin.com

Printed in U.S.A.

CONTENTS

EMMA'S WEDDING

Chapter 1

There were three people in the room: an elderly man with a fringe of white hair surrounding a bald pate and a neat little beard, a lady of uncertain years and once very pretty, her faded good looks marred by a look of unease, and, sitting at the table between them, a girl, a splendid young woman as to shape and size, with carroty hair bunched untidily on top of her head and a face which, while not beautiful or even pretty, was pleasing to look at, with wide grey eyes, a haughty nose and a wide mouth, gently curved.

The elderly man finished speaking, shuffled the papers before him and adjusted his spectacles, and when her mother didn't speak, only sat looking bewildered and helpless, the girl spoke.

'We shall need your advice, Mr Trump. This is a surprise—we had no idea... Father almost never mentioned money matters to either Mother or me, although some weeks before he died…' her voice faltered for a moment '…he told me that he was investing in some scheme which would make a great deal of money, and when I asked him about it he laughed and said it was all rather exciting and I must wait and see.'

Mr Trump said dryly, 'Your father had sufficient funds to live comfortably and leave both your mother and you provided for. He invested a considerable amount of his capital in this new computer company set up by a handful of unscrupulous young men and for a few weeks it made profits, so that your father invested the rest of his capital in it. Inevitably, the whole thing fell apart, and he and a number of the other investors lost every penny. In order to avoid bankruptcy you will need to sell this house, the car, and much of the furniture. You have some good pieces here which should sell well.'

He glanced at her mother and added, 'You do understand what I have told you, Mrs Dawson?'

'We shall be poor.' She gave a little sob. 'There won't be any money. How are we to live?' She looked around her. 'My lovely home—and how am I to go anywhere if we haven't any car? And clothes? I won't be shabby.' She began to cry in real earnest. 'Where shall we live?' And before anyone could speak she added, 'Emma, you must think of something…'

'Try not to get upset, Mother. If this house and everything else sells well enough to pay off what's owing, we can go and live at the cottage in Salcombe. I'll get a job and we shall manage very well.'

Mr Trump nodded his bald head. 'Very sensible. I'm fairly certain that once everything is sold there will be enough to pay everything off and even have a small amount leftover. I imagine it won't be too hard to find work during the summer season at least, and there might even be some small job which you might undertake, Mrs Dawson.'

'A job? Mr Trump, I have never worked in my life and I have no intention of doing so now.' She dissolved into tears again. 'My dear husband would turn in his grave if he could hear you suggest it.'

Mr Trump put his papers in his briefcase. Mrs Dawson he had always considered to be a charming little lady, rather spoilt by her husband but with a gentle, rather helpless manner which appealed to his old-fashioned notions of the weaker sex, but now, seeing the petulant look on her face, he wondered if he had been mistaken. Emma, of course, was an entirely different kettle of fish, being a sensible young woman, full of energy, kind and friendly—and there was some talk of her marrying. Which might solve their difficulties. He made his goodbyes, assured them that he would start at once on the unravelling of their affairs, then went out to his car and drove away.

Emma went out of the rather grand drawing room and crossed the wide hall to the kitchen. It was a large house, handsomely furnished with every mod con Mrs Dawson had expressed a wish to have. There was a daily housekeeper too, and a cheerful little woman who came twice a week to do the rough work.

Emma put on the kettle, laid a tea tray, found biscuits and, since the housekeeper had gone out for her half-day, looked through the cupboards for the cake tin. She and her mother might have been dealt a bitter blow, but tea and a slice of Mrs Tims's walnut cake would still be welcome. For as long as possible, reflected Emma.

Mrs Dawson was still sitting in her chair, dabbing her wet eyes.

She watched Emma pour the tea and hand her a cup. 'How can I possibly eat and drink,' she wanted to know in a tearful voice, 'when our lives are in ruins?'

All the same she accepted a slice of cake.

Emma took a bite. 'We shall have to give Mrs Tims notice. Do you pay her weekly or monthly, Mother?'

Mrs Dawson looked vague. 'I've no idea. Your father never bothered me with that kind of thing. And that woman who comes in to clean—Ethel—what about her?'

'Shall I talk to them both and give them notice? Though they'll expect something extra as Father's death gave them no warning.'

Emma drank some tea and swallowed tears with it. She had loved her father, although they had never been close and the greater part of his paternal affection had been given to her brother James, twenty-three years old and four years her junior. And presently, most unfortunately, backpacking round the world after leaving university with a disappointing degree in science.

They weren't even quite sure where he was at the moment; his last address had been Java, with the prospect of Australia, and even if they had had an address and he'd come home at once she didn't think that he would have been of much help.

He was a dear boy, and she loved him, but her mother and father had spoilt him so that although he was too nice a young man to let it ruin his nature, it had tended to make him easygoing and in no hurry to settle down to a serious career.

He had had a small legacy from their grandmother when she died, and that had been ample to take care of his travels. She thought it unlikely that he would break off his journey, probably arguing that he was on the other side of the world and that Mr Trump would deal with his father's affairs, still under the impression that he had left his mother and sister in comfortable circumstances.

Emma didn't voice these thoughts to her mother but instead settled that lady for a nap and went back to the kitchen to prepare for their supper. Mrs Tims would have left something ready to be cooked and there was nothing much to do. Emma sat down at the table, found pencil and paper, and wrote down everything which would have to be done.

A great deal! And she couldn't hope to do it all herself. Mr Trump would deal with the complicated financial situation, but what about the actual selling of the house and their possessions? And what would they be allowed to keep of those? Mr Trump had mentioned an overdraft at the bank, and money which had been borrowed from friends with the promise that it would be returned to them with handsome profits.

Emma put her head down on the table and cried. But not for long. She wiped her eyes, blew her nose and picked up her pencil once more.

If they were allowed to keep the cottage at least they would have a rent-free home and one which she had always loved, although her mother found the little town of Salcombe lacking in the kind of social life she liked, but it would be cheaper to live there for that very reason. She would find work; during the summer months there was bound to be a job she could do—waitressing, or working in one of the big hotels or a shop. The winter might not be as easy, the little town sank into peace and quiet, but Kingsbridge was only a bus ride away, and that was a bustling small town with plenty of shops and cafés...

Feeling more cheerful, Emma made a list of their own possessions which surely they would be allowed to keep. Anything saleable they must sell, although she thought it was unlikely that her mother would be prepared to part with her jewellery, but they both had expensive clothes— her father had never grudged them money for those—and they would help to swell the kitty.

She got the supper then, thinking that it was a pity that Derek wouldn't be back in England for three more days. They weren't engaged, but for some time now their future together had become a foregone conclusion. Derek was a serious young man and had given her to understand that once he had gained the promotion in the banking firm for which he worked they would marry.

Emma liked him, indeed she would have fallen in love with him and she expected to do that without much difficulty, but although he was devoted to her she had the idea that he didn't intend to show his proper feelings until he proposed. She had been quite content; life wasn't going to be very exciting, but a kind husband who would cherish one, and any children, and give one a comfort- able home should bring her happiness.

She wanted to marry, for she was twenty-seven, but ever since she had left school there had always been a reason why she couldn't leave home, train for something and be independent. She had hoped that when James had left the university she could be free, but when she had put forward her careful plans it had been to discover that he had already arranged to be away for two years at least, and her mother had become quite hysterical at the idea of not having one or other of her children at home with her. And, of course, her father had agreed...

Perhaps her mother would want her to break off with Derek, but she thought not. A son-in-law in comfortable circumstances would solve their difficulties...

During the next three days Emma longed for Derek's return. It seemed that the business of being declared bankrupt entailed a mass of paperwork, with prolonged and bewildering visits from severe-looking men with briefcases. Since her mother declared that she would have nothing to do with any of it, Emma did her best to answer their questions and fill in the forms they offered.

'But I'll not sign anything until Mr Trump has told me that I must,' she told them.

It was all rather unnerving; she would have liked a little time to grieve about her father's death, but there was no chance of that. She went about her household duties while her mother sat staring at nothing and weeping, and Mrs Tims and Ethel worked around the house, grim-faced at the unexpectedness of it all.

Derek came, grave-faced, offered Mrs Dawson quiet condolences and went with Emma to her father's study. But if she had expected a shoulder to cry on she didn't get it. He was gravely concerned for her, and kind, but she knew at once that he would never marry her now. He had an important job in the banking world, and marrying the daughter of a man who had squandered a fortune so recklessly was hardly going to enhance his future.

He listened patiently to her problems, observed that she was fortunate to have a sound man such as Mr Trump to advise her, and told her to be as helpful with 'Authority' as possible.

'I'm afraid there are no mitigating circumstances,' he

told her. 'I looked into the whole affair when I got back today. Don't attempt to contest anything, whatever you do. Hopefully there will be enough money to clear your father's debts once everything is sold.'

Emma sat looking at him—a good-looking man in his thirties, rather solemn in demeanour, who had nice manners, was honest in his dealings, and not given to rashness of any sort. She supposed that it was his work which had driven the warmth from his heart and allowed common sense to replace the urge to help her at all costs and, above all, to comfort her.

'Well,' said Emma in a tight little voice, 'how fortunate it is that you didn't give me a ring, for I don't need to give it back.'

He looked faintly surprised. 'I wasn't aware that we had discussed the future,' he told her.

'There is no need, is there? I haven't got one, have I? And yours matters to you.'

He agreed gravely. 'Indeed it does. I'm glad, Emma, that you are sensible enough to realise that, and I hope that you will too always consider me as a friend. If I can help in any way… If I can help financially?'

'Mr Trump is seeing to the money, but thank you for offering. We shall be able to manage very well once everything is sorted out.'

'Good. I'll call round from time to time and see how things are…'

'We shall be busy packing up—there is no need.' She added in a polite hostess voice, 'Would you like a cup of coffee before you go?'

'No—no, thank you. I'm due at the office in the morning and I've work to do first.'

He wished Mrs Dawson goodbye, and as Emma saw

him to the door he bent to kiss her cheek. 'If ever you should need help or advice…'

'Thank you, Derek,' said Emma. Perhaps she should make a pleasant little farewell speech, but if she uttered another word she would burst into tears.

'How fortunate that you have Derek,' said Mrs Dawson when Emma joined her. 'I'm sure he'll know what's best to be done. A quiet wedding as soon as possible.'

'Derek isn't going to marry me, Mother. It would interfere with his career.'

A remark which started a flood of tears from her mother.

'Emma, I can't believe it. It isn't as if he were a young man with no money or prospects. There's no reason why you shouldn't marry at once.' She added sharply, 'You didn't break it off, did you? Because if you did you're a very stupid girl.'

'No, Mother, it's what Derek wishes.' Emma felt sorry for her mother. She looked so forlorn and pretty, and so in need of someone to make life easy for her as it always had been. 'I'm sorry, but he has got his career to consider, and marrying me wouldn't help him at all.'

'I cannot think what came over your father…'

'Father did it because he wanted us to have everything we could possibly want,' said Emma steadily. 'He never grudged you anything, Mother.'

Mrs Dawson was weeping again. 'And look how he has left us now. It isn't so bad for you, you're young and can go to work, but what about me? My nerves have never allowed me to do anything strenuous and all this worrying has given me a continuous headache. I feel that I am going to be ill.'

'I'm going to make you a milky drink and put a warm

bottle in your bed, Mother. Have a bath, and when you're
ready I'll come up and make sure that you are comfortable.'

'I shall never be comfortable again,' moaned Mrs
Dawson.

She looked like a small woebegone child and Emma
gave her a hug; the bottom had fallen out of her mother's
world and, although life would never be the same again,
she would do all that she could to make the future as
happy as possible.

For a moment she allowed her thoughts to dwell on
her own future. Married to Derek she would have had
a pleasant, secure life: a home to run, children to bring
up, a loving husband and as much of a social life as she
would wish. But now that must be forgotten; she must
make a happy life for her mother, find work, make new
friends. Beyond that she didn't dare to think. Of course
James would come home eventually, but he would plan
his own future, cheerfully taking it for granted that she
would look after their mother, willing to help if he could
but not prepared to let it interfere with his plans.

The house sold quickly, the best of the furniture was
sold, and the delicate china and glass. Most of the table
silver was sold too, and the house, emptied of its contents,
was bleak and unwelcoming. But there was still a great
deal to do; even when Emma had packed the cases of
unsaleable objects—the cheap kitchen china, the saucepans, the bed and table linen that they were allowed to
keep—there were the visits from her parents' friends,
come to commiserate and eager, in a friendly way, for details. Their sympathy was genuine but their offers of help
were vague. Emma and her mother must come and stay

as soon as they were settled in; they would drive down to Salcombe and see them. Such a pretty place, and how fortunate that they had such a charming home to go to…

Emma, ruthlessly weeding out their wardrobes, thought it unlikely that any of their offers would bear fruit.

Mr Trump had done his best, and every debt had been paid, leaving a few hundred in the bank. Her mother would receive a widow's pension, but there was nothing else. Thank heaven, reflected Emma, that it was early in April and a job, any kind of job, shouldn't be too hard to find now that the season would be starting at Salcombe.

They left on a chilly damp morning—a day winter had forgotten and left behind. Emma locked the front door, put the key through the letterbox and got into the elderly Rover they had been allowed to keep until, once at Salcombe, it was to be handed over to the receivers. Her father's Bentley had gone, with everything else.

She didn't look back, for if she had she might have cried and driving through London's traffic didn't allow for tears. Mrs Dawson cried. She cried for most of their long journey, pausing only to accuse Emma of being a hard-hearted girl with no feelings when she suggested that they might stop for coffee.

They reached Salcombe in the late afternoon and, as it always did, the sight of the beautiful estuary with the wide sweep of the sea beyond lifted Emma's spirits. They hadn't been to the cottage for some time but nothing had changed; the little house stood at the end of a row of similar houses, their front gardens opening onto a narrow path along the edge of the water, crowded with small boats and yachts, a few minutes' walk from the main street of the little town, yet isolated in its own peace and quiet.

There was nowhere to park the car, of course. Emma stopped in the narrow street close by and they walked along the path, opened the garden gate and unlocked the door. For years there had been a local woman who had kept an eye on the place. Emma had written to her and now, as they went inside, it was to find the place cleaned and dusted and groceries and milk in the small fridge.

Mrs Dawson paused on the doorstep. 'It's so small,' she said in a hopeless kind of voice, but Emma looked around her with pleasure and relief. Here was home: a small sitting room, with the front door and windows over-looking the garden, a smaller kitchen beyond and then a minute backyard, and, up the narrow staircase, two bed-rooms with a bathroom between them. The furniture was simple but comfortable, the curtains a pretty chintz and there was a small open fireplace.

She put her arm round her mother. 'We'll have a cup of tea and then I'll get the rest of the luggage and see if the pub will let me put the car in their garage until I can hand it over.'

She was tired when she went to bed that night; she had seen to the luggage and the car, lighted a small log fire and made a light supper before seeing her mother to her bed. It had been a long day, she reflected, curled up in her small bedroom, but they were here at last in the cottage, not owing a farthing to anyone and with a little money in the bank. Mr Trump had been an elderly shoulder to lean on, which was more than she could say for Derek. 'Good riddance to bad rubbish,' said Emma aloud.

All the same she had been hurt.

In the morning she went to the pub and persuaded the landlord to let her leave the car there until she could hand it over, and then went into the main street to do the shopping. Her mother had declared herself exhausted after their long drive on the previous day and Emma had left her listlessly unpacking her clothes. Not a very good start to the day, but it was a fine morning and the little town sparkled in the sunshine.

Almost all the shops were open, hopeful of early visitors, and she didn't hurry with her shopping, stopping to look in the elegant windows of the small boutiques, going to the library to enrol for the pair of them, arranging for milk to be delivered, ordering a paper too, and at the same time studying the advertisements in the shop window. There were several likely jobs on offer. She bought chops from the butcher, who remembered her from previous visits, and crossed the road to the greengrocer. He remembered her too, so that she felt quite light-hearted as she made her last purchase in the baker's.

The delicious smell of newly baked bread made her nose quiver. And there were rolls and pasties, currant buns and doughnuts. She was hesitating as to which to buy when someone else came into the shop. She turned round to look and encountered a stare from pale blue eyes so intent that she blushed, annoyed with herself for doing that just because this large man was staring. He was good-looking too, in a rugged kind of way, with a high-bridged nose and a thin mouth. He was wearing an elderly jersey and cords and his hair needed a good brush...

He stopped staring, leaned over her, took two pasties off the counter and waved them at the baker's wife. And now the thin mouth broke into a smile. 'Put it on the bill, Mrs Trott,' he said, and was gone.

Emma, about to ask who he was, sensed that Mrs Trott wasn't going to tell her and prudently held her tongue.

He must live in the town for he had a bill. He didn't look like a fisherman or a farm worker and he wouldn't own a shop, not dressed like that, and besides he didn't look like any of those. He had been rude, staring like that; she had no wish to meet him again but it would be interesting to know just who he was.

She went back to the cottage and found a man waiting impatiently to collect the car and, what with one thing and another, she soon forgot the man at the baker's.

It was imperative to find work but she wasn't going to rush into the first job that was vacant. With a little wangling she thought that she could manage two part-time jobs. They would cease at the end of the summer and even one part-time job might be hard to find after that.

'I must just make hay while the sun shines,' said Emma, and over the next few days scanned the local newspapers. She went from one end of the town to the other, sizing up what was on offer. Waitresses were wanted, an improver was needed at the hairdressers—but what was an improver? Chambermaids at the various hotels, an assistant in an arts and crafts shop, someone to clean holiday cottages between lets, and an educated lady to assist the librarian at the public library on two evenings a week...

It was providential that while out shopping with her mother they were accosted by an elderly lady who greeted them with obvious pleasure.

'Mrs Dawson—and Emma, isn't it? Perhaps you don't remember me. You came to the hotel to play bridge. I live at the hotel now that my husband has died and I'm delighted to see a face I know...' She added eagerly, 'Let's go and have coffee together and a chat. Is your husband with you?'

'I am also a widow—it's Mrs Craig, isn't it? I do re-member now; we had some pleasant afternoons at bridge. My husband died very recently, and Emma and I have come to live here.'

'I'm so very sorry. Of course you would want to get away from Richmond for a time. Perhaps we could meet soon and then arrange a game of bridge later?'

Mrs Dawson brightened. 'That would be delightful...'

'Then you must come and have tea with me sometimes at the hotel.' Mrs Craig added kindly, 'You need to have a few distractions, you know.' She smiled at Emma. 'I'm sure you have several young friends from earlier visits?'

Emma said cheerfully, 'Oh, yes, of course,' and added, 'I've one or two calls to make now, while you have coffee. It is so nice to meet you again, Mrs Craig.' She looked at her mother. 'I'll see you at home, Mother.'

She raced away. The rest of the shopping could wait. Here was the opportunity to go to the library...

The library was at the back of the town, and only a handful of people were wandering round the bookshelves. There were two people behind the desk: one a severe-looking lady with a no-nonsense hair style, her compan-ion a girl with a good deal of blonde hair, fashionably tousled, and with too much make-up on her pretty face. She looked up from the pile of books she was arrang-ing and grinned at Emma as she came to a halt and ad-dressed the severe lady.

'Good morning,' said Emma. 'You are advertising for an assistant for two evenings a week. I should like to apply for the job.'

The severe lady eyed her. She said shortly, 'My name is Miss Johnson. Are you experienced?'

'No, Miss Johnson, but I like books. I have A levels

in English Literature, French, Modern Art and Maths. I am twenty-seven years old and I have lived at home since I left school. I have come here to live with my mother and I need a job.'

'Two sessions a week, six hours, at just under five pounds an hour.' Miss Johnson didn't sound encouraging. 'Five o'clock until eight on Tuesdays and Thursdays. Occasionally extra hours, if there is sickness or one of us is on holiday.' She gave what might be called a lady-like sniff. 'You seem sensible. I don't want some giddy girl leaving at the end of a week…'

'I should like to work here if you will have me,' said Emma. 'You will want references…?'

'Of course, and as soon as possible. If they are satisfactory you can come on a week's trial.'

Emma wrote down Mr Trump's address and phone number and then Dr Jakes's who had known her for years. 'Will you let me know or would you prefer me to call back? We aren't on the phone yet. It's being fitted shortly.'

'You're in rooms or a flat?'

'No, we live at Waterside Cottage, the end one along Victoria Quay.'

Miss Johnson looked slightly less severe. 'You are staying there? Renting the cottage for the summer?'

'No, it belongs to my mother.'

The job, Emma could see, was hers.

She bade Miss Johnson a polite goodbye and went back into the main street; she turned into a narrow lane running uphill, lined by small pretty cottages. The last cottage at the top of the hill was larger than the rest and she knocked on the door.

The woman who answered the door was still young,

slim and tall and dressed a little too fashionably for Salcombe. Her hair was immaculate and so was her make-up.

She looked Emma up and down and said, 'Yes?'

'You are advertising for someone to clean holiday cottages...'

'Come in.' She led Emma into a well-furnished sitting room.

'I doubt if you'd do. It's hard work—Wednesdays and Saturdays, cleaning up the cottages and getting them ready for the next lot. And a fine mess some of them are in, I can tell you. I need someone for those two days. From ten o'clock in the morning and everything ready by four o'clock when the next lot come.'

She waved Emma to a chair. 'Beds, bathroom, loo, Hoovering. Kitchen spotless—and that means cupboards too. You come here and collect the cleaning stuff and bedlinen and hand in the used stuff before you leave. Six hours' work a day, five pounds an hour, and tips if anyone leaves them.'

'For two days?'

'That's what I said. I'll want references. Local, are you? Haven't seen you around. Can't stand the place myself. The cottages belonged to my father and I've taken them over for a year or two. I'm fully booked for the season.'

She crossed one elegantly shod foot over the other. 'Week's notice on either side?'

'I live here,' said Emma, 'and I need a job. I'd like to come if you are satisfied with my references.'

'Please yourself, though I'd be glad to take you on. It isn't a job that appeals to the girls around here.'

It didn't appeal all that much to Emma, but sixty pounds a week did...

She gave her references once more, and was told she'd
be told in two days' time. 'If I take you on you'll need
to be shown round. There's another girl cleans the other
two cottages across the road.'

Emma went home, got the lunch and listened to her
mother's account of her morning with Mrs Craig. 'She
has asked me to go to the hotel one afternoon for a rub-
ber of bridge.' She hesitated. 'They play for money—
quite small stakes...'

'Well,' said Emma, 'you're good at the game, aren't
you? I dare say you won't be out of pocket. Nice to have
found a friend, and I'm sure you'll make more once the
season starts.'

Two days later there was a note in the post. Her references for the cleaning job were satisfactory, she could
begin work on the following Saturday and in the meantime call that morning to be shown her work. It was
signed Dulcie Brooke-Tigh. Emma considered that the
name suited the lady very well.

She went to the library that afternoon and Miss Johnson told her unsmilingly that her references were satisfactory and she could start work on Tuesday. 'A week's
notice and you will be paid each Thursday evening.'

Emma, walking on air, laid out rather more money
than she should have done at the butchers, and on Sunday went to church with her mother and said her prayers
with childlike gratitude.

The cleaning job was going to be hard work. Mrs
Brooke-Tigh, for all her languid appearance, was a hard-
headed businesswoman, intent on making money. There
was enough work for two people in the cottages, but as
long as she could get a girl anxious for the job she wasn't
bothered. She had led Emma round the two cottages she

would be responsible for, told her to start work punctually and then had gone back into her own cottage and shut the door. She didn't like living at Salcombe, but the holiday cottages were money-spinners...

The library was surprisingly full when Emma, punctual to the minute, presented herself at the desk.

Miss Johnson wasted no time on friendly chat. 'Phoebe will show you the shelves, then come back here and I will show you how to stamp the books. If I am busy take that trolley of returned books and put them back on the shelves. And do it carefully; I will not tolerate slovenly work.'

Which wasn't very encouraging, but Phoebe's cheerful wink was friendly. The work wasn't difficult or tiring, and Emma, who loved books, found the three hours had passed almost too quickly. And Miss Johnson, despite her austere goodnight, had not complained.

Emma went back to the cottage to eat a late supper and then sit down to do her sums. Her mother had her pension, of course, and that plus the money from the two jobs would suffice to keep them in tolerable comfort. There wouldn't be much over, but they had the kind of expensive, understated clothes which would last for several years... She explained it all to her mother, who told her rather impatiently to take over their finances. 'I quite realise that I must give up some of my pension, dear, but I suppose I may have enough for the hairdresser and small expenses?'

Emma did some sums in her head and offered a generous slice of the pension—more than she could spare. But her mother's happiness and peace of mind were her first concern; after years of living in comfort, and being

used to having everything she wanted within reason, she
could hardly be expected to adapt easily to their more
frugal way of living.

On Saturday morning she went to the cottages. She
had told her mother that she had two jobs, glossing over
the cleaning and enlarging on the library, and, since Mrs
Dawson was meeting Mrs Craig for coffee, Emma had
said that she would do the shopping and that her mother
wasn't to wait lunch if she wasn't home.

She had known it was going to be hard work and it
was, for the previous week's tenants had made no effort
to leave the cottage tidy, let alone clean. Emma cleaned
and scoured, then Hoovered and made beds and tidied
cupboards, cleaned the cooker and the bath, and at the
end of it was rewarded by Mrs Brooke-Tigh's nod of ap-
proval and, even better than that, the tip she had found
in the bedroom—a small sum, but it swelled the thirty
pounds she was paid as she left.

'Wednesday at ten o'clock,' said Mrs Brooke-Tigh.

Emma walked down the lane with the girl who cleaned
the other two cottages.

'Mean old bag,' said the girl. 'Doesn't even give us a
cup of coffee. Think you'll stay?'

'Oh, yes,' said Emma.

The future, while not rosy, promised security just so
long as people like Mrs Brooke-Tigh needed her services.

When she got home her mother told her that Mrs Craig
had met a friend while they were having their coffee and
they had gone to the little restaurant behind the boutique
and had lunch. 'I was a guest, dear, and I must say I enjoyed myself.' She smiled. 'I seem to be making friends.
You must do the same, dear.'

Emma said, 'Yes, Mother,' and wondered if she would

have time to look for friends. Young women of her own age? Men? The thought crossed her mind that the only person she would like to see again was the man in the baker's shop.

Chapter 2

Emma welcomed the quiet of Sunday. It had been a busy week, with its doubts and worries and the uncertainty of coping with her jobs. But she had managed. There was money in the household purse and she would soon do even better. She went with her mother to church and was glad to see that one or two of the ladies in the congregation smiled their good mornings to her mother. If her mother could settle down and have the social life she had always enjoyed things would be a lot easier. I might even join some kind of evening classes during the winter, thought Emma, and meet people...

She spent Monday cleaning the cottage, shopping and hanging the wash in the little backyard, while her mother went to the library to choose a book. On the way back she had stopped to look at the shops and found a charming little scarf, just what she needed to cheer up her grey dress. 'It was rather more than I wanted to spend, dear,' she explained, 'but exactly what I like, and I get my pension on Thursday...'

The library was half empty when Emma got there on Tuesday evening.

'WI meeting,' said Miss Johnson. 'There will be a rush after seven o'clock.'

She nodded to a trolley loaded with books. 'Get those back onto the shelves as quickly as you can. Phoebe is looking up something for a visitor.'

Sure enough after an hour the library filled up with ladies from the WI, intent on finding something pleasant to read, and Emma, intent on doing her best, was surprised when Miss Johnson sent Phoebe to the doors to put up the 'Closed' sign and usher the dawdlers out.

Emma was on her knees, collecting up some books someone had dropped on the floor, when there was a sudden commotion at the door and the man from the baker's shop strode in.

Miss Johnson looked up. She said severely, 'We are closed, Doctor,' but she smiled as she spoke.

'*Rupert Bear*—have you a copy? The bookshop's closed and small William next door won't go to sleep until he's read to. It must be *Rupert Bear*.' He smiled at Miss Johnson, and Emma, watching from the floor, could see Miss Johnson melting under it.

'Emma, fetch *Rupert Bear* from the last shelf in the children's section.'

As Emma got to her feet he turned and looked at her.

'Well, well,' he said softly, and his stare was just as intent as it had been in the baker's shop.

She found it disturbing, so that when she came back

with the book she said tartly, 'May I have your library ticket?'

'Have I got one? Even if I knew where it was I wouldn't have stopped to get it, not with small William bawling his head off.'

He took the book from her, thanked Miss Johnson and was off.

Emma set the books neatly in their places and hoped that someone would say something. It was Phoebe who spoke.

'The poor man. I bet he's had a busy day, and now he's got to spend his evening reading to a small boy. As though he hadn't enough on his plate...'

Miss Johnson said repressively, 'He is clearly devoted to children. Emma, make a note that the book hasn't been checked out. Dr van Dyke will return it in due course.'

Well, reflected Emma, at least I know who he is. And on the way home, as she and Phoebe walked as far as the main street she asked, 'Is he the only doctor here?'

'Lord, no. There's three of them at the medical practice, and he's not permanent, just taken over from Dr Finn for a few months.'

Why had he stared so, and why had he said, 'Well, well,' in that satisfied voice? wondered Emma, saying goodnight and going back home through the quiet town.

It wouldn't be quiet for much longer. Visitors were beginning to trickle in, most of them coming ashore from their yachts, mingling with those who came regularly early in the season, to walk the coastal paths and spend leisurely days strolling through the town. More restaurants had opened, the ice cream parlour had opened its doors, and the little coastal ferry had begun its regular trips.

Emma was pleased to see that her mother was already starting to enjoy what social life there was. She played bridge regularly with Mrs Craig and her friends, met them for coffee and occasionally did some shopping. But her gentle complaints made it clear that life in a small, off-the-beaten-track town was something she was bravely enduring, and whenever Emma pointed out that there was little chance of them ever leaving the cottage, Mrs Dawson dissolved into gentle tears.

'You should have married Derek,' she said tearfully. 'We could have lived comfortably at his house. It was large enough for me to have had my own apartment...'

A remark Emma found hard to answer.

As for Emma, she hadn't much time to repine; there was the cottage to clean, the washing and the ironing, all the small household chores which she had never had to do... At first her mother had said that she would do all the shopping, but, being unused to doing this on an economical scale, it had proved quite disastrous to the household purse, so Emma had added that to her other chores. Not that she minded. She was soon on friendly terms with the shopkeepers and there was a certain satisfaction in buying groceries with a strict eye on economy instead of lifting the phone and giving the order Mrs Dawson had penned each week with a serene disregard for expense...

And Miss Johnson had unbent very slightly, pleased to find that Emma really enjoyed her work at the library. She had even had a chat about her own taste in books, deploring the lack of interest in most of the borrowers for what she called a 'good class of book'. As for Phoebe, who did her work in a cheerful slapdash fashion, Emma liked her and listened sympathetically whenever Phoebe found the time to tell her of her numerous boyfriends.

But Mrs Brooke-Tigh didn't unbend. Emma was doing a menial's job, therefore she was treated as such; she checked the cottages with an eagle eye but beyond a distant nod had nothing to say. Emma didn't mind the cleaning but she did not like Mrs Brooke-Tigh; once the season was over she would look around for another job, something where she might meet friendly people. In a bar? she wondered, having very little idea of what that would be like. But at least there would be people and she might meet someone.

Did Dr van Dyke go into pubs? she wondered. Probably not. He wouldn't have time. She thought about him, rather wistfully, from time to time, when she was tired and lonely for the company of someone her own age. The only way she would get to know him was to get ill. And she never got ill...

Spring was sliding into early summer; at the weekends the narrow streets were filled by visiting yachtsmen and family parties driving down for a breath of sea air and a meal at one of the pubs. And with them, one Sunday, came Derek.

Mrs Dawson was going out to lunch with one of her bridge friends, persuaded that Emma didn't mind being on her own. 'We will go to evensong together,' said her mother, 'but it is such a treat to have luncheon with people I like, dear, and I knew you wouldn't mind.'

She peered at herself in the mirror. 'Is this hat all right? I really need some new clothes.'

'You look very smart, Mother, and the hat's just right. Have a lovely lunch. I'll have tea ready around four o'clock.'

Alone, Emma went into the tiny courtyard beyond the kitchen and saw to the tubs of tulips and the wallflowers growing against the wall. She would have an early lunch and go for a walk—a long walk. North Sands, perhaps, and if the little kiosk by the beach there was open she would have a cup of coffee. She went back into the cottage as someone banged the door knocker.

Derek stood there, dressed very correctly in a blazer and cords, Italian silk tie and beautifully polished shoes. For a split second Emma had a vivid mental picture of an elderly sweater and uncombed hair.

'What on earth are you doing here?' she wanted to know with a regrettable lack of delight.

Derek gave her a kind smile. He was a worthy young man with pleasant manners and had become accustomed to being liked and respected.

He said now, 'I've surprised you…'

'Indeed you have.' Emma added reluctantly. 'You'd better come in.'

Derek looked around him. 'A nice little place—rather different from Richmond, though. Has your mother settled down?'

'Yes. Why are you here?'

'I wanted to see you, Emma. To talk. If you would change into a dress we could have lunch—I'm staying at the other end of the town.'

'We can talk here. I'll make cheese sandwiches…'

'My dear girl, you deserve more than a cheese sandwich. We can talk over lunch at the hotel.'

'What about?'

'Something which will please you…'

Perhaps something they hadn't known anything about had been salvaged from her father's estate… She said slowly, 'Very well. You'll have to wait while I change, though, and I must be back before four o'clock. Mother's out to lunch.'

While she changed out of trousers and a cotton top into something suitable to accompany Derek's elegance, she wondered what he had come to tell her. Mr Trump had hinted when they had left their home that eventually there might be a little more money. Perhaps Derek had brought it with him.

When she went downstairs he was standing by the window, watching the people strolling along the path.

'Of course you can't possibly stay here. This poky little place—nothing to do all day.'

She didn't bother to answer him, and he said impatiently, 'We shall have to walk; I left the car at the hotel.'

They walked, saying little. 'I can't think why you can't tell me whatever it is at once,' said Emma.

'In good time.' They got out of the road onto the narrow pavement to allow a car to creep past. Dr van Dyke was sitting in it. If he saw her he gave no sign.

The hotel was full. They had drinks in the bar and were given a table overlooking the estuary, but Derek ignored the magnificent view while he aired his knowledge with the wine waiter.

I should be enjoying myself, reflected Emma, and I'm not.

Derek talked about his work, mutual friends she had known, the new owner of her old home.

Emma polished off the last of her trifle. 'Are you staying here on holiday?'

'No, I must return tomorrow.'

'Then you'd better tell me whatever it is.' She glanced at the clock. 'It's half past two...'

He gave a little laugh. 'Can't get rid of me soon enough, Emma?'

He put his hand over hers on the table. 'Dear Emma, I have given much thought to this. The scandal of your father's bankruptcy has died down; there are no debts, no need for people to rake over cold ashes. There is no likelihood of it hindering my career. I have come to ask you to marry me. I know you have no money and a difficult social position, but I flatter myself that I can provide both of these for my wife. In a few years the whole unfortunate matter will be forgotten. I have the deepest regard for you and you will, I know, make me an excellent wife.'

Emma had listened to this speech without moving or uttering a sound. She was so angry that she felt as though she would explode or burst into flames. She got to her feet, a well brought up young woman who had been reared to good manners and politeness whatever the circumstances.

'Get stuffed,' said Emma, and walked out of the restaurant, through the bar and swing doors and into the car park.

She was white with rage and shaking, and heedless of where she was walking. Which was why she bumped into Dr van Dyke's massive chest.

She stared up into his placid face. 'The worm, the miserable rat,' she raged. 'Him and his precious career…'

The doctor said soothingly, 'This rat, is he still in the hotel? You don't wish to meet him again?'

'If I were a man I'd knock him down…' She sniffed and gulped and two tears slid down her cheeks.

'Then perhaps it would be a good idea if you were to sit

in my car for a time—in case he comes looking for you. And, if you would like to, tell me what has upset you.'

He took her arm and walked her to the car. He popped her inside and got in beside her. 'Have a good cry if you want to, and then I'll drive you home.'

He gave her a large handkerchief and sat patiently while she sniffed and snuffled and presently blew her nose and mopped her face. He didn't look at her, he was watching a man—presumably the rat—walking up and down the car park, looking around him. Presently he went back into the hotel and the doctor said, 'He's a snappy dresser, your rat.'

She sat up straight. 'He's gone? He didn't see me?'

'No.' The doctor settled back comfortably. 'What has he done to upset you? It must have been something very upsetting to cause you to leave Sunday lunch at this hotel.'

'I'd finished,' said Emma, 'and it's kind of you to ask but it's—it's…'

'None of my business. Quite right, it isn't. I'll drive you home. Where do you live?'

'The end cottage along Victoria Quay. But I can walk. It is at the end of Main Street and you can't drive there.'

He didn't answer but backed the car and turned and went out of the car park and drove up the narrow road to the back of the town. It was a very long way round and he had to park by the pub.

As he stopped Emma said, 'Thank you. I hope I haven't spoilt your afternoon.'

It would hardly do to tell her that he was enjoying every minute of it. 'I'll walk along with you, just in case the rat has got there first.'

'Do you think he has? I mean, I don't suppose he'll

want to see me again.' She sniffed. 'I certainly don't want to see him.'

The doctor got out of the car and opened her door. It was a splendid car, she noticed, a dark blue Rolls-Royce, taking up almost all the space before the pub.

'You have a nice car,' said Emma, feeling that she owed him something more than thanks. And then blushed because it had been a silly thing to say. Walking beside him, she reflected that although she had wanted to meet him she could have wished for other circumstances.

Her mother wasn't home and Emma heaved a sigh of relief. Explaining to her mother would be better done later on.

The doctor took the key from her and opened the door, then stood looking at her. Mindful of her manners she asked, 'Would you like a cup of tea? Or perhaps you want to go back to the hotel—someone waiting for you...?'

She was beginning to realise that he never answered a question unless he wanted to, and when he said quietly that he would like a cup of tea she led the way into the cottage.

'Do sit down,' said Emma. 'I'll put the kettle on.' And at the same time run a comb through her mop of hair and make sure that her face didn't look too frightful...

It was tear-stained and pale and in need of powder and lipstick, but that couldn't be helped. She put the kettle on, laid a tray, found the cake tin and made the tea. When she went back into the sitting room he was standing in front of a watercolour of her old home.

'Your home?' he wanted to know.

'Until a month or so ago. Do you take milk and sugar?'

He sat down and took the cup and saucer she was offering him. 'Do you want to talk about the—er—rat?

None of my business, of course, but doctors are the next best thing to priests when one wishes to give vent to strong feelings.'

Emma offered cake. 'You have been very kind, and I'm so grateful. But there's nothing—that is, he'll go back to London and I can forget him.'

'Of course. Do you enjoy your work at the library?'

She was instantly and unreasonably disappointed that he hadn't shown more interest or concern. She said stiffly, 'Yes, very much. Miss Johnson tells me that you don't live here, that you are filling in for another doctor?'

'Yes, I shall be sorry to leave…'

'Not yet?'

His heavy-lidded eyes gleamed. 'No, no. I'm looking forward to the summer here.' He put down his cup and saucer. 'Thank you for the tea. If you're sure there is nothing more I can do for you, I'll be off.'

Well, he had no reason to stay, thought Emma. She was hardly scintillating company. Probably there was someone—a girl—waiting impatiently at the hotel for him.

'I hope I haven't hindered you.'

'Not in the least.'

She stood in the doorway watching him walking away, back to his car. He must think her a tiresome hysterical woman, because that was how she had behaved. And all the fault of Derek. She swallowed rage at the thought of him and went back to clear away the tea tray and lay it anew for her mother.

Mrs Dawson had had a pleasant day; she began to tell Emma about it as she came into the cottage, and it wasn't until she had had her tea and paused for breath that she noticed Emma's puffy lids and lightly pink nose.

'Emma, you've been crying. Whatever for? You never cry. You're not ill?'

'Derek came,' said Emma.

Before she could utter another word her mother cried, 'There—I knew he would. He's changed his mind, he wants to marry you—splendid; we can leave here and go back to Richmond...'

'I would not marry Derek if he was the last man on earth,' said Emma roundly. 'He said things—most unkind things—about Father...'

'You never refused him?'

'Yes, I did. He took me to lunch and I left him at the table. I met one of the doctors from the health centre and he brought me home. Derek is a rat and a worm, and if he comes here again I shall throw something at him.'

'You must be out of your mind, Emma. Your future— our future—thrown away for no reason at all. Even if Derek upset you by speaking unkindly of your father, I'm sure he had no intention of wounding you.'

'I'm not going to marry Derek, Mother, and I hope I never set eyes on him again.'

And Emma, usually soft-hearted over her mother's whims and wishes, wouldn't discuss it any more, despite that lady's tears and gentle complaints that the miserable life she was forced to lead would send her to an early grave.

She declared that she had a headache when they got back from evensong, and retired to bed with a supper tray and a hot water bottle.

Emma pottered about downstairs, wondering if she was being selfish and ungrateful. But, even if she were, Derek was still a worm and she couldn't think how she had ever thought of marrying him.

Mrs Dawson maintained her gentle air of patient suffering for the rest of the following week, until Emma left the house on Saturday morning to clean the cottage. The week's tenants had had a large family of children and she welcomed the prospect of hard work. As indeed it was; the little place looked as though it had been hit by a cyclone. It would take all her time to get it pristine for the next family.

She set to with a will and was in the kitchen, giving everything a final wipe-down, when the cottage door opened and Mrs Brooke-Tigh came in, and with her Dr van Dyke and a pretty woman of about Emma's own age.

Mrs Brooke-Tigh ignored her. 'You're so lucky,' she declared loudly, 'that I had this last-minute cancellation. Take a quick look round and see if it will suit. The next party are due here in half an hour but the girl's almost finished.'

'The girl', scarlet-faced, had turned her back but then had to turn round again. 'Miss Dawson,' said Dr van Dyke, 'what a pleasant surprise. This is my sister, who plans to come for a week with her children.'

He turned to the woman beside him. 'Wibeke, this is Emma Dawson; she lives here.'

Emma wiped a soapy hand on her pinny and shook hands, wishing herself anywhere else but there, and listened to Wibeke saying how pleased she was to meet her while Mrs Brooke-Tigh, at a loss for words for once, tapped an impatient foot.

Presently she led them away to see round the cottage, and when they were on the point of leaving Mrs Brooke-Tigh said loudly, 'I'll be back presently to pay you, Emma. Leave the cleaning things at my back door as you go.'

The perfect finish for a beastly week, thought Emma, grinding her splendid teeth.

And Mrs Brooke-Tigh hardly improved matters when she paid Emma.

'It doesn't do to be too familiar with the tenants,' she pointed out. 'I hardly think it necessary to tell you that. Don't be late on Wednesday.'

Emma, who was never late, bade her good afternoon in a spine-chilling voice and went home.

It would have been very satisfying to have tossed the bucket and mop at Mrs Brooke-Tigh and never returned, but with the bucket and mop there would have gone sixty pounds, not forgetting the tips left on the dressing table. She would have to put up with Mrs Brooke-Tigh until the season ended, and in the meantime she would keep her ears open for another job. That might mean going to Kingsbridge every day, since so many of the shops and hotels closed for the winter at Salcombe.

Too soon to start worrying, Emma told herself as she laid out some of the sixty pounds on a chicken for Sunday lunch and one of the rich creamy cakes from the patisserie which her mother enjoyed.

To make up for her horrid Saturday, Sunday was nice, warm and sunny so that she was able to wear a jersey dress, slightly out of date but elegant, and of a pleasing shade of blue. After matins, while her mother chatted with friends, a pleasant young man with an engaging smile introduced himself as Mrs Craig's son.

'Here for a few days,' he told her, and, 'I don't know a soul. Do take pity on me and show me round.'

He was friendly and she readily agreed. 'Though I have part time jobs...'

'When are you free? What about tomorrow morning?'

'I must do the shopping…'

'Splendid, I'll come with you and carry the basket. We could have coffee. Where shall I meet you?'

'At the bakery at the bottom of Main Street, about ten o'clock?'

'Right, I'll look forward to that. The name's Brian, by the way.'

'Emma,' said Emma. 'Your mother is waiting and so's mine.'

'Such a nice boy,' said her mother over lunch, and added, 'He is twenty-three, just qualified as a solicitor. He's rather young, of course…' She caught Emma's eye. 'It is a great pity that you sent Derek away.'

Emma quite liked shopping, and she enjoyed it even more with Brian to carry her basket and talk light-heartedly about anything which caught his eye. They lingered over coffee and then went back through the town to collect sausages from the butcher. His shop was next to one of the restaurants in the town and Brian paused outside it.

'This looks worth a visit. Have dinner with me one evening, Emma?'

'Not on Tuesday or Thursday; I work at the library.'

'Wednesday? Shall we meet here, inside, at half past seven.'

'I'd like that, thank you.' She smiled at him. 'Thank you for the coffee; I've enjoyed my morning.'

Miss Johnson was grumpy on Tuesday evening and Mrs Brooke-Tigh was more than usually high-handed the following day. She couldn't find fault with Emma's work, but somehow she managed to give the impression that it wasn't satisfactory. Which made the prospect of an evening out with Brian very inviting. Emma put on the jersey dress once more and went along to the restaurant.

Brian was waiting for her, obviously glad to see her, and sat her down at the small table, ordering drinks.

In reply to her enquiry as to what he thought of the town he smiled wryly. 'It's a charming little place, but after London's bright lights... What do you do with yourself all day long?'

'Me? Well, there's the library and the shopping, and all the chores, and we're beginning to know more people now.'

'You don't get bored? My mother likes living here; it's a splendid place for elderly widows: nice hotels, bridge, coffee, reading a good book in the sun, gossiping—but you are rather young for that.'

'I've been coming here ever since I was a small girl. It's a kind of a second home, although most of the people I knew have left the town. But I'm quite content.'

They went to their table and ate lobster and a complicated ice cream pudding, and finished a bottle of white wine between them, lingering over their coffee until Emma said, 'I really must go home. Mother insisted that she would wait up for me and she sleeps badly.'

'I'm going back on Friday. But I'm told there's a good pub at Hope Cove. Will you have lunch with me there? I'll pick you up around twelve-thirty?'

'Thank you, that would be nice. If you like walking we could go along the beach if the tide's out.'

'Splendid. I'll walk you back.'

They parted at the cottage door in a friendly fashion, though Emma was aware that he only sought her company because he was bored and didn't know anyone else...

Her mother was in her dressing gown, eager for an account of her evening.

'You'll go out with him again if he asks you?' she enquired eagerly.

'I'm having lunch with him on Friday.' Emma yawned and kicked off her best shoes. 'He's going back to London; I think he is bored here.'

'Mrs Craig was telling me that she wishes he would settle down...'

'Well, he won't here; that's a certainty.' Emma kissed her mother goodnight and went to bed, aware that her mother had hoped for more than a casual friendship with Brian.

He is still a boy, thought Emma sleepily, and allowed her thoughts to turn to Dr van Dyke who, she suspected, was very much a man.

Miss Johnson was still grumpy on Thursday evening, but since it was pay day Emma forgave her. Besides, she was kept busy by people wanting books for the weekend. She felt quite light-hearted as she went home, her wages in her purse, planning something tasty for the weekend which wouldn't make too large a hole in the housekeeping.

Friday was warm and sunny, and she was out early to do the weekend shopping for there would be no time on Saturday. Her mother was going out to lunch with one of her new-found friends and Emma raced around, getting everything ready for cooking the supper and, just in case Brian wanted to come back for tea, she laid a tea tray.

He came promptly and they walked through the town to the car park. He drove up the road bordering the estuary onto the main road and then turned off to Hope Cove. The road was narrow now, running through fields, with a glimpse of the sea. When they reached the tiny village and parked by the pub there were already a number of cars there.

The pub was dark and oak-beamed and low-ceilinged inside, and already quite full.

Brian looked around him. 'I like this place—full of atmosphere and plenty of life. What shall we eat?'

They had crab sandwiches, and he had a beer and Emma a glass of white wine, and since there was no hurry they sat over the food while he told her of his work.

'Of course I could never leave London,' he told her. 'I've a flat overlooking the river and any number of friends and a good job. I shall have to come and see Mother from time to time, but a week is about as much as I can stand.' He added, 'Don't you want to escape, Emma?'

'Me? Where to?'

'Mother told me that you lived in Richmond. You must have had friends…'

'My father went bankrupt,' she said quietly. 'Yes, we had friends—fair-weather friends. And we're happy here. Mother has made several new friends, so she goes out quite a lot, and I'm happy.' She went on, 'If you've finished, shall we walk along the cliff path for a while? The view is lovely…'

She hadn't been quite truthful, she reflected, but she sensed that Brian was a young man who didn't like to be made uneasy. He would go back to his flat and his friends, assuring himself that her life was just what she wanted.

They drove back to Salcombe presently, parked the car at the hotel and walked back through the town.

Outside the bakery Emma stopped. 'Don't come any

further,' she suggested. 'If you are going back today I
expect you want to see your mother before you go. I enjoyed lunch; Hope Cove is a delightful little place. I hope
you have a good journey back home.'

'I'll leave within the hour; it's quite a long trip. I'll be
glad to get back. Life's a bit slow here, isn't it? I wish we
could have seen more of each other, but I expect you'll
still be here if and when I come again.'

'Oh, I expect so.' She offered a hand and he took it
and kissed her cheek.

Dr van Dyke, coming round the corner, stopped short,
wished them a cheerful hello and gave Emma a look to
send the colour into her cheeks. It said all too clearly
that she hadn't wasted much time in finding someone to
take Derek's place.

He went into the baker's, and she bade a final hasty
goodbye to Brian and almost ran to the cottage. The doctor would think... She didn't go too deeply into what he
would think; she hoped that she wouldn't see him again
for a very long time.

It was a brilliant morning on Saturday, and already
warm when she got to Mrs Brooke-Tigh's house, collected her cleaning brushes and cloths and started on
her chores. From a bedroom window she watched Mrs
Brooke-Tigh go down the lane, swinging her beach bag.
On Saturday mornings she went to the hotel at the other
end of the town, which had a swimming pool and a delightful terrace where one could laze for hours. The moment she was out of sight the girl in the other cottage
crossed over and came upstairs.

'Thought I'd let you know I've given in my notice.
She's furious; she'll never get anyone by Wednesday.

Wouldn't hurt her to do a bit of housework herself. Mind she doesn't expect you to take on any more work.'

Emma was stripping beds. 'I don't see how she can...'

'She'll think of something. I'd better get on, I suppose. Bye.'

Mrs Brooke-Tigh came back earlier than usual; Emma was setting the tea tray ready for the next tenants when she walked in.

'That girl's leaving,' she told Emma without preamble. 'She never was much good but at least she was a pair of hands. I'll never get anyone else at such short notice. We will have to manage as best we can. I shall notify the next two weeks' tenants that they can't come in until six o'clock. If you come at nine o'clock and work until six you can do both cottages. I'll pay you another fifteen pounds a day—thirty pounds a week more.'

Emma didn't answer at once. The money would be useful... 'I'm willing to do that for the next week and, if I must, the second week. But no longer than that.'

Mrs Brooke-Tigh sniffed. 'I should have thought that you would have jumped at the chance of more money.' She would have said more, but the look Emma gave her left the words dying on her tongue. Instead she said ungraciously, 'Well, all right, I'll agree to that.' She turned to go. 'Bring your stuff over and I'll pay you.'

There was a car outside the door as she left. It appeared to be full of small children, and a friendly young woman, the one who had been with the doctor, got out. 'I say, hello, how nice to meet you again. We're here for a week so we must get to know each other.' She smiled. 'Where's that woman who runs the place?'

'I'll fetch her,' said Emma, 'and I'd love to see you again.'

Chapter 3

It was quite late in the evening when the phone rang. 'It's me, Wibeke Wolff. There wasn't time to talk so I got that woman to give me your phone number. I do know who you are, Roele told me, so please forgive me for ringing you up. I don't know anyone here. Roele's only free occasionally, and I wondered if you would show me the best places to take the children. A beach where they can be safe in the water? If you would like, could we go somewhere tomorrow? I'll get a picnic organised. This is awful cheek...'

'I'd love a picnic,' said Emma. 'There are some lovely beaches but we don't need to go far tomorrow; there's South Sands only a few minutes in a car. Would that do for a start?'

'It sounds ideal. You're sure you don't mind?'

'No, of course not. Where shall I meet you?'

'Here at this cottage? About ten o'clock? I thought we might come back about three o'clock. You're sure I'm not spoiling your day?'

'No, I'm looking forward to it. And I'll be there in the morning.'

'Who was that, Emma?' Her mother looked hopeful. 'Someone you have met taking you out for lunch?'

'A picnic. Mrs Wibeke Wolff with three children; we're having a picnic lunch at South Sands tomorrow.'

'Oh, well, I suppose it's a change for you. I shall be out in the afternoon; I'll make a sandwich or something for my lunch.'

Emma took this remark for what it was worth. Her mother had no intention of doing any such thing. She said cheerfully, 'I'll leave lunch all ready for you, Mother, and cook supper after we've been to church. Unless you want to go to Matins?'

'You know I need my rest in the morning. Just bring me a cup of tea and I'll manage my own breakfast.'

'If you want to,' said Emma briskly. 'There'll be breakfast as usual in the morning, but if you would rather get up later and cook something?'

'No, no, I'll come down in my dressing gown. I don't have much strength in the morning, but then of course I have always been delicate.'

Emma, her head full of the morrow's picnic, wasn't listening.

Sunday was another glorious morning. Emma got into a cotton dress and sandals, found a straw hat and a swimsuit, got breakfast for her gently complaining parent and made her way through the still quiet streets to the holiday cottages.

Wibeke was loading the car and waved a greeting. As

Emma reached her she said, 'I've got the children inside. Everyone here seems to be asleep and they're noisy.'

Emma glanced at Mrs Brooke-Tigh's house. There was no sign of life there and the curtains were still drawn. A good thing, since she didn't approve of the cleaners mixing with the tenants. Emma said, 'Hello, it's going to be a warm day; the beach will be pretty crowded.'

'The children will love that.' Wibeke opened the door and they piled out. 'Hetty, George and Rosie,' said Wibeke as Emma shook hands with them. They were three small excited kids, bursting with impatience to get their day on the beach started. Without waste of time they crowded into the back of the car and, with Emma beside her, Wibeke drove through the town and along the coast road. It was a short drive.

'It's really only a short walk away,' said Emma as they began the business of parking the car and unloading the children and picnic basket, the buckets and spades, the swimsuits...

The beach was full but not crowded. They settled against some rocks and got into their swimsuits, and Wibeke and the children raced to the water's edge while Emma guarded their belongings. It was pleasant sitting there, for the sun was warm but not yet hot enough to be uncomfortable, and there was no one near by. This, she reflected, was the first day out she had had since they'd come to Salcombe. She didn't count Derek or Brian, for she hadn't been at ease with either of them, but Wibeke and the children were friendly and undemanding; she had only just met them and yet she felt that she had known Wibeke for years. Of course they would all be gone in a week, but still she would have pleasant memories...

They came trooping back and Wibeke said, 'It's your

turn now. A pity we can't all go together. Do you suppose we might? There's no one very close and we could see our belongings easily...'

'Let's wait and see if the beach fills up.'

The water was chilly, but within seconds Emma was swimming strongly away from the beach and then idling on her back until the thought of Wibeke coping with three small children sent her back again.

Time passed, as it always did when one was happy, far too quickly. They built sandcastles, dug holes and filled them with buckets of water, and went swimming again. This time Wibeke stayed on the beach.

Wibeke was peering into the picnic basket when Dr van Dyke joined her.

'Roele, how lovely. Have you come to lunch? You're wearing all the wrong clothes.'

'I've been to see a patient and I've another call to make; no one is going to take advice from a man in swimming trunks.' He was watching the children and Emma prancing around at the water's edge, her magnificent shape enhanced by her simple swimsuit, her bright hair tied up untidily on the top of her head.

'She's rather gorgeous, isn't she?' Wibeke peeped at her brother. 'She should be out in the fashionable world, with a string of boyfriends and lovely clothes.'

'Never.'

The doctor spoke so emphatically that she stared at him, and then smiled.

'Why, Roele...'

But by then the bathing party were within a few feet of them, and while the children rushed at their uncle Emma hung back, taken by surprise, feeling suddenly shy.

'Hello,' said the doctor easily. 'I see you've been

landed with these tiresome brats—sandcastles and looking for crabs and digging holes—you'll be exhausted.
Don't let them bully you.' He got up, the children cling-
ing to him. 'I must go—have a lovely day and don't get
too much sun.'

He hadn't really looked at her, she reflected, just a
casual smile and a wave as he went. She had been silly
to feel shy.

By mid-afternoon the children were tired, and they left
the now crowded beach and drove back to the cottage.

'Come in and have a cup of tea,' begged Wibeke, but
Emma shook her head.

'It's been a lovely day but I really must go home. If you
would like me to babysit one evening I'll do that gladly.
It'll give you a change to go out if you want to.'

'Would you really? That would be great. What are you
doing tomorrow?'

'Shopping, washing, ironing, household chores—but
would you all like to come to tea? We're right by the
water and there's lots for the children to see.'

'We'd like that. Where exactly do you live?'

Emma told her, bade the sleepy children goodbye,
and went home.

Her mother was there, complaining in her gentle voice
that it had been far too warm at the hotel, where she had
had tea with Mrs Craig. 'I'm not sure that I have the energy to go to evensong.'

'You'll feel better when I've made another cup of
tea—China, with a slice of lemon.'

'You enjoyed your day?' asked her mother.

'Very much. The sea's a bit chilly but it was lovely to
swim… I've invited Mrs Wolff and the children to tea
tomorrow. You might enjoy meeting them.'

'Small children? Emma, dear, you know how quickly I get a headache if there's too much noise, and children are so noisy.'

'You'd like Wibeke—Mrs Wolff...'

'Shall I? How did you meet?'

Emma had glossed over her second job; her mother would have been horrified to know that she was doing someone else's housework. 'Oh,' she said vaguely, 'she is staying for a week in a rented cottage.'

There was no need to say more for her mother had lost interest.

As it turned out, the tea party was a success. Wibeke was a lively talker, full of the light-hearted gossip Mrs Dawson enjoyed, and willing to discuss the latest fashions, the newest plays and films, who was marrying whom and who was getting divorced. When she and the children had gone, Mrs Dawson pronounced her to be a very nice young woman.

'Obviously married well and leading a pleasant social life.' She looked reproachfully at Emma as she spoke. 'Just as you would have if you hadn't been so foolish about Derek.' And when Emma didn't reply she added, 'I must say the children were quiet.'

Well, of course they were, reflected Emma, who had made it her business to keep them occupied—first with a good tea and then with a visit to her bedroom, where they had been allowed to open cupboards and drawers, try on her hats and shoes while George took the books from her bookshelf and piled them in neat heaps. For a three-year-old he was a bright child, so she had hugged him and told him that he was a clever boy, and that had led to hugs for the little girls, too. She felt a stab of envy of Wibeke...

* * *

The doctor called on his sister in the late evening.

She gave him a drink and sat down opposite him in the little living room.

'We all went to Emma's cottage and had tea. Have you met her mother? Darling, she's a ball and chain round Emma's neck. Charming, small and dainty and wistful, harping on about having to live here after an obviously comfortable life at Richmond. Told me that Emma had chosen to reject some man or other who wanted to marry her.'

The doctor smiled. 'Ah, yes, the rat…'

Wibeke sat up. 'You know about him? Have you met him?'

'I happened to be handy at the time. He would never have done for Emma.'

'Perhaps she will meet a man here, though she doesn't have much of a social life. Not that she says much; it's what she doesn't say…'

'Quite. Is Harry coming down on Saturday to see you back home?'

This was a change of conversation not to be ignored. 'Yes, bless him. He'll take George and most of the luggage, and I'll have the girls. We plan to leave quite early.' She peeped at the doctor. 'Before Emma starts her cleaning.'

And if she had expected an answer to that, she didn't get it.

When Emma got to the cottages in the morning there was a good deal of bustle. The children, reluctant to go, were being stowed into their mother's car, and Wibeke was fastening George into his seat behind his father, who was packing in the luggage.

'We're off,' cried Wibeke as soon as she saw Emma. 'This is Harry. Come and say hello and goodbye!'

Which Emma did, uncaring of the fact that she would be late starting her day's cleaning and sorry to see them go. She had liked Wibeke and Wibeke had liked her; they could have been friends…

The little lane seemed very quiet when they had driven away, as Emma fetched her bucket and brushes and started work.

It was a scramble to be finished by six o'clock, and the second lot of tenants drove up as she closed the door. She had managed to get one cottage ready in time for the early arrival of its occupants, but she told herself that, despite the extra money, one more week of doing two persons' work was all she intended to do.

She told Mrs Brooke-Tigh that when she stowed away her cleaning things.

'You young women are all the same,' said Mrs Brooke-Tigh nastily. 'Do as little as you can get away with for as much as possible.'

'Well,' said Emma sweetly, 'if you cleaned two of the cottages you would only need to find one young woman.'

Mrs Brooke-Tigh gave her a look of horrified indignation. Emma didn't give her a chance to reply but wished her good evening and went home. She was tired and, not only that, she was dispirited; the future, as far as she could see, was uninviting. The pleasant hours she had spent with Wibeke and the children had made that clear.

As though that wasn't bad enough, she was met by her mother's excited admission that she had seen the most charming dress at the boutique. 'Such a sweet colour, palest blue—you know how that suits me, dear—I just had to have it. I've not had anything new for months. When your dear father was alive he never grudged me anything.'

Emma took off her shoes from her aching feet. 'Mother, Father had money; we haven't—only just enough to keep us going. How much was the dress?'

Her mother pouted. 'I knew you'd make a fuss.' She began to weep tears of self-pity. 'And to think that everything could have been so different if only you hadn't sent Derek away.'

Too tired to argue, Emma went to the kitchen to start the supper, and while she cooked it she drank a mug of very strong tea—a bottle of brandy would have been nice, or champagne. In fact anything which would drown her feeling of frustration. Something would have to be done, but what? Her mother had made up her mind to be unhappy at Salcombe; she had always taken it for granted that anything she wanted she could have and she had made no attempt to understand that that was no longer possible. If only something would happen...

She was coming out of the bakery on Monday morning when she met Dr van Dyke going in. He wasted no time on polite greetings. 'The very person I wanted to see. Wait while I get my pasties.'

Outside the shop, Emma asked, 'Why do you fetch pasties? Haven't you got a housekeeper or someone to look after you?'

'Yes, yes, of course I have, but when I have a visit at one of the outlying farms I take my lunch with me. Don't waste time asking silly questions. One of my partners is unexpectedly short of a receptionist and general dogsbody. No time to go to an agency or advertise. He's a bit desperate. Would you care to take on the job, Monday to Friday, until he can get things sorted out? Half past eight until eleven o'clock, then five in the afternoon until half past six.'

She stood gaping at him. 'You really mean it? Would I really do?'

'I don't see why not; you seem a sensible girl. Oh, and there's no evening surgery on Tuesdays and Thursdays.'

'So I could still work at the library?'

'Yes. Come up to the surgery after eleven o'clock and see Dr Walters. Talk it over with him.'

He nodded goodbye and strode away. Emma watched him go, not quite believing any of it but knowing that after eleven o'clock she would be at the surgery, doing her best to look like a suitable applicant for the post of receptionist.

She did the rest of the shopping in a hopeful haze, hurried home to tidy her unruly hair and get into her less scruffy sandals, told her mother that she would be back for lunch and made her way through the town.

The surgery was at the back of the town, away from the main street. It was pleasantly situated in a quiet street, and even if the surgery hours were over it was still busy. Bidden to wait, since Dr Walters was seeing his last patient, Emma sat down in the waiting room and whiled away ten minutes or so leafing through out-of-date copies of country magazines, at the same time rehearsing the kind of replies she might be expected to give. Since she had no idea of the questions she would be asked, it was a fruitless occupation.

The moment she entered Dr Walters's surgery she knew that she need not have worried. He was a small middle-aged man, with the kind of trustful face which made women want to mother him. He was also a very good doctor, though untidy, and forgetful of anything which wasn't connected with his work or his patients. His desk was an untidy mass of papers, patients' notes, various forms and a pile of unopened letters.

He got up as she went in, dislodging papers and knocking over a small pot full of pens.

'Miss Dawson.' He came round the desk to shake hands. 'Dr van Dyke told me that you might consider helping out—my receptionist and secretary, Mrs Crump, had to leave at a moment's notice—her daughter has had an accident. She will return, of course, but I need help until she does.'

He waved Emma to a chair and went back behind the desk. 'Have you any experience of this type of work?'

'None at all—' there was no point in pretending otherwise '—but I can answer the telephone, file papers, sort out the post, make appointments and usher patients in and out.'

Dr Walters peered at her over his old-fashioned spectacles. 'You're honest. Shall we give it a trial? I'm desperate for help with the paperwork. I can't pay you the usual salary because you aren't trained. Could we settle for— let me see...' He named a sum which made Emma blink.

'I'm not worth that much,' she told him, 'but I'd like the job.'

'It's yours until Mrs Crump gets back. If after a week I think that you don't deserve the money I'll reduce it. No references—Dr van Dyke seems to know enough about you. Start tomorrow? Half past eight? We'll see how we get on.'

For all his mild appearance, Emma reflected, he certainly knew his own mind.

* * *

The next few months were the happiest Emma had spent since her father died. She sorted patients' notes from letters, and letters from the endless junk mail, she kept the doctor's desk tidy, and saw that the day's patients were clearly listed and laid on his blotter where he couldn't possibly mislay the list, she answered the phone and booked patients in and out. She didn't attempt to do any of Mrs Crump's skilled jobs, and she had no doubt that that lady would have a great deal of work to deal with when she returned, but she did her best and Dr Walters, once he realised her limitations, made no complaint.

And in all that time she barely glimpsed Dr van Dyke. A brief good morning if they should meet at the surgery, a wave of the hand if she passed him on her way home... She told herself that there was no reason for him to do more than acknowledge her, but all the same she was disappointed.

All the wrong men like me, she thought crossly, and when I do meet a man I would like to know better he ignores me.

The season was at its height when Mrs Dawson received an invitation to go and stay with an elderly couple who had been friendly with her and her husband before his death. The friendship had cooled, but now it seemed that sufficient time had glossed over the unfortunate circumstances following his death and they expressed themselves delighted at the prospect of a visit from her.

'So kind,' declared Mrs Dawson. 'Of course I shall accept! How delightful it will be to go back to the old life, even if it is only for a few weeks. You will be able to manage on your own, won't you, Emma? You are so seldom home these days, and although I'm sure you don't mean to neglect me I am sometimes lonely. There is so little to do,' she added peevishly.

There were several answers to that, but Emma uttered none of them.

'I shall be perfectly all right, Mother. You'll enjoy the change, won't you? When do they want you to go? We must see about travelling. Someone will meet you at Paddington?'

'Yes, I couldn't possibly manage on my own. I shall need some new clothes...'

Emma thought of the small nest egg at the bank. 'I'm sure we can manage something; you have some pretty dresses...'

'Last year's,' snapped her mother. 'Everyone will recognise them.' She added, 'After all, you take half my pension each week.'

They mustn't quarrel, thought Emma. 'You will have all of it while you are away,' she pointed out gently, 'and we'll put our heads together about some new clothes for you.'

'I must say that since your father died, Emma, you have become very bossy and mean. I suppose it's the result of living here in this poky little cottage with no social life.'

'Now I'm working at the medical centre I haven't much time to be sociable. And, Mother, we couldn't manage unless I had a job. When do you plan to go?'

'On Friday. I'll collect my pension on Thursday; that will give me a little money in my purse. I want to go to the boutique tomorrow and see if there is anything that I can afford.' She looked at Emma. 'How much money can I spend?'

When Emma told her, she said, 'Not nearly enough, but I suppose I'll have to manage.'

A most unsatisfactory conversation, thought Emma, lying in bed and doing sums in her head that night. Mrs Crump wasn't going to stay at home for ever. Sooner or later she would lose her job, and with summer coming to an end so would the kind of jobs she could apply for. Of course she could live more cheaply when her mother had gone, but once summer was over there would be the cottage to keep warm and lighted.

She shook up her pillows again, determined to think of something else. And that wasn't at all satisfactory, for all she could think about was the complete lack of interest in her evinced by Dr van Dyke.

Mrs Dawson spent a good deal more money than Emma had bargained for. There had been such a splendid choice, her mother enthused, and really the prices were so reasonable it would have been foolish to ignore such bargains. At least she was happy getting ready for her visit, talking about nothing else.

Emma, tidying books on the library shelves, listening to Phoebe's cheerful gossip, thought about her day with Dr Walters. He had been untidier than usual, and his morning patients had taken longer than usual too. It had been almost one o'clock before she had been ready to leave, and then she had discovered his scribbled note asking her to return for an hour that afternoon as he had arranged to see a patient privately.

She had hurried home, got lunch and rushed to the shops with her Mother's wispy voice echoing in her ears; there was so much to tell her about the letter she had received from her friends and Emma couldn't be bothered to stay and listen. Emma, racing in and out of the butcher, the greengrocer and the bakery, prayed for patience…!

Getting her mother away on time, properly packed and the journey made as easy as possible, hadn't been the problem she had feared. Mrs Craig had offered to drive her mother to Totnes to catch the train, and the prospect of leaving Salcombe had changed her from a disgruntled woman to a charming lady who, having got what she wanted, was prepared to be nice to everyone. All the same Emma, who loved her mother, missed her.

Life became more leisurely as there was less of everything to do: meals didn't need to be on time, the cottage, with only her in it, was easy to keep clean and tidy, and it no longer mattered if she needed to stay late at the surgery.

Her mother was happy too; she had met several old friends, all of whom wanted her to visit them. 'I shan't be home yet,' she told Emma gleefully. Emma, relieved to know that her mother was once more living the life she enjoyed, permitted herself to forget the worries of the forthcoming winter. The summer was sliding gently into autumn, and although there were still plenty of visitors very soon now the shops would close for the winter. And still there was no news of Mrs Crump's return…

Her mother had been gone for two weeks when Dr Walters, sipping coffee after the morning surgery, began tossing the papers on his desk all over the place. He found what he wanted, a letter, and he put on his glasses.

'News, Emma. I have heard from Mrs Crump. She at last sees her way clear to returning to work.' He glanced at the letter. 'In a week's time. That brings us to Friday, which is most convenient for there is no surgery on Saturday, so you will be able to leave after Friday evening surgery.'

He beamed at her across the desk. 'I must say I shall be sorry to see you go; you have been of great help to me. I'm sure I don't know how I would have managed without you. You will be glad to be free again, no doubt?'

'Yes,' said Emma steadily, 'that will be nice, Dr Walters, although I have enjoyed working here for you. I expect Mrs Crump will be delighted to come back to work and you will be equally pleased to have her.'

'Indeed, I shall.' He put down his cup. 'I must be off. I'll leave you to clear up and I'll see you this evening.'

Emma set about putting the place to rights, her thoughts chaotic. She should have been prepared for the news but she had been lulled by several weeks of silence from Mrs Crump so that leaving had become a comfortably vague event which she didn't need to be worried about just yet. She would have to set about finding another job, for her hours at the library would hardly keep body and soul together.

She finished her chores and left the medical centre just as Dr van Dyke got out of his car. For once he stopped to speak to her.

'Rather late leaving, aren't you? Not being overworked, are you?'

'No, no, thank you.' She tried to think of something casual to say, but her mind was blank and at any moment now she was going to burst into tears.

'I must hurry,' she told him, and almost ran down the road.

He stood watching her fast retreating back, frowning; he had been careful to avoid her during the past months,

aware that she attracted him and just as aware that he
would be returning to Holland within a few weeks and
that to allow the attraction to grow would be foolhardy.
Perhaps it was a good thing that she showed no signs of
even liking him.

He went along to his surgery and forgot about her.
But later that evening he allowed his thoughts to return
to her, smiling a little at her rage at the hotel and then
again at the quite different Emma, playing with the children on the sands.

Back at the cottage, Emma gave way to her feelings.
The situation called for a good cry, not a gentle flow
of tears easily wiped away with a dainty hanky and a
few sighs. She sat bawling her eyes out, her face awash,
sniffing and snuffling and wiping away the tears with
her hands, catching her breath like a child. It was a great
relief, and presently she found a hanky and mopped her
face and felt better. It was something which she had
known would happen, and she told herself that it wasn't
the end of the world; she would soon find another job—
probably not as well paid, but enough to live on. It was
a good thing that her mother was away...

She washed her sodden face, tidied her hair and made
a sandwich and a pot of tea, and, not wishing to show
her red nose and puffy lids to the outside world, spent
the afternoon doing the ironing. By the time it was necessary to go back to work she was almost herself again,
fortified by yet more tea and careful repairs to her face.

There were a lot of patients, and Dr Walters was far
too busy to do more than glance at her. Confident that
she looked exactly as usual, she ushered patients in and

out, found notes and made herself generally useful. Only to come face to face with Dr van Dyke.

She tried sidling past him and found her arm gently held.

'So you will be leaving us, Emma. Dr Walters is sorry to see you go, but I dare say you will be glad of more leisure?'

'Oh, I shall, I shall... I can't stop. Dr Walters wants some notes.'

He took his hand away and she skipped off to hide behind a cupboard door until he had gone. The less she saw of him the better, she told herself, and knew that that wasn't true. But he would be gone in a few weeks and she would forget him.

The week went too rapidly, and her last day came. She said goodbye to everyone—everyone except Dr van Dyke, who had gone across the estuary to East Portlemouth to deliver a baby.

'You're bound to see him around the town before he leaves,' observed Dr Walters. 'We shall miss him, but of course he wants to go back to his own practice, and naturally we shall all be glad to see Dr Finn back again. Probably he will bring back a number of new ideas from the States.'

There was a letter from her mother when she got home; she wouldn't be coming home for the next week or so, she wrote.

And Alice Riddley—remember her, my old school-friend—has made an exciting suggestion to me, but I will let you know more about that later, when we have discussed it thoroughly. I'm sure you are enjoying yourself without your tiresome old mother

*to look after. Make lots of young friends, Emma,
and buy yourself some pretty dresses. You can afford them now that I'm not at home to buy food for.*

Emma folded the letter carefully. Why was it that her
mother always made her feel guilty? As for new clothes,
every penny would need to be hoarded until she had more
work. She would start looking on Monday...

Mrs Craig stopped her after church on Sunday. 'I have
had a letter from your mother; she hints at all kinds of
exciting happenings for the future. Do you know what
she means, dear?'

'No, I've no idea, Mrs Craig. She mentioned that she
would have something to tell me later, but I've no idea
what it is. She won't be coming home for another week
or two.'

'You're not lonely, Emma?'

'Not a bit; the days are never long enough...'

A pity she couldn't say the same of the nights. Why is
it, she wondered, that one's brain is needle-sharp around
three o'clock in the morning, allowing one to make impossible plans, do complicated mental arithmetic and see
the future in a pessimistic light?

She started her job-hunting on the Monday. The season was coming to an end, temporary jobs would finish
very soon, and since so many of the shops would shut
until the spring there was no question of them taking on
more staff. The holiday cottages to rent would lock their
doors and the few for winter-letting were maintained by
their owners.

After several days Emma realised that she would have
to go to Kingsbridge and find work there. It would mean
a daily bus ride, and not much leisure, but if she could

find something full-time that would see them through the winter. There was a large supermarket there which sounded promising...

She had seen nothing of Dr van Dyke. Perhaps he had already left, she wondered, and found the thought depressed her. He might not have liked her but she would have liked to have known him better. And he had been very kind about Derek.

She went to the library on Thursday evening, and as they packed up Miss Johnson called her over. 'After this week we shall be closing down the evening session and I'm afraid there won't be enough work for you to continue, Emma. We shall be sorry to let you go but there wouldn't be anything for you to do. If you would come on Tuesday evening and help us go through the shelves and generally tidy up...'

Emma found her voice. It didn't sound quite like hers but at least it was steady. 'I shall miss working here. Perhaps I could come back next year? And of course I'll come on Tuesday.' She said goodnight, called a cheerful greeting to Phoebe and went home.

This was something she hadn't foreseen. The money from the library wasn't enough to live on, but it would have helped to eke out her savings until she was working again. This time she didn't cry; she hadn't time for that. She would have to plan for the next few weeks, pay one or two outstanding bills, think up some cheap menus. At least she had only herself to think about.

She was getting into bed much later when she heard a faint whine. It sounded as though it was coming from the front garden and she went downstairs to have a look, opening the door cautiously, forgetful that she was in her nightie and with bare feet.

There was a very small dog peering at her through the closed gate, and she went at once to open it. The cottage next door was empty of visitors so there was no one about. The dog crept past her and slid into the cottage, its tail between its legs, shivering.

Emma fetched a bowl of bread and milk and watched the little beast wolf it down. It was woefully thin, its coat bedraggled, and there was a cut over one eye. There was no question of sending it on its way. She fetched an old towel and rubbed the skinny little body while the dog shivered and shook under her gentle hands.

'More bread and milk?' said Emma. 'And a good night's sleep. Tomorrow I shall give you a good wash. I always wanted a dog and it seems I'm meant to have one.'

She carried him upstairs to bed then, wrapped in a towel, and he fell asleep before she had turned out the light. She went to sleep too, quite forgetful of the fact that she was out of work and, worse, was never going to see Dr van Dyke again.

Chapter 4

It was raining when she woke up in the early morning and the little dog was still asleep, wrapped in the towel. But he opened frightened eyes the moment she moved and cowered away from her hand.

'My poor dear,' said Emma. 'Don't be frightened. You're going to live here and turn into a handsome dog, and in any case this is no weather to turn you out into the street.'

He pricked up his ears at her voice and wagged a wispy tail, and presently, rendered bold by the promise of breakfast, went cautiously downstairs with her.

She had intended job-hunting directly after breakfast, but that would have to wait for a while. Full of a good breakfast, the dog accepted her efforts to clean him up, sitting on his towel in the little kitchen, being washed and dried and gently brushed. When she had finished he looked more like a dog, and cautiously licked her hand as she cleaned the wound over his eye. By that time it was mid-morning and he was ready for another meal...

Emma found an old blanket, arranged it in one of the chairs, and with the aid of a biscuit urged him into it.

'I'm going out,' she told him. 'You need food and so do I.'

A marrow bone was added to the sausages for her own lunch, suitable dog food and dog biscuits and, in one of the small shops which sold everything, a collar and lead. She went back in the rain and found him asleep, but he instantly awoke when she went in, cowering down into the blanket.

She gave him another biscuit and told him that he was a brave boy, then fastened the collar round his scrawny neck and went into the garden with him and waited patiently while he pottered among the flowerbeds and then sped back indoors.

'Time for another meal,' said Emma, and opened a tin. Since he was still so frightened and cowed she stayed home for the rest of the day, and was rewarded by the lessening of his cringing fear and his obvious pleasure in his food. By bedtime he was quite ready to go upstairs with her and curl up on her feet in bed, anxious to please, looking at her with large brown eyes.

'Tomorrow,' she told him, 'I must go looking for work, but you'll be safe here and we will go for a little walk together and you'll learn to be a dog again. I have no doubt that before long you will be a very handsome dog.'

The rain had stopped by morning. The dog went timidly into the garden, ate his breakfast and settled down on his blanket.

'I won't be long,' Emma told him, and went into the town to buy the local paper. There weren't many jobs going, and the two she went after had already been taken. She went home dispirited, to be instantly cheered by the dog's delight at seeing her again.

'Something will turn up,' she told him, watching him eat a splendid dinner. 'You'll bring me luck. You must have a name…' She considered that for a minute or two. 'Percy,' she told him.

She took him for a short walk later, trotting beside her on his lead, but he was quickly tired so she picked him up and carried him home.

And it seemed as though he *was* bringing her luck for there were two jobs in the newsagent's window the next day. She wrote down their addresses and went home to write to them. She wasn't sure what a 'general assistant' in one of the hotel's kitchens might mean, but the hotel would be open all winter. And the second job was part-time at an antiques shop at the end of an alley leading off Main Street. She was tempted to call there instead of writing, but that might lessen her chances of getting the job.

She posted her letters, saw to Percy's needs, had her supper and went to bed, confident that the morning would bring good news.

It brought another letter from her mother, a lengthy one, and Emma wondered at her Mother's opening words. 'At last you will be free to live your own life, Emma.'

Emma put down her teacup and started to read and when she had read it, she read it again. Her mother and her old schoolfriend had come to a decision; they would share life together.

We shall live at the cottage, but since she has a car we can go to Richmond, where she will keep her

*flat, whenever we want a change. I'm sure you will
agree with me that this is an excellent idea, and
since I shall be providing a home for her she will
pay all expenses. So, Emma, you will be free to do
whatever you like. Of course we shall love to see
you as often as you like to come. Such a pity that
there are only two bedrooms, but when we go to
Richmond you can use the cottage.*

Emma drank her cooling tea. She had no job, she had
received her very last pay from Miss Johnson, and now,
it seemed, she was to have no home.

'Well, things can't get worse,' said Emma, and offered
the toast which she no longer wanted to Percy. 'So things
will get better. I'll advertise in the paper for a live-in job
where dogs are welcome.'

Brave words! But Emma was sensible and practical as
well. There was work for anyone who wanted it; it was
just a question of finding it. Since her mother now didn't
intend to return for another week or so she had all the
time in the world to go looking for it.

There were no replies to her two letters, but there was
still time for their answers. She didn't give up her search,
though, and filled in her days with turning Percy into a
well-groomed, well-fed dog. He would never be handsome, and the scar over his eye had left a bald patch, but
she considered that he was a credit to her. More than
that, he helped her to get through the disappointing days.

She had written to her mother, and it had been a difficult letter to write. That her mother had had no intention of upsetting her was obvious, but circumstances had
arisen which would make it possible for her to live in
comfort with a congenial companion and she had brushed

aside any obstacles which might stand in her way. She had had no difficulty in persuading herself that Emma would be glad to be independent and she had written cheerfully to that effect, unconcerned as to how Emma would achieve that independence.

It might take a little time, Emma had pointed out, before she could find work which would pay her enough to give her her independence, but no doubt that was something which had been considered in their plans and in any case Salcombe was still full of visitors. Which wasn't quite true, but Emma had felt justified in saying so. The longer her mother delayed coming back to Salcombe the better were her chances of getting a job.

The days went by. She went to Kingsbridge by bus and spent the day searching out agencies and scanning the adverts in the newspaper shops, and finally she tried the supermarket. No chance of work, she was told roundly. They were shedding seasonal staff, and if a vacancy occurred it would go to someone local.

It was early evening by the time she got back and Percy was waiting impatiently. She fed him and took him for a walk, and went to get her own supper. Almost another week, she reflected. Unless something turns up tomorrow I shall have to write to Mother and tell her I can't leave until I can find a job…

She wasn't hungry; Percy gobbled up most of her supper and went back to sleep on his blanket and she sat down to peruse the local paper. Work was getting scarce now that the season was almost over and there was nothing there for her. She sat in the darkening evening, doing nothing—for once her cheerful optimism had left her.

Someone knocking on the door roused her and Percy

gave a small squeaky bark, although he didn't get off the blanket.

Dr van Dyke was on the doorstep.

Emma was conscious of the delight and relief she felt surge through her person at the sight of him—like finding a familiar tree in a wood in which she had been lost. She stood there looking at him, saying nothing at all.

When he asked, 'May I come in?' she found her tongue.

'Yes, of course. Did you want to see me about something?'

He followed her into the living room and closed the door. He said coolly, 'No, I was walking this way and it seemed a good idea to call and see how you are getting on.' His eye fell on Percy. He lifted an eyebrow. 'Yours?'

'Yes. His name is Percy.'

He bent to stroke Percy's untidy head. 'Your mother is not home?'

'Mother's away, staying with friends in Richmond. Won't you sit down? Would you like a cup of coffee?'

She must match his coolness with her own, she thought, and sat down composedly, facing him, forgetful of the table-lamp which highlighted her face.

'What is the matter, Emma?'

The question was unexpected, and she said far too quickly, 'The matter? Why, nothing. Have you been busy at the medical centre?'

'No more than usual. I asked you what is the matter, Emma?'

He sounded kind and friendly in an impersonal way, but he watched her from under his heavy-lidded eyes. The weeks without a regular sight of her carroty topknot and their occasional brief meetings had made it plain to him that the strong attraction he felt for her had become something beyond his control; he had fallen in love with her.

He smiled at her now and she looked away quickly. 'Oh, it's nothing. I'm a bit disappointed at not finding another job, and the library doesn't want me now that summer's over...'

When he remained silent, she said with barely concealed ill-humour, 'I'll make some coffee.'

'You have no work, no money and you are lonely.'

She said waspishly, 'You've put it very clearly, and now, you know, I think you should go...'

'You will feel better if you talk to someone, and I am here, am I not? What is more, I have the added advantage of leaving Salcombe in the very near future. After all, I am a good listener; that is something which my profession has taught me—and you need a pair of ears.'

'Well, there is nothing to tell you,' said Emma rather defiantly, and burst into tears.

Dr van Dyke, by a great effort of will-power, stayed sitting in his chair. Much as he would have liked to take her into his arms, now was not the moment to show more than friendly sympathy, but presently he leaned across and stuffed his handkerchief into her hand and watched while she mopped her face, and blew her nose in an effort to return to her normal sensible manner. But her voice was a bit wobbly and she was twisting his handkerchief into a travesty of its snowy perfection.

'Well,' began Emma, and it all came tumbling out— not always in the right order, so that he had to sort out the details for himself. And when at last she had finished she muttered, 'Sorry I've made such a fool of myself. I do think it would be better if you went now; I am so ashamed of being such a cry-baby.'

Already at the back of the doctor's clever head a vague plan was taking shape. Far-fetched, almost for certain to be rejected by Emma, yet it was the obvious answer. To leave her to the uncertainties of her mother's plans, workless and more or less penniless... It was something he would think over later, but for now he said cheerfully, 'I'll go if you want me to, but I think a cup of coffee would be nice first.'

She jumped up. 'Of course. I'm sorry. It won't take long.'

She went into the kitchen and laid a tray, and was putting the last few biscuits in the tin onto a plate when he followed, the dog at his heels.

'This is a charming little house. I've often admired it from the outside, and it's even nicer indoors. I like kitchens, don't you?' He glanced round him. She had left a cupboard door open and it looked empty; she was very likely not having quite enough to eat. He carried the tray back to the living room and sat for another half an hour, talking about nothing in particular, feeding a delighted Percy with some of his biscuit, taking care not to look at Emma's tearstained face.

'Wibeke wanted to know how you were,' he told her. 'They enjoyed their holiday here. The children have all got chicken pox now; she's thankful that they're all having it at the same time.'

'They were dears, the children,' said Emma, and smiled at last. 'They must be such fun.'

'They are.' He got up to go. 'Have dinner with me tomorrow evening and we'll talk about them. Eight o'clock? Shall we see if the Gallery has any lobsters?' And when she hesitated, he added, 'I'm not asking you because I'm sorry for you, Emma, but a meal and a pleasant talk is a comfortable way to end an evening.' He glanced at Percy. 'I dare say we might be allowed to hide him under the table—the manager owes me; I stitched up his cut hand late one night.'

He didn't wait for her to answer.

As she closed the door she decided that it would be most ungracious to refuse his invitation since he had been so kind.

She went to bed and slept soundly and set off once more on her fruitless search for work in the morning, to return home to the pleasant prospect of dinner with Dr van Dyke.

Aware that she had hardly looked her best on the previous evening, she took pains with her appearance. The evenings were cool now, so she got into a dress and jacket in a soft uncrushable material. It was a subdued silvery green which made the most of her hair, which she had twisted into an old-fashioned bun at the nape of her neck. 'Out-of-date but respectable,' she told Percy, who was sitting on the bed watching her dressing.

Dr van Dyke was waiting for her, studying the board outside the restaurant. His 'Hello,' was briskly friendly. 'I see we're in luck; there's lobster on the menu.'

'Hello,' said Emma breathlessly. 'I've brought Percy—you said…'

'All arranged. Let's go in; I'm famished.'

The lobster was delicious, served simply on a bed of lettuce with a Caesar salad. They talked as they ate, unhurriedly. The place was almost empty and would close for the winter in a few days' time. Peach Melba followed, and a pot of coffee which was renewed while they talked. As for Percy, sitting silently under the table, he had a bowl of water and, quite contrary to the house rules, a plate of biscuits.

It was well after ten o'clock when they left. Walking back to the cottage, Dr van Dyke glanced at Emma in the semi-darkness of the little quay. His plans had become reality. It was now a question of convincing Emma that they were both practical and sensible. No hint of his feelings for her must be allowed to show. This would be a businesslike arrangement with no strings attached. Now it was merely a matter of waiting for the right moment.

He unlocked the cottage door, switched on the lights, bade Percy goodnight and listened gravely to her little speech of thanks.

'It is I who thank you, Emma. Lobster is something one should never eat alone and I have much enjoyed your company.'

'I've never been compared with a lobster before,' said Emma tartly.

'I wouldn't presume to compare you with anyone or anything, Emma. Sleep soundly.'

'Oh, I will.' As he turned away she asked, 'When do you go back to Holland?'

'Very soon now. Goodnight, Emma.'

Not a very satisfactory answer.

The doctor had kindly Fate on his side; two evenings later the lifeboat was called out to go to the aid of a yacht off Prawle Point. He had just sat down to his supper when the maroon sounded and within ten minutes he was in oilskins and heavy boots, putting to sea with the rest of the crew. It was a stormy evening, with squalls of heavy rain and a strong wind. This was something he would miss, he reflected, taking up his station. When he had first come to Salcombe a crew member had fallen ill; he had volunteered to take his place and been accepted as a man who could be useful when the need arose.

Two hours later they were back in harbour, the yacht in tow, its crew led away to the Harbour Master's office for warm drinks and plans for the night. Half an hour later the doctor said goodnight and went out into the narrow lane behind the boat house. He glanced along Victoria Quay as he reached it and then lengthened his stride. Emma and Percy were just turning into the cottage gate.

She was at the door when he reached the cottage.

She saw him then, and waited at the door until he reached her, took the key from her hand, opened the door and switched on the light. She saw him clearly then: wet hair, an old pullover.

'What's happened?' she asked, and then 'You were in the lifeboat…?'

'Yes, I was on the way home when I saw you both.'

'I went up to the boat house to see if there was anything I could do. You're all safe?' When he nodded, she added, 'Would you like a hot drink? Cocoa?'

That was a drink he associated with his childhood, gulped down under Nanny's sharp eye. 'That would be most welcome. The weather's pretty rough outside the estuary.'

The little room looked cosy and smelled strongly of furniture polish. Indeed, looking round him, he could see that everything gleamed as though waiting for a special occasion, and in one corner there was a small box neatly packed with books.

Emma came back presently, with the cocoa and a tin of biscuits, and he studied her face narrowly as he got up. She looked sad, but not tearfully so, and there was a kind of quiet acceptance in her face. He had seen that look many times before on a patient's face when they had been confronted with a doubtful future.

He sipped his cocoa, pronounced it delicious, and asked, carefully casual, 'Have you heard from your mother? She plans to return soon?'

'They will be coming next week—on Wednesday.'

'And you? You have plans?'

'I'll find a job.'

'For some time now,' said the doctor casually, 'I have been badgered by my secretary in Holland to find someone to give her a helping hand. She does have too much to do, and when I return there will be even more work. It has occurred to me that perhaps you would consider working for her? It is rather a menial job: filing letters and running errands and dealing with phone calls if she is engaged. She is a fierce lady but she has a heart of gold. She speaks English, of course. The money won't be much but there's a room in the house where she lives which I think you could afford.' He added, 'A temporary measure, of course, just to tide you over.'

'You're offering me a job in Holland? When?'

'As from the middle of next week. Should you consider accepting, we could leave on the day your mother returns here, so that you could spend some time with her. I plan to go over to Holland on the late-night ferry from Harwich. We wouldn't need to leave here before five o'clock.'

'I can't,' said Emma. 'I won't leave Percy.'

'He can come with us; there's time to deal with the formalities. Do you have a passport? And do you drive a car?'

'Yes, to both.' She put down her mug. 'You do mean it, don't you?'

He said evenly, 'Yes, I mean it, Emma. You would be doing Juffrouw Smit a good turn and save me hunting around for someone when I get home.'

'Where do you live?'

'Near Amsterdam. My rooms are in the city, as are the hospitals where I work. You would live in Amsterdam itself.'

He put down his mug, lifted a somnolent Percy off his knee and got up.

'It's late. Think about it and let me know in the morning.' And as she went to open the door he said again, 'The cocoa was so delicious.' He smiled down at her bewildered face. 'Sleep well.'

And strangely enough she did, and woke in the morning with her mind made up. Here was her opportunity to make a life for herself. Moreover, it meant that she would still see Dr van Dyke from time to time. He was kind and thoughtful, he liked dogs and children, and he had offered her a job...

'It's a pity that I don't appeal to him as a woman,' said Emma to Percy. 'It's my hair, of course, and bawling my eyes out all over him.'

She would have to let him know and without waste of time. But first she made sure that she had her passport, and then she sat down to tot up her money. She would leave half of it in the bank and take the rest with her; she might not be paid for a month and she would have to live until then.

It wasn't much but it would give her security, and she would arrange with the bank that her mother could use the money there. She would have to bear in mind that her mother and her friend might agree to part later on, in which case she would have to return. But there was no

point in thinking about that; her mother had been quite
positive about her plans and made it clear that Emma
had no part in them.

The doctor's surgeries would be over by eleven
o'clock; she went to the medical centre and waited until
the last patient had gone and then knocked on Dr van
Dyke's door. He was sitting at his desk but he got up as
she went in.

'Emma—sit down.' When she did, he sat back in his
chair again. 'And what have you decided?'

'When I went to bed last night,' said Emma carefully,
'I decided to make up my mind this morning—think
about it before I went to sleep. Only I went to sleep first,
and when I woke up this morning my mind had made
itself up. If you think I could do the job you offered me,
I'd like to accept.'

'Good. Now, as to details: you will work from eight
o'clock in the morning until five in the afternoon. An
hour and a half for lunch at noon, half an hour for tea at
half past three. You must be prepared to turn your hand
to anything which Juffrouw Smit or I ask of you. You
will be free on Saturday and Sunday, although if the occasion should arise you might need to work on either of
those two days. You will be paid weekly.' He named a
sum in guilders and then changed it into English pounds.
It seemed a generous amount, and when she looked questioningly at him, he said, 'It's the going rate for a job such
as yours, and you will earn it. Juffrouw Smit expects the
best. Do you still want to come?'

He was friendly, but he was brisk too. This was a businesslike meeting, she reminded herself. She said quietly,
'Yes, I still want to come. If you will tell me where to
go and when...'

'You will go over to Holland with me. You will need your passport, of course, not too much luggage—and Percy. You will perhaps let your mother know that we will leave in the late afternoon on Wednesday, so that she can arrange to be here before you leave? You are quite sure that is what she wants?'

'Yes. She—she has never been happy living here with me, but I think she will settle down with her friend. They like the same things: bridge and driving around the country and being able to go back to Richmond when they want to. And if it doesn't turn out as they hoped, then I'll come back here…'

'Just so,' agreed the doctor. If he had a hand in it that would be the last thing his darling Emma would do.

He said smoothly, 'Shall we settle some of the details? I'll see about Percy and arrange the journey. I'll come down to the cottage at five o'clock on Wednesday. It will be quite a long drive and we shan't get to Amsterdam until well after midnight. Will you have much luggage?'

'A case and a shoulder bag.'

Going home presently, she thought how coolly businesslike he had been. Since he was to be her employer, perhaps that was a good thing. She took Percy for a brisk walk and set about the task of sorting out her clothes. She wouldn't need much; she doubted if she would have much social life…

Her tweed jacket and skirt, the cashmere twin-set, a grey jersey dress which she thought might do for her work, another skirt—jersey again because it could be squeezed into a corner without creasing—blouses and a thin sweater, and, as a concession to the social life she didn't expect, a sapphire-blue dress which could be

folded into almost nothing and remained bandbox-fresh.
'Shoes,' said Emma to a watchful Percy. 'And I'll wear
my winter coat and cram in a raincoat, gloves, handbag,
undies and dressing gown...'

She laid everything out on the bed in her mother's bedroom and, being a sensible girl, sat down and wrote out
all the things she had to do before Wednesday.

There was a letter from her mother in the morning.
She and Mrs Riddley would arrive during the morning
on Wednesday.

*We shall spend the night on the way, and get to you
in good time for coffee. Just a light lunch will do
because we shall eat out in the evening. I expect
you have arranged everything; I'm sure that by
now you must have found just the kind of job you
would like. Far be it from me to stand in the way
of your ambition...*

Emma put down the letter. She loved her mother, and
she hoped that her mother loved her, but that lady had a
way of twisting circumstances to suit herself, ignoring
the fact that those same circumstances might not suit anyone else. Emma had known that since she was a small girl
and had accepted it; her mother had been a very pretty
woman, and charming, and Emma had grown up taking it for granted that she must be shielded from worry
or unpleasantness. There had been little of either until
her father had died, and she didn't blame her mother for
wishing her former carefree life to continue.

She went the next day to say goodbye to Miss Johnson
and Phoebe. Miss Johnson wished her well and told her

to be sure and visit the splendid museums in Amsterdam, and Phoebe looked at her with envy.

'Lucky you, going to work for Dr van Dyke. What wouldn't I give to be in your shoes? Going for keeps or coming back here later?'

'I'm not going for keeps,' said Emma, 'and I dare say I'll come back later on.'

She met Mrs Craig the next day.

'My dear Emma, the very person I want to see. I had a card from your mother. How excited you must be. It's good news that she is going to stay in Salcombe—bringing a friend with her, she tells me.' She gave a little laugh. 'The cottage is rather small for three of you...'

'I won't be here,' said Emma. 'I'm going to work for Dr van Dyke when he goes back to Amsterdam. At least, I shall be working with his secretary. I'm to have lodgings with her. I've been working at the medical centre and I liked the work. It would have been difficult fitting three of us into the cottage, as you say.'

'Your mother will miss you.'

'Her friend is delighted to take my place—they have known each other since schooldays. She's very much looking forward to being here and meeting you and Mother's other friends.'

Mrs Craig studied Emma's face. There was no sign of worry or annoyance on it, all the same she didn't sound quite right.

Emma bade her a cheerful goodbye and hurried home to take Percy for his walk. He was becoming quite handsome, with a gleaming coat, melting brown eyes and a long feathery tail. Only his ears were on the large side, and she suspected that he wasn't going to grow much larger. She had told him that he was going to live in another country with her and he had wagged his tail in a pleased fashion. This was only to be expected, considering the doubtful life he had been leading in Salcombe.

Her mother and Mrs Riddley arrived in a flurry of greetings and embracing and gentle grumbling because they'd had to leave the car by the pub and there was no one to carry their luggage.

'Do find someone, darling,' said Mrs Dawson plaintively. 'And I quite forgot to ask you to find someone to clean the place for us.'

Emma accepted the car keys. 'Well, it's a bit late for me to do anything about that now,' she said cheerfully, 'but there are plenty of adverts in the newsagent's. I'll see what I can do about your luggage. Don't let Percy out of the gate, will you?'

'Such an ugly little dog,' said Mrs Riddley. 'But of course you'll take him with you?'

'Yes,' said Emma. 'We shall be gone this afternoon.'

She didn't like Mrs Riddley. Emma had heard of her from her mother from time to time but they had never met, though she could quite see that she would be an ideal companion for her mother. Another one skimming over the surface of life, making light of anything serious or unpleasant, being fashionable and excellent company; her mother would be happy with her.

The odd-job man at the pub helped with the luggage and Emma lugged it upstairs. She left the two ladies to begin their unpacking while she got the lunch, and over that meal she listened to their plans and intentions.

'We two old ladies intend to keep each other company while you go off and enjoy yourself. You're only young once, Emma. How wise of you to decide to see something of the world.'

Just as though I had planned the whole thing, reflected Emma. She felt bitterly hurt at her mother's bland acceptance of her leaving home, and felt as guilty as though she had actually arranged the whole thing herself. But there was no doubt that her mother was happy; she had convinced herself that Emma was pleasing herself, and beyond saying that it was so fortunate that Emma was going to work for someone she already knew she didn't want to know about the job itself.

After lunch Mrs Dawson said, 'You must tell me what you have done about the bank account. Dear Alice will see to the bills, since she is living here rent-free, but I must contribute towards the housekeeping, I suppose, and that will leave me almost penniless.'

'There's an account in your name at the bank. I've put in all the money I've earned except for the last two weeks' wages. I don't know what expenses I'll have until I've been in Amsterdam for a while and I won't get paid until the end of the month.'

'A good salary? You'll be able to help me out if I get short, darling?'

'Don't depend on that, mother. I shan't be earning much and I'll have to pay for food and lodgings.'

Her mother pouted. 'Oh, well, I suppose I'll just have to manage as best I can. Your father would turn in his grave, Emma...'

Emma didn't speak because she was swallowing tears. But presently she said, 'I must take Percy for a walk. I'll prepare tea when I come back.'

She took quite a long walk: round the end of Victoria Quay and round the back of the town and back through the main street. She wasn't sure when she would see it again, with its small shops and the friendly people in them. She waved to the butcher as she went past, and even the cross-faced woman at the bakery smiled.

They had finished their tea and Emma had washed up and put everything ready for the morning when Dr van Dyke came.

She introduced him, and she could see that the two ladies were impressed. He looked—she sought for words—respectable, and he said all the right things. But he didn't waste time; he told her that they must leave and made his goodbyes with the beautiful manners which her mother and Mrs Riddley obviously admired.

And then it was her turn to make her farewells, sent on her way with cheerful hopes that she would have a lovely time and to be sure and send a card when she had time. 'And don't forget your poor old mother,' said Mrs Dawson in a wispier voice than usual—which sent Emma out of the door feeling that she was an uncaring daughter deserting her mother.

She walked beside the doctor, with Percy on his lead, and he took her case and shoulder bag. He didn't look at her, and it wasn't until she was in the car beside him that she muttered, 'I feel an absolute heel…'

He still didn't look at her. 'Your mother is a charming lady, Emma, but you mustn't believe all she says. She was merely uttering a remark which she felt suited the occasion. She will be very happy with her friend—I believe that and so must you—far happier than living with you; you must see that for yourself. You may love each other dearly but you are as unlike as chalk from cheese.'

Emma sniffed; she had no intention of crying although she felt like it.

His large comforting hand covered hers for a moment. 'You must believe me; she will be happy and so will you.'

Chapter 5

Emma sat beside the doctor, watching the quiet Devon countryside flash past as he made for the A38 and Exeter. He had told her that everything would be all right and she had to believe him, although she was beset by doubts. Juffrouw Smit might dislike her on sight; she might not be able to cope with the work. She would have to acquire at least a smattering of Dutch—and would she be able to live on her wages?

And over and above all that there was the unhappy thought that somehow or other she must make a success of the job, stay there until she had experience and some money saved before she could return to England. And what then? Her mother would be glad to see her as long as she didn't upset her life. Perhaps she would never be able to go back to the cottage at Salcombe...

'Stop worrying,' said Dr van Dyke. 'Take each day

as it comes, and when you have found your feet you can make your plans. And I promise you that if you are unhappy in Amsterdam then I will see that you get back to England.'

'You're very kind,' said Emma. 'It's silly of me to fuss, and actually I'm rather looking forward to working for your Juffrouw Smit.'

He began to talk then, a gentle meandering conversation which required few answers on her part but which somehow soothed her. By the time they had bypassed Exeter, left the A30 and joined the A303, she actually felt quite light-hearted.

At the doctor's speed it didn't take long to reach the M25 and take the road to Harwich, but first they stopped at Fleet, parked the car, took Percy for a run and went to the café for coffee and sandwiches.

'We can get something else on board,' said the doctor, 'and of course there will be someone waiting for us when we get home.'

'In Amsterdam? Not at Juffrouw Smit's house?'

'No, no, I wouldn't dare to disturb her night's sleep. I live a few miles outside the city. You'll spend the night at my house and go to Juffrouw Smit in the morning.' He glanced at his watch and sent the great car surging forward. 'We are almost at Harwich. You're not tired?'

'No. I've enjoyed the trip; it's a lovely car.' She peered over her shoulder. 'Percy's asleep.'

They were very nearly the last on board the ferry. The doctor drove on, tucked Percy under one arm and ushered Emma to a seat.

'Make yourself comfortable. It's a short crossing—about three and a half hours. It may be a bit choppy but

it is most convenient with the car, and the catamaran is
as steady as an ordinary ferry.'

'I'm not nervous.'

'Coffee and a brandy, I think, and something to eat.
I'll order while you trot off...'

How nicely put, thought Emma, making a beeline for
the ladies'.

They ate their sandwiches, drank their coffee and
brandy, and presently the doctor got some papers out of
his briefcase. 'You don't mind if I do some work?'

She shook her head, nicely drowsy from the brandy,
and, with her arms wrapped round a sleeping Percy, presently she slept too.

The doctor's hand on her arm woke her. 'We're about
to dock. Better give me Percy.'

It was dark and chilly and she could see very little of
her surroundings.

'Not long now,' said Dr van Dyke, and swept the car
onto a lighted highway. After a few minutes there were
no houses, just the road ahead of them, and Emma closed
her eyes again.

When she woke she could see the lights of Amsterdam, but before they reached the outskirts the doctor took
an exit road and plunged into the darkness of the countryside. But not for long, for there were a few trees, and
then a house or two, and then a village—nice old houses
lining the narrow road. She glimpsed a church—closed
now, of course—and a tall iron railing, before he turned
the car between brick pillars, along a short straight drive
and stopped before the house.

'You had better go straight to bed. I'll see to Percy.' He
got out of the car, lifted Percy off the back seat, opened
her door and urged her out.

She stood a minute, looking around her, for a moment wide awake. The house was large and square, with white walls and a steep gabled roof. The massive door was open and there were lights in some of the windows.

'Is this your home?' asked Emma.

'Yes.' He sounded impatient, so she trod up the steps to the door beside him and went into the hall. It was large and square, with doors on all sides and a vast expanse of black and white tiled floor. There was a rather grand staircase curving up one wall, and a chandelier which cast brilliant light over everything. She saw all that in one rapid glance before the doctor at her elbow said, 'This is my housekeeper, Mevrouw Kulk—Katje, this is Miss Emma Dawson.' And when they had shaken hands, he spoke to Katje in Dutch.

Mevrouw Kulk was tall, stout and dignified, but she had a cheerful smiling face. She was answering the doctor when a door at the back of the hall opened and a middle-aged man came towards them.

He went to the doctor and shook hands, saying something in an apologetic voice. The doctor laughed and turned to Emma. 'This is Kulk. He and his wife run my home. He is apologising because he wasn't here to greet us. He was shutting my dog into the kitchen.'

Emma shook hands and looked anxiously at Percy, standing obediently by the doctor's feet. 'Shall I take him with me? He'll only need a minute or two outside...'

'Go with Mevrouw Kulk. She will show you your room, bring you a hot drink and see you safely into bed. I'll see to Percy and she will bring him up when you're in bed. He'd better be with you tonight.'

Mevrouw Kulk smiled and nodded and beckoned, and

the doctor said briskly, 'Sleep well, Emma. Breakfast at half past eight, before I take you to Juffrouw Smit.'

Emma followed the housekeeper upstairs. I'm twenty-seven, she thought sleepily, and he's ordering me around as though I were a child. But she was too tired to bother about that.

The stairs opened onto a gallery with doors on every side. Mevrouw Kulk opened one and ushered Emma inside.

Emma had an instant impression of warmth and light. The mahogany bed had a soft pink quilt, matching the curtains at the window. There was a small table, with a triple mirror on it and a slender-legged stool before it, and on either side of the bed there was a small table bearing pink-shaded lamps. A lovely room, but surely not one in which Percy would be allowed to sleep?

The housekeeper turned down the coverlet. 'Bed,' she said firmly, and smiled and nodded and went away.

Emma kicked off her shoes and dug her feet into the soft white carpet. Someone had already brought her luggage to her room. She found a nightie and, since it seemed the only thing to do, had a quick shower in the small, splendidly equipped bathroom next door. She got into bed just in time; Mevrouw Kulk was back again, this time with Percy prancing beside her and a blanket over one arm, which she spread at the end of the bed. She nodded and smiled once more, to return within a minute with a small tray, containing hot milk and a plate of biscuits.

'Dr van Dyke says, "Eat, drink and sleep!"'

She patted Emma's shoulder in a motherly fashion and went away again.

So Emma drank the milk, shared the biscuits with Percy, put her head on the pillow and slept—to be wakened in the morning by a buxom girl with a tea tray. There was a note on the tray: *Let Percy go with Anneke; she can take him for a run in the garden.*

Breakfast was at half past eight and it was already eight o'clock. She showered and dressed, wishing she had more time to take pains with her face and hair, and went downstairs, wondering where she should go.

Kulk was in the hall. His 'Good morning, Miss', was uttered in a fatherly fashion as he opened a door and invited her to go past him into the room beyond. This was a small room with a bright fire burning in the steel fireplace, its windows open onto the gardens beyond. There was a round table set for breakfast, a scattering of comfortable chairs, bookshelves overflowing with books, and small tables just where they were needed. The walls were panelled and the ceiling was a magnificent example of strap work.

Emma rotated slowly as the doctor came in from the garden. There was a mastiff beside him and, trotting as close as he could get, Percy.

His good morning was brisk. 'Percy and Prince are the best of friends, as you can see. You slept well? Shall we have breakfast?'

Emma had bent to stroke Percy. 'What a beautiful dog you have.' She held out a fist and Prince came close and breathed gently over it, then went back to stand by his master. Kulk came in then, with a loaded tray, and the doctor sent the dogs outside into the garden while they ate.

Emma was hungry. It seemed a long time since she had sat down to a decent meal, and as if he had read her thoughts Dr van Dyke observed, 'I do apologise for depriving you of a meal yesterday. You must allow me to make up for that once you have settled in.'

An invitation to dinner, thought Emma, loading marmalade onto toast. What a good thing I brought that dress. But all she said was, 'That would be very nice,' in a non-committal voice. It might be one of those half-meant, vague invitations exchanged so often amongst friends and acquaintances when she lived in Richmond, which never materialised. But no one had expected them to anyway.

Given no more than a few minutes in which to collect her things and thank the Kulks for their kindness, she was urged into the car, her luggage put in the boot, and Percy, waiting on the doorstep, was put on the back seat. Since the doctor had nothing to say, she held her tongue. She knew him well enough by now to understand that if there was nothing she should know she should be quiet.

Amsterdam was surprisingly close: first the modern outskirts and then the real Amsterdam—narrow streets and gabled houses leaning against each other lining the canals.

The doctor stopped before a row of old redbrick houses with imposing fronts.

'I shall be a few minutes,' he told her, before he got out and went inside one of the houses, which gave her time to look around her. There were several brass plates beside the door; this would be his consulting rooms, then. Very stylish, thought Emma.

He got back into the car presently. 'My consulting rooms,' he told her. 'You will work here with Juffrouw Smit.'

He swung the car down a narrow lane with small houses on either side of it and stopped again before one of them. He helped her out, scooped up Percy and rang the old-fashioned bell. The door was opened immediately by a lady who could have been a close relation of Miss Johnson: the same stiff hairstyle, white blouse and cardigan and sensible skirt, the same severe expression. Emma felt a surge of relief; it was like meeting an old friend...

'Good morning, Doctor, and I presume, Miss Dawson?' Her eyes fastened on Percy. 'And the little dog. Come in. Will you have coffee? You have an appointment at ten o'clock, Doctor...'

'How nice to see you again, Smitty. I must go to the hospital first, so I had better get along. Bring Emma round with you, will you? Give her some idea of her work. She can settle in this afternoon.' He smiled down at Emma. 'Juffrouw Smit, this is Emma Dawson. I'm sure she will be an apt pupil.' And when the two women had shaken hands, he said, 'I'll be off.'

Juffrouw Smit shut the door behind his vast back. 'Coffee first, then a quick look at your room before we go round to the doctor's rooms. We will speak English, but once you have found your feet you must learn a little Dutch.'

She led the way out of the tiny hall into a small sitting room, rather too full of old-fashioned furniture but very cosy. 'Sit down. I'll fetch the coffee.'

When it was poured Emma said, 'Did you know that I had Percy?'

'Yes, Dr van Dyke told me. I have a small garden with a very high wall and I shall leave the kitchen door open for him. He will be alone, but not for long, for I come home for my meals and if there are no patients you can slip back for a few minutes. He will be happy?'

'He was a stray, and I've had to leave him alone from

time to time, but I'm sure he'll be happy. You don't mind?'

'Not at all. Drink your coffee, then come and see your room. The doctor took your luggage up before he went.'

It was a small low-ceilinged room, overlooking the lane, very clean and cheerful, with simple furniture and a bed against one wall.

'My room is at the back of the house and there is a bathroom between. And if you should wish to be alone there is a small room beside the kitchen.'

Emma looked out of the window, trying to find a suitable way of asking about the rent; Juffrouw Smit wasn't like the usual landlady.

It was her companion who said briskly, 'Dr van Dyke is paying me for your room and board; that is why your wages are small.'

'Oh, thank you. Your English is so perfect, Juffrouw Smit—have you lived in England?'

'For several years some time ago. You will find that most people here speak English, although we appreciate foreigners speaking our language.'

Of course I'm a foreigner, reflected Emma, although I don't feel like one.

They settled Percy on a blanket in the kitchen, with the door open into the neat garden, and walked to the doctor's rooms. Two or three minutes brought them to the imposing door and across the equally imposing hall to another door with his name on it. Juffrouw Smit had a key and led the way into a short hallway which opened into a well-furnished waiting room—comfortable chairs, small tables with magazines, bowls of flowers and a desk in one corner.

'Through here,' said Juffrouw Smit, and opened the

door by the desk. 'This is where we keep patients' notes, the account book, business letters and so on.' She shut the door, swept Emma across the room and opened another door. 'Dr van Dyke's consulting room. The door over there leads to the examination room.'

She led the way out again. 'This last door is where we make tea and coffee, and here is a cloakroom.'

Emma took it all in, rather overwhelmed. She had never thought of the doctor as being well-known and obviously wealthy. She thought of the understated luxury of his consulting room and remembered his rather bare little room at the medical centre in Salcombe. His lovely house, too. He had never given her an inkling—but then, why should he? She had come over here to work and as such would hardly be expected to take a deep interest in his personal life. He had, of course, got one; she wished she knew more about it.

'Sit here, by my desk,' said Juffrouw Smit, 'and watch carefully. You must learn the routine before you will be any use to me.'

Emma, obediently making herself unobtrusive, reflected that Juffrouw Smit was every bit as severe as Miss Johnson.

The first person to arrive was Dr van Dyke, crossing to his own room with a brief nod, and five minutes later an imposing matron who replied graciously to Juffrouw Smit's greeting and ignored Emma. She was followed at suitable intervals by a fat man with a red face, a thin lady looking frightened, and lastly a sulky teenager with a fierce-looking parent.

When they had gone, Juffrouw Smit said, 'This is a typical morning. Dr van Dyke goes next to one or other of the hospitals where he is a consultant, and returns here around mid-afternoon, when he will see more patients. Very occasionally he sees patients in the evening. Now, if you will make the coffee and take him a cup, we will have ours and I will explain your work to you.'

'Do I knock?' asked Emma, cup and saucer in hand.

'Yes, and no need to speak unless he does.'

She knocked and went in. He was sitting at his desk, writing, and he didn't look up. She put the coffee on his desk and went out again, vaguely disappointed. He could at least have lifted his head and smiled…

She and Juffrouw Smit had their coffee and she took the cups back to the little cubbyhole. When she got back it was to see the doctor's back disappearing through the door.

'Now,' said Juffrouw Smit, 'listen carefully…'

Her tasks were simple: fetching and carrying, making coffee, answering the phone if Juffrouw Smit was unable to do so with the quickly learned words *'een ogenblik'*, which it seemed was a polite way of saying 'hold on'. She must see that the doctor's desk was exactly as he liked it each morning, tidy the newspapers and magazines, and, once she felt at ease with these jobs, she was expected to find and file away patients' notes and sort the post.

'Many small tasks,' observed Juffrouw Smit, 'of which I shall be relieved so that I can attend to the administration—the paperwork.'

They went back to her house for their lunch, and then Emma took Percy for a quick run before they went back to the consulting rooms and another afternoon of patients. The doctor, coming and going, did no more than nod as he went, with a brief, 'Settling in?' not waiting for an answer.

Quite a nice day, thought Emma, curling up in bed

that night. Under Juffrouw Smit's severe exterior, she felt sure lurked a nice middle-aged lady who would one day become a friend. And the work, so far, wasn't beyond her. She had a pleasant room, and enough to eat, and Percy had been made welcome. The niggardly thought that the doctor seemed to have forgotten all about her she dismissed. Any fanciful ideas in that direction were to be eschewed at once...

The next day went well, despite the fact that the patients seemed endless. Excepting for a brief lunch there was no respite, so that when the last patient had gone, soon after five o'clock, and Juffrouw Smit told her to get her coat and go to the post office with a pile of letters, she was glad to do so.

It was an early dusk, and chilly, but it was lovely to be out of doors after the warmth of the waiting room. The post office was five minutes' walk away; Emma went over the little bridge at the end of the street, turned left and followed the canal. The post office was on the corner, facing a busy main road thick with traffic, trams and people. She would have liked to have lingered, taken a quick look around, but that would have to wait until she was free tomorrow. She hurried back and found Juffrouw Smit still at her desk, with no sign of the doctor.

'Take the key,' said Juffrouw Smit, 'and go to my house. Perhaps you would put everything ready for our meal? *Zuurkool* and potatoes and a smoked sausage. Put them all on a very low gas and feed Percy. I shall be another ten minutes. While I cook our meal you can take him for his walk.'

So Emma went back to the little house, to be greeted by a delighted Percy and deal with the saucepans and wait for Juffrouw Smit.

* * *

Juffrouw Smit was sitting opposite the doctor's desk, listening to him.

'Yes,' she told him, 'Miss Dawson—who wishes to be called Emma—has settled in without fuss. A sensible girl with nice manners, and quick to grasp what is wanted of her.' Juffrouw Smit fixed the doctor with a sharp eye. 'Do you wish me to train her to take my place, Doctor?'

'Take your place? Smitty, you surely don't want to retire? There are years ahead of you. You surely never supposed that that was in my mind? I cannot imagine being without you. No, no, I will explain...'

Which he did, though giving away none of his true feelings, but as Juffrouw Smit got up to go and reached the door she turned to look at him.

'You wish to marry Emma, Doctor?'

He glanced up from the papers he was turning over. 'That is my intention, Smitty.'

The smile he gave her warmed her spinster's heart.

Emma, unaware of the future planned for her, took Percy for a brisk walk, noting the names of the streets as she went. The ranks of tall old houses all looked rather alike, and so did the canals. As she went back she passed the consulting rooms and saw the lights were still on. She hoped the doctor wasn't sitting there working when he should be at home with that magnificent dog. Kulk should be offering him a stiff drink after his day's work while Mevrouw Kulk cooked him a delicious meal. It would be nice to see the house again, but she doubted if she would.

That evening she listened to Juffrouw Smit's suggestions—clearly to be taken most seriously—concerning her washing and ironing, the time of the day when she might consider the bathroom to be hers, and the household chores she was expected to do—which weren't many, for a stout woman came twice each week to clean. Emma must keep her room clean and tidy, and help with the cooking and tidying of the kitchen.

Armed with a Dutch dictionary, and a phrasebook Juffrouw Smit gave her, Emma spent a good deal of her evening in the small room beside the kitchen. Only just before bedtime did she join Juffrouw Smit in the sitting room for a last cup of coffee before saying goodnight. They talked a little then, and watched the news, before she let Percy into the garden prior to taking him upstairs with her.

For the moment Emma was content; it was all new to her and it would be several weeks before she would feel anything other than a lodger. A day out tomorrow—Saturday—she decided. She would get a map of the city and find her way around at her leisure, and on Sunday she would go to church—there would surely be an English Church? And she would write letters in the little room, out of Juffrouw Smit's way.

She had written home once already, a brief letter telling her mother of her safe arrival, with the address and phone number. She would buy postcards too, and send them to Phoebe and Miss Johnson and Mrs Craig. And find a bookshop…

She went to bed with a head full of cheerful plans. Juffrouw Smit had listened to them and nodded and offered a street map, and told her where she would find the English church. She had observed that she herself would be spending Saturday with a cousin and on Sunday would be going to her own church in the morning.

'So you must feel free to spend your days as you wish,

Emma. You have a key, and I hope you will do as you wish and treat my house as your home.'

Emma told herself that she was a very lucky girl; she had a job, a home, and Percy—and, as well as that, her mother was once more happy.

She helped to wash up and tidy the little house in the morning and then went to her room to get her jacket and her handbag. When she went downstairs Percy was in the hall waiting for her. So were Juffrouw Smit and Dr van Dyke.

His good morning was genial. 'If you feel like a walk I thought I might show you some of Amsterdam. It can be a little confusing to a stranger…'

She stared up at him. 'Thank you, but I wouldn't dream of wasting your time. I have a street map…'

'Oh, but I'm much easier to understand than a street map.' He smiled at her. 'The canals can be very confusing, don't you agree, Smitty?'

'Oh, undoubtedly, Doctor. And it will be much quicker for Emma to find her way around once she has been guided by someone who knows the city.' She said briskly to Emma, 'You have your key?'

Emma nodded, trying to think of something to say which wouldn't sound rude; she was having her day arranged for her, and although it would be delightful to spend it with the doctor she couldn't help but feel that he was performing a charitable act prompted by good manners. To refuse wasn't possible; rudeness was something she had been brought up to avoid at all costs, so she said quietly, 'You're very kind. May I bring Percy?'

'Of course. He'll be company for Prince.'

They bade Juffrouw Smit goodbye and went out into

the street. The Rolls was there, with Prince in the driver's seat, and Emma came to a halt.

'I was going to explore Amsterdam...'

'So we will, but first we will go back to my place and have coffee, and leave Prince and Percy in Kulk's charge; neither of them would enjoy sightseeing, you know.'

This statement was uttered in such a reasonable voice that there was no answer...besides, it was obvious when they reached his house that Percy was delighted to be handed over to the care of Kulk and Prince's fatherly company.

She was ushered into the room where they had had breakfast and the dogs rushed out into the garden as Kulk came in with the coffee tray. Emma, pouring coffee from the silver pot into paper-thin cups, allowed herself to enjoy the quiet luxury of the doctor's household. A pity, she thought as she nibbled a wafer-thin biscuit, that she couldn't see behind the ornate double doors on the other side of the hall. It was a large house, and doubtless full of lovely furniture...

She made polite small talk, encouraged by the doctor's grave replies, but it was a relief when he suggested that she might like to tidy herself before they went back to Amsterdam.

He parked the Rolls outside his consulting rooms. 'I shall show you the lay-out of the city,' he told her, 'so that you are familiar with the main streets. We shall walk first to the station. Think of it as the centre of a spider's web. The main streets radiate from it and the canals encircle it. Always carry Juffrouw Smit's address with you, and my telephone number, and keep to the main streets until you know your way around.'

He walked her briskly to the station, then down Dam-

rak to Damrak Square, where he allowed her a moment
to view the royal palace and the memorial before taking her through Kalverstraat, lined with shops, to the
Leidesgracht, into the Herengracht and into Vizelstraat
back towards the Dam Square.

He took her to lunch then, in a large hotel close to the
flower market and the Mint, and Emma, her appetite
sharpened by their lengthy walking, ate smoked eel—
which she hadn't expected to like but which turned out
to be simply delicious—followed by sole *meunière* with
a salad and a dessert of profiteroles and whipped cream.
Pouring coffee, she said in her sensible way, 'That was
a lovely lunch. Thank you!'

'Good. Now I will show you where the museums are,
and the churches, the Town Hall, the hospitals and the
post office and banks.'

So off they went once more. It was hardly a social out-
ing, reflected Emma, conscious that her feet were beginning to ache, excepting for the lunch, of course. On the
other hand it was going to make finding her way around
the city much easier.

It was four o'clock when he said finally, 'You would
like a cup of tea,' and ushered her to a small elegant café.
She sank into a chair and eased her feet out of her shoes,
drank the tea and ate a mountainous pastry swimming
in cream and then pushed her feet back into her shoes
once again.

It was a relief to find that they were only a short walk
from Juffrouw Smit's house, and when they were in sight
of it the doctor said, 'I've tired you out. Go indoors; I'll
fetch Percy.'

If her feet hadn't been hurting so much perhaps she
might have demurred. As it was she went thankfully into

the house and he went at once. 'Fifteen minutes,' he told her, and was gone.

She had her shoes off and her slippers on, her outdoor things put away and everything ready for coffee by the time he returned with Percy.

She opened the door to him, embraced Percy and politely offered coffee.

The doctor stood looking at her. The bright overhead light in the little hall had turned her fiery head into a rich glow, and the long walk had given her a splendid colour. The temptation to gather her into his arms and kiss her was great, but he resisted it, well aware that this wasn't the time or the place.

'Would you like coffee?' asked Emma.

'I've an appointment,' he told her. 'I do hope I haven't tired you too much?'

'No, no. I've enjoyed every minute of it—and it will be so helpful now that I've a good idea of the city. It was a lovely day. Thank you very much.'

He smiled, then bade her goodbye and went away.

It seemed very quiet in the little house when he had gone. She made dark coffee, fed Percy and thought about her day. Being with the doctor had been delightful, for he was a good companion and she felt quite at ease in his company, but she doubted if there would be many occasions such as today. He had felt it his duty, no doubt, to make her familiar with Amsterdam, since she had had no chance to do anything about it herself, and probably he felt responsible about her since she was in his employ. And that was something she must never forget, for all his friendliness.

Juffrouw Smit had said that she would be late home, so Emma got her own supper presently, and wrote a letter to her mother. She had plenty to write about, and she had only just finished it when Juffrouw Smit came back. They sat together for an hour over coffee, exchanging news of their day until bedtime.

Tomorrow, thought Emma sleepily, curling up in her bed, I shall go to church, have lunch somewhere and explore. The quicker she felt at home in Amsterdam the better.

She found the little church in the Beguine Court, which the doctor had told her about, and after the service wandered around looking at the charming little houses surrounding it before going in search of a small café.

Much refreshed by a *kaas broodje* and coffee, she found her way to the station, bought a timetable with an eye to future expeditions, and then boarded a sightseeing boat to tour the canals.

The boat was full, mostly with Americans and English, and the guide kept up a running commentary as they went from one canal to the other. It gave her a splendid back-to-front view of the city, with the lovely old houses backing onto the canals, some with high-walled gardens, some of their windows almost at water level. If she had had the time she would have gone round again for a second time, but it was almost four o'clock and she intended to have tea before she went back to Juffrouw Smit.

She found the café where the doctor had taken her, and, reckless of the prices, had tea and an enormous confection of cream and meringue and chocolate. Then, well satisfied with her day, she went back to Juffrouw Smit's little house.

They spent a pleasant evening together, talking about nothing much while Juffrouw Smit knitted a complicated pattern with enviable ease. Beyond hoping that she had enjoyed her day she asked no questions as to what Emma had done with it, nor did she vouchsafe any information as to her own day. Emma sensed that although they liked each other they would never become friendly enough to exchange personal feelings. But it was enough that they could live together in harmony.

The days went smoothly enough. As the week progressed Emma found herself taking on more and more of the trivial jobs at the consulting rooms, so that Juffrouw Smit could spend more time at her desk, dealing with the computer, the e-mails and the fax machine. For all her staid appearance, there was nothing lacking in her modern skills.

These were things Emma supposed she would have to master if she wished to make a career for herself, but first she supposed that she must learn at least a smattering of the Dutch language. She must ask Juffrouw Smit if there were evening classes. But for the moment it was enough that she had a roof over her head, a job and her wages.

Towards the end of the week she had a letter from her mother. Mrs Dawson was happy—something she had never been with her, thought Emma wistfully, but it was good to know that she was finding life fun again. She and Alice, she wrote, had settled in well. They had found a woman to look after the place, and they had joined a bridge club. They had coffee with Mrs Craig and various friends each morning, and the boutique had such lovely clothes for the winter. At the end of the letter Mrs Dawson hoped that Emma had settled in happily and was getting to know some young people and having fun. *You really must learn to enjoy life more, darling!* She didn't ask about Emma's work.

Emma, stifling hurt feelings, was glad that her mother

was once again living the kind of life she had always enjoyed. She wrote back cheerfully.

Otherwise she spent her evenings poring over the Dutch dictionary, and replied with a cool politeness to the doctor's brief greetings as he came and went each day.

She had been there almost a month when she decided that she could afford to buy a winter coat. She had learned her way around Amsterdam by now, and there were side streets where there were little dress shops where one might pick up a bargain...

Her pay packet crackling nicely in her pocket, she was getting out the case sheets for the day's patients when the doctor came out of his room. He put a letter on the desk and turned to go back.

'Please see that your letters are addressed to Juffrouw Smit's house and not to my rooms,' he observed pleasantly, and had gone again before Emma could utter an apology.

She picked up the letter. It looked official, typewritten and sent by the overnight express mail. She opened it slowly—had she left an unpaid bill? Or was it something to do with the bank?

She began to read.

Chapter 6

It was from Mr Trump. This would be a severe shock to her, he wrote, but her mother and her friend Mrs Riddley had died instantly in a car crash while making a short visit to friends at Richmond. Fortunately, someone who knew them had phoned him at once and he was dealing with the tragic matter. He had not known how to reach her on the phone but begged her to ring him as soon as possible. It was a kind letter and he assured her of his support and assistance.

She read it through again, standing in the cubbyhole, until Juffrouw Smit's voice, a little impatient, penetrated the blankness of her mind. Would she take the doctor's coffee in at once, or he would have no time to drink it before the first patient arrived.

She made the coffee, filled his cup and carried cup and saucer across to his door, knocked and went in. As she set them down on his desk he looked up, saw her ashen face and promptly got up to take her in his arms.

'Emma, what's wrong? Are you ill?' He remembered the letter. 'Bad news?'

She didn't trust herself to speak but fished the letter out of her pocket. Still with one arm round her, he read it.

'My poor dear girl. What shocking news.' He sat her down in the chair facing his desk and pressed the button which would light the discreet red light on Juffrouw Smit's desk. When that lady came, he said, 'Smitty, Emma has had bad news from England. Will you bring her some brandy, then delay my first patient if she comes on time?'

When she brought the brandy he explained in Dutch, and then asked, 'Is Nurse here yet?'

'Any minute now.'

'She must cope here while you take Emma back to your house. Stay with her for as long as you need to, get her a hot drink and try to get her to lie down.' Then, in English, he said, 'Drink this, Emma. Juffrouw Smit will take you back to her house in a moment. Leave the letter with me. I will telephone Mr Trump and discover all I can, then let you know what is best to be done.'

'I must go...'

'Of course. Don't worry about that. I'll arrange everything. Now, drink the rest of the brandy like a good girl.'

A little colour had crept into her cheeks and he took her hands in his.

'Do as Juffrouw Smit suggests and wait until I come, Emma.' His quiet voice pierced her numb senses, firm and comforting, letting her know that he would do everything he could to help her. She gave him a small bleak smile and went with Juffrouw Smit.

There were five minutes before his patient would arrive, and the doctor spent them sitting at his desk. By the
time she was ushered in by the nurse he knew exactly
what had to be done.

Emma, like an obedient child, did just what Juffrouw
Smit bade her do: drank the tea she was offered and lay
down on her bed with a blanket tucked around her. She
was aware that Juffrouw Smit was talking to her in a
quiet, comforting voice, sitting by the bed holding her
hand. Presently, she told herself, she would think what
must be done, but somehow her thoughts slid away to
nothing...

She had no idea how long she had been lying there
when Dr van Dyke came in.

Juffrouw Smit slipped away and he sat down in her
chair and took Emma's hand in his. She opened her eyes
and looked at him, and then sat up in bed as the realisa-
tion of what had occurred penetrated her shock.

'Mother,' she said, and burst into tears...

The doctor sat on the bed beside her and took her in his
arms again and let her cry until she was exhausted. When
she had finally come to a stop, he mopped her face and
said, 'There's my brave girl—and you must stay brave,
Emma. I shall take you over to England this evening. We
shall go to Mr Trump's house, where you will stay for a
few days. He will help you and advise you and make all
the necessary arrangements. So, now I want you to come
downstairs and eat something and pack a bag. We shall
leave here as soon after five o'clock as possible.'

She peered at him through puffy eyelids. 'Am I not
to come back here?'

'Of course you're coming back. I shall come over and

fetch you. But we will talk about that later. Just take enough with you for five or six days. I'm going to take Percy with me now; he will stay with Prince and Kulk until you come back.'

'Did you phone Mr Trump? I'm sorry to give you so much trouble...'

'Yes, I rang him and he is expecting you to stay. Don't worry, Emma, he will explain everything to you this evening.'

'But you can't leave here—your patients, the hospital...'

'Leave that to me.' He gave her a reassuring pat on the shoulder. 'I'm going now. Be ready for me shortly after five o'clock.'

For Emma the day was endless. She packed her overnight bag, did her best to swallow the food Juffrouw Smit offered her and tried to think sensibly about the immediate future. But time and again her thoughts reverted to her mother and the awful suddenness of it all. She wanted desperately to know exactly what had happened. Perhaps she wouldn't feel so grief-stricken once she knew that. She knew it was useless, but she longed to run from the house and go back to England without wasting a moment.

But five o'clock came at last and she stood ready to leave the moment the doctor came for her. She neither knew or cared how she got to Mr Trump; the doctor had said he would see to everything and she had thought no more about it.

When she had been waiting for ten minutes he finally came, but her nerves were on edge and when Juffrouw Smit offered him coffee and something to eat she could have screamed at the delay.

He took a quick look at her tense face, declined the offer and picked up her case. He was tired and hungry, for he had spent time arranging their journey as well as doing his hospital round and then leaving his registrar to deal with anything urgent.

Emma bade a hasty goodbye to Juffrouw Smit and made for the door, impatiently listening to the doctor telling his secretary that he would be there in the morning for his patients. He spoke in Dutch, but as far as Emma was concerned it could have been any language under the sun; if only they could start their journey...

She wondered from where they would get a ferry— and surely it would be far into the night before they got to Mr Trump's house?

As though he had read her thoughts, Dr van Dyke said, 'Just a short drive. There's a plane waiting for us at Schipol; we will be at Heathrow in an hour or so.'

She hardly noticed anything of their journey; she was deeply thankful that she would be back in England so quickly, and at any other time she would have been thrilled and delighted at the speed with which they travelled, but now all she could think of was to get to Mr Trump as quickly as possible.

It seemed perfectly natural that a car should be waiting at Heathrow. She had thanked the pilot when they left the plane and hardly noticed the ease with which they went from it to the car.

The doctor, who had had very little to say on their journey, asked now, 'You know where Mr Trump lives? I have his address but I am not familiar with Richmond.'

Half an hour later they were sitting in Mr Trump's drawing room, drinking coffee while his wife plied them with sandwiches. To her offer of a bed for the night the doctor gave a grateful refusal. 'I've arranged to fly back at eleven o'clock; I have appointments I cannot break in the morning.'

The quiet normality of Mr Trump's home had restored some of Emma's habitual calm. 'But you can't,' she declared. 'You'll be tired. Surely there is someone who could take over for you…?'

She wished she hadn't said that; he had gone to a great deal of trouble to get her to Mr Trump but of course he wanted to get back to his home and his practice as soon as possible. She had disrupted his day most dreadfully.

She said quickly, 'I'm sorry. Of course you know what is best. I'm very grateful—I can never thank you enough… Of course you must go back home as quickly as possible.'

The doctor got up to go. 'I shall be back for your mother's funeral, Emma.' He took her hands in his. 'Mr Trump will take care of everything for you.' He bent and kissed her cheek. 'Be a brave girl, my dear.'

He shook hands with Mrs Trump and went out of the room with Mr Trump. The two men had talked on the phone at some length during the day, and now the doctor said, 'I will arrange things so that I can get here for the funeral and stay for several days. It is very good of you to have Emma to stay.'

'My wife and I are very fond of her, and we have always thought that she had less fun out of life than most girls. She was splendid when her father died. There's Salcombe to decide about, of course.'

'If you think it a good idea I'll drive her there.'

'That might be a very good idea. I'm grateful to you for getting her here so quickly.'

They shook hands and the doctor drove back to Heathrow and was flown back to Schipol, to get thankfully into his car and take himself home. Tomorrow he would get his plans made so that he could go back to England for as long as Emma needed him.

Mr Trump vetoed Emma's request for an account of her mother's death. 'You are tired,' he told her. 'Go to bed and sleep—for I'm sure that you will, whatever you think. In the morning we will sit quietly and I will tell you all that I know. I can promise you that your mother and her friend died instantly; they would have known nothing.'

Emma, worn out by grief and the nightmare day, went to her bed and fell at once into exhausted sleep.

Facing her as she sat opposite him in his study the next morning, Mr Trump saw that she was composed and capable of listening to what he had to say. 'I will tell you exactly what happened, and then we must discuss what arrangements you will wish to be made...'

It was almost a week later, on the evening before her mother's funeral, that Emma went into Mr Trump's drawing room and found Dr van Dyke there.

He got up and went to her at once and took her hands in his.

'Emma—how are you? Mr Trump tells me that you have been such a help to him...'

'Have you come...? That is, will you be here tomorrow?'

'Yes. Mr Trump and I have talked it over and he agrees with me that, if you agree, I should drive you down to Salcombe after the funeral. You will have several matters to deal with there.'

'Oh, would you do that? Thank you.' She found her

hands were still in his and withdrew them gently. 'But you will want to get back to Holland...'

'No, no. I don't need to return for several days. Ample time in which you can attend to matters.' He smiled down at her. 'When everything is settled to your satisfaction, I'll take you back to Amsterdam.'

Mrs Trump bustled in then. 'Had your little chat?' she asked comfortably. 'I'll bring in the tea tray; I'm sure we could all do with a cup.'

The doctor went after tea, saying that he would be back in the morning. The funeral was to be at eleven o'clock and he proposed driving Emma down to Salcombe shortly afterwards. From what Mr Trump had told him there would be small debts to pay in the town, and an interview with the bank manager.

'I suspect,' Mr Trump had said thoughtfully, 'that there is no money—indeed, there may be an overdraft. Of course, the bank were not able to tell me this on the phone, but I feel I should warn you.'

'Will you let me know if there is any difficulty? You may count on me to deal with any.'

Mr Trump had given him a sharp glance. 'I don't think that Emma would like to be in your debt, even though you have proved yourself to be such a good friend.'

The doctor had only smiled.

It was a grey afternoon by the time he drove away from Mr Trump's house with a silent Emma beside him. The funeral had been quiet; there were no close relatives to attend, although there had been friends who had known her mother when she had lived at Richmond. They had been kind to Emma, saying all the right things but careful not to ask as to her future. It had only been the Trumps who'd wished her a warm goodbye, with the assurance that she was to come and stay with them whenever she felt like it. And Mr Trump had added that she could count on him for advice and help in any way.

There was no will; her mother had delayed making one, declaring that making a will was a morbid thing to do, and he had explained that there might be very little money.

'The cottage will be yours, of course, and I'll see to that for you, and its contents, but I know of nothing else. You will need to see your bank manager... Ask him to get in touch with me if there are any difficulties.'

So Emma had a lot to think about, but the first muddle of her thoughts must be sorted out, so it was a relief when the doctor said cheerfully, 'Do you want to talk? Perhaps you would rather have your thoughts?'

'I've had them all week,' said Emma bleakly, 'and they've got me nowhere.'

'Then think them out loud; perhaps I can help?'

'You've done so much already. I can never repay you.' All the same she went on, 'I've forgotten to do so much. The cottage—I should have written to Mrs Pike, who used to clean it for us—and asked her to go and turn on the water and the electricity; it's always turned off when there is nobody there...'

'That's been dealt with,' he told her, 'and there will be food in the fridge and the beds made.'

'Oh, did Mrs Trump think of it? She's been so kind.'

He didn't correct her. 'So that's one problem settled. What's next?'

Slowly, all her doubts and fears came tumbling out, but she stopped short at her biggest fear: her own future. The doctor hadn't said any more about her going back to Amsterdam and she could hardly blame him; she had been enough trouble to him. But if, as Mr Trump had hinted, there wasn't much money in the bank, she would have to find work quickly. 'What about Percy?' she asked suddenly.

'I left him in splendid spirits. He and Prince are devoted; he even climbs into Prince's basket and sleeps with him. They may not look alike but they are obviously soul mates.'

It was on the tip of her tongue to observe that they would miss each other when Percy came back to England, but she stopped herself in time; the doctor might think she was trying, in a roundabout way, to find out if he intended to employ her. Instead she said, 'I must see to things at the cottage.' A task she dreaded—sorting out her mother's possessions, her clothes, looking through her papers.

'Only after you have seen your bank manager and Mr Trump has advised you.'

He gave her a quick sideways glance. 'Mr Trump told me how splendidly you coped when your father died; you will cope splendidly now, Emma.'

They were on the A303 by now, going fast through an early dusk, but as a roadside service station came into sight he slowed.

'Tea, don't you think? We still have quite a way to go.'

Over tea and toasted teacakes she asked him anxiously, 'You don't have to drive back this evening, do you? And won't you be too late for the evening ferry? I didn't think—I'm sorry I've made things so difficult for you.'

'Not at all. I'm staying at Salcombe until you've got things settled as you want them.'

'Staying in Salcombe? But it might be days...'

'Don't worry, I've taken a week or so off.' He smiled
at her across the table—such a kind smile that her heart
gave a happy little skip; he would be there, helpful and
self-assured, knowing what had to be done and how to
do it. She smiled widely at him. 'Oh, how very nice—
and how kind of you. It will be all the quicker with two,
won't it?'

He agreed gravely and passed his cup for more tea, and
Emma, feeling happier than she had done for days, bit
with something like an appetite into her toasted teacake.

It was a dark evening by the time he parked the Rolls
by the pub, took out her case and his own, and went with
her to the cottage. He took the key from her and opened
the door, switched on the lights and ushered her inside.

There were logs ready to light in the small fireplace,
and he put a match to them before she had closed the
door, and although the little room was chilly it was cheerful.

'While you put the kettle on,' he said briskly, 'I'll take
the cases up. Which was your room?'

'On the left... Cases? But there's only my overnight
bag—the case is in the car.'

He was halfway up the narrow stairs. 'I'll have the
other room.' He looked over his shoulder at her surprised
face. 'Did you really suppose that I would dump your
things and leave you on your own?'

'Well,' said Emma, 'I don't think I'd thought about it.'
She paused. 'No, that's not true. I've been dreading being
alone here. I thought you would have booked a room in
one of the hotels and driven back in the morning.'

'You must think me a very poor-spirited friend. But
now we've cleared the matter up, go and make the tea;

while we drink it we will decide what we will cook for supper.'

She took off her coat and went into the kitchen. She put the kettle on and got a teapot and mugs, then peered into the fridge. There was milk there, eggs and butter, bacon and a small loaf of bread.

'There's bacon and eggs and bread and butter,' she told him as he came into the kitchen, and he saw with relief that the shadow of sorrow had lifted from her face. She was pale and tired and unhappy, but the sharpness of her grief had been melted away by familiar surroundings and his matter-of-fact acceptance of events. Without thinking about it, she had accepted his company as a perfectly natural thing. Which was what he had hoped for.

She cooked their supper presently, while he laid the table, and when they had washed up they sat by the fire talking. There were plans to be made but he wouldn't allow her to get too serious about them. Beyond agreeing with her that seeing the bank manager was something which needed to be done as soon as possible, he began to discuss what groceries they would need to buy and the necessity of visiting Mrs Pike.

It was only much later, when she was in bed and on the edge of sleep, that she remembered that if she was to stay in Salcombe she wouldn't need that lady's services. And tomorrow, she promised herself, she would ask the doctor if he still wished to employ *her*.

She was awakened by his cheerful bellow urging her to come down to the kitchen and have her early-morning tea. She had slept all night, and although at the moment of waking she had felt a remembering grief, it was no longer an unbearable ache. She dragged on her dressing gown and went downstairs, and found the doctor, in a vast pullover, with his hair uncombed and a bristly chin, pouring the tea into mugs. His good morning was cheerfully impersonal. 'I can see you've slept well. While you drink your tea I'll go and shave.'

'Have you been up long? I didn't hear you.'

'Proof that you slept well; your shower is the noisiest I've ever come across. While you cook breakfast I'll go and get some rolls; they should be hot from the oven.'

It was a cold bright morning when, after breakfast, they walked through the town to the bank. At its door Emma said hesitantly, 'Would you mind coming with me? I'm sure there's nothing I can't understand or deal with, but just in case there's something...'

The manager received them gravely, uttering the established condolences, enquiring after Emma's health, and acknowledging the doctor's presence with a thoughtful look. He opened the folder on his desk and coughed.

'I'm afraid that what I have to tell you is of a rather disturbing nature, although I am sure we can come to some decision together. There was a small sum of money in your joint account with your mother to which you added before you went to Holland. Not a great deal of money, but sufficient to give your mother a modicum of security. She had her pension, of course, and she gave me to understand that she had no need to contribute to household expenses so that the pension was an adequate amount for her personal needs. Unfortunately she spent her money freely, and when the account was empty persuaded me to allow her an overdraft, assuring me that you would repay it. In short, she spent a good deal more than the overdraft and there are a number of debts outstanding.'

Emma asked in a small shocked voice, 'But what could

she have spent the money on? Her pension was enough for clothes and spending money—there was a few hundred in our account. Are you sure?'

'Quite sure. I'm sorry, Miss Dawson, but I was assured by your mother that there were funds she could call upon, and since I have known your parents for a number of years I saw no reason to question that.'

'Besides the bank, do you know to whom she owed money?'

'I hold a number of cheques which the bank have refused to pay. It would be quite in order for you to have them and settle them personally. I suggest that I should open an account here in your name so that you can settle the accounts at your convenience.'

'But I haven't...' began Emma, but was stopped by Dr van Dyke's calm voice.

'That is sound advice, Emma. Allow Mr Ansty to open a new account in your name, and perhaps he would be good enough to tell me how much is needed to cover any payments.' When Emma opened her mouth to protest, he said, 'No, Emma, allow me to deal with this for the moment.'

There was something in his voice which stopped her saying anything more. Only she gave a little gasp when Mr Ansty told the doctor how much was needed to cover the debts and the overdraft. After that she didn't listen while the two men dealt with it, for her mind was wholly occupied with the ways and means of paying back so vast a sum. How on earth was she going to do it?

It wasn't until they were out on the street again that she stopped suddenly.

'I must be mad—whatever have I let you do? We must go back and tell him that you've changed your mind.'

The doctor said nothing, but whisked her into the nearby patisserie and ordered coffee.

'Didn't you hear what I said?' hissed Emma.

'Yes, I did. And when we get back to the cottage I will explain everything to you. Now, drink your coffee like a good girl and we will do the shopping.'

He sounded matter-of-fact, and quite unworried, and that served to calm her down a little. All the same, going in and out of the shops buying their lunch and supper, and listening politely to sympathetic condolences, at the back of her mind was the uneasy feeling that she wasn't quite sure what was happening...

There was a message on the answerphone from Mr Trump when they returned to the cottage. Mrs Riddley's niece would be driving down to Salcombe on the following day to collect her aunt's possessions. She hoped that Miss Dawson had left everything untouched so that she could check for herself that everything was as it should be.

'Well, really,' exclaimed Emma crossly. 'Does she suppose I'd take anything which wasn't Mother's?' She sliced bread with a good deal of unnecessary energy. 'And do I have to stay here all day waiting for her?'

'Very likely. And I must go to the medical centre tomorrow. What's for lunch?'

'Welsh Rarebit. I must go and see Mrs Pike and Miss Johnson...' She was buttering toast. 'And you are going to explain to me about paying the bills.'

He had intended to explain a good deal more than that, but as they finished their meal there was a knock on the door and there was Mrs Craig standing on the doorstep, expecting to be asked in.

'I heard you were here.' She looked at Dr van Dyke,

'With the doctor. I had to come to see you to express my sympathy and have a little chat. I saw your mother frequently, you know, and I'm sure you would wish to know what a happy life she was leading. Such a sad thing to happen, and you so far from her at the time, although I hear that she died instantly.'

Mrs Craig settled herself comfortably in a chair. 'I would have gone to the funeral if it had been here, but of course she wished to be buried with her husband.'

She doesn't mean to be unkind, thought Emma, sitting rigid in her chair, but if she doesn't go soon I shall scream.

It was the doctor who came to the rescue. 'You are the very person we wanted to see,' he told Mrs Craig. 'May I come back with you to the hotel? There is someone there I believe had dealings with Mrs Dawson, and it would make it so much easier if you could introduce me. I'm sure you must know her...'

Mrs Craig got up at once. 'Of course, Doctor. I'm so delighted to be of help. I've lived here for some time now and know almost everyone here. Emma, you will forgive me if I don't stay, for I'm sure Dr van Dyke is anxious to settle his business.'

Emma was left alone, to cry her eyes out in peace, so that when the doctor came back she was tolerably cheerful again, in the kitchen getting their tea.

'There were one or two small bills at the hotel,' he told her. 'I've settled them.' He didn't tell her that he had telephoned Mr Trump, paid a visit to the rector and talked at length with Kulk.

When she suggested again that they had to talk about his arrangements with the bank he brushed it aside. 'You have had enough to think about today,' he told her. 'We will get a meal at the pub and not be too late in bed, for we don't know how early this niece will arrive.'

They ate fresh-caught fish and a mountain of chips, and since there was no one else in the little dining room behind the bar the landlord came and talked to them while they ate, gathering up their plates when they had finished and promising them apple pie and cream.

The doctor kept up a casual flow of talk during their meal, urged her to have a brandy with her coffee and walked her briskly back to the cottage. She was pleasantly sleepy by now, and needed no urging to go to her bed. Tomorrow they would have that talk, and once Mrs Riddley's niece had taken her aunt's things she would pack away her mother's possessions. That left only Mrs Pike to see...

She woke in the small hours and sat up in bed, struck by a sudden thought. What a fool I am, she reflected. I can sell the cottage and pay back the money. I must tell him in the morning.

She fell asleep again, satisfied that the problem was solved.

They had barely finished breakfast when Mrs Riddley's niece arrived. Emma disliked her on sight; she was a youngish woman, fashionably thin, expensively dressed and skilfully made-up.

She answered Emma's polite greeting with a curt nod. 'You're Emma Dawson? I haven't much time; I intend to drive back as soon as possible.' She went past Emma into the cottage. 'I hope you haven't touched any of my aunt's possessions...'

Emma said quietly, 'No. I'm sorry that Mrs Riddley died.'

The doctor, at the kitchen sink, rattled a few plates.

'Someone else is here?'

'A friend who brought me back to England. Would you like coffee, or would you prefer to go straight to your aunt's room?'

'Oh, I'll get her stuff packed up first. Which room is it?'

'I'll show you, and when you are ready perhaps you will look around the cottage and make sure that there is nothing you have overlooked?'

'Certainly I shall.' She closed the door firmly in Emma's face.

The doctor was drying plates with the air of one who had been doing it all his life. He lifted an eyebrow at Emma as she went into the kitchen.

'Keep a sharp eye on her; she might filch the spoons!'

Emma, a bit put out, giggled, feeling suddenly light-hearted.

After a while the niece came downstairs. 'I've packed up my aunt's things. There are several dresses and hats too old to bother with. I dare say you can take them to a charity shop.'

She looked at the doctor, all at once smiling.

'Dr van Dyke—this is Miss or is it Mrs Riddley?' said Emma. 'And actually I think you should take everything with you.'

'Oh, undoubtedly,' said the doctor smoothly. 'One needs to be careful about these matters. I'll fetch a plastic sack and you can bundle everything in it.'

'Would you like coffee?' asked Emma. 'And then you must go round the cottage.'

Miss Riddley refused coffee. 'I left the car at the end of the quay...'

'I'll carry your bags to it,' offered the doctor. 'We will

let Mr Trump know that you have been and removed everything of your aunt's.' He stood up. 'Shall we go? I dare say you are anxious to get back home?'

Chilling good manners, thought Emma, watching Miss Riddley mince along on her high heels beside the doctor. He looks very nice from the back, reflected Emma, and then she thought, I'll tell him about selling the cottage and how I'll pay back his money, and then he can go back to Amsterdam and not feel he has to do anything more for me. Of course there's Percy. Perhaps he wouldn't mind giving me a lift back so that I can bring Percy back here...

Much taken with this half-witted idea, she went upstairs to make quite sure that Mrs Riddley's possessions had really gone.

There was no sign of the doctor when she went back downstairs and she remembered that he had intended to go to the medical centre. She had her coffee and started on a task she had been putting off: going through the desk her mother had used and clearing out the papers in it. It was something which had to be done, and it seemed likely that now everything was more or less settled the doctor would wish to return to Holland. That was something else she must talk to him about without delay. She had been living in a kind of limbo, doing what he suggested, not allowing herself to think too much about the future, but it was time she faced up to that.

She finished clearing the desk and set the table for lunch, which would be cheese and pickles and the rolls he had fetched early that morning—there was to be no lingering over lunch, she decided. There was too much to talk about.

But she wasn't to have her wish. The doctor came in

briskly, observed that he had seen the niece drive away and then gone to see his former colleagues, then added as a kind of afterthought, 'What do you call me, Emma?'

'Call you? Why, Dr van Dyke.'

'My name is Roele.'

'Yes, I know, but I can't call you that; I've been working for you. Which reminds me...'

He gave her no chance to continue. 'Yes, you can.' He sat back in his chair and smiled at her. 'Will you marry me, Emma?'

She put the roll she was buttering back on her plate, staring at him.

'Why?' she asked.

He was amused, but all he said was, 'A sensible question. I am thirty-six, Emma. I need a wife to run my home, entertain my friends and—er—support me.'

'But Kulk runs your home beautifully and your friends might not like me. Besides, you don't need supporting. Indeed, you've been supporting me.' She added politely, 'Thank you for asking me. I've had a very good idea this morning. I shall sell the cottage and then I can pay you back all that money you gave the bank.'

'And?'

'Then I'll get a job.'

'For such a sensible girl you have some odd ideas, Emma. What job? And where will you live? And how will you pay the rent and feed yourself on the kind of wages you are able to earn?'

'Well, I must say,' said Emma crossly, 'I thought you'd be pleased to be free to go back home.' She frowned. 'This is a very strange conversation.'

'Indeed it is. Shall we start again. Will you marry me, Emma?'

Chapter 7

She stared at him across the table. 'But you don't—that is, you can't possibly be in love with me...'

'I have made no mention of love, or falling in love, Emma. Indeed, a happy marriage is as likely to be the result of compatibility, a real liking for each other, and the slow growing of deep affection which would surely follow. Sound bases on which to build. Whereas all too often marrying on impulse whilst in the throes of a love which so often turns into infatuation turns into disaster.'

He smiled at her. 'Do I sound like an elder brother giving you advice? I don't mean to; I'm only trying to make the situation clear to you without pretending to a romance that doesn't exist.'

'And if I should say yes?'

'We will marry as soon as possible and go back to Amsterdam. You will, of course, keep this cottage. We both like Salcombe, don't we? And it would be nice to keep a foot in the door here.'

'Have you ever been in love?' asked Emma. If he was surprised at her question he didn't show it.

'Oh, countless times. Young men do, you know, it's all part of growing up. And you?'

'Oh, yes. With film stars and the music master at school and my best friend's brother—only they went to live abroad and I forgot about him. And of course there was Derek, but I didn't love him—only got used to him. Mother liked him and he was always very attentive— until Father died and he discovered that he was bankrupt and it would damage his career if he married me. Would I damage *your* career?'

He answered her with perfect gravity. 'No. Indeed, I suppose it would be a great advantage to me. A married man always seems so much more reliable!'

'You might meet someone and fall in love... So might I...'

'There is that possibility, but remember that I am no longer an impetuous youth and you, if I may say so, have reached the age of reason.'

'I'm twenty-seven,' snapped Emma, 'and if you suppose that I'm a staid spinster you're mistaken.'

'No, no, I wouldn't imagine anything of the sort. I merely meant to imply that we are both of us ideally suited to be man and wife.'

'You're not asking me because you are sorry for me?'

His, 'Good Lord, no,' had a satisfyingly genuine ring to it. All the same she frowned.

'Ought we to wait and think about it?'

'For my part, I've done my thinking, but by all means take all the time you need, Emma. I'll go back to Amsterdam in a while, and you can make up your mind at your leisure.'

This was a prospect she didn't fancy; to be here in the cottage on her own and Roele not there to advise her... But of course she couldn't ask his advice about marrying him, could she?

'You don't know anything about me...'

'On the contrary, I know that you are capable, sensible, have similar tastes and interests to mine, you are a good listener, have the ability to face up to life, and, as a bonus, you are a very attractive young woman. And let me make it quite clear to you that I do not wish for or expect you to strive for a romantic attachment until such time as you feel ready for it.'

'Just friends to start with?'

'You see what I mean? Sensible and matter-of-fact. Just friends—good friends.'

'There's another thing. I think you must be comfortably off, but I want you to know that I'm not marrying you for your money.'

Roele gave a small inward sigh of relief. His darling Emma was going to marry him, and sooner or later would learn to love him. In the meantime he had more than enough love for them both. He said firmly, 'I know you aren't, and, yes, I do have rather a lot of money. It will be nice to share it with someone.'

His smile was warm and friendly and utterly reassuring. 'Will you marry me, Emma?'

'Yes, I will. I like you very much and I know that I would miss you very much if you were to go away, and—and when you're not here I feel a bit lost. Only I hope I won't be a disappointment to you.' She looked at him with a question in her eyes. 'You would tell me?'

'Yes, I promise you that I will.' He leaned across the table and took one of her hands in his. 'Would you object to getting married by special licence as soon as possible? Here in Salcombe? And we'll return to Amsterdam as soon as possible afterwards.'

'I still have Mother's things to pack up...'

'Then start on that while I go and see Mrs Pike and talk to the rector.'

'Does it take a long time to get a special licence?'

'It should be in the post tomorrow morning; all we need to do is fix a time and a day.'

'Just us?'

'Well, I think Dr Walters might like to be at the church, and what about Miss Johnson and Mrs Craig?'

'Oh, witnesses. Of course. All right. And now everything is settled we had better get started.'

She got up and began to clear the table, but he took the dishes out of her hands and put his hands on her shoulders. 'How very unromantic of me to propose to you over the remnants of a meal. I must make up for that...' He bent and kissed her gently. 'We shall be happy, Emma, I promise you...'

His kiss sent a glow of warmth through her; she was honest enough to admit that she enjoyed it, and for the first time since her mother's death she felt a surge of content and happiness.

As soon as he had gone in search of the rector and Mrs Pike she went to her mother's room and began the sad task of packing up her clothes.

The cupboards and drawers were stuffed full. In the short time in which Emma had been away Mrs Dawson had indeed spent a good deal of money on dresses, hats and shoes—most of them hardly worn. They would have to go to a charity shop.

She picked out one or two of the more sober garments in case Mrs Pike might like to have them, bundled everything else in sacks and then opened her mother's jewel box. There was a pearl necklace, rings and brooches and earrings. They were hers now, Emma supposed. She closed the box. She would wear the pearls on her wedding day but the rest she would put away until an occasion when she might need to wear them.

She wept a little as she thought of her mother and father. I'm an orphan, she thought, drowning in sudden self-pity, until her sensible self took over again and she reminded herself that she was going to get married to a man she liked very much and go and live in a splendid house and share his life. And she was going to make a success of it too.

Roele came back then, with the news that the rector would marry them in two days' time at ten o'clock in the morning, if she was agreeable to that. And as for Mrs Pike, he had arranged for her to go to the cottage once a week and keep it in good order. 'For of course we shall come here from time to time, even if it is only for a few days. Now, what do you want me to do with your mother's clothes?' he asked.

She had been crying, poor girl. The quicker the cottage was empty of things which would remind her of her grief the better.

'There are three sacks full. Could you take them to the charity shop? The nearest one is in Kingsbridge.'

'A good idea. Get your hat and coat; we'll both go. I'll take them along to the car while you get ready.'

By the time she had done that, and tidied her face and

hair, she looked quite cheerful again. As they drove the few miles to Kingsbridge he kept up a steady flow of cheerful remarks, so that by the time they reached the shop and handed everything over she was quite ready to go to a tea room at the bottom of the high street and linger over tea and hot buttered crumpets.

They were married two days later, on a morning of tearing wind and persistent rain, despite which a surprising number of people came to the church to see them wed. Dr Walters and his colleagues, Miss Johnson and Phoebe, Mrs Craig and Mrs Pike, several members of the lifeboat crew, even the cross-looking baker's wife.

They gathered round when the simple ceremony was over, offering good wishes and waving goodbyes as they got into the Rolls. They drove through the little town and on to the road to Exeter on the first stage of their journey back to Holland.

They had had an early breakfast. Roele had taken the luggage to the car and locked the cottage door with the cheerful remark that they would be back in the spring, and then popped her into the car and driven to the church without giving Emma time to feel regret or sadness. And now he kept up a steady flow of talk: the unexpected pleasure of seeing friends and acquaintances at the church, the stormy weather, the pleasure of seeing Prince and Percy again.

'You won't see much of me for a few days,' he told her. 'I'll have a backlog of work, but that will give you time to get used to the house and do some shopping. I should warn you that the nearer we get to Christmas the more social life there will be. Which will give you a chance to meet my friends.'

'Oh, do you have a lot of friends and go out a great deal?'

'Plenty of friends, yes. And I do have a social life, but a very moderate one.'

They were on the A303, driving into worsening weather. As they approached Middle Wallop Roele said, 'We will stop for lunch.' He turned to smile at her. 'Breakfast seems a long time ago. There's rather a nice place where we can get a meal.'

He took a side-turning and stopped before a handsome manor house on the edge of a village. After the gloomy skies and heavy rain its comfortable warmth was welcoming. Emma, led away by a pleasant waitress, returned to find that Roele was sitting at the bar.

'I hope you're hungry; I am.' The bartender put two champagne cocktails before them. 'To our future together, Emma.'

It was probably the champagne which gave her such a pleasurable feeling of excitement.

They lunched on sautéed mushrooms, duckling and orange sauce and bread and butter pudding and a pot of delicious coffee. Looking out at the wild weather, Emma felt very reluctant to leave.

'I'll phone from the car,' Roele told her. 'I doubt if the Harwich Ferry will be running in this weather. If that's the case, we'll make for Dover.'

It was the case; the Harwich Ferry was cancelled. But the Dover ferries were still running, so the doctor drove on to the M25 and presently took the Dover road.

It was well into the afternoon now, and already getting dark with no sign of the weather improving. Emma, sitting in the car, waiting to go on board the ferry, looked at the rough seas and hoped for the best.

On board, she drank the tea she was offered and opened the magazine Roele had bought her. They should be home by midnight, he assured her. It was a long drive to Amsterdam, but the roads were good and fast and Kulk would be waiting for them. She smiled and nodded and tried not to notice the heaving deck. They were halfway across when she put the magazine down.

'I'm going to be sick,' said Emma.

The doctor took a quick look at her white face, heaved her gently to her feet and led her away. And she, feeling truly awful, wouldn't have cared if he had thrown her overboard.

Instead he dealt with things with an impersonal kindness which made it less awful than it was, finally gently washing her face and settling her in her seat again with an arm round her. He made her drink the brandy the steward brought, then tucked her head onto his shoulder. 'Go to sleep,' he told her, 'we are nearly there. Once we're on land you'll be quite yourself again. My poor girl, I should never have brought you—we should have stayed until tomorrow.'

Emma mumbled into his coat, feeling better already. 'That wouldn't have done; you told me that you had an appointment tomorrow.' She hiccoughed as a result of the brandy, and closed her eyes. She was quite safe with Roele's arm around her, and not only safe but happy.

He was right, of course, once on dry land she was quite herself again. It was dark night now, the rain lashing down, blown hither and thither by the wind, but the road was good and almost empty of traffic. Roele drove fast, relaxed behind the wheel of the big car, not saying much, only telling her from time to time where they were—along the coast to Ostend and then inland onto the E40. He turned off again onto the motorway to Antwerp, and then over the border into Holland to Utrecht and finally the outskirts of Amsterdam.

But before they reached the city the doctor turned off to go to his home, driving slowly now along the narrow road until he reached the village and a moment later drew up before his front door. There were lights shining out from the downstairs windows and the front door opened wide to reveal more light, with Kulk and Mevrouw Kulk standing there.

The doctor got out, opened Emma's door and swept her into the house through the rain and wind, to be greeted by handshaking and beaming smiles and a rush of excited talk. She was borne away by Mevrouw Kulk to have her coat taken, and ushered into the cloakroom at the back of the hall. She was tired and very hungry, and the prospect of bed was enticing, but she washed her face to wake herself up, tidied her hair and went back in to the hall.

Kulk was bringing in their luggage and Roele had gone out again to put the car in the garage. She stood for a moment, feeling uncertain. But only for a moment, for Mevrouw Kulk appeared through a door behind the staircase. With her was Percy, and close on his heels Prince.

Emma was kneeling on the floor, her arms round the two dogs, when the doctor came back. He threw his coat onto a chair, received the lavish affection offered by Prince and Percy and helped her to her feet.

'Welcome home, Emma. Mevrouw Kulk has a meal ready. You must be hungry—and longing for your bed. Sleep for as long as you like in the morning; I shall be away all day until early evening, forgive me for that, but the Kulks will look after you.'

He took her hand and led her through an arched double

door into a room with a high-plastered ceiling and long windows. The walls were white and hung with paintings in heavy gilt frames, and the furniture matched the room—a rectangular mahogany table ringed by ribband-backed chairs, a massive sideboard bearing a display of silver, and a wide fireplace surmounted by an elaborate chimneypiece.

'This is a beautiful room,' said Emma, forgetting her tiredness for a moment as Roele sat her down at the table, where two places had been laid. Despite the lateness of the hour, she noted, silver and crystal gleamed on the lace tablemats and there were fresh flowers in a Delft blue bowl. And their supper, when it came, was delicious: beef bouillon, a creamy golden soufflé and finally a fruit tart, the pastry light as a feather.

'And, since it is our wedding day, champagne is obligatory,' said the doctor. He smiled at her across the table. 'You were a beautiful bride, Emma.'

She gaped at him. 'In last year's suit and the only hat I could find in the town?'

'And still a beautiful bride. An unusual wedding day, perhaps, but I have enjoyed every minute of it.'

'Really? Well, yes, I suppose I have too—not the ferry, though!'

'I'm sorry about that too, but at least you will never forget your wedding day.' He studied her tired face. 'You would like to go to bed, wouldn't you? No coffee; it might keep you awake. Mevrouw Kulk shall take you to your room.' He got up and walked to the door with her, and bent and kissed her cheek. 'Sleep well, Emma.' After a pause, he added, 'I'll see to Percy.'

Already half asleep, she followed Mevrouw Kulk up

the wide staircase, along a gallery and into a softly lit bedroom.

'I must explore it in the morning,' muttered Emma as Mevrouw Kulk drew curtains and opened doors and cupboards, switched on another bedside light and patted the turned-down coverlet before beaming with a *'wel te rusten'* as she went away.

Emma cleaned her teeth, washed her face, tore off her clothes and got into bed—to fall asleep instantly.

When she woke there was a sturdy young girl drawing back the curtains to reveal a dull morning. She sat up in bed and ventured a *'Goeden morgen'* with such success that the girl answered with a flood of Dutch.

Emma tried again. 'I don't understand' had been one of first useful phrases she had learnt. The girl smiled, picked up the tray she had set on the table under the window and brought it to the bed. Emma, struggling to find the words she wanted, was relieved to see a note propped up against the teapot. Roele in an almost unreadable scrawl, wished her good morning, recommended that she ate a good breakfast and then took the dogs for a walk, and said he would be home at about six o'clock.

Emma drank her tea, read the note again and got up. The bathroom held every incentive to linger, with its deep bath and shelves loaded with towels, soap and everything else she could possibly want, but she resisted its luxury after a pleasurable time lying in a scented bath and dressed once more in the suit. Nicely made up, and with her hair in its usual topknot, she went downstairs.

Kulk was hovering in the hall to wish her good morning and lead her to the small room where she had breakfasted on her earlier visit. The table had been drawn near the brisk fire and Prince and Percy were waiting for her.

This was her home, she reflected as Kulk set a coffee pot down before her, moved the toast rack a little nearer and asked her if she would prefer bacon and eggs, scrambled eggs, or perhaps an omelette...

And I actually belong here, thought Emma, devouring the scrambled eggs with appetite and deciding that toast and marmalade would be nice, with another cup of coffee. She handed out morsels of toast to both dogs, and when Kulk came to see if there was anything else she would like she asked, 'The doctor, did he leave very early?'

His English was good, although the accent was pronounced. 'At half past seven, *mevrouw*. I understand he has a number of patients to see before going to the hospital, where he has a clinic and ward rounds.'

'You have been with the doctor for a long time?'

'I taught him to ride a bicycle, *mevrouw*, when I was a houseman at his parents' home. When they retired to a quiet life I came as his houseman and my wife as his cook.'

Emma set down her coffee cup. 'Kulk, this is all strange to me. I would be glad if you will help me...'

'With the greatest pleasure, *mevrouw*. Katje and I will do everything to assist you in any way. If you have finished your breakfast you might like to come to the kitchen and we will explain the running of the household to you. Katje speaks no English but I will translate, for you will wish to order the meals and inspect the linen and cutlery as well as the stores she keeps.'

'Thank you, Kulk. I should like to know as much as possible, but I have no intention of taking over.' She hesitated; Kulk was an old family servant and to be trusted. She said carefully, 'You see, Kulk, the doctor and I married without waiting for an engagement. I have recently lost my mother and I had no reason to stay in England.'

'Katje and I are happy that the doctor is happily married, *mevrouw*. For a long time we have wished that, and now we are delighted to welcome you and serve you as we serve him.'

That sounded incredibly old-fashioned, but she had no doubt that it was spoken in all sincerity. 'Thank you—and Katje. May I call her that? I know that I—we are going to be very happy here. I'll come with you now, shall I? May Prince and Percy come, too?'

'Of course, *mevrouw*.'

He led the way into the hall, through a door beside the staircase and along a short passage which led to the kitchen. This was a large room, with windows overlooking the grounds behind the house. It was old-fashioned at first glance, but as well as the vast wooden dresser against one wall and the scrubbed table at its centre there was an Aga flanked by glass-fronted cupboards and shelves gleaming with shining saucepans. There was a deep butler's sink under one window and a dishwasher beside it, and on either side of the Aga were two Windsor armchairs, each with a cat curled up on its cushion.

'The cats!' exclaimed Kulk. 'Perhaps you do not care for them…?'

'Oh, but I do—and what a lovely kitchen.'

Mevrouw Kulk wasn't there, but she had heard them for she called something to Kulk from an open door in one wall. She came a moment later, holding a bowl of eggs. She put them down, wished Emma good day and offered a chair.

Emma sat at the table, listening to Kulk talking to his wife, trying to understand what was being said. But presently she gave up. As soon as possible she would take lessons; her smattering of the language wouldn't be of much use if she were to join in Roele's social life. Besides, she would want to shop; he had never mentioned her clothes, but she was quite sure that as his wife she would be expected to dress with some style.

Mevrouw Kulk interrupted her thoughts, standing beside her with a pad and a pencil.

'Dinner for tonight,' said Kulk. 'Is there something you would wish for? Katje has it planned, but perhaps you would wish for other things.'

'No, no, of course not. But I'd like to know what we are to have…'

She left the kitchen after an hour with a good idea of the day's routine kept by the Kulks. There was a girl to help—she who had brought her early-morning tea, Bridgette—and a gardener, and once or twice a year local women came in from the village to help with the bi-annual cleaning of the house. 'If there is to be a social occasion,' explained Kulk, 'then we get extra help.'

Obviously it was a well-run house which needed no help from her.

She put on a coat and went into the grounds with the dogs. There was a terrace behind the house, with steps leading down to a formal garden, and beyond that a great stretch of lovingly laid out shrubs and ornamental trees, and narrow stone paths with unexpected rustic seats and stone statues round every corner. Whoever had planned it had done it with meticulous attention to detail. She wandered round for some time, with Percy and Prince chasing imaginary rabbits and racing back to see if she was still there. It was a beautiful place even on a wintry morning; in summer it would be somewhere where one would want to sit and do nothing.

She went back indoors then and had the coffee Kulk had ready.

If *mevrouw* wished, he suggested, he would show her round the house. But perhaps she would prefer to wait for the doctor?

She thanked him. 'I would rather wait for the doctor to come home, and then we can go round it together, Kulk.'

'Quite right and proper, too,' said Kulk to Katje later, 'and them newlyweds and having plans and so forth. Such a nice young lady he's found for himself. Used to nice living, I can see that, but it must be very strange for her. A bit of help from us from time to time won't come amiss.'

There were books in the small sitting room, as well as newspapers in both Dutch and English. Besides that there was a television, discreetly tucked away in a corner. Emma, not easily bored, had plenty to keep her occupied, but after lunch she sat down by the fire, hemmed in by the dogs, and allowed her thoughts free rein.

It was apparent that Roele was more than just very well off, he had what her old schoolmistress had always referred to as 'background'—a background which, she suspected, stretched back for generations. She must ask him about that—but she must also remember not to plague him with endless questions for the time being. Having worked at his consulting rooms, she was aware of the number of patients he saw each day and the length of his visits to the hospital—more than one hospital, Juffrouw Smit had told her. Only when he had the leisure to talk to her would she question him.

There was a great deal unsaid between them, but she had expected that; they might have married, but they didn't know each other well. At least, she didn't know Roele, and she supposed that he didn't know her as a person. That they liked each other was a solid fact and that they would, in time, have a happy life together was something she didn't doubt. Until then she would be content...

She went upstairs to change into the jersey dress after tea, and when she came downstairs Roele was taking off his coat in the hall, fending off the dogs' delighted greeting. When he saw her he came to the bottom of the stairs and held out a hand.

'How nice to find you here, have you been bored or lonely?'

'Neither. It would be impossible to be lonely with the dogs, and I could never be bored in this house.'

'You have explored?'

'No.'

He was quick to see her hesitate. 'You waited for me? Splendid. We will go round now, and while we are having a drink before dinner you can tell me what you think of it.'

He put an arm round her shoulders and turned her smartly towards the big arched doorway on one side of the hall.

'The drawing room,' he said, and opened the door.

It was a large room, with walls hung with pale green silk between white-painted panels. There were brass sconces between the pillars and a cut-glass chandelier hung from the strapwork ceiling. The three tall windows were curtained in old-rose velvet and the floor was covered by a dark green Aubusson carpet with a floral design at its centre. Above the fireplace was an elaborate Rococo chimneypiece with an enormous mirror.

It was a very grand room, and its furniture reflected

its grandeur: William and Mary settees on either side
of the fireplace, two Georgian winged armchairs with
a Pembroke table between them, a group of armchairs
around a veneered rosewood tripod table and a scattering
of small tables, each with its own lamp. There were two
walnut display cabinets, filled with porcelain and silver,
and a long-case clock facing the windows.

Emma stood in the middle of the room, taking it all in.
'What a wonderful room!' She caught sight of the pile of
magazines and an open book lying on one of the tables.
'Do you use it often?'

'Oh, yes. It's remarkably cosy with a good fire burning
in the winter. Tea round the fire on a Sunday afternoon
with a good book and the right music. And for social occasions, of course.'

He crossed to the door and opened it. There was a con-
servatory beyond, and Emma lingered among the wealth
of plants and shrubs before he ushered her through a further door and back into the hall. 'We've seen the dining
room, now here is my study.' This proved to be another
panelled room, its walls lined with bookshelves and a
vast desk under its window.

Emma gazed around, wondering if she would be welcome in it. Probably not, she thought.

'You know the morning room,' said Roele, 'but there's
one more room here.' He crossed the hall again and
opened a door onto a quite small room, with two easy
chairs by a small steel grate and a sofa table standing
behind a big sofa under the window. 'My mother always
used this room. She wrote her letters here and sat in that
chair, knitting and working at her tapestry. I do hope you
will make it your own, Emma.'

'Your mother?'

'She and my father live just outside Den Haag now. My father is retired—like me, he was a medical man— and they have a house in the country. We will go and visit them shortly.'

'Do they know that you married me?'

'Of course, and they are delighted to welcome you into the family.'

They were now halfway up the staircase, but she paused, her hand on the carved wood balustrade. 'If I were them,' she declared, letting grammar go to the winds, 'I wouldn't want to welcome me, coming in from nowhere—I might be an adventuress.'

The doctor laughed. 'An adventuress wouldn't have carroty hair,' he told her. 'Besides, they trust my judgement. Don't worry about them, Emma; they will like you and I think that you will like them.'

He led her across the gallery to the front of the house, opened a door and urged her inside. The room was large, with two tall windows opening out onto a wrought-iron balcony. A four-poster bed faced them, its coverlet in the same satin chintz as the curtains. There was a mahogany dressing table between the windows, with an elaborate carved framed triple mirror on it, a cabinet chest against one wall and a tallboy facing it. On either side of a small round table there were small tub chairs, and at the foot of the bed a Regency chaise longue. It was a beautiful room, and Emma said so.

'You must love your home, Roele,' she said.

'As you will love it too, Emma. We can go through here…' He led the way through a bathroom to a smaller room, simply furnished, and then out into the gallery again to open another door.

Emma lost count of the rooms after a time. When they

had inspected those opening onto the gallery there were
the side passages, leading to even more rooms, and then
a staircase to the floor above.

'The nurseries,' said the doctor, sweeping her in and
out of doors. Children's bedrooms, more guest rooms.
And then up another staircase. 'Kulk and Katje have
rooms here, and Bridgette too, and along here are the
attics and a door onto the roof.'

There was a narrow parapet and an iron staircase
down to the ground.

'We keep the door locked but the key hangs above it.
Kulk has another key and so have I.'

'I had no idea...' began Emma.

He understood her at once. 'It is a large house, but it
is also home—our home, Emma. You will learn to love
it as I do.'

They went back downstairs and had drinks and a
splendid dinner, and shortly afterwards Roele went to
his study to work. Emma spent a blissful few hours in
the drawing room, examining everything in it. Percy was
with her, but Prince had gone with his master. Presently
she was joined by the two cats, who wandered in and
settled onto one of the settees with the air of welcome
guests. That was what was so delightful about the house,
reflected Emma, it *was* a home as well.

Roele came back then, asked her if there was anything
she would like before going to bed and suggested that
she might like to go and see Juffrouw Smit on the following day. 'She would like you to go to her house for
lunch. Kulk will drive you in about midday. I shall be
at the hospital for most of the day, but I'll call for you at
about half past one and bring you back here.'

He smiled at her. 'I shall be free at the weekend and we can be together. You're not too lonely?'

'No, of course not. There's such a lot to see. Tomorrow I had thought I'd walk to the village, but now I'm going to Juffrouw Smit, so I'll go to the village the next day. The days won't be long enough.'

She sounded so convincing that she almost convinced herself, and tried hard not to mind when he made no effort to keep her after she suggested that she should go to bed.

Chapter 8

Emma was relieved to see Juffrouw Smit's severe countenance break into a smile when she arrived for lunch the next day. It could have been an awkward meeting, but somehow her hostess gave the impression that she had expected Dr van Dyke and Emma to marry, and it was something of which she entirely approved.

'The doctor is coming for you at half past one so we do not have much time for a chat, but perhaps you will come again? I am interested to hear of your wedding and the cottage at Salcombe—as you know, the doctor has very little time to chat. A quiet wedding, I expect?'

So Emma sat down and drank very dry sherry and described her wedding; not that there was much to describe, but she made the most of it, enlarged upon their journey back and the awful weather, and, over lunch, described the cottage in detail.

'Perhaps you would like to stay there when you have a holiday? It is a charming little town and the people are friendly—besides, your English is so good.' She added impulsively, 'You were so kind to me when I came here to work for the doctor, and I never thanked you for that. But I do now. I'm glad I did work here, even in such a humble capacity, because now I can understand how hard Roele works.'

'You will be a good wife to him,' pronounced Juffrouw Smit. 'Now, we will have coffee here at the table, for the doctor will be here very shortly and I must go back to work. But you will come again, I hope?'

'Yes, please. There is such a lot I need to know— about the shops and all the everyday things one takes for granted in one's own country.'

Roele was punctual and she was glad that she was ready for him for, although he was his usual quiet self, she sensed that he was impatient to be back at work. So she shook hands with Juffrouw Smit, thanked her for her lunch without lingering and got into the car.

'I could have found my own way home,' she told him as they drove off.

'So you could, and I'll tell you how best to do that some time.' He smiled at her, thinking that she had called his house home quite unconsciously; they had been married for only a day or so and she was already fitting into his life as though it had been made for her. 'I'll be home earlier today,' he told her. 'We will have tea together and then take the dogs to the village.'

It was a short walk to the village. He took her to see the church, which was small and austere outside but the interior held high carved wood pews and a magnificent pulpit and its walls were covered by black and white marble plaques, many of them from Roele's family. And underfoot there were ancient gravestones, inscribed in flowery Latin. He showed her the front pew under the pulpit, with its red velvet cushions and hassocks. 'This is where we come on Sundays,' he told her.

The village was small, its little houses and cottages having shining windows and spotless paintwork. Here and there were larger houses, set haphazardly between the cottages. There was a small shop too, selling, as far as Emma could see, absolutely everything.

'And yet the village is so close to Amsterdam...'

'Yes, but off the beaten track, and a good many of the people living here are elderly and don't want the hassle of a bus ride to the shops. Come and meet Mevrouw Twist.'

The shop was dark inside, and it smelled of onions and of the smoked sausages hanging from the ceiling, with a whiff of furniture polish and washing powder. The doctor introduced her, bought dog biscuits and listened courteously to Mevrouw Twist's gossip, then shook hands, waited while Emma did the same, and then they went back into the small square.

'Tomorrow we have been asked to the *dominee's* house so that I may introduce you to him and his wife. In the evening at about six o'clock. We shall drink home made wine and stay for an hour.' He tucked her arm in his. 'You see, I lead two lives, Emma. I know everyone in the village but I have friends in Amsterdam, too.'

They were walking up the drive to the house, the dogs running ahead.

'Bear with me for a few more days and then we will go shopping. You always look nice, but you will need warm clothes and some pretty dresses...'

* * *

The following evening they walked to the *dominee's* house arm-in-arm, talking of everyday ordinary events, and Emma realised that she felt like a wife...

The *dominee* was tall and thin and rather earnest, while his wife was blonde, wholesomely good-looking and friendly. She took Emma away to see the baby—a boy, lying sleeping in his cot. 'Roele is his godfather,' she told Emma. She led the way into an adjoining room. 'Anna, Sophia and Marijke,' she said and waved towards the three small girls sitting at the table, schoolbooks spread around them.

Emma said hello, and their mother blew them a kiss then took Emma back to the men. The *dominee* gave her a glass of wine, saying, 'My wife is clever; she makes the wine. This is from rhubarb.'

He came and sat beside her. 'I am sorry to hear that you have had a good deal of unhappiness, but now you are married to Roele you will be happy again.'

'Yes, I know,' said Emma, and knew that that was true.

Walking back presently, she told Roele, 'I liked the *dominee* and his wife, and the baby and the little girls. Have you known them for a long time?'

'Years and years. He and I were at school together. Jette is an old friend too.'

Towards the end of the week Roele told her over dinner, 'I'll be free until the evening tomorrow. Shall we go shopping?'

Emma, heartily sick of the few clothes she had brought with her, agreed with enthusiasm.

'You will need a winter coat and a good raincoat— get yourself whatever you wear in the winter, and some pretty dresses for the evening and anything else you need.'

'Thank you, but how much may I spend?'

'You can use my account at some of the shops, but at the smaller shops I'll settle the bills as we go. I'll arrange for you to have an allowance as soon as possible, but in the meantime leave the paying to me.'

In bed that night, Emma thought uneasily that she needed a great deal, and that perhaps Roele hadn't realised how much even a basic wardrobe would cost him. But she had stayed awake worrying about that to no purpose; the next morning he drove her to Amsterdam, parked the car and walked her briskly to a street of small fashionable shops. The kind of shop, she saw, which displayed one or two mouthwatering garments in its narrow window with no price ticket in sight.

The doctor stopped before an elegant shop window. 'My sisters go here,' he observed, and ushered her into its dove-grey interior.

The elegant woman who glided towards them took in Emma's out-of-date but expertly tailored suit, the well polished equally out-of-date shoes and handbag, and recognised a good customer.

'Dr van Dyke—you were here with your sister some time ago.'

'Indeed I was. My wife would like some dresses. We shall be entertaining, so something for dinner parties.'

'I have the very thing for *mevrouw*, and so fortunate that a consignment of delightfully pretty outfits arrived only this week. If *mevrouw* will come with me?'

So Emma went behind elegant brocade curtains and had her useful suit and sweater taken from her and replaced by a dark green velvet dress, very plain, with long sleeves and a high neck, and a skirt which just skimmed her knees and showed off her shapely legs to great advantage.

She showed herself rather shyly to Roele, sitting comfortably in a gilt chair reading a newspaper.

'Very nice. Have it.'

'But I'm sure it's very expensive,' hissed Emma.

'Just right for dinner parties; get another one...blue...'

The saleslady had splendid hearing; she had a blue crêpe dress with short sleeves, a low square neck and a wide pleated skirt ready to slip over Emma's head.

When she went back to Roele again, he nodded. 'Very nice, have it, and get a couple of warm dresses...'

Emma, slightly light-headed, allowed herself to be fitted into a soft brown cashmere dress, and then a green jersey dress, a two-piece, and, since Roele approved of them both, she added them to the others. Once more in her old suit, she waited while Roele paid for everything and arranged for them to be sent round to his consulting rooms.

'We will pick them up before we go home,' he told her. 'Now, if I remember rightly there is a place here where they stock Burberry...'

With a short pause for coffee, Emma acquired a raincoat and hat, two tweed skirts she'd admired, a couple of cashmere sweaters and a handful of silk blouses. By then it was time for lunch.

Over lobster thermidor at Thysse and Dikker, she pointed out that she now had a splendid wardrobe—and shouldn't they go home?

'We are by no means finished,' the doctor pointed out. 'You need shoes, a couple of evening dresses, a wrap of some kind for the evening, a winter coat, a hat—for church—and undies. There's a small shop where my sisters always go, not too far away.'

Emma stopped worrying about the cost of everything, for it was obvious that Roele was unmoved by the bills. She bought shoes and slippers and boots, and a brown cashmere coat, and, after much searching, a plain, elegant felt hat with a narrow brim which she set at an angle on her carroty hair—the effect of which made the doctor stare so hard at her that she blushed and asked him if he didn't like it.

'Charming—quite charming!' he told her, and thought how beautiful she looked.

As for the undies, he left her for half an hour, and when he returned the saleswoman handed him a bag the size of which was evidence of her success in finding what she wanted.

He took her to an elegant little café for tea, and then presently drove to his consulting rooms, stowed her shopping in the boot and then drove home. Emma sat beside him, rehearsing the thank-you speech she intended to make once they were indoors. It had been a wonderful day, she reflected, and Roele appeared to have enjoyed it as much as she had. Let there be more days like this one, she prayed silently, doing things together...

She went to her room once they had reached the house, leaving Kulk to bring in the parcels while Roele stood in the hall, looking through the letters on the tray on the console table.

'I'll be down in a minute,' she told him, and flew upstairs to throw off her coat and tidy her hair, add a little lipstick and powder her nose. She was less than five minutes, and when she got downstairs again the doctor was still in his coat, talking to Kulk, who, when he saw her, tactfully slid away.

'Roele, thank you for a lovely day'—began Emma, to be interrupted.

'Delightful, wasn't it? I won't be in for dinner and don't wait up; I shall be late home. I'm glad you enjoyed the day; we must do it again some time.' He crossed the hall to her and bent and kissed her cheek. 'I won't be home until early morning; we can have breakfast together. Sleep well, Emma.'

She conjured up a smile and watched him go, her lovely day in shreds around her; he had probably hated every minute of it, but his beautiful manners had prevented him from showing his wish for the tiresome day to be over. And where was he going now, and with whom?

Emma felt a sudden and unexpected surge of resentment. And she felt ashamed of that, for he had been very patient with her and spent a great deal of money.

She went to find Katje and ask if she might have dinner a little earlier, so that she had time to spend the evening unpacking her clothes and trying them on before she went to bed. She even tried to explain what a splendid day she had had, and Katje nodded encouragingly and Kulk said what a pity it was that the doctor should have to spend the evening out of the house.

He shrugged his shoulders. 'But of course it is his work, *mevrouw.*'

So what right had she to feel so disgruntled? She told herself that she was becoming selfish and thoughtless.

After dinner she told Kulk that she would go to her room and would need nothing further that evening. 'The doctor told me that he would be very late back. Do you usually wait up for him?'

'No, *mevrouw*. Coffee and sandwiches are left ready for him and he lets himself into the house. I'll take Prince and Percy out for their final run, but the doctor doesn't like me to stay up later than midnight.'

Unpacking her new clothes and trying everything on took a long time. Emma was surprised to find that it was midnight by the time the last garment had been carefully hung away. She bathed and got ready for bed and then, on an impulse, went quietly down the stairs. The *stoel* clock in the hall chimed one as she reached it, dimly lit by a wall-light above the console table. She stood for a moment, listening. Perhaps Roele was in his study or the kitchen. But he was in neither. Only Prince and Percy, curled up together, lifted sleepy heads as she went into the kitchen.

There was coffee on the stove and a covered plate on the table. Sandwiches—slivers of ham between thin buttered slices of bread. Emma took one and sat down by the Aga to eat it. She was wearing her new dressing gown, pale pink quilted silk, her feet thrust into matching slippers, and she admired them as she ate. She wasn't sure why she had come down to the kitchen, but it was warm and comfortable and Roele might be glad of company when he got home. She took another bite of sandwich and turned round at the faint sound behind her.

Roele was standing in the doorway. He looked tired, but he was smiling.

'What a delightful surprise to find you here, Emma, eating my sandwiches...'

He came into the kitchen, acknowledging the dogs' sleepy greeting, and sat down opposite her.

'You don't mind? I don't know why I came down. Well, I suppose it was because I thought you might want to talk to someone. But I'll go back to bed if you don't want company.'

'My dear Emma, I am delighted to have company. But are you not tired?'

She was pouring coffee into two mugs and had put the sandwiches within his reach.

'Not a bit.' She sat down and added quietly, 'It was so kind of you to waste a whole day shopping with me. I enjoyed it, but all the while you must have been thinking about your patients and the hospital and wanting to be there.' Before he could speak she added, 'I want to thank you for everything, Roele. All my lovely clothes, and showing me the shops, and lunch and tea…'

It was tempting to tell her then that the day had been a delight for him too, that buying all the clothes she wanted had given him the greatest delight, and that if it were possible he would buy her the most splendid jewels he could find. But it was too soon; she was at ease with him, trusted him, but that was all. It was a strange situation, wooing Emma with a courtship after they were married, but he had no doubt of its success, provided he could possess his soul in patience.

He settled back in his chair and between sandwiches told her about the patient he had driven miles to see that evening: a public figure whose illness needed to be kept secret; even the faintest whisper of it would send the Stock Market into a state of chaos.

'He'll recover?'

'I believe so, and no one will be the wiser.' He ate the last sandwich. 'How satisfying it is to come home to someone and talk.'

Emma took the mugs to the sink. 'Well, that's why we married, wasn't it, to be good companions?'

He got up, too. 'Yes, Emma. Is that thing you're wearing new? It's very pretty.' He kissed her cheek, a cool kiss which she had come to expect. 'Thank you for being here. Now go to bed and sleep. We will see each other at breakfast.'

She smiled at him sleepily, aware that something had happened between them although she had no idea what it was. In bed presently, she thought about it, but she was too sleepy to think clearly—knowing only that remembering the hour in the kitchen gave her a warm glow deep inside her.

She wore one of the cashmere jumpers and a new skirt to breakfast, and felt pleased when he remarked upon them.

'Will you be home for tea?' she asked him.

'I'll do my best. I've a clinic this afternoon, and sometimes we have to run overtime, but I'll be back in good time for dinner. I'll be free on Saturday, as well as Sunday, so we will go and see my mother and father. They are anxious to meet you. They wanted us to stay the night but I thought we might have Sunday to ourselves. We'll go for lunch and stay for tea, and perhaps for dinner. We can take Percy and Prince.' He picked up his letters and came round the table to bend and kiss her. 'Have you any plans for today?'

'I'm to inspect the linen cupboard with Katje and then I'm going for a walk with the dogs.'

'Don't get lost. But if you do say who you are and someone will see you safely home.'

The countryside round the village was quiet, despite the fact that Amsterdam was only a few miles away, and, warmly wrapped in the new winter coat, she and the dogs walked along the narrow brick roads. They met few peo-

ple, but those she did, greeted her cheerfully. She came
to a canal presently, and walked beside it for some distance. The country was very flat, and she could see the
village churches dotted here and there in the landscape.
They were further away than they appeared to be, however, and so she turned for home.

The walk had given her an appetite, and she ate lunch
and then settled down to read by the fire, with the dogs
snoozing at her feet. Presently she snoozed off herself,
her rather untidy head lolling on the chair cushions.

Which was how Roele found her, sprawled awkwardly,
her shoes kicked off, her mouth slightly open. He sat
down opposite her, watching her until she stretched and
woke and sat up.

'Oh, goodness, I fell asleep. Have you been here long?'
She was scrabbling around for her shoes and tucking odd
wisps of hair tidily away. 'I went for a long walk and ate
too much lunch. I'll go and tidy myself and tell Kulk to
bring the tea.'

'You are very nice as you are, and Kulk will be here in
a few minutes. Where did you go? As far as the canal?'

Emma decided on the green jersey two-piece for their
visit on Saturday. It was simple, the colour flattered
her, and if they stayed for dinner it would pass muster.
Wrapped in her new winter coat, she got into the car beside Roele, telling herself that she wasn't at all nervous.
He had settled Percy and Prince on the back seat and now
turned to look at her.

'Nervous? Don't be. They are longing to meet you and
I believe that you will like them. They're elderly, but interested in just about everything. They are enthusiastic
gardeners, they love the theatre and concerts and they

still travel. You met Wibeke—and I have another sister, married with children, living in Limburg, and a brother. He's a doctor too, not married yet. He's at Leiden.'

Which gave her plenty to think about.

Roele drove down towards Den Haag and turned off to Wassenaar on the coast north of that city. Wassenaar was so close to Den Haag that it might be called a suburb, peopled by the well-to-do. But once past the elegant tree-lined roads and villas there was the old village, and past that a stretch of fairly open country bordering the wide sands stretching out to the North Sea. The doctor turned into a narrow lane with a pleasant rather old-fashioned lot of houses on either side, and at one of these he stopped.

Nice, thought Emma, getting out and taking a look. Homely and solid. As indeed the house was. It was red brick, with shutters at the windows and an iron balcony above a solid front door. And the garden, even in winter, was one to linger in.

Not that she was allowed to linger. Roele took her arm and whisked her through the large stout door which a woman was holding open. He flung an arm around her and kissed her plump cheek. 'Klar...' He said something to make her laugh and turned to Emma.

'Klar looks after my mother and father,' he told her. 'She has been with us for even longer than the Kulks.'

Klar shook hands and beamed, and led the way through the hall to a door at its end and opened it. The room beyond was large, with a great many windows giving a view of the garden beyond. There were plants arranged in it, as well as comfortable chairs and tables and an old-fashioned stove at one end of it. It was warm, light and old-fashioned. Children, thought Emma, would love it.

She gave a small sigh of relief as the two people in it came to meet them. Roele, thought Emma, in thirty years' time: a nice old gentleman in elderly tweeds, still handsome, his eyes as bright and searching as his son's. And his mother—she had tried to imagine her without much success, and she had come nowhere near the plump little lady with hair in an old-fashioned bun and a pretty face, unashamedly wrinkled. Her eyes were blue and she was wearing a dress of the same colour, not fashionable, but beautifully made.

'Mother, Father,' said the doctor, 'here is my wife, Emma.'

She had not known such warmth since her father died. She was welcomed as though they had known and loved her all their lives. She swallowed back unexpected tears and was kissed and hugged and made to sit down beside Mevrouw van Dyke, and over coffee and sugary biscuits she listened to her mother-in-law's gentle kind voice.

'You poor child, you have had little happiness for the last year or so, but now Roele will make you happy again. We are so delighted to have you for another daughter. He has taken a long time to find a wife to love and to be loved by her.'

Presently Emma found herself sitting with the old gentleman. 'Roele has told us so much about you; we feel we know you well already. We don't see as much of him as we should like, for he is a busy man. You will know that already. But you must come and see us as often as you wish. Do you drive? Then he will get you a car so that you can be independent of him.'

Emma murmured agreement, not sure that she wanted to be independent. Roele's company wasn't only a pleasure, she had a feeling that she didn't wish to do without it. Surely he didn't want her to be one of those women who had so many interests outside the home that they were hardly ever there?

She caught his eye across the room and had the feeling that he knew just what she was thinking. That made her blush, and that in turn made Mevrouw van Dyke smile.

Lunch was a light-hearted meal, with cheerful talk about the wedding, and afterwards Emma walked round the garden with her father-in-law. Since she was quite knowledgeable about plants, flowers and shrubs, they got on famously.

Later, he told his wife that Roele had married a splendid girl. 'She knows the Latin names of almost everything in the garden but doesn't boast about it. He's met his match!'

His wife knew just what he meant. She said comfortably, 'Yes, dear. He's met his love too.'

It was late when Roele and Emma got home, for they had stayed for dinner and sat talking long after the meal was finished. The house was quiet, for the Kulks had gone to bed, and they went into the kitchen to sit at the table drinking the hot chocolate Katje had left on the Aga, not saying much, sitting in companionable silence. Prince and Percy, curled up together in Prince's basket had given them a sleepy greeting and dozed off again, and Emma yawned.

'A lovely day,' she said, sleepily content—only to have that content shattered a moment later when Roele told her that he was going to Rome in the morning.

Emma swallowed the yawn. 'Rome? Whatever for? For how long?'

In her sudden dismay she didn't see the gleam in the

doctor's eyes. There had been more than surprise on her face; his Emma was going to miss him...

'I have been asked to examine a patient who lives there. I shall be gone for four or five days, perhaps longer. It depends upon her condition.'

'A woman?' said Emma, and he hid a smile.

'Yes, a famous one too. In the entertainment world.'

'How interesting,' said Emma tartly, and got to her feet. 'Shall I see you tomorrow before you go?'

'I'll leave here tomorrow about nine o'clock. Shall we have breakfast about eight?'

She nodded. 'I'll leave a note for Katje.' She went to the door and he went with her and opened it, bending to kiss her cheek as she went past him.

'Goodnight, Emma, sleep well.'

Well, I shan't, thought Emma crossly, intent on lying awake and feeling sorry for herself. Leaving her alone in a strange country while he jaunted off to Italy. And who was this patient? Some glamorous film star, bewitchingly beautiful, no doubt, lying back on lacy pillows in her bed, wearing a see-through nightie...

Emma allowed her imagination full rein and cried herself to sleep.

She went down to breakfast feeling quite contrary, wearing a tweed skirt and a cashmere jumper, wishing to look as much unlike the hussy in the nightie as possible. She had dabbed powder on her nose but forgotten her lipstick, and swept her colourful hair onto the top of her head in an untidy bunch.

The doctor thought she looked adorable, but from the look on her face he judged it hardly the time to tell her so. He enquired instead as to whether she had slept well, passed the toast rack and told her that he would phone her that evening.

'What time will you arrive in Rome?'

'Early afternoon.'

'Then you can phone me when you get there.' That sounded like a suspicious wife, so she added hastily, 'That is, if you have the time.'

'I'll ring from the airport.'

The matter settled to her satisfaction, Emma finished her breakfast, remarking upon the weather, the garden, the dogs—anything but his trip to Rome.

When he had gone, with Kulk beside him so that he could drive the Rolls back from Schipol, she took the dogs for a walk. She was beginning to find her way around now. The countryside wasn't dramatic but it was restful, and there was little traffic. She walked a long way, meeting no one and feeling lonely.

Roele phoned after lunch. His voice reassured her that the flight had been uneventful and he was about to be driven into Rome.

'I hope you will find your patient not too ill,' said Emma, 'and that you will have some time to enjoy Rome.'

They had had orgies in ancient Rome, she reminded herself. Did they still have them, and would Roele be tempted to go to one? She wasn't exactly sure what one did at an orgy but there would be bound to be beautiful girls there...

Such thinking wouldn't do at all, she told herself. Her imagination was running away with her again. It was only because she liked Roele so much that she wanted him to take care. It was a pity that she couldn't picture him, calm and assured, bending over the bed of a famous singer who had been struck down by some obscure illness which, so far, no one had diagnosed. The bed of the hospital variety, without a lace pillow in sight, and his patient's wan face as white as the all-enveloping garment she was wearing. And, since she was feeling very ill, the doctor could have been an ogre with two heads for all she cared.

There was plenty to keep Emma occupied during the next few days. The *dominee* called to ask her to go with his wife to Amsterdam to buy the small toys to be handed out to the schoolchildren on Sint Nikolaas Eve, and the following day they had to be wrapped in bright paper and stowed away ready for the party. When Roele phoned Emma told him about it, not taking too long, in case he was anxious to ring off. But it seemed he wasn't, for he wanted to know what else she had done, whether the dogs were behaving themselves and had she taken any long walks?

She wanted very much to ask when he was coming home, but surely he would tell her? She was on the point of bidding him a cheerful goodbye when he said, 'I shall be home tomorrow, Emma.'

Before she could stop herself she said, 'Oh, I'm so glad; I've missed you...'

She hung up then, wishing she hadn't said it.

She went to find Kulk and tell him, and discovered that he already knew. He was to take the car to Schipol to pick up the doctor from the plane landing at three o'clock. And would *mevrouw* like to see Katje about dinner for the following day? The doctor was bound to be hungry...

Emma felt hurt. Roele could have told *her* at what time he would arrive, and she could have gone to Schipol to meet him. But he hadn't wanted her.

For the first time since they had married she wondered if she had made a dreadful mistake. Somehow the close friendship she had felt at Salcombe was dwindling away. Perhaps he was disappointed in her, although she had done her best to be what he wanted. He had said he wanted a friend and a companion, someone who would ease his social life for him and preside at his dinner table when they had guests.

She worried at her thoughts like a dog worrying a bone for the rest of the day, and a good deal of the night. But by the following afternoon she had pulled herself together, deciding she was being silly, imagining things which didn't exist. She put on one of the pretty warm dresses, took pains with her face and subdued her hair into a French pleat. She went downstairs and sat in the drawing room with Prince and Percy and, so as not to look too eager, had a book open on her lap.

She didn't read a word but sat, her ears stretched for the sound of the heavy front door closing, so that the doctor, coming into his house by a side door, caught her unawares.

He stood in the doorway and said, 'Hello, Emma,' in a quiet voice.

She dropped the book and spun round and out of her chair to meet him. She forgot that she was going to be pleased to see him in a cool friendly way; instead she shot across the room and he came to meet her and take her in his arms.

'Well, what a warm welcome,' he said, smiling down at her. He held her a little way from him. 'And how pretty you look. For my benefit, I hope?'

'No, of course not. Well, yes. I mean, you were coming home…' She saw his slow smile and added hastily, 'Was it a success, your visit?'

'I hope so. An obscure chest condition which might bring an end to the lady's singing career.'

He came and sat down opposite her and Kulk brought in the tea tray. Emma felt a very warm contentment.

It was on the following day that he told her that they had been invited to have drinks at the hospital director's house. 'We have known each other some time now, and he has a charming wife. Will you be ready if I get home around six o'clock.'

'Then I'll tell Katje to have dinner ready at eight?'

'Yes, by all means. I should warn you that this is the beginning of an obligatory social round so that you may meet everyone—my colleagues, their wives, old family friends. I did tell you that I knew a number of people.'

'My Dutch…' began Emma.

'No need to worry; they all speak English. I must rely upon you to deal with invitations, and of course we shall have to invite everyone back again.' He smiled at her. 'You can see why I need a wife!'

For some reason his remark depressed her.

Chapter 9

She must look her best, decided Emma, getting ready for the drinks party that evening. She brushed her hair to shining smoothness, took pains with her face and got into the dark green velvet dress. Which, even under her critical gaze, was without fault. And Roele's admiring look clinched the matter.

Although she was by no means unused to social occasions, Emma felt nervous. The director of the hospital was an important person, and she wanted to make a good impression and not let Roele down. But she need not have worried. Their host was a middle-aged, scholarly man who appeared to be on the most friendly terms with Roele, and as for his wife, an imposing lady with a rigid hairstyle and ample proportions, she was kindness itself, taking Emma under her wing and introducing her to several other people there.

Going back home later, Emma asked anxiously, 'Was I all right? I wish I could speak Dutch—your kind of Dutch, not just the odd word.'

'You were a great success, Emma. I have been envied by the men and congratulated by the women and, should you wish, you have a splendid social life ahead of you.'

'Well,' said Emma, 'I like meeting people and going to the theatre and all that sort of thing, but not by myself and not too often. And only if you're there, too.'

'I shall do my best to be on hand, but you will have to go to numerous coffee mornings on your own.'

'I'm going to one in the village tomorrow. A kind of coffee morning the children have got up to raise money for Christmas. All the mothers are going and the *dominee* asked if I would go too. It'll be fun and I can practise my Dutch on the children. I asked Katje to make some biscuits so that I could take something. You don't mind?'

'My dear Emma, of course I don't mind. This is your home in which you may do whatever you like, and I'm glad that you like the village. My mother did a great deal to help the *dominee* and he will be delighted to have your interest.'

The visit to the village was a success; the children accepted Emma's fragmented Dutch in the unsurprised way that children have, and even though she seldom managed to complete a whole articulate sentence no one laughed.

No one laughed at the various coffee mornings she attended either, but then everyone spoke English to her. They were kind to her, these wives of Roele's colleagues, introducing her to an ever-widening circle of acquaintances, concealing their well-bred curiosity about her, making sure that she went to the right shops, dropping hints as to what to wear at the various social functions.

Emma took it all in good part, sensing that they wanted to be friends and had no intention of patronising her.

But she didn't allow the social round to swallow her up. She was beginning to understand the running of Roele's house, under Katje's tuition: the ordering of food, the everyday routine, the careful examination of its lovely old furniture, checking for anything that needed expert attention, the checking of the vast linen cupboard. All things which needed to be done without disturbing Roele's busy day.

Besides that, there was the village. She went at least once a week, always with the dogs—to have coffee at the *dominee's* house, to talk to the middle-aged school teacher at the primary school, and join the committee engaged in organising first Sint Nikolaas and then Christmas. Her days were full and she was happy. Though not perfectly happy, for she saw so little of Roele.

It sometimes seemed to her that he was avoiding her. True, they went to a number of dinner parties, and he once took her to the theatre to see a sombre play in Dutch. She hadn't enjoyed it, but sitting by him had made her happy; she saw so little of him…

There was to be a drinks party at the hospital. 'Black tie and those slippery bits and pieces to eat,' Roele had told her. 'Wear something pretty. That green thing with the short skirt. It won't only be hospital staff; there will be the city dignitaries there as well.' He had smiled at her. 'Mother and Father will be there, and quite a few people who know you quite well by now.'

On the evening of the party she went downstairs to the small sitting room and found him already there, immaculate in black tie, standing at the open door into the garden where the dogs were romping.

As she went in he whistled them indoors and closed the French windows, shutting out the cold dark evening.

'Charming,' he said, and crossed the room to her. 'And it's about time we got engaged.'

'But we're already married,' said Emma.

'Ah, yes, but I have always fancied a long engagement, buying the ring and so on.'

Emma laughed. 'Don't be absurd, Roele. You do all that before you marry!'

'So we must do it after, must we not? I cannot offer to buy you a ring, but perhaps you will wear this one? A family heirloom which gets handed down to each successive bride.'

He had a ring in his hand, a glowing sapphire surrounded by diamonds set in a plain gold band. He slipped it onto her finger above her wedding ring.

'There, they go well together.'

Emma held up her hand to admire it. 'It's very beautiful—and it fits.'

'I remembered the size of your wedding ring and had this one altered.'

He was matter-of-fact, rather like someone who was aware of something which had to be done and did it with as little fuss as possible.

I have no reason to feel unhappy, thought Emma. He had given me a gorgeous ring and I'm a very lucky girl. So she thanked him with just the right amount of pleasure, careful not to gush. Sentiment seemed to have no part in his gift.

The party was a grand and dignified affair, with champagne being offered on silver trays by correctly dressed waiters and sedate women in black dresses and white aprons proffering canapés from wide dishes. It wasn't long before Emma became separated from Roele and taken under the wing of the director's wife, handed from one guest to the next. They were all kind to her, and the younger men were flatteringly attentive while the younger women bombarded her with questions about the wedding.

She would have liked Roele to be with her but he was at the far end of the large room, deep in conversation with a group of other men, so she did her best to give light-hearted replies without saying much. Roele was a re-served man and wouldn't want the circumstances of their marriage broadcast. She felt a wave of pleasure, remembering his obvious admiration in the drawing room, and earlier, just before they had gone to greet their host and hostess, he had said softly, 'I'm proud of my wife, Emma.'

The evening was half over when she found herself standing beside an older woman, elegantly dressed and discreetly made up. She had a beaky nose and rather small dark eyes. Emma didn't think she liked her, but since she had made some trivial remark it needed to be answered politely.

'So you are Roele's wife. I am surprised that he has married at last, and to an English girl. I wish you both a happy future. You will find everything strange, no doubt.'

'Well, not really,' said Emma, being polite again but wishing the lady would go away. 'Life here is very much as it is in England, you know.'

'It is perhaps a good thing that he has chosen someone not from his own country. I—we all—thought he was a confirmed bachelor. After all, he was devoted to Vero-nique. He was a changed man when she went to America. But of course he needs a wife, a domestic background.

For a man in his profession that is necessary. I am sure that he has made a very good choice in you.'

The woman was being spiteful and gossipy, thought Emma to herself. She said sweetly, 'I suppose it is natural for people to be curious about our marriage. But everyone I have met so far has been so kind and friendly. I feel quite at home. And I never listen to gossip…'

She was saved from saying more by one of the younger doctors coming to ask her if she would be coming to the hospital ball.

'You must come. Now that Dr van Dyke has you for a partner I don't see how he can make an excuse. He comes and dances once with the director's wife and then goes away again, but now he can dance all night with you. Although he won't get the chance; we shall all want to dance with you!'

'A ball? How lovely. Of course we shall come. When is it to be?'

The beaky-nosed woman said sourly, 'It is an annual event—Roele hasn't done more than put in a token appearance since Veronique went to America.'

'Then we shall have to change that,' said Emma brightly, and was thankful when the young doctor suggested that she might like to go to the buffet with him and have something to eat.

'Mevrouw Weesp is a little—how shall I say?—sour. She is the widow of a former director and now I think she is lonely and not much liked.'

'Poor soul,' said Emma, and forgot her for the moment, for Roele was coming towards her.

'Oh, I'll make myself scarce,' said the young doctor cheerfully.

'Enjoying yourself?' Roele was piling a plate for her

with smoked salmon and tiny cheese tartlets. 'You've scored another triumph, Emma.'

'It must be this dress.'

They were joined by some of his friends and their wives and she had no chance to speak to him again.

'A pleasant evening,' observed the doctor later, ushering her into the house and the welcoming flurry of dogs. 'The ball is the next event to which we have to go.'

'That young man I was talking to said you don't stay— only for one dance.' Which reminded her of something.

They had gone to the small sitting room, where Katje had laid out coffee and sandwiches, and she cast down her wrap and kicked off her shoes.

'Someone called Mevrouw Weesp talked to me. Roele, who was Veronique?'

She watched his face become still. 'A girl I once knew. Why do you ask?'

Emma said crossly, 'May I not ask? I'm your wife, aren't I? Husbands and wives don't have secrets from each other.'

'Since you ask, I will tell you. She was—still is—a beautiful woman, and I fell in love with her—oh, ten years ago. She went to America and married there and is now divorced. I met her again last year when I was over there at a seminar.'

'So she wouldn't marry you and you made do with second best. Me.'

'If you think that of me, then perhaps we should discuss the matter when you aren't so uptight.'

'Me? Uptight?' said Emma in a voice which didn't sound quite like her own. 'Of course I'm not. I asked a perfectly civil question about someone you should have told me about ages ago.'

'Why?' he asked slowly. 'It isn't as if you are in love with me, so my past can be of little interest to you. Just as your affair with Derek is of no interest to me.'

Emma exploded. 'Affair with Derek! You know it wasn't an affair… I couldn't bear the sight of him.' She drew a shaky breath, 'But you met her again last year, and she's divorced.'

He was staring at her rather hard. 'Do you mind so much, Emma?'

She was grovelling around for her shoes. 'I don't mind in the least. I'm going to bed.'

In her room she flung her clothes off, got into bed and cried herself to sleep. Even then she didn't realise that she was in love with Roele.

But Roele knew. He knew too that he would have to handle the situation very carefully, and say nothing for a day or so while she realised her feelings for him. He had been patient; he would continue being patient for as long as need be.

Emma went down to breakfast the next morning, half hoping that Roele would have already left the house. But he was there, wishing her good morning in his calm, friendly fashion, passing her the toast, remarking on the mild weather.

'I shall be at the hospital for a good deal of today, but I'll be free to go with you for the St Nikolaas party in the village tomorrow afternoon. Have they got all they want for the children?'

Emma replied suitably, wondering if they were to forget about last night. Well, he might, but I shan't, she reflected, and to make matters worse as he picked up his post, ready to leave, she saw that the top letter bore a USA stamp.

He put a hand on her shoulder as he went, but he didn't give her the light kiss she had come to expect.

She took herself and the dogs for a long walk that morning, and after lunch wrote a long letter to Miss Johnson and a still longer one to Phoebe. After tea Emma went to her room and examined her clothes, finding that it gave her no satisfaction at all; she might just as well wear an old skirt and jumper, for there was no one to see the lovely things she had bought with such pleasure. Wallowing in self-pity, she went downstairs.

Roele was in the small sitting room, stretched out on one of the comfortable armchairs. He was asleep, his tired face relaxed, the lines in it very marked.

Emma, standing there looking at him, knew then.

Her bad temper, uncertainty and bewilderment and self-pity were swept away. She was in love with him—and why hadn't she realised it sooner? She had always loved him, from that first meeting in the bakery shop at Salcombe.

Now they were in a pretty pickle, weren't they? This woman in America, now free to marry him, and he was tied to a wife he had married for all the wrong reasons. She had been feeling sorry for herself when in fact she should be sorry for Roele. He would do nothing about it even if he had given his heart to this other woman, for that was the kind of man he was. So she would have to do something about it. For him to be happy was the one thing which mattered.

He opened his eyes and sat up. 'Hello, I got home earlier than I expected. Have you had a pleasant day?'

'Yes, I took the dogs through the village and along the road by the canal. Would you like tea? Or coffee? Dinner won't be for an hour or so...'

He got to his feet. 'Just time for me to go and see the *dominee* about the Christmas trees…'

So she was alone again, and even if she had wanted to talk to him he hadn't given her the chance.

They talked over dinner, of course, trivialities which didn't give her an opening to say what she wanted to say, and after the meal he told her that he had work to do and went away to his study. He was still there when she opened the door and wished him goodnight. Perhaps that would have been a good moment, but he was engrossed in a sheaf of papers, and although he got to his feet he had the papers in his hand, obviously waiting to get back to them.

Perhaps tomorrow, thought Emma before she slept.

True, he was home early, and went with her to the village, where she helped distribute plates of food and mugs of lemonade. She was aware that he was having a word with everyone there, listening gravely to the elderlies who had come to have a look, laughing with the younger women, admiring their babies, and then finally handing out the prizes. She could see that he was enjoying himself among people that he had known for most of his life, and that they accepted him as one of themselves. Just as they accepted her, she discovered with pleasure and surprise.

There was an hour or more before dinner when they got home. Emma went into the small sitting room and Roele followed her. He shut the door and said quietly, 'I think that we might have a talk, Emma…'

'Yes, but before you start, did you know that Veronique was free to marry again when you married me?'

The doctor hadn't expected that. He answered quietly, 'No, Emma.'

Emma sat down and Percy climbed onto her lap. 'You see,' she observed, 'that is important…'

He said, suddenly harsh, 'It is not of the slightest importance—' The phone stopped him. He picked it up, said savagely, 'Van Dyke,' and listened. 'I'll take the car to Schipol—give me an hour,' he said finally.

He put the phone down. 'I'm going to Vienna. I'm not sure how long I'll be away.' He was halfway to the door. 'Get Kulk to pack a bag, will you?'

He went into his study and shut the door and she went to find Kulk and ask Katje to have sandwiches and coffee ready.

Fifteen minutes later he had gone.

The next day she was to go to a coffee morning one of the doctor's wives was giving. Since it was being held for charity, she knew that she would have to go.

There were familiar faces there, and several of them knew that Roele had gone to Vienna.

'An emergency,' one of the older women told her. 'All a bit hush-hush—a political VIP shot in the chest, and of course Roele's splendid with chests.' She smiled kindly at Emma. 'But you know that already. You've not heard from him yet?'

'No, he left in a tremendous hurry. He'll ring just as soon as he can spare a minute.'

Her companion laid a kindly hand on her arm. 'I know just how anxious you feel, my dear. Even now, after years of being married to a medical man, I still fuss privately if he goes off somewhere. We are all fond of Roele, we older wives. He is still so young, and brilliantly good at his job. We were so relieved when that woman Veronique—you know about her, of course?' Emma nodded. 'When she went off to America. A most beautiful woman, but with a cold, calculating heart, greedy and selfish.'

Emma said lightly, 'Roele tells me that she is divorced now...'

'Well, thank heaven that he found you. We all think that you are exactly the right wife for him.'

She was, she knew now that she was, but did he know it? She had fitted in very nicely to his life but there was more to it than that...

She was to meet Kulk with the car at the consulting rooms, and she made her way there, passing Juffrouw Smit's house on the way. On impulse, she rang the old-fashioned bell. Juffrouw Smit opened the door, her severe expression softening to a smile.

'Emma, come in. I don't need to go to the consulting rooms until two o'clock and I've just made coffee. You'll have a cup?'

It was more of a command than a query. Emma, awash with coffee already, meekly said that she would love that.

They sat each side of the old-fashioned stove and talked. One didn't gossip with Juffrouw Smit; the weather was discussed, the government torn to shreds, the high price of everything in the shops condemned, and all in a very refined manner, until at last, these subjects exhausted, Emma said, 'May I ask you something, Juffrouw Smit? In the last day or so I have twice been told about someone called Veronique—someone the doctor knew some years ago. I have no wish to pry into his past life, and I know that he would tell me about her, but each time he is about to do so he has to go away in a hurry. If I knew a little more about her it would be easier for me when people talk to me about her.' She looked hopefully at her companion's severe face. 'You do see that, don't you? And you would know about her, because Roele regards you as his right hand.'

Juffrouw Smit's face remained severe, and Emma said in a rather sad voice, 'I dare say you don't wish to talk about it, and I quite understand. I know it isn't important, but I might say the wrong thing. Everyone takes it for granted that I know about her...'

Juffrouw Smit sniffed delicately. 'There is always gossip, and you have probably got the wrong impression from it. I do not feel that it is any business of mine to discuss it with you, Emma. All I will say is that this woman went to America a long time ago and that if the doctor sees fit to tell you about her then he will do so. There is always gossip at these social gatherings, some of it quite unfounded.'

Emma swallowed disappointment. 'I'm sure you're right,' she agreed politely. 'I don't really enjoy coffee mornings and tea parties, but Roele told me to meet as many people as I could so that I would feel at home quickly.' She glanced at her watch. 'I must go. Kulk will be waiting for me. I do hope that I haven't hindered you.'

'No. I'm always glad to see you, Emma. I hope the doctor will be back home soon. You will be going to Wassenaar for Christmas?'

'Yes. All the family will be there. And you? You spend it with family, too?'

'My brother in Utrecht, just for two days, but I shall go again for the New Year.'

At the door she put a hand on Emma's arm. 'You mustn't worry,' she said.

Which was a useless bit of advice, for there was another letter with an American stamp on top of the pile waiting for Roele's return, and, as if that wasn't enough, that evening there was a phone call. It had gone to the consulting rooms and the porter had switched it through to the house, as he always did.

When Emma answered his ring he said gruffly, 'A call from Washington, *mevrouw.* I'm putting it through for you.'

She had understood most of what he had said, but the woman's voice in her ear took her by surprise.

As she was speaking in Dutch, Emma waited until there was a pause in the rather shrill voice.

'I'm sorry, Dr van Dyke is away and I don't speak Dutch. Will you leave a message? He will be back in a few days.'

The voice sounded annoyed, snapping, 'No message.' Then the caller replaced the receiver.

Perhaps whoever it was would ring again, thought Emma. When the porter went off duty he would switch the answering machine on and Juffrouw Smit would check it in the morning as she always did.

Emma got her coat and went into the garden with the dogs. Two letters from America and a phone call within days? They had to be more than coincidence, and surely whoever it was could have at least given their name or a message?

Emma, usually so matter-of-fact and sensible, allowed her imagination to run riot. If only Roele would phone...

He did, just as she had finished dinner. He sounded just as he always did, friendly, unhurried. How was she? What had she done with her day?

She told him, then added, 'There is another letter for you from America, and this evening a—woman—phoned from Washington. She spoke Dutch. She didn't give a name and she wouldn't leave a message.'

He sounded unconcerned. 'Oh, yes. I was expecting a call. I'll get on to Smitty about it. I can't get away for several days, Emma. I hope that when I do get home we shall have a chance to talk. I'm not prepared to go on as we are.'

'Me too. Goodnight, Roele.'

Emma knew what she was going to do. She went and sat down at the little walnut Davenport in the sitting room and began to write a letter. The first attempt was no good, nor was the second, while the third was brief, almost businesslike.

She was going back to Salcombe, she wrote in her rather large writing. She quite realised that their marriage had been a mistake which could luckily be put right. It would have been nice if he had told her himself about Veronique, but luckily she had been told by several people. She quite understood that now Veronique was free he could be happy with his real love.

It would be quite easy, wrote Emma, writing fast and untidily. She would tell everyone that she had to go back and settle some family business and when she had been away for a week or two he could explain.

She didn't pause to consider if he might object to doing this, but signed herself, 'Your friend Emma', before putting the letter in an envelope and into a pocket. She would leave it on his desk in the study when she went.

She sat for a while at the little desk, doodling on the blotting paper, writing his name in various ways, drawing a heart with an arrow piercing it and then adding 'I love you' several times.

'I'm a fool,' said Emma to Percy and Prince, who were watching her anxiously, and she tucked the blotting paper behind the fresh sheets on the pad.

The letter written, she went to her room and packed a small case and her overnight bag. She counted her money and found her passport, then went back to the small sitting room and lifted the phone.

It was too late for a flight, but the overnight ferry from the Hoek didn't leave until midnight. If Kulk drove her in the Rolls she had ample time to get there. There was a helpful girl on the telephone enquiry line who put her through to the ferry offices, and there was no trouble booking a berth.

Next she went in search of Kulk. She told him she had had an urgent message from England and must get there as soon as possible. 'I've booked on the Hoek ferry. If you'll drop me there, Kulk, I can be ready in less than half an hour.'

'The doctor, *mevrouw*—can you let him know?'

Emma, embarked on her impetuous plan, allowed the lies to flow easily from her ready tongue. 'I couldn't get him, Kulk. He wasn't at any of the places I enquired at. I left a message and I'll phone as soon as I reach England.'

She felt quite sick at the muddle she was weaving, but to get away as quickly as possible was paramount. She had no plan other than that. The future, for the moment, meant nothing to her.

A worried Kulk drove her to the Hoek, saw her safely on board and turned for home, feeling uneasy.

At one o'clock in the morning the ferry was making heavy work of the rough weather, and Emma, longing for sleep, was seasick.

And at one o'clock in the morning the doctor got back home, ruthlessly cutting short the various social occasions and meetings laid on for him now that his patient

was on the way to recovery. He hadn't liked the sound
of Emma's voice on the phone, and his patience was exhausted. He would shake her until her teeth rattled, and
then kiss her...

He frowned as he put his key in the lock of the small
side door which he used if he was called out at night.
There was a light on in the passage leading to the kitchen,
and as he went in Kulk came to meet him.

'*Mijnheer*, you are back. Thank heaven...'

'*Mevrouw?* She's ill? There's been an accident?'

'No, no.' Kulk explained, then added, 'It didn't seem
right that she should go off like that at a moment's notice.
But she insisted. I've only been back half an hour or so.'

They were in the kitchen and Roele sat down at the
table.

'Sit down and tell me exactly what happened,' he
begged calmly.

Kulk put a cup of coffee before him. 'Upset, she was.
Said she couldn't get you on the phone and in such a
hurry to be away.'

The doctor drank his coffee. He said with outward
calm, 'I dare say there is a letter...'

He went along to the sitting room and saw the envelope propped up on the Davenport. He sat down to read
it. When he had finished he was smiling. This was a tangle easily untangled...

His eye lighted on the screwed-up papers in the waste-
paper basket and he smoothed them out and read them
too. Emma had written in a good deal of agitation but
her meaning was clear. He saw the pristine blotting paper
too, and thoughtfully turned it over.

He was a tired man, but his wide smile erased the lines
etched on his handsome face.

Kulk came presently, with more coffee and sandwiches.

'Go to bed, Kulk. I shall need you in the morning.'

He drank his coffee, ate the sandwiches, and went to bed himself, to sleep for the last few hours of the night, knowing exactly what he would do.

He was up early, but Kulk was waiting, offering breakfast.

'I am going over to England this morning. I've arranged for a plane from Schipol and I'll fly to Plymouth. This is what I want you to do. Take the car over tomorrow morning and drive to Salcombe. Let me know when you get there. I shall be at the end cottage on the Victoria Quay. Take an early ferry and get to Salcombe by early afternoon if you can. I'll drive back in time to get the late-evening ferry. I shall have *mevrouw* with me and you can catch up on your sleep in the back of the car.'

Kulk listened gravely. 'Very well, *Mijnheer*. You will need an overnight bag?'

In the kitchen he confided in Katje that whatever it was that had gone wrong was being put right without loss of time.

'And a good thing, too,' said Katje. 'Such a nice young lady she is.'

Emma, her feet once more on dry land, couldn't wait to get to the cottage. It would be quiet there and she would be able to think clearly. It had been borne in upon her that she had acted hastily, and perhaps unwisely, but it was too late to have regrets as she began the tedious journey to Salcombe: first to London, on a train which had no refreshment car, let alone coffee or tea, queuing for a taxi to cross London, then finding that she would have to wait for an hour for a fast train to Totnes.

She had a meal, made up her face, bought magazines which she didn't read and finally got into the train. It left late and stopped every now and then in the middle of nowhere for no apparent reason, so that by the time she reached Exeter and found the train to Totnes she was hard put to it not to scream. But at last she was in Totnes, and getting into a taxi to take her the last twenty miles or so to Salcombe.

It was early evening now, and all she could think of was a large pot of tea and the chance to take off her shoes.

The taxi dropped her off by the pub and she walked the last short distance along the quay to the cottage. She had the key ready in her hand and unlocked the door with a rush of relief, to be taken aback for the moment by the pleasant warmth of the little room. She switched on the light and caught her breath.

Lounging comfortably in one of the armchairs was Roele.

He got to his feet as she stood staring at him. 'There you are, my dear. You must have had a very tiresome journey.'

Emma burst into tears and he took her in his arms and held her close. 'You shouldn't be here,' sobbed Emma. 'I've left you. Don't you understand?'

'One thing at a time,' said the doctor calmly. 'I'm here because I love you and you're here because you love me. Isn't that right?'

Emma gave a watery snort. 'But you don't love me. There's this Veronique…'

He sighed. 'Ten years ago I believed that I loved her; then she went to America and I haven't given her a thought since.'

'You met her last year.'

'At a friend's house—and I hardly remembered her. Just as you don't remember Derek.'

'She rang up…'

'No, she didn't. That was the secretary of someone I know in Washington who wants me to do a series of lectures.'

Emma mopped her face on the handkerchief he offered her. 'Do you really love me?'

He looked down at her tired tearstained face. 'Yes, my darling, I really love you. I fell in love with you at the bakery and from that moment you have taken over my life.'

'Have I? Have I really? Do you know I didn't know that I loved you, even though I know now that it was when I first saw you? You bought a pasty.'

'My darling girl… And that reminds me. There are pasties for our supper.'

'I'm hungry. Can one be so in love and be hungry too?'

'Undoubtedly.' He smiled down at her as he unbuttoned her coat and pulled off her gloves. 'There's a bottle of champagne too.'

Later, replete with pasty, pleasantly muzzy with champagne, Emma asked, 'How do we get home?'

'Kulk is bringing the car; we will drive home tomorrow.'

'Back home,' said Emma, in a voice so full of content that he felt compelled to sweep her into his arms once more.

She peered into his face—such a handsome face, tired now, so that he looked older than he was, but happy…

'I am so very happy,' said Emma, and she kissed him.

* * * * *

MARRYING MARY

Chapter 1

Mary Pagett, stripping a bed with energy, was singing at the top of her voice. Not because she was happy, but to quell the frustration within. For her father—that charming but absent-minded man—to invite Great Aunt Thirza to spend her convalescence at his home had been a misplaced kindness, bringing with it a string of inconveniences which would have to be overcome.

For a start Mrs Blackett, who came daily to oblige and suffered from a persistent ill temper, was going to object to peeling more potatoes and scraping more carrots, not to mention the extra work vacuuming the guest bedroom. And Mr Archer, the village butcher, was going to express hurt feelings at the lack of orders for sausages and braising steak, since Great Aunt Thirza was a vegetarian, and for reasons of economy the rest of the household would have to be vegetarian too.

There was her mother too—Mary's voice rose a few decibels—a lovable, whimsical lady, whose talent for designing Christmas cards had earned her a hut in the garden to which she retired after breakfast each day, only appearing at meals. Lastly there was Polly, her young sister, who was a keen and not very accurate player of the recorder; her loving family bore with the noise but Great Aunt Thirza was going to object...

Mary finished making the bed, cast an eye over the rather heavy furniture in the high-ceilinged room, with its old-fashioned wallpaper and wooden floor, sparsely covered by elderly rugs, and hoped that the draughts from the big sash windows opposite wouldn't be too much for her elderly relation.

The house—a mid-Victorian rectory built for an incumbent with a large family—wasn't all that old. After standing empty for some years it had been bought by her father, since it had been a bargain at its low price. But he, an unworldly man, had not taken notice of the size of its rooms, which made heating the place almost hopeless, or the lack of maids, or the fact that coal for the enormous grates was a constant drain on the household purse—nor had he considered the amount of gas and electricity which was needed.

He had his study, where he worked on his book, and Mary's pleas for someone to clear the drains, paint the doors and put tiles back on the elaborate roof fell on deaf ears.

Her father was a dear man, she reflected, but unworldly. He was devoted to his wife and children, but that had never prevented him from delegating the mundane responsibilities of a married man to someone else and, since Mary was so conveniently there, they had fallen to her.

It had happened very gradually; she had left school with hopes of going on to university, but her mother had been ill and her two brothers had been home, and someone had had to feed and look after them—besides which Polly had still been a little girl. Her mother had got better, the boys had gone to Cambridge, but no one had suggested that Mary might like to do anything but stay home and look after them all. She had stayed quite willingly since, despite its drawbacks, she loved the shabby old house, she liked cooking, and she even liked a certain amount of housework.

So the years had slipped quietly by, and here she was, twenty-four years old, a tall, splendidly built girl with a lovely face, enormous brown eyes and an abundance of chestnut hair, her face rendered even more interesting by reason of her nose, which was short and tip-tilted. It went without saying that the men of her acquaintance liked her, admired her and in two cases had wished to marry her. She had refused them kindly and remained firm friends, acting as bridesmaid at their weddings and godmother to their children.

There was Arthur, of course, whom she had known for years—a worthy young man who rather took it for granted that one day she would marry him, and indeed from time to time she had considered that possibility. He would be a splendid husband—faithful and kind even if a bit bossy. He was also a shade pompous and she had doubts as to what he would be like in ten years' time.

Besides, she had no intention of marrying anyone at the moment; the boys were away from home but Polly was thirteen—too young to be left to the care of a fond but unworldly mother and a forgetful father. Right at the back of her head was the half-formed wish that something exciting would happen—something so exciting and urgent that her prosaic plans would be dashed to pieces...

The only thing that was going to happen was Great Aunt Thirza, who was neither of these things, but a cantankerous old lady who liked her own way.

Mary went down to the kitchen and broke the news to Mrs Blackett, who paused long enough in her cleaning of the kitchen floor with far too wet a mop to scowl at her and grumble with such venom that her dentures got dislodged.

'As though we 'aven't got enough on our 'ands. And it's no good you expecting me to do more for you than what I do now.' She gave a snort of ill humour and sloshed more water over the floor.

Mary, side-stepping the puddles, made soothing noises. 'When you've finished the floor,' she said cheerfully, 'we'll have a cup of tea. I wouldn't expect you to do more than you do already, Mrs Blackett, and I dare say that Great Aunt Thirza will spend a good deal of time resting.'

Knowing that lady, she thought it unlikely, but Mrs Blackett wasn't to know that, and the latter, calmed with a strong cup of tea and a large slice of cake, relating the latest misdemeanour of Horace, her youngest, became sufficiently mollified to suggest doing a bit extra around the house. 'I'd stay for me dinner and do a couple of hours in an afternoon—it'd 'ave to be a Tuesday or a Wednesday, mind.'

Mary accepted her offer gratefully. 'It will only be for a week or two, Mrs Blackett.'

'Where's she coming from, then?'

'She's in St Justin's. Her housekeeper will take whatever clothes she needs to the hospital and an ambulance will bring her here.' Mary gave a very small sigh. 'Tomorrow.'

'You'll want more spuds,' said Mrs Blackett. 'Going ter get a nice bit of 'am?'

'Well, I'm afraid that Mrs Winton is a vegetarian...'

'I don't 'old with them,' said Mrs Blackett darkly.

Nor did Mary, although she sympathised with their views.

She took a basket from the hook behind the kitchen door and went down the garden to pick beans, pull new carrots and cut spinach. Thank heaven it was early summer and her small kitchen garden was flourishing, although she would have to go to the greengrocer presently and get more vegetables, as well as beans and lentils and spaghetti. She hoped that Great Aunt Thirza would like that, though she was doubtful if anyone else would.

Before going back into the house she stopped to look around her. The house was on the edge of Hampstead Heath, with Golders Green not far away, and the garden offered a pleasant view and she stood admiring it. It would be nice to spend a day in the country, she reflected, and thought of her childhood, spent in a rambling cottage in Gloucestershire.

They might still be there but for the fact that her father had needed to be nearer the British Museum so that he could do his research and her mother had wanted a closer contact with the agent who sold her cards. Polly hadn't been born then, and although it hadn't mattered much to the boys, who had been at boarding-school anyway, Mary had taken some time to settle down at her new school and make new friends.

She went back indoors and presently out to the butcher, where, since it was likely to be the last meat they would have for a while, she bought steak and kidney in a generous amount and bore it home. It was a warm day for steak and kidney pudding but she was rewarded that evening by the pleasure with which it was received.

'Everything all right, dear?' asked her mother, and before she could reply added, 'I've had a letter from Mr Thorne—the agent—he's got me a splendid commission. I shall have to work at it, though—you'll be quite happy with Great Aunt Thirza?'

Mary assured her that she would. She wasn't surprised to hear from her father that he would be away all day at the British Museum. 'But I'll be home in time to welcome Thirza,' he said. 'Make her comfortable, won't you, my dear?'

'I'll play her "Greensleeves",' offered Polly.

'That'll be lovely, darling,' said Mrs Pagett. 'It's so nice that you're musical.'

Mrs Winton arrived the next day in nice time for tea. She was tall and thin with a high-bridged nose, upon which rested her pince-nez, and she wore a beautifully cut coat and skirt of the style fashionable in the early decades of the century, and crowned this with a wide-brimmed straw hat. She had the same kind of hat, only in felt, during the winter months.

Mary had gone to the door to meet her and watched while the ambulancemen settled her into a chair and trundled her over.

'That will do, thank you,' said Great Aunt Thirza. 'My niece will help me into the sitting-room.' She turned to look at her. 'Well, Mary, here I am.'

Mary kissed the offered cheek. 'We are delighted to have you to stay, Aunt.' She stopped as the men turned away. 'If you'd like to go to the kitchen—the door over there—there's tea and sandwiches. Thank you both so much.'

She had a lovely smile and they beamed back at her. 'If that's not troubling you, miss, we could do with a cuppa.'

'Would you like tea, Aunt Thirza? It's all ready in the sitting-room.' She gave the old lady an arm and settled her in an armchair by the small tea-table. 'Father's at the British Museum; he'll be back at any moment. Mother's very busy; she's just had an order for Christmas cards.'

'Ridiculous,' said Mrs Winton. 'Christmas cards, indeed—child's play.'

'Actually they need a great deal of skill, and Mother's very good at them.'

Her aunt sipped her tea. 'Why aren't you married, Mary?'

'Well, I don't think I've met anyone I want to marry yet. There's Arthur, of course...'

'A girl should marry.' She pronounced it 'gel'. 'I don't hold with this independence. My generation had more sense; we married and settled down to be good wives and mothers.'

Aunt Thirza was in her eighties. Mary wondered what it had been like to be young then—corsets and hats and gloves, not just on Sundays and occasions but even to go shopping, and not to be able to drive a car or wear trousers...

On the other hand there had been no television and there had been dances—not the leaping around that was the fashion now, but foxtrotting and waltzing. Waltzing with a man you loved or even liked must have been delightful. The clothes had been pretty awful, but they were pretty awful nowadays among the young. Mary, who sometimes felt older than her years, sighed.

Great Aunt Thirza was quite a handful. She had brought a good deal of luggage with her which had to be unpacked and disposed around the house according to her fancy. She poked her nose into the kitchen and made scathing remarks about Mrs Blackett's terrible old slippers with the nicks cut out for the comfort of her bunions; she inspected the fridge, lectured Polly on her untidiness, interrupted her nephew in his study and swept down to the hut to see her niece-in-law, where she passed so many critical remarks that that lady was unable to pick up her brush for the rest of the day.

It didn't matter how ingenious Mary was with the lentils, dried peas and beans, her elderly relation always found something wrong with them.

At the end of a week, having escorted her to her room, shut the windows, refreshed the water jug, gone downstairs again for warm milk, found another blanket, run a bath and listened to her aunt giving her opinion of the drawbacks of the house, Mary went downstairs to where her mother and father were sitting in the drawing-room—a room seldom used since it was large, draughty and, despite Mary's polishing, shabby.

'When is Great Aunt Thirza going home?' she asked her father, sounding cross.

He looked up from the book he was reading, peered over his glasses at her and said mildly, 'I really don't know, my dear. She's no trouble, is she?'

Mary sat down. 'Yes, Father, she is. She has made Mrs Blackett even more bad-tempered than usual—she's threatened to leave—and Polly is rebellious and I can't blame her. I haven't cooked a square meal for more than a week; I don't expect that you've noticed but there's not been an ounce of meat in the house for days and I, for one, am sick of spinach and lettuce leaves.'

Her mother looked up from the sketches she was making. 'A nice steak with mushrooms, and those French fries you do so well, darling.' She added hopefully, 'Could we go out for a meal?'

'It would cost too much,' said Mary, who knew more about the housekeeping money than her mother. 'We need a miracle…'

It came with the postman in the morning. Great Aunt Thirza was bidden to attend at St Justin's in Central London where she had been treated for a heart condition—nine o'clock on the following morning. Should her examination prove satisfactory she could make arrangements to return to her home and resume a normal life.

'I shall, of course, abide by the specialist's advice,' said Great Aunt Thirza. 'He may consider it more beneficial to my health for me to return here for a further few weeks.' She poured herself another cup of tea—the special herbal one that she preferred. 'You can drive me there, Mary. It will save the expense of a taxi.'

Mary didn't answer. Mrs Winton was comfortably off, well able to afford as many taxis as she could want; she could afford to pay for the peas and beans too, thought Mary peevishly.

To waste most of a day, certainly a whole morning, taking her aunt to the hospital was tiresome when there was a stack of ironing waiting to be done, besides which she needed to thumb through the cookery book she had borrowed from the library and find another way to cook kidney beans...

Polly, back from school at teatime, gobbling bread spread with an imitation butter, heavily covered with peanut butter, voiced the opinion that Great Aunt Thirza was quite well enough to go home. 'Let her housekeeper cook that rabbit food.' She rolled her large blue eyes dramatically. 'Mary, I'll die if I don't have some chips soon.'

'Perhaps I could have a word with the specialist,' mused Mary.

'Yes, do. Wear something pretty and flutter your eyelashes at him. You're quite pretty, you know.'

'I don't expect that kind of man—you know, wildly clever and always reading books like Father, only younger—notices if one is pretty or not. If I had a heart attack or fainted all over him he might, I suppose.'

She spent a moment imagining herself falling gracefully into the arms of some doddering old professor. It wouldn't do; she wasn't the right shape. Fainting was for small, ethereal girls with tiny waists and slender enough to be picked up easily. Whoever it was who caught her would need to be a giant with muscles to match. 'But I will wear that green dress and those sandals I bought in the sales.'

St Justin's Hospital wasn't far as the crow flew, but driving there during the rush hour was a different matter. Great Aunt Thirza, roused from her bed at an early hour, was in a bad temper. She sat beside Mary, her lips firmly closed, wearing the air of someone who was being shabbily treated but refused to complain, which left Mary free to concentrate on getting to the hospital by nine o'clock.

The outpatients department was already full. They

were told where to sit and warned that Mr van Rakesma had not yet arrived but was expected at any moment. 'I am probably the first to be seen,' said Great Aunt Thirza. She edged away from an elderly man beside her who was asleep and snoring gently. 'Really, the people one meets; I find it distasteful.'

'You could always be a private patient,' suggested Mary.

'My dear Mary, you talk as though I had a fortune. Besides, why should I pay for something I can obtain for nothing?'

Mary wondered if having money made one mean. She wasn't interested in her aunt's finances. She changed places with the old lady and found that the snoring man was watching her. 'Morning, love,' he said cheerfully. 'Don't tell me someone as pretty as you needs to come to this halfway house.'

'Halfway house?'

He winked. 'Take a look, love. We're all getting a bit long in the tooth and needing a bit of make do and mend to help us on our way!' He winked again and added, 'Who's the old biddy with you? Not your ma, that's for sure.'

'An aunt—a great aunt actually. Shall we have to wait for a long time?'

He waved a vague arm. 'Starts at eight o'clock, does his nibs, but, seeing that he's not here yet and it's gone nine o'clock, I'd say we'll still be here for our dinner.'

'You mean the first appointment is for eight o'clock?' When he nodded she said, 'My aunt thought she would be the first patient.'

His loud laugh caused Great Aunt Thirza to bend for-

ward and look around Mary so that she could give him
an icy stare.

'I cannot imagine why this man hasn't come, Mary.
Possibly he is still in his bed...'

He wasn't, though. There was a wave of interest in the
closely packed benches as he walked past them—a very
tall, heavily built man, his gingery hair tinged with grey,
his handsome face without expression, looking ahead of
him just as though there was no one else there but himself
and his registrar beside him. Mary had ample opportunity to study him. He was, she realised, the man she had
been waiting for, and she fell instantly in love with him.

After that she didn't mind the long wait, and sat between the now sleeping man and an irate great aunt. She
had plenty to think about, and most of her thoughts were
of a highly impractical nature, but just for the moment
she allowed day-dreaming to override common sense. He
would look at her and fall in love, just as she had done...

'At last,' hissed Great Aunt Thirza. 'Come with me,
Mary.'

The consulting-room was quite small and Mr van
Rakesma seemed to take up most of it. He glanced up
briefly as they went in, asked them to sit down in a pleasant, impersonal voice and finished his writing.

'Mrs Winton? You have been referred to me by Dr
Symes and I am glad to see you looking so well.' He
glanced at the notes before him. 'You wish to return
home, I understand, and if I find you quite recovered I
see no reason why you shouldn't do so.'

'Young man,' said Great Aunt Thirza sternly, 'I had
an appointment for nine o'clock this morning. It is now
ten minutes past twelve. I consider this a disgraceful
state of affairs.'

Mary went pink and stared at her feet. Mr van Rakesma smiled; Sister, standing beside his desk, gave an indignant snort.

'Circumstances occasionally arise which prevent our keeping to our original plans,' he said mildly. 'Would you be good enough to go with Sister to the examination-room so that I can take a look?'

'You will stay here,' she told Mary as she went. Mary didn't look up, which was a pity for she would have found his eyes on her. He couldn't see her face, but her glorious hair was enough to attract any man's eye…

'Is there something wrong with your shoe?' he asked gently.

She looked at him then, still pink. 'No—no.' She went on rapidly, 'My aunt's tired; she didn't mean what she said.'

He smiled and her heart danced against her ribs. 'No? A disappointment; I rather liked being called "young man".' He got up and went into the examination-room, and when he came out again presently he didn't so much as glance at her but sat down and began to write. When Mrs Winton reappeared he told her that for her age she was very fit and there was no reason why she shouldn't resume a normal lifestyle.

'You have someone to look after you? A housekeeper? A daughter?'

'A housekeeper and, of course, should I require extra help, my niece—' she nodded at Mary '—would come.'

He nodded. 'Then everything seems most satisfactory, Mrs Winton.' He stood up and shook hands with her and bade her a grave goodbye, gave Mary a brief, unsmiling nod, then sat down and took up his pen once more.

It was Sister who said, 'You'll need an appointment

for six months' time, Mrs Winton; go and see Reception as you go out. Professor van Rakesma will want to keep an eye on you.'

Great Aunt Thirza stopped short. 'Professor? You mean to tell me that he's a professor?'

'Yes, and a very clever one too, Mrs Winton. We're lucky to have him for a consultant.'

Over lunch at a nearby café, Great Aunt Thirza observed that for a foreigner his manners had been surprisingly good. Mary murmured a reply, busy with her own thoughts.

'Presumably,' went on Great Aunt Thirza, 'he is reliable.'

'Well, he's a professor. I expect he had to take exams or something before he could be one.'

'I trust the exams were taken here in England. Our standards are high.'

'Wasn't the seat of medical learning Leiden? I believe it is still considered one of the best medical schools...' She added, 'He is Dutch.'

'That is as may be,' observed the old lady. 'I shall check with Dr Symes.'

Mary, who had been wondering how she could find out more about the professor, said casually, 'What a good idea. You must let me know what he says. Probably he's over here on some exchange scheme.'

It was a slender chance, she thought wistfully; it was unlikely that she would ever see him again. How silly she was to fall in love with a complete stranger. 'We'd better start back,' she said briskly. 'You'll want to ring your housekeeper and arrange things.'

'Naturally. I intend to leave your father's house in two days' time; that will give us the opportunity to pack my things. You will, of course, drive me home.'

At the thought of eating sausages and the weekend joint again Mary sighed with relief; she would have driven her great aunt to the furthest corner of the land...

Her mother and father expressed pleasure at Mrs Winton's recovery, and pressed her to stay as long as she wished, unaware of Mary's speaking glance. Mary could see her wavering. Something had to be done—and quickly. 'Polly, fetch your recorder and play something for Great Aunt Thirza.'

A wobbly rendering of 'Greensleeves', followed by an unrecognisable piece full of wrong notes, which Polly assured them was 'The Trout' by Schubert, put an end to the old lady's indecision; she would return home, as she had first intended, in two days' time.

It fell to Mary's lot, naturally enough, to pack for her aunt, and then unpack everything again because that lady suddenly remembered that she would need a particular cardigan to wear. She did it all cheerfully, quite unmoved by her aunt's fault-finding and lack of thanks, and two days later she got the car out, loaded the cases and settled Mrs Winton on the back seat.

Her father had come out of his study to say goodbye and her mother, in her painting smock and holding a brush in her hand, had joined him on the doorstep. Polly wasn't back from school but Mrs Blackett, obliging with an extra afternoon's work, glowered from the kitchen window.

Great Aunt Thirza said her goodbyes graciously, omitting to thank anyone, giving the impression that she had honoured them greatly by her visit and pausing long enough in the hall to find fault with several things around the house. 'I'm sure, though, that you did your best,' she added, 'and on the whole the meals were palatable.'

These remarks were met in silence. 'I dare say I shall see improvements when I next visit you,' she said and swept out to the car.

The Pagetts watched their daughter drive away. 'Perhaps we should wait a little before we invite dear Aunt Thirza to stay again, my dear,' observed Mr Pagett, and added, 'I do hope Mary will cook something tasty for supper...'

Mrs Winton lived in Richmond in a red-brick terraced house, which was much too large for her and stuffed with mid-Victorian furniture, heavy plush curtains and a great many ornaments. Her housekeeper had been with her for a good number of years—a silent, austere woman who kept her distance, ran the house efficiently and never talked about herself, which wasn't surprising really since Mrs Winton never asked.

She opened the door as Mary stopped the car, wished them good afternoon and took Mrs Winton's luggage from the boot. 'We'd like tea at once, Mrs Cox,' said Great Aunt Thirza, and swept indoors with a brisk, 'Come along, Mary; don't dawdle!'

Mary wasn't listening; she had gone back to the car to give Mrs Cox a hand with the luggage.

She hadn't wanted to stay for tea but good manners made it necessary; she sat on an uncomfortable horse-hair chair—a museum piece if ever there was one—and drank weak tea from a beautiful Minton cup and ate a dry Madeira cake which she suspected had been in the tin ever since Great Aunt Thirza's illness.

While she ate she thought of the sausages and the mountains of chips she would cook when she got home. She had no doubt that her mother and father and Polly would enjoy them as much as she would.

Driving back presently, it wasn't sausages and chips

on her mind, it was love—the sheer excitement of it, the wonder of it, just to look at someone and know that he was the one… Her euphoria was short-lived. 'Fool,' said Mary. 'You'll never see him again—it was pure chance; besides, he didn't even look at you.'

She edged past a slow-moving Ford Anglia, driven by an elderly man in a cloth cap. 'He'll be married to some gorgeous wisp of a girl who he'll treat like fragile porcelain.' She sighed; no one, however kindly disposed, could describe her as fragile. 'All the same, it would be nice to find out about him.'

She was talking to herself again, waiting at traffic lights, and the driver of the car alongside hers gave her a startled look. She looked sane enough, but he couldn't see anyone else in the car…

Professor van Rakesma, unlike Mary, wasn't talking to himself—he was going through the notes of his patients.

'Mrs Winton,' he said at length in a satisfied voice, and made a note of her address. He had no doubt at all that he would discover more of the girl who had been with her—a niece, the old lady had said, and one in the habit of giving extra help and therefore to be tracked down at some future date.

He handed the notes back to the patient nurse waiting for them and left the hospital. He was dining out with friends and anticipating a pleasant evening as well as an excellent dinner.

Mary and her family had an excellent dinner too; the sausages and chips were greeted with whoops of joy from Polly, and even her mother, a dainty eater, welcomed them with pleasure. There was a wholesome roly-poly

pudding for afters too, and a bottle of red wine, pronounced delicious by everyone.

Her father, of course, hardly noticed what he drank,
and her mother was too kind to do more than remark on
its good colour. The professor, had he been there, would
have poured it down the sink.

Never mind that—it was a celebration; they were a
family again without Great Aunt Thirza to meddle and
complain. No one actually said that; only Polly remarked
that she hoped that her great aunt wouldn't pay them another visit for a very long time.

'Well, she only comes when she wants something,'
said Polly, 'and she's well again now isn't she?'

'She saw a specialist the other day?' asked her mother,
who, always being in her hut working at her cards, had
missed the tale of Great Aunt Thirza's hospital appointment.

Mary, to her great annoyance, blushed. 'Yes—he said
that she was able to resume normal life again and that
she was very fit for her age.'

'Was he nice?'

'He seemed very nice,' said Mary cautiously.

Polly asked, 'What did he look like?'

Mary longed to describe him in every small detail but
that would never have done. 'Oh, well, quite young—he
was Dutch...'

'But what did he look like?' persisted Polly.

'Very tall and big with gingery hair, only it was grey
too, and he had very blue eyes.' She remembered something and smiled. 'Great Aunt Thirza called him "young
man"!'

Her father said, 'Your aunt was always outspoken.'

'Did he mind?' asked her mother.

'No, he said that he rather liked it.'

'He doesn't sound like a specialist. Do you suppose that if I'm ill he'd look after me?' Polly looked hopeful.

'Well, no—he looks after people with bad hearts.'

'Supposing you broke your heart—would he look after you?'

Mary said in a level voice, 'No, I don't suppose that he's got time to waste on broken hearts, only ill ones.' She got up from the table. 'I'll bring the coffee in here, shall I?'

Life settled down into its accustomed pattern once more. Mary's days were full. Her father had dropped a pile of notes all over his study floor and it took hours of work to get them in order again; her mother floated in and out of the house, absorbed in her painting, and Polly was away most of the day.

Mrs Blackett, free to do as she liked again, was her usual ill-tempered self, although she no longer threatened to leave, and Mary slipped back into her customary routine. And if her thoughts dwelt wistfully upon Professor van Rakesma she didn't allow them to show; she had plenty of common sense and she was aware that day-dreams, though pleasant, had nothing at all to do with real life.

There was Arthur too. He had been away on a course and now he was back and, though she was reluctant to do so, she had agreed to go out to dinner with him—to a nice little place in Hampstead, he had told her; they would be able to get a good meal very reasonably.

The idea that she was only worth a reasonably priced dinner rankled with Mary, but she got out a pretty if somewhat out-of-date dress, put polish on her nails, did her face and piled her glorious hair on top of her head. She made sure that the casserole for the family supper was safely in the oven, and went to remind her father that she was going out.

He looked up from his writing. 'Out? Well, enjoy yourself, my dear. Have you a key?'

She went down to the hut next. 'I'm going out to dinner with Arthur, Mother. The supper's in the oven; it'll be ready at half-past seven. I've told Polly.'

'Dear child,' said her mother fondly, 'go and enjoy yourself—who with?'

'Arthur.'

'Oh, Arthur, of course. Tell me, do you like robins on this card, or do you suppose a bunch of holly would be better?'

'Robins,' said Mary.

Polly was in the hall. 'I'll see to supper, Mary. Did you feed Bingo?'

The family cat had made himself scarce while Great Aunt Thirza had been there, only skimming in for his meals, but now he was in possession of the house once more, commandeering laps and eating heartily.

'Yes—here's Arthur...'

Polly caught her arm. 'Don't say yes, Mary,' she whispered urgently. 'He might propose!'

'Arthur has never done anything hastily in his life; he'll have to give a proposal a lot of thought, and he'll lead up to it so gradually that I'll have plenty of time to think about it.'

'You like him?'

Mary said guardedly, 'I've known him for a long time, love; he's a good man but I don't want to marry him.'

She added thoughtfully, 'I don't think he really wants to marry me...'

Arthur had got out of the car and thumped the door-knocker; she kissed Polly and went to meet him.

Arthur's 'Hello, old girl,' had nothing lover-like about it. She said, 'Hello, Arthur,' and got into the car beside him and enquired about his course.

Telling her about it took up the entire drive and he still hadn't finished when they sat down at a table in the restaurant. It was a pleasant place but not, she decided, the right background for romance. Its pale green walls were too cool, and the white tablecloths and little pot of dried flowers echoed the coolness, but since Arthur obviously had no thought of romance that didn't matter.

Mary ate her plaice, French fries and macédoine of vegetables, chose trifle for pudding and listened to him. She was a kind girl, and it was obvious that he needed to tell someone everything which had occurred at the course. She said 'Oh, splendid,' and 'Really?' at suitable intervals, and wondered what Professor van Rakesma was doing...

She thanked Arthur when he took her back home, offered him coffee, which he refused, and accepted his kiss on her cheek. 'A splendid evening, Mary—we've had a good talk.' He added, in a rather condescending tone which grated on her ear, 'When I can find the time we must do it again.'

What about my time? thought Mary, and murmured politely.

Getting into bed, she decided that in ten years' time Arthur would definitely be pompous.

She was getting the breakfast ready the next morning when the phone rang. Mrs Cox, usually so calm, sounded

agitated. 'Miss Mary? The doctor's here; your aunt's took
bad. She wants you—ever so restless she is. The doctor
said if you could come to ease her mind. Won't go to the
hospital, she says, at least not until you come.'

'I'll be there as soon as I can, Mrs Cox. Tell Great
Aunt Thirza, will you?'

Mary switched off the gas under the frying-pan and
went to find her mother.

Chapter 2

There were cars parked on either side of the road where Mrs Winton lived. Mary wedged the elderly Austin into the space between a new Rover and a Rolls Royce and nipped smartly across the pavement and up the steps to the front door.

'I thought you'd never get here,' said Mrs Cox, no longer the silent and austere housekeeper now that she was thoroughly put out. 'Your aunt's real poorly; the doctor's with her now.'

'If she's so ill she must go back to hospital or have a nurse here—where's this doctor?'

'Ah—the niece,' said a voice gently beside her. There he was—the man she had been thinking of all day and every day, standing a foot from her, smiling. 'Mrs Winton's doctor is with her; I thought it best if I were to have a word with you…' He glanced at Mrs Cox. 'If we might go somewhere quiet?'

They were ushered into the drawing-room and Mary sat down on the self-same horsehair chair that she had so happily vacated so short a time ago. She was glad to sit down; she had never believed that nonsense about knees turning to jelly when one was confronted by the loved one, but hers were jelly now.

'Fancy seeing you again,' she said, and added, 'That's a silly thing to say.' And she blushed because he was smiling again, although he said nothing.

He stood by the door, watching her, and presently said, 'Your aunt has had a mild heart attack. Not serious enough for her to return to hospital but she will need to stay quietly at home for a few days. As you may know, the treatment is now quite an active one, but she is old which largely precludes it. If it is difficult for you to stay with her I'm sure Dr Symes will be able to find a nurse from one of the agencies, but I understand from Mrs Winton that you are a very capable young woman, and, of course, a nurse—a private nurse—is a costly expense in these days.'

I don't cost a penny, reflected Mary bleakly.

'There will be very little for you to do,' said the Professor smoothly, watching her expressive face from under heavy lids. 'See that she takes gentle exercise each day, eats sensibly, doesn't become agitated…' Mary gave him a cold look. 'Yes, I quite understand that Mrs Winton is used to having her own way, but she appears to like you and will probably do what you ask of her.'

He came and sat down opposite her on another horse-hair chair. 'You are needed at home?' He sounded casually sympathetic. 'You live close by?'

'No, no, I don't; at least, Hampstead isn't far, but it's an awkward journey. Besides, there's no one to see to the house.'

He raised his eyebrows. 'You live alone? I gathered from the hospital that Mrs Winton was staying with a nephew—your father?'

'Yes, but Father's writing a book and my mother paints. My sister's only thirteen and she's at school all day. Mrs Blackett could manage for a day or two, but she's always on the point of leaving.'

'Mrs Blackett?' prompted the professor gently, greatly enjoying himself.

'Our daily. At least, she comes four mornings a week, but—she didn't get on well with Great Aunt Thirza.'

'Just so.' The professor might have been only thirty-five years old, but his manner was that of a man twice his age, seemingly prepared to listen sympathetically and give suitable advice. Mary responded to that; she had plenty of friends of her own age, but it wouldn't have entered her head to bore them with her worries, but here was a sympathetic ear, and it seemed the most natural thing in the world to unburden herself.

'Mother—' she began. 'Mother's a darling, and so clever with a paintbrush, but of course she's artistic and she doesn't really like cooking and that kind of thing; besides, the money she gets for the cards is most useful. And Father's very clever; he doesn't notice what's going on around him. I wouldn't change them for the world but they simply can't manage unless someone is there to see to the house. Polly's splendid, but she's at school and there's homework. So you see it is a bit awkward if I have to stay here...' She added snappily, 'Not that I'm indispensable...'

'No, no,' soothed Professor van Rakesma. 'Of course not, but I see that you have problems. Would it help if you were to go home for a few hours each day? Perhaps while your aunt rests in the afternoons?'

'Have you any idea what the traffic is like between here and Hampstead—the other end of Hampstead?'

He tucked this useful piece of information away at the back of his mind and said that he had a very good idea. 'If a nurse were to relieve you for a few hours each day would that help?' And at her look of surprise he added, 'I'm sure the National Health Service would be prepared to pay for her; she would cost a lot less than having your aunt in hospital, besides giving us another empty bed. Always in short supply.'

'Would they? Who should I ask?'

'Leave that to me. Now, I think we might join Dr Symes and his patient.'

Great Aunt Thirza was sitting, propped up by pillows, in a vast mahogany bed; she looked pale and tired and Mary forgot how tiresome the whole thing was and bent to kiss her cheek. 'I'm sorry, Aunt Thirza, but a few days' rest and you'll be as right as rain.'

'So that foreign man tells me. Dr Symes is of no use at all—nice enough, but of course all doctors are fools, and don't contradict me, miss!' She caught Mary's hand. 'You'll stay, Mary?'

'Until you are better, yes, Aunt Thirza.'

Mrs Winton closed her eyes. 'Then go away and leave me in peace.'

Mary looked at the two men. Dr Symes nodded to her to go with him, leaving the professor at the bedside. Outside the door he said, 'She'll listen to him. Are you sure you can manage? I'll be in every day and I dare say

Professor van Rakesma will visit again. It was a piece of luck that I happened to be on the other phone to him when the housekeeper rang up—said he'd seen her at St Justin's and asked if he might come and see her. Very civil of him.'

She agreed, and added sedately, 'I'm sure it will be a great relief to Aunt Thirza to know that she is being looked after so well. You'll be here in the morning?'

'After surgery, but phone me if you are worried.'

They were joined by the professor then, who, beyond wishing her good morning, had nothing further to say before the two men went out to their cars and drove away. She shut the door and went to find Mrs Cox.

'You're staying, Miss Mary? I told the doctor and I'm telling you that I'm the housekeeper, not the nurse. I've enough to do without fetching and carrying all day and half the night.'

'Yes, of course I'll stay, Mrs Cox. Professor van Rakesma thinks that Mrs Winton will be fully recovered in a short time. I'm sure that it must have been a nasty shock to you when she became ill again. I'll look after my aunt so please don't worry; I'm sure that you have enough to do.'

Mrs Cox bridled. 'Well, as to that, I'm sure I'm willing to give a hand when necessary—though I won't be left alone with Mrs Winton.'

'No, no. No one would ask you to do that. I'm sure we'll manage very well between us. I'll go and see my aunt now. I dare say she's tired after being examined.'

Great Aunt Thirza was asleep. Mary stealthily opened a window, and sat down on a little spoon-back chair and went over her conversation with the professor. He had said that she was to leave things to him, that he would arrange for someone to come each day so that she could go home, but he was a busy man and, however well meant, she doubted if anything would come of that.

It had been a delightful surprise seeing him again, she reflected, not that he had been over-friendly. Well, she conceded, he's been kind and helpful, but she rather thought that he would be that to anyone with a problem. She had to admit that he had shown no special interest in her, but then why should he? Probably he was happily married...

'Why are you sitting there?' demanded Great Aunt Thirza. 'There's surely something you can be doing? I don't approve of idle hands.'

'I was waiting for you to wake up,' said Mary. 'Dr Symes wants you to have a warm drink—tea or milk or cocoa?'

Great Aunt Thirza was feeling cantankerous. 'I don't want a drink...'

Mary got to her feet. 'I'll bring you a tray of tea—Earl Grey—and do you fancy a little fish for your lunch?'

'Fish! Fish? I'm very ill, girl, probably dying...'

'Professor van Rakesma said that you will be up and about in a few days. You've had a nasty fright, Aunt Thirza, but there's no question of your dying. A nice little piece of sole, with a morsel of creamed potato and perhaps a purée of new peas?'

'You may bring it to me,' said the old lady ungraciously, 'but I shall most likely be unable to eat it.'

It seemed a very long day to Mary; her aunt kept her busy, for she was a bad patient, prone to do exactly the opposite to what she was asked to do, so that Mary got into bed quite worn out with hanging on to her patience. She had phoned her mother that evening, and was relieved that everything was going smoothly at home—although Mrs Pagett's efforts at cooking supper seemed to have been rather chaotic.

'You won't have to stay there long?' her mother had asked.

'No, I don't think so.' She recounted what the doctor had said but didn't mention the professor's offer to find a relief for her each day. It had been a kind thought, she reflected sleepily, but he would have forgotten by now.

He hadn't though. Mary was carrying her aunt's lunch tray downstairs the next day when Mrs Cox admitted an elderly woman in a nurse's uniform.

Mary, poised on the bottom tread of the stairs, stared at her. 'He actually meant it,' she exclaimed.

The woman smiled. 'Indeed he did. Professor van Rakesma seldom says much, but when he does he means it. He has arranged for me to come each day while you are here—two o'clock until half-past five.'

Mary put down her tray and shook hands. 'That's very kind and thoughtful of him—and kind of you too. It's not interfering with your work? I didn't realise that the Health Service were so helpful.'

'Well, you must have time to yourself. I'm Maisie Stone.' She glanced at Mrs Cox, who was standing by the door looking rather sour.

'This is Mrs Cox, my aunt's housekeeper,' said Mary hastily. 'She runs the house beautifully and is such a help.'

Mrs Cox looked smug. 'I'm sure I do my best but, as I told Miss Mary here, I won't do no nursing or lifting or suchlike.'

'Well, I wouldn't expect you to do that,' said Mrs Stone

comfortably. 'I'm sure we shall get on very well together.' She turned to Mary. 'If I might take a look at the patient?'

Ten minutes later Mary was in the car, driving home. It was an awkward journey, but she had discovered several shortcuts and the traffic wasn't too heavy and it was worth it; her mother was delighted to see her—it wasn't one of Mrs Blackett's days and the kitchen needed urgent attention. Mary put on a pinny. 'If you'll make us a cup of tea—there's a cake in the tin on the dresser— I'll just clear these dishes and saucepans. What had you planned for the evening?'

'There's that chicken you were going to roast…'

'I'll casserole it. Then all you'll have to do is put it in the oven a couple of hours before you want it.' Mary picked up a teatowel. 'Mother, supposing I write down what you need to buy each day? Then when I come home I'll get it ready to cook.'

'Oh, darling, would you? I've been so busy I've hardly had a moment to do any painting. Perhaps Polly…?'

'Well, no, love, she's got a lot of prep to do when she gets home, hasn't she? If you pop down to the shops each morning you'll have the rest of the day to work—you and Father can have a cold lunch. Is he at home?'

'No. He said he'd be back about five o'clock.'

Mary hung the teacloth to dry and sat down at the table. 'So we'll have tea and decide what to buy tomorrow.'

'Will you be away long?' asked her mother wistfully. 'We don't seem able to get on very well when you're not here, dear.'

'Not long, and I can come home each afternoon—well, most of them; I don't know about weekends.'

But when Sunday came Mrs Stone arrived at her usual

hour, and this time the professor was with her. He took a quick look at Mrs Winton, pronounced her greatly improved, suggested that she could take some exercise each day and, as they went downstairs, observed casually that since he had heard that Mary lived at Hampstead, and he was on his way there, he would give her a lift.

Mary paused on the bottom tread. 'Thank you; that's kind of you to offer but I've got our car—I have to get back again, you see.'

'I'm invited to tea with my godson—his parents live near the Heath. I'll pick you up at around five o'clock and collect Maisie.'

Even though she was so much in love with him and could hardly bear him out of her sight Mary took a few moments to agree to this. Her heart might be his, but common sense told her that allowing herself to get involved wouldn't do at all. A prudent refusal was on the tip of her tongue when he said, 'Well, run along and get your coat and we can be off.'

He sounded just like the older of her two brothers; besides, if she refused to go she might never see him again...

She went out to the car with him and he opened the door for her to get in. There was a dog sitting behind the steering-wheel—a Jack Russell, white and black with a whiskered face full of intelligence. He eyed her beadily and the professor said, 'A friend, Richard,' and went round to his door and got in.

Richard moved to sit between them, panting and uttering short happy barks. Mary rubbed his ears and asked, 'Why Richard? It's an unusual name for a dog.'

'He has a lion's heart. Don't let him crowd you; you like dogs?'

'Yes, but we haven't got one. We have a cat called Bingo.'

He began to talk about her aunt then; he sounded exactly like a family doctor, which made him remote so that she couldn't find the courage to ask him about his work, let alone his personal life. Even though he talked about Mrs Winton it was surprising the amount of information he gleaned from her without giving the least inkling of his own life.

They were very nearly at her home when she asked shyly, 'Do you live here in England or go back to Holland?'

'My home is in Holland but I spend a good deal of time here.' He added lightly, 'A foot in either camp, as it were.'

Which left her knowing no more about him than that.

He stopped before her home and she thanked him with a hand on the door ready to jump out, but he was there before her, holding her door open—something Arthur wouldn't have dreamt of doing even if she'd had her arms full of parcels. Arthur would have sat behind the wheel and said, 'So long, old girl.'

Professor van Rakesma was older and wiser than Arthur, besides the fact that he had nice manners. He opened the gate, glanced at the shabby house with its elaborate gables and said, 'There must be a splendid view from the back of your home.'

'Oh, there is—the Heath, you know.'

They stood facing each other, either side of the gate, and he smiled suddenly. 'I'll be back around five o'clock, Miss Pagett.'

She went up the overgrown drive to the front door and turned round to look when she reached it. He was still there, and she wondered uneasily if he had expected to

be asked in. He had said that he was going to have tea
with his godson… She opened the door and went inside.

Polly came into the hall to meet her. 'Mary, I haven't
seen you for days. Mother's in the hut and Father's in the
study. I cooked most of the lunch. Can you stay for tea?
I made some rock cakes.'

'Lovely, Polly, and I can stay for tea, but I have to be
ready to leave at five o'clock.' She went on with a slightly
heightened colour, 'I have a lift here and back.'

'Not Arthur?'

'Heavens, no. What I mean is, I don't think he knows
I'm at Aunt Thirza's house.'

'Then who?'

'Professor van Rakesma brought Mrs Stone, who relieves me each day, and since he was visiting someone
in Hampstead he said he'd bring me home and drive me
back.'

'What's he like? I know you said he had ginger hair
and blue eyes but is he nice?'

'Very nice.'

'Is he married?'

'I really don't know. He's—he's not a man to talk about
himself, I think.'

'Well, then, he's a nice change from Arthur,' observed
Polly. 'It would be nice if he fell in love with you and
married you, and that would be one in the eye for Arthur.'

'Arthur is a good, steady man,' said Mary as they went
into the kitchen and began to gather things ready for tea.

'Oh, pooh,' said Polly. 'Can you imagine what he'll
be like in ten years' time?'

Mary knew exactly what she meant.

On Sundays, when they were all at home, they had tea
in the drawing-room—a large, lofty-ceilinged place and

very draughty since the old-fashioned windows were ill-
fitting and allowed the air to seep in round their frames.
In winter, of course, the door was shut and no one went
near the place; it would have cost a fortune to light a fire
large enough to warm the room and there was a damp
patch in one corner which dried out during the summer
and reappeared each autumn.

Today was dry and warm, however, and the room,
though shabby and on the chilly side, was pleasant
enough; the chairs were elderly but comfortable and Mary
and Mrs Blackett kept the tables and cabinets polished.
They laid the tea things on a table by the big bay window
at the back of the room and Mary cut sandwiches while
Polly cut the cake and boiled the kettle.

As Mary sliced and spread she allowed her thoughts
to wander. Professor van Rakesma was probably at that
very moment eating his tea somewhere in Hampstead.
It would be a more elegant meal than she was preparing,
of course—good china and silver teaspoons and cake-
stands. He must be glad to get away from the hospital,
which was jammed tight among narrow, busy city streets.
Would he live there? she wondered, and dismissed the
idea. Consultants would only be at the hospital at certain
times; he must have a flat...

'Mary.' Polly had raised her voice. 'I've been talking
to you for ages and you haven't heard a word. Are you
in love? You look quite moony.'

'Good heavens, no.'

Mary spoke so sharply that Polly said, 'Well, you don't
have to snap my head off. P'haps you are tired. Great
Aunt Thirza's pretty grim, isn't she?'

'She's old. Will you be a darling and fetch Mother
from the hut? And I'll get Father.'

Tea was a pleasant, leisurely meal. Mrs Pagett wondered in her dreamy way when Mary would be home again, and her father remarked in a vexed voice that when she was away he could never find anything that he wanted.

'I'll be home soon,' soothed Mary. 'Aunt Thirza is much better and she's to start doing more tomorrow.'

'That's nice, dear. Don't let her tire you too much,' observed her mother. 'I suppose you have to go back after tea?'

'Yes. Five o'clock. Professor van Rakesma gave me a lift here and is calling for me then.'

'He could have come to tea…'

'He was going to have tea with his godson, somewhere in Hampstead.'

'Will he be coming in? I still have one or two cards—'

'He won't come in, Mother. I'll wait for him at the gate—he'll want to get back.'

Mrs Pagett got up. 'Then you won't mind if I go back to the hut and get on with my painting, darling. I'll see you tomorrow, I expect.'

She wandered away down the garden and presently Mr Pagett got up too. 'I'll leave you two to tidy up; I'll only be in the way.'

Polly ate the last sandwich. 'I'll wash up,' she volunteered, 'after you've gone.'

'We'll do it together—there's fifteen minutes before he'll be here.'

They cleared the table together and went into the kitchen. Mary turned on the sink taps and waited patiently for the water to get warm—the boiler was beginning to get temperamental—and Polly went off to feed Bingo. She went out of the back door to call him in and found him lying comfortably in a rose bed by the gate. Professor van Rakesma was leaning over the gate, doing nothing.

'Hello,' Polly danced up to him. 'Have you come for Mary? She's in the kitchen, washing up.' She scooped up Bingo and added, 'Open the gate and follow me.'

The professor smiled down at her. 'Shall I be welcome?'

'Why ever not? If you're a professor shouldn't you be old or at least elderly?'

'Er—you know, I'd never thought about it. I shall, of course, in due time be elderly and hopefully old.'

'How old are you?'

'Thirty-five.' He sounded amused.

'I'm thirteen. Mary's twenty-four, getting on a bit; if she doesn't marry Arthur she'll be an old maid.'

'Then let us hope that there is an alternative.'

They had arrived without haste at the kitchen door and he stood for a moment watching Mary, who was attacking a saucepan with a great deal of energy so that her hair was coming loose as she rubbed and scoured. She didn't see him at once but when Bingo let out an impatient miauw said, 'You found him. Good. I can't think why this saucepan is burnt—what...?'

Something made her turn her head then. Feeling very much at a disadvantage, and aware that she hardly looked her best, she said peevishly, 'You should have come to the front door.'

He said meekly, his heavy lids hiding the gleam of amusement in his eyes, 'I do apologise. I'll go back and ring the bell while you tuck your hair up and assume your usual calm manner!'

She smiled then, and Polly laughed. 'I'm sorry—I didn't mean to be rude.'

'Think nothing of it; I am convinced that a burnt saucepan is enough to upset any housewife worth her salt.'

Polly said suddenly, 'I like you. You're not a bit like a professor. Are you married? Because if you aren't you might—'

Mary, with a heightened colour, interrupted her briskly. 'Polly, be an angel and tell Father I'm just going, will you?' She was washing her hands and wishing that she could get to a comb and a looking-glass. Heaven alone knew what she looked like. 'I'll get my handbag...'

Polly went with them to the car and the professor waited patiently while she admired it. 'I've never ridden in a Rolls Royce,' she observed wistfully.

'Then I will come and take you for a ride one day.'

'You will? You promise?'

'I promise.'

'You're great—I do wish that Mary—' She caught her sister's look of outrage and went on airily, 'Well, perhaps I'd better not say that.' When they were in the car she poked her head through the open window. 'If you take a good look at Mary she's quite pretty!'

The professor spoke gravely. 'I agree with you absolutely, Polly.' He waved goodbye and drove off and Mary, very red in the face, was relieved when he didn't even glance at her.

She said presently, 'You mustn't take any notice of Polly—she's a bit outspoken.'

'One forgets how delightful it was when one could speak honestly—something quickly smothered by the conventions. Have you ever considered how much happier we would be if we uttered our real feelings instead of the well-mannered platitudes expected of us?'

'Well, it would be nice sometimes to say just what one wished to say...' She stared ahead of her. 'I expect you have to—to—wrap up your words to your patients.'

'Indeed I do, but if I'm asked a straight question then I give an honest answer.'

'You like being a doctor?'

He smiled faintly. 'Yes, it has been, until very recently, the one great interest in my life.'

She thought about this. 'Are you going to get married?'

'Shall we say, rather, that I have from time to time considered it?' He glanced at her. 'And you?'

'Me? No...' She cast around to find some light-hearted remark about that, and was relieved when Richard, perched between them, decided that her lap would be more comfortable. After that they said very little until he stopped at Great Aunt Thirza's front door.

After he and Maisie had gone Mary, preparing her aunt's supper since Mrs Cox had gone to church, allowed her thoughts to dwell on the professor. His goodbye had been polite but uninterested, just as though, she thought bitterly, he had discharged a task and was thankful that it was done. Well, she would take care to keep out of his way in future; she would badger Dr Symes to allow her to go home within the next day or two.

She carried out her plan on the following morning when Dr Symes arrived. There was really no reason for her to stay any longer; Great Aunt Thirza was quite re-covered, she told him. Dr Symes agreed.

'I can arrange for a practice nurse to come in each morning, just to keep an eye on things, and both Professor van Rakesma and I are agreed that the sooner your aunt returns to her normal, quiet way of living the better. You do understand that there may be further heart attacks, but living an invalid's life is no guarantee against that?'

'So it would be quite all right for me to go home in a day or two? Of course I'll come over and see my aunt—I could come each day if you thought that I should—but I really need to be at home...'

'Yes, of course; shall we say the day after tomorrow?'

Mary told Maisie that afternoon. 'I expect Dr Symes will tell Professor van Rakesma, won't he?'

Maisie nodded. 'Sure to—after all, the professor was consulted in the first place, although of course your aunt is Dr Symes's patient. Don't worry, my dear. You could stay here for months and your aunt would be as fit as a fiddle, on the other hand she could die tomorrow; you never know with heart cases, and she is an old lady.'

As if in complete agreement with Maisie's words, Great Aunt Thirza died peacefully in her sleep that night.

It was Mary, taking her an early morning cup of tea, who found her. She put the small tray she was carrying slowly down on to the bedside table. The cup rattled in the saucer because her hands were shaking but she stayed calm, aware of regret that the old lady had died and at the same time glad that her end had been so peaceful.

She wasn't going to pretend to a sorrow she didn't feel; Great Aunt Thirza had been a difficult and despotic member of the family, but all the same she had been family. Mary murmured a childish prayer and went to phone Dr Symes.

Mary had plenty to occupy her for the next few days. Her father reluctantly undertook to make all the necessary arrangements, but she and Mrs Cox were left to deal with all the details. Maisie had come, alerted by Dr

Symes Mary supposed, and proved invaluable, but although Mary's father had dealt with the undertakers he had left a great deal for her to do.

'I've let Aunt Thirza's solicitor know,' he told her. 'He'll see to everything, my dear. The funeral is on Friday; did I tell you?'

'No, Father. Do you want everyone to come back here afterwards? It's usual. Mrs Cox will see to that side of things.'

'Do what you like, Mary. I told the solicitor to let any friends know.' He smiled briefly. 'I don't think your Great Aunt Thirza had many.' He added vaguely, 'She was twelve years older than my mother and the last of her generation.'

He patted her arm, 'Well, my dear, I think I've seen to everything. Arrange things with your mother, won't you? I have an appointment later on today…'

There weren't many people at the funeral other than the family. There was Mrs Cox, of course, tight-lipped and dour in black; she had said little to Mary but Mary guessed that she was worried about her future—she had been with Great Aunt Thirza for many years and another job might be hard to find now that she was past middle age. There were several old ladies there too—Great Aunt Thirza's bridge companions. They said little, but ate Mrs Cox's splendid tea with relish.

It was when they had all gone that Mr Shuttleworth, Great Aunt Thirza's solicitor, observed that he would now read the will. He was an old man, and Mary, who had a vivid imagination, thought that he looked as if someone had taken him out of a cupboard and dusted him down for the occasion.

Great Aunt Thirza having been Great Aunt Thirza,

her will held no pleasant surprises. Mrs Cox was to have the contents of the wardrobe and two thousand pounds, Mr Pagett three thousand pounds, Polly the full set of *Encyclopaedia Brittanica* and Mary an early edition of Mrs Beeton's cookery book, with the hope that by its perusal she might improve her cooking.

The house, its contents and the remainder of her not inconsiderable fortune were to be given to various charities.

Mrs Pagett received nothing, which caused her no distress at all. Great Aunt Thirza had never approved of her designing Christmas and greetings cards; she had once observed that it was no suitable occupation for a lady. Mrs Pagett, even if she was whimsical, didn't lack spirit; she had laughed and muttered, 'Pooh,' before going away to her shed.

Mary watched Mr Shuttleworth tidy away his papers. It was a pity that Great Aunt Thirza hadn't left her father a larger portion of her fortune. All the same, perhaps now the roof might get a few necessary tiles and the old boiler could be replaced with something modern. She saw Mr Shuttleworth to the door, her mind busy with domestic problems.

Chapter 3

It was days later, when Mary took the household bills to her father, that he told her that he didn't intend to pay them. 'That is to say, of course, they will be paid, but they can easily be left for a few weeks. My credit is good...'

'I do need some petty cash, Father—Polly's bus fares and Mrs Blackett—and the window cleaner is due this week.'

He frowned. 'Yes, yes, of course, Mary. Your mother had a cheque this morning; ask her to let you have whatever you need—I'll repay her.'

Her mother, absorbed in the painting of Christmas elves in a snow scene, told her to find her handbag. 'It's somewhere in the bedroom, Mary—there's some money there. Take what you need, dear, and let me know how much so that I can get it back from your father.' She paused for a moment and looked up. 'Are we short of money?'

'No, Mother. I need some petty cash and Father hasn't enough.'

She didn't like running up bills at the local shops but, as her father had pointed out, they were known to the local tradespeople and his credit was good. All the same, at the end of another week, when the butcher asked for something on account Mary waylaid her father as he prepared to leave the house.

'I'm already late,' he told her testily. 'I have an important appointment—very important.' His testiness was suddenly replaced by a broad smile. 'Be sure that I'll give you the money you require this evening, Mary.'

With that she had to be content. There was no need to worry, she told herself. It would be some weeks before her father received Great Aunt Thirza's bequest, but when he did she could settle up the bills.

She frowned, for even without that money there had always been enough—just enough—for her to run the household. It hadn't been easy, but with careful management she had contrived, but now, mysteriously, her father's private income seemed to have dwindled; she had been told to borrow from her mother's purse once more, and she knew for a fact that until the next batch of cards was sent away there would be very little money left in it.

She went along to the kitchen and found Mrs Blackett scowling.

'Met yer pa in the hall,' she said angrily. 'Told me I don't need to come no more—give me the sack, 'e 'as.'

'The sack? Mrs Blackett you must be mistaken...'

'Course I'm not; I got ears, ain't I? What I wants ter know is, why?'

'I've got no idea. Could you forget about it? For I'm

sure he didn't mean a word of it. I'll see him when he gets home this evening and I'm sure everything's all right.'

She glanced at Mrs Blackett's cross face. 'Let's have a cup of tea before you start on the kitchen. I'll get the washing machine going and make the beds.'

Mrs Blackett, mollified, drank her tea—strong with a great deal of sugar—and began on the kitchen, and Mary loaded the washing machine and went upstairs. There was something wrong, something amiss somewhere, and she wished she had someone in whom she could confide.

There wasn't anyone—Polly was too young, Arthur would be bored and impatient, her mother wasn't to be worried, she decided lovingly, and the only person she really wanted to pour out her doubts and troubles to was miles away, gone for good.

Indeed, Professor van Rakesma was miles away, in Holland. He hadn't, however, gone for good.

Her father usually came home around five o'clock when he'd spent the day at the British Museum, had a cup of tea and went straight to his study to work on his notes until supper. So Mary was surprised when he arrived home in the middle of the afternoon. She went into the hall to meet him with the offer of coffee or a late lunch, but the words died on her lips. Mr Pagett, never a robust man, had shrunk inside his clothes; a man in his fifties, he had aged twenty years.

'Father—you're ill.' She took his coat and hat. 'Go and sit down in the study; I'll bring you a cup of tea—better still, if there's any whisky left you'd better have that first. I'll ring Dr Hooper.'

'No, I'm not ill, Mary, but I'll have that whisky. I have had some bad news.'

She went with him to the study, fetched the whisky

and sat down near his chair. 'Do you want to tell me, Father? Or shall I fetch Mother?'

'No, not your mother, not until I can think of what is to be done. She mustn't be upset…'

He told her then, about a man he had met at the British Museum, researching for a book he was writing about ceramics. 'He seemed a very pleasant fellow, who knew several of the people I had known at Cambridge—or so he said, and I didn't think to doubt him. Mentioned my book on the Dead Languages, asked about the book I'm writing now; in fact we became friendly.

'Some weeks ago he told me that he had a brother in the Stock Exchange who occasionally gave him tips. There were some shares coming on the market, he said, at a rock-bottom price; if I had some capital lying idle it would be a very sound investment. It seemed a splendid way in which to use Aunt Thirza's little windfall. I said that I had three thousand pounds to invest and gave him a cheque—yes, I know I haven't received my bequest yet but I withdrew some of my capital; this investment he was to make for me was going to earn twice as much interest.

'He showed me the listed shares in the *Financial Times* and indeed the price was going steadily up. He suggested that I might like to put another thousand or two to the first investment and I withdrew another six thousand.'

Mary said slowly, 'So that's nine thousand pounds…'

Her father said heavily, 'He has gone—this man—together with the money. The shares he showed me had nothing to do with it; he probably guessed that my knowledge of them is negligible.'

'So you have to repay the bank with Aunt Thirza's money?'

'Indeed, yes, and over and above that I shall have to employ a solicitor to take the matter to court.'

'What is the use of that if the man has gone, Father? Probably he's in Australia or South America by now. Did you report it to the police?'

'Yes, yes, of course, and they tell me that there is almost no chance of reclaiming the money.'

'We'll manage,' said Mary in a voice she strove to make cheerful. 'After all we always have, and you've still got the income from your investments.' She gave him a reassuring hug. 'Besides, your book will be finished in another six months or so, won't it?'

'My dear, you do not know the whole. Some of my shares have fallen; we have been living from capital for some months now. I have not yet had the time to go into the matter thoroughly, but my income is sadly depleted. We must cut down on expenses. I'm sure that you can do that; you manage so well.'

Mr Pagett was looking better; whisky and the comfortable knowledge that Mary would cope as she had been doing for years had somewhat restored his peace of mind. He would leave everything to her. He patted her hand and said vaguely, 'We'll say nothing—eh, my dear? And now I have some notes to write up, and I'm sure you have the supper to cook.'

It was too early to start the supper; her mother was still painting and Polly was in the dining-room, doing her homework. Mary sat down at the table and allowed herself the luxury of feeling scared and doubtful.

No way could she be more economical than she was now. They could sell the car, she supposed, but that would mean fares each time anyone had to go somewhere. They could give up Mrs Blackett, but she quailed at the prospect of running the place unaided; it was a large and awkward house, and she lacked the modern appliances to make running it easier.

'I'll get a job,' said Mary aloud. 'Mrs Blackett can stay, and I can get up earlier and go to bed later.' She frowned, 'What kind of job? It'll have to be close by, and part-time if I can earn enough. Mother's help? A shop? Housework?'

Mother's help, she decided, and, having done so, instantly felt better. After all, it need only be for six months or so; once her father's book was published everything would be all right.

Feeling quite cheerful, she went to the fridge—the remains of the lamb joint they had had could be turned into a shepherds pie. The sight of it reminded her that the butcher wanted to be paid—she would have to get a job as soon as possible.

She scanned the local paper the next morning and saw with satisfaction that there were several advertisements for mother's helps, all of them local. She cut them out and decided to phone them all for an appointment.

She put the phone down after her fourth call—fulltime, she had been told, and no dependents. The next call was more promising—part-time, ten in the morning until four o'clock in the afternoon, Sundays free, sixty pounds a week and her midday dinner. Two children, said the voice. Four years old and five, boy and girl, lively and happy. The voice made an appointment for that afternoon and rang off.

Sixty pounds a week, reflected Mary, and it was only a short bus ride—one of the large houses overlooking the Heath. She could pay off the tradespeople, keep Mrs Blackett, and lay out the rest of the money as economically as possible. The reluctant thought that she hadn't much liked the voice she decided to ignore.

Her father was out, her mother absorbedly painting and Polly not yet back from school. Mary, very neat, and hoping that she looked like a mother's help, got on to a bus.

The house was just as she had expected—large, red-brick and solid, with a big garden separating it from the road. She rang the bell.

The door was opened by a small, thin girl in a grubby apron and suffering from a heavy cold. 'Come on in,' she invited, not waiting for Mary to speak. 'The missus is expecting you.'

The girl opened a door in the large hall. 'In here— Mrs Bennett, here's the young lady.'

She padded off down the hall and Mary walked into the room. It was as she had secretly feared—the person matched the voice. She was a handsome young woman, if one didn't mind the small eyes and the down-turned mouth, dressed in the height of fashion and wearing too much jewellery.

She was sitting in a deep chair by the window and said pleasantly enough, 'Come in and sit down. I do hope you'll do; the children are utterly charming, but they're rather out of hand and I'm not much good with them. Have you brought your references with you?'

'No, Mrs Bennett, but I can give you the names and addresses of several people who will vouch for me.'

'You live in Hampstead?'

'On the other side of the Heath.'

'So you can get here by ten o'clock each morning? I go out a good deal—you'll see to the children's dinners, of course. No housework—there's a daily woman as well as Maggie, who opened the door to you. She lives in. I expect you to keep the children amused and clean and tidy—and a walk every day; I'm a great believer in fresh air.'

'They don't go to school?'

'No, Ben's five, but he's highly strung, and Grace is only four. Come up to the nursery and meet them.'

The nursery was up two flights of stairs, behind a baize door, and the two children were throwing toys around the room as they went in.

'They are so high-spirited,' said Mrs Bennett, and dodged the stuffed rabbit that her small son flung at her. 'They get bored and Maggie can't control them.'

Mary eyed them; the boy was big for his age, dark and too plump. He would grow into a handsome man, she decided, but perhaps not a very nice one. She resisted the impulse to stick her own tongue out in response to his and looked at Grace. A small girl, with light brown hair and large blue eyes, she was snivelling and her nose needed wiping. Mary felt a rush of pity for her; she needed a bath and clean clothes and her hair needed washing.

Maggie did her best, no doubt, but Mary suspected that she had more than enough to do in the house. She followed Mrs Bennett downstairs again, and was told that, provided her references were satisfactory, she could start in two days' time—a Monday.

'You'll be paid weekly,' said Mrs Bennett. 'It's an easy job and well paid.'

Mary murmured politely; she didn't think it would be easy and she wasn't sure that it was well paid, for she knew no one with a similar position, but it was the straw that the proverbial drowning man clutched at. Perhaps it wasn't quite what she had hoped for but the thought of being able to look the butcher in the eye and pay him at the end of the week sent her spirits soaring.

She caught the bus home, her eyes sparkling, her pretty face alight with relief, so that the other passengers took a second look at her—to see someone so obviously pleased with life on a London bus was unusual and heart-warming.

Some of her euphoria ebbed away when she reached home. She had already decided to tell her mother that she felt the urge to do more than be at home all day; a little outside interest would be nice, she would say, and her mother would agree placidly. Her father would tell her to do whatever she wanted, his clever head so full of his learned book that he would have quite forgotten that if she hadn't done something about it they would have been in a sorry way.

Not that she blamed either one of them; they were made that way, content with each other and their lives, never allowing unpleasantness to interfere with the placid way of life. The boys were no longer at home, Polly was nicely settled at her school, and Mary saw to everything…

It was Polly who would ask questions and raise objections, and Mrs Blackett, once more installed as the household help, would certainly have her say. Mary rehearsed suitable answers for the pair of them and hoped for the best.

'It's not fair,' blazed Polly when she was told. 'You ought to be out every night, dining and dancing in pretty dresses with someone super like Professor van Rakesma; I bet he'd take you somewhere grand and you'd eat caviare…'

'It's only for a few months, Polly—Father was deceived into putting money into bogus shares; it really wasn't his fault and I don't mind a bit. I always have time to spare during the day; it'll be fun to be paid for using it up.'

'You're fibbing. I think it's beastly for you—you can have my pocket money…'

'Thank you, love; that's very generous of you, but I'll have some pocket money each week, truly I shall.' She began to improvise, to rid her sister's face of its look of doubt. 'If Arthur asks me out I'll be able to go and have my hair done…'

'Arthur,' said Polly with scorn. 'I wouldn't waste my money on a decent hair-do for him!'

Mrs Blackett, when told the following morning, was outspoken. 'It's not for the likes of me to ask why you should go gallivanting round the place with a parcel of children, as though you 'aven't enough to do 'ere. I'll not deny I'm glad ter be coming as usual, but extra time I can't and won't offer; I've got that old Mrs Caldwell two afternoons a week and Mr Trevor on Fridays—it's as much as I can manage.'

'If you'd just come as usual, Mrs Blackett, I'm sure we can cope. It's only part-time.'

'There's part-time and part-time,' said Mrs Blackett, 'and a very elastic thing it can be, as you'll no doubt discover, Miss Mary.'

Mrs Blackett was always gloomy, reflected Mary. It wasn't going to be as bad as she had hinted; in fact, it would be a splendid way of solving the temporary problems which had arisen so swiftly and unexpectedly.

Only later, in bed in the shabby room she had slept in for years, did she allow her thoughts to return to the professor. It was silly to spend time thinking about him but it was difficult not to, since he was indelibly printed on to her brain. She wondered if in time she would be able to forget him, if he would become dim in her memory. Of one thing she was quite certain: Arthur—indeed any man—would never take his place.

Arthur came the next day. Mary had just got back from church and was wrapping an apron around what Polly called her 'Sunday dress', preparatory to cooking the midday dinner, when he parked his car by the front door and walked in.

'Thought we'd go for a drive,' he said, strolling into the kitchen. 'I need to relax; I've had a busy week. Cut some sandwiches, Mary, and we'll be off.'

He hadn't said, 'Hello, Mary,' or asked how she was, or even if she wished to go with him. She didn't, and she bade him a cool good morning.

'I'm cooking the dinner, Arthur; I can't drop everything and come just like that.'

'Polly can cook, for heaven's sake.' He added bossily, 'Come on, old girl.'

'I may be a girl but I'm not yet old,' she said tartly. 'Besides, I don't want to; I haven't the time...'

He laughed. 'Rubbish. You're here all day with nothing much to do.'

She let that pass. 'There are things I have to do today,' she told him evenly. 'I'm starting a job tomorrow.'

'A job? Whatever for?'

'You have just reminded me that I am here all day with nothing much to do—I think a job will be rather interesting.'

Arthur frowned. 'Well, when we're married don't think you're going to be a career woman.'

'Is this a proposal?' asked Mary, and prodded the potatoes, turned down the gas and turned to face him.

He looked awkward. 'Well, no, I'm not ready to marry yet. It's something which needs careful consideration; I need another year or two before I settle down.'

'I might possibly change my mind within the next year or two,' said Mary gently. She emptied a bowl of peas into a pan of boiling water. 'In fact, Arthur, I think I've changed it now, so you won't need to worry about whether you're ready to marry me or not.'

'I say, old girl, you don't mean that? I'd got quite used to the idea of our marrying when it was convenient.'

'I do mean it. You see, Arthur, when I marry it won't be because it's convenient but because I'm so in love that I can't imagine being anything else but married, if you see what I mean.'

'Good Lord, what's come over you, Mary? You're not behaving normally.'

'Yes, I am. Arthur, dear, go away and find another girl—someone young enough not to mind waiting until you're ready to marry her.' She left the stove and went and kissed his cheek. 'Go along to the rectory; Millie's home for the weekend and she's had her eye on you for months.'

Arthur looked pleased. 'Yes! Well, I might just call in. Mind you, I'm deeply hurt, Mary.'

'Yes, Arthur—all the more reason to have a soothing companion to help you get over it. Millie's very soothing.'

He had been gone for ten minutes before Polly came into the kitchen. 'I've been up in the attic looking for a bit of old blanket for Bingo's basket; Aunt Thirza threw the other one away—she said it smelt. I heard a car...'

'Arthur. He wanted me to go out with him...'

'Well, why didn't you? I know he's not a bit exciting—

anyone less sexy…' declared Polly. 'You could have had a super meal somewhere.'

'He wanted me to cut sandwiches.'

'Sandwiches? Is that man mean? Don't marry him, Mary, will you?'

'No, love. He didn't exactly propose, but he wanted to put me on hold until he felt like marrying me, so I refused him and told him to go and find someone else.'

Polly stared at her. 'You don't mind?'

'Not one little bit. Nor, I think, did he. Will you get Mother and Father? Everything is ready.'

Going home again on the bus after her first day at Mrs Bennett's, Mary wondered for a brief moment if she had been wise to reject Arthur's ideas for their future.

She had set out that morning all agog to make a success of her job. She hadn't known what to expect, although she had been cheerfully optimistic—she would get to know the children, enjoy taking care of them, playing with them and reading them stories, and seeing that they ate their meals.

It hadn't been like that at all. The untidy little maid had let her in and told her that she was to go straight to the nursery. 'She's not up yet,' she had observed, and sniffed. 'Took her breakfast up not half an hour ago. The kids 'ad theirs in the nursery.'

The nursery had been a shambles; the children had been left to eat alone, that was obvious; moreover Grace had had an unfortunate accident and wet her knickers, and Ben was spooning the remains of his cornflakes over the floor.

Mary had done the obvious—cleaned Grace, led Ben away to wash his face and hands and then set about restoring order to the room. The house had been so quiet that they might have been alone in it, the three of them. Presumably Mrs Bennett had still been in her room, and the little maid had had enough to do without Mary bothering her for information. She'd found the children's bedroom—the beds unmade, clothes all over the place—sought for sandals, put them on protesting small feet and had led the children downstairs.

'Where are we going?' said Ben and kicked her ankle.

'For a walk.' If ever a child needed his bottom smacked, Ben did. Perhaps if she walked for long enough and far enough they would both tire and be easier to manage.

The Heath was just across the road; she kept to the more frequented paths and presently let them run free and, sure enough, as they tired they became more manageable, so that by the time they reached the road again they were behaving like normal small children.

Mary, waiting to cross between the traffic, was hot and tired and longing for a cup of coffee. Her hair was coming loose from its French pleat and she was sure her nose shone. Professor van Rakesma, driving past, blinked and looked again. What on earth was the girl doing, clutching two children and looking a good deal less serene than usual? It was a pity he had no time to stop and find out. Mary didn't see him, which, seeing that she felt herself not to be looking her best, was a good thing.

Mrs Bennett was up when they got back. 'I expect to be told when you take the children out,' she observed coldly.

'If you had been here to tell I would have done so,' said Mary reasonably. 'The children were in the nursery; they had eaten their breakfast alone, Ben was throwing the cornflakes about and Grace had needed the lavatory and there had been no one to help her... It seemed the best thing to do was to clean them up and take them out on the Heath.'

Mrs Bennett had the grace to look uncomfortable. 'I overslept. They had better have their morning milk. I suppose you want a cup of coffee...? They have their dinner at half-past twelve and then they're supposed to rest for an hour. I suppose you can find something to do—have you made their beds and tidied the room?' She caught Mary's eye. 'Well, no, I suppose you haven't had the time—you could do that later. I'm going out to lunch and do some shopping. I'll be back before four o'clock.'

The rest of the day went quickly enough—too quickly in fact; it seemed that she was to be responsible for the children's clothes and their bedroom, as well as the nursery where they ate their dinner. She helped Maggie carry it upstairs, and although she was hungry there was little opportunity to eat since Ben, unlike his small sister, was determined to do everything he could to be obnoxious.

Mary, who hadn't taken to Mrs Bennett, nevertheless was relieved to see her a few minutes after four o'clock.

At home she set about preparing the supper while Polly, just back from school, made the tea. 'What was it like?' she wanted to know.

'Quite interesting...' Mary was at the sink, peeling the potatoes.

'Were they awful, the children? Did you have them all day?'

'Well, yes. They did rest for an hour after their dinner—I read to them.'

'It's not as nice as you hoped,' observed Polly. She

poured the tea. 'Here, drink this, Mary—tell me about it; Mother and Father needn't know.'

'Well, it wasn't too bad. In fact, if I can tame the little boy and get organised I might quite like it.' She smiled suddenly. 'I shall like it on Saturday when I get paid.'

It would be all right once she had got used to the job, she told herself as she got into bed and lay thinking about the professor until she went to sleep.

He was the first thing she thought of when she woke too, but there was no time to moon around. She got up and crept downstairs and started on the necessary house-work.

It was a lovely morning—the birds were singing, the Heath beyond the garden looked delightful and the early morning traffic was just a distant hum. She made a mug of tea and took it on to the back doorstep. The professor would still be in bed, she reflected; probably he had spent the previous evening at some grand house as a dinner guest or had dined with some charming girl.

Mary gulped down her tea and went back to dusting the sitting-room—an occupation which allowed for free thought. Of course he lived in a splendid flat some-where—and perhaps had a girlfriend. Her imagination took off...

The professor was shaving, making a good job of it with the cut-throat razor held in a steady hand. Despite the fact that he had been up most of the night, called to the bedside of an eminent public figure who had suffered a severe heart attack, he was preparing for another busy day at the hospital.

He was tired—there were lines of weariness etched in his handsome face—but presently he went down to breakfast, to all outward appearances a man who had had a good night's sleep and the leisure to don the superbly cut grey suit and fine silk tie. He looked pleasant and impersonal—a man to be trusted.

He had little time for breakfast, but while he ate it he wondered about Mary. But only briefly—he had a long day ahead of him and there would be no time to indulge in private thoughts. Beyond deciding to find out more about her when he had the time to do so, he dismissed her from his mind.

Tuesday was only slightly better than Monday. True, the children had been given their breakfast in the kitchen with Maggie but she had too much to do to bother with them. Mary took them to the nursery, dealt with their needs, sat them down at the table with picture books and crayons and nipped around tidying the place, making their beds and collecting their clothes for the washing machine. By then Mrs Bennett had come into the nursery.

'You can take them for a walk now, Mary—while they're resting after lunch you can do the ironing. I've guests for lunch; you'll see the children are up here, won't you?'

She kissed the children and went away again, ignoring Grace's whimper of 'Mummy'. Ben hadn't looked up from his crayoning. Mary's charming bosom heaved with indignation; they were by no means little cherubs, but Mrs Bennett was their mother—surely she loved them.

She had no doubt that they would be quite delightful children if they weren't so neglected. It wasn't wilful neglect. They had nice clothes, their food was exactly what it should be, they had more toys than they could play with—but they hadn't got their mother's love, not all of it anyway. They needed cuddling, laps to sit on, a mother to romp with sometimes. Ben was five years old, but despite his aggressive ways she guessed that he was a lonely child.

As if to bear out her thoughts he was more aggressive than ever that morning... All the same, she walked them across the road and on to the Heath, this time with a ball in her pocket. They soon tired of tossing it about and suddenly Ben took to his heels and ran towards the thicket some way off. 'Stay where you are,' said Mary to Grace, and went after him.

She ran well and he was no match for her long legs. She caught him easily enough and marched him back, not saying anything even when he delivered a few kicks on her shins and tried to bite her hand.

Still without a word she took them home, tidied them up for their dinner and sat them down to eat it.

'The lady who looked after us before you came smacked us,' volunteered Grace, shovelling mince into her small mouth.

'She called Mummy "an old cow",' observed Ben, giving Mary a sidelong look, puzzled because she hadn't seemed to mind his running away.

'That was rude and I don't want to hear you say it again, Ben. You're not a baby; you must behave like a boy—you'll be going to school soon with other boys.'

'I don't care...'

'Don't care was made to care, don't care was hung, don't care was put in the pot and cooked till he was done,' said Mary, which sent the children off into peals of delighted laughter.

'Aren't you cross?' asked Ben as she settled them on their beds.

'Not in the least. Close your eyes and go to sleep, my

dear.' She tucked the quilt round Grace's small face and left the door open while she did the ironing in the nursery.

Tea was a peaceful meal and she had left soon afterwards, anxious to get to the shops before she went home. She was tired but the day had been no worse than the previous one, and tomorrow was Wednesday, halfway through the week, and on Saturday she would be paid.

The week wound to its close with its few ups and far too many downs, but she forgot that in the satisfaction of paying the butcher's bill. There was very little money left in the housekeeping purse; she added her wages to it, assured her father that she would manage very well without asking him for her usual allowance—even though she knew that he had no intention of offering it—paid Mrs Blackett, gave Polly her pocket money and sat down to plan the housekeeping for the next week. Provided that no bills came in, she could manage.

Halfway through the next week Mrs Bennett put her head round the nursery door as Mary was clearing up after the children's breakfast. No one, it seemed, thought it necessary to collect the plates and mugs, wipe the children's faces and hands and tidy the room. At first she had resented it but, since Maggie had more than enough to do and Mrs Bennett didn't rise from her bed until ten o'clock, she had accepted it as something that would have to be done whatever she felt about it.

To see Mrs Bennett up and, moreover, dressed in the height of fashion was a surprise; she was quite taken aback when that lady said briskly, 'Get the children decently dressed, Mary; I've an appointment for them with my dentist. You will come with them, of course. You can have twenty minutes while I get the car and see Maggie.'

It needed patience and strength to coax the children

into clean clothes. Grace, being small and female, had no objection to wearing one of her prettier frocks and her red sandals, but forcing Ben into a shirt and shorts and his favourite trainers without actually causing him bodily harm was quite another matter.

All the same, by the time Mrs Bennett called sharply for them to go down to the hall Mary had achieved her purpose. There would be a few bruises on her shins and a few nasty scratches on her arms later on, but that was neither here nor there.

Mrs Bennett drove a Mercedes, and, ordered on to the back seat with the children, Mary wondered once again if her employer had a husband. Was she divorced, or did he work away from home? she wondered. It wasn't her business, of course, but it would be nice to know...

Mrs Bennett drove well and rather too fast, and she didn't speak at all until, some time later, she stopped outside one of the tall red-brick houses in Harley Street, put money into a parking meter and told Mary to get out and bring the children with her.

Naturally the pair of them hung back—Grace in tears because she didn't understand why she was there and Ben kicking and screaming since that was his normal behaviour when faced with a situation he didn't fancy.

Mary had reached the dignified entrance when the door was opened to Mrs Bennett's ring and she swept inside to the elegant vestibule. There were two men standing to one side of it and Mrs Bennett paused and smiled charmingly at them, secure in the knowledge that she was a handsome woman beautifully dressed—although the effect was rather spoiled by her son bawling his head off.

She said over her shoulder, far too sharply, 'For heaven's sake, Mary, control the children. Really, you must manage them better than this.'

She made a pretty little grimace, shrugged and looked at the two men again. The elder of them wasn't worth more than a glance but his companion... She tried to catch his eye but he was looking past her, his face without expression.

Mary, wrestling Ben into the vestibule, had been too occupied to look around her. Mrs Bennett's waspish remark had filled her with rage and her cheeks were flushed; her wish to turn round and go out into the street and leave her employer and her children to fight it out between them was so overpowering that she had to clench her teeth together and remind herself that at the end of the week there would be another sixty pounds.

She took a firmer grip of Ben's hand, soothed the weeping Grace, and looked up to encounter Professor van Rakesma's cool stare.

Chapter 4

Mary's instant delight at the sight of Professor van Rakesma gave way to embarrassment; she was already hot-cheeked; now the slowly ebbing colour crept back, giving him the chance to admire it. She blushed charmingly, and that, combined with eyes blazing with her rage, turned her into an arresting beauty.

What good fortune had sent her here for him to meet again so unexpectedly? he wondered, and gave her a smiling nod. It was the smiling nod he gave to his patients, courteous and impersonal, and Mary, recognising it as just that, gave him a stiff, unsmiling nod in answer as she went past him.

Of course he had gone when, after a trying hour, she got into the car with Ben and Grace, both weeping and scarlet in their faces with childish rage.

Mrs Bennett was disposed to be friendly. 'That's

over for another year,' she observed over her shoulder.
'Why the children have to make such a fuss I don't know.
They'll be home late for their dinners, but that can't be
helped. They've had enough excitement for one day; they
can go straight to rest once they've eaten. They don't need
to go out again. Give them their tea before you go, Mary.'

It didn't enter her head to say please or thank you. 'Did
you notice that man in the vestibule as we went in? Not
the old one, the other one—I wonder who he is? I might
be able to find out; I wouldn't mind meeting him some-
time.' She added defiantly, 'One gets lonely when one's
husband is away for weeks at a time.'

It was a remark that Mary decided it was better not
to answer.

Thankfully the children were too tired to be naughty;
even Ben settled down to take a nap after his dinner, leaving her free to tidy up and finish the ironing, which was
an occupation conducive to thought, she had discovered.
It had been exciting and delightful to see the professor
again, and in such an unlikely place. Perhaps he had been
to the dentist too? With a spurt of tenderness she hoped
that he hadn't had the toothache.

Professor van Rakesma had watched Mary disap-
pear into the dentist's waiting-room, bade his companion a civil goodbye and had taken himself up to the floor
above, where he had his consulting-rooms.

It was only when the last of his patients had left that
he allowed his thoughts to dwell on her.

It was obvious to him that she must give up her job
and find something more congenial. He had no doubt
that beneath her patient handling of the little boy she
was hiding a desire to smack his bottom. Professor van

Rakesma, who liked children, had considered Ben to be a holy terror much in need of parental discipline.

He wondered idly if there was a Mr Bennett and just how long Mary would stay there. There must be a good reason for her having to do so…

His receptionist put her head round the door to tell him that she was off home. 'You're booked solid tomorrow,' she warned him cheerfully, 'and the first patient is that nervous Mrs Payne.'

'Ah, yes…' He bade her goodnight and began to consider the nervous Mrs Payne, and he thought no more about Mary.

Mary received her sixty pounds at the end of the second week, feeling that she had earned every penny of it and more. She had made progress with little Grace, although she cried a great deal and showed no interest in her toys—expensive dolls with wardrobes, a doll's house of magnificent proportions, and any number of picture books.

But what use were they, reflected Mary, when there was no mother around to play with her and a bullying brother who took pleasure in breaking her things? But once or twice Grace had smiled, even laughed, and they had had a splendid time spring-cleaning the doll's house together, despite Ben's efforts to interfere.

Ben, she considered, needed to go to a strict pre-prep school where there would be other children to cut him down to size. He was a tyrant now; what he would be like as he grew older she shuddered to think. All the same, she had to stay; the sixty pounds was a lifeline until things got better at home.

She said nothing to her mother and father about her

job, giving them the impression that it was all rather fun; only Polly guessed that it was far from ideal. Mary, starting her third week, allowed herself the luxury of day-dreaming on the bus. She had done her best to forget Professor van Rakesma but somehow he wouldn't go away; besides, she found it comforting to think about him.

He hadn't given her another thought. His days were full and so were his leisure hours; besides, he was starting on a learned book about cardiac arrest—something which was dear to his heart and taxed his very clever brain—so that everything which had nothing to do with that received scant attention.

Meeting Polly on the following Saturday morning on the Heath reminded him of Mary once more.

Polly was with friends, but she spied him at once, striding along with Richard racing ahead, and she ran to meet him.

'I knew I'd see you again one day,' she told him happily, 'and it's all right about not having come to take me for a drive; Mary said you might not have enough time and I dare say you haven't.'

He stood looking down at her cheerful young face wreathed in smiles. 'Mary is quite right; I have been very busy.' He glanced around him. 'You're alone?'

'No, with friends. I'm not allowed to come here by myself, but they're over there; I can catch them up easily.'

She threw a twig for Richard. 'Mary's got a job, looking after two horrid children on the other side of the Heath. The little boy is simply beastly; he bites her and kicks her and yesterday he cut her with a knife he'd found. Not a bad cut, but it bled on to her only decent skirt. I suppose you couldn't do anything about it?'

'I? I'm sorry your sister has such an unpleasant job but I can hardly interfere. Surely she is capable of changing jobs and getting something more to her liking?'

'Of course she is. But jobs aren't that easy to get and she has to get some money…' She paused. 'I'm not supposed to talk about it,' she mumbled.

He gave her a kind smile. 'You know, people tell me all kinds of things when they come to see me; it relieves their minds, you see, and I forget everything they have said. I think if you want to talk to me about it it will be quite in order. I'll forget it too.'

She stared up at him, nodded and said, 'I think that, inside you, you are a very nice man. It would be nice to tell you, and Mary won't know…

'You see, Father was cheated of almost all his money; Great Aunt Thirza left him some too, and the man took that as well. It wasn't really Father's fault; he's very clever and writing a book and he forgets about things. Mother's clever too, but she doesn't worry about money. So Mary got a job so that we could go on living…'

She added fiercely, 'But I know she hates it although she never says so.' She put a hand on his sleeve. 'You won't tell anyone, will you?'

He said gently, 'No, Polly, you have my word. I'm not going to promise that I'll help her, because I can't see how I can, but if I should hear of anything more suitable I will let you know.'

'How?'

'A letter would be best, but don't be too hopeful. I haven't forgotten our drive either; maybe I'll just turn up and hope that you are at home.'

'Oh, great! You really are rather nice. I don't suppose... No, of course not.' She had gone rather red. 'I'd better go before the others get too far away.' She put out her hand. 'Thank you very much.'

They shook hands and she ran off, and he stood and watched her rejoin her friends in the distance before he resumed his own walk. For a little while he thought about Mary, regretful that there was little that he could do.

In that he was mistaken; two days later, browsing in the bookshop he frequented—a dark, low-ceilinged series of rooms housing literary treasures—he came upon its owner, an elderly man, untidy as to dress, wearing old-fashioned spectacles on his long, thin nose and with a wreath of white hair surrounding a bald patch.

They wished each other good day and the old man said, 'There are some more interesting books I've just received—part of a private library. Unfortunately I haven't had the time to unpack them. My assistant has left suddenly in order to be with his mother, who lives, I believe, somewhere in the south of France. I have advertised in various journals but so far I have had not one applicant. I am not sure how I shall manage.'

Professor van Rakesma said slowly, 'Indeed, how unfortunate. Must your assistant have qualifications of any kind?'

'Qualifications? No, no. A willingness to please the customers and learn something of my trade. Well-spoken, of course, and honest.'

Professor van Rakesma observed, 'I believe that I may be able to help you. A young lady, educated—you may know her father by name—Pagett...'

'Indeed I do; erudite and a great scholar. If she has a

fraction of his learning I would be more than pleased to give her employment.'

'I'll see what I can do,' said the professor, and wondered what he was letting himself in for. Ten to one, if Mary discovered that he was instrumental in finding her a job she would refuse, not wishing to be beholden to anyone, certainly not him.

All the same, later that day, sitting in his drawing-room with Richard's whiskery chin on his shoes, he pondered his chances. It was past midnight when he went to bed, tolerably satisfied with his plans.

Polly, mooning around the garden on the following Saturday afternoon, was enchanted to see Professor van Rakesma making his way up the short drive to the house. She ran to meet him. 'I knew you'd come.' She paused. 'But perhaps you want to see Mary? She's working this afternoon because Mrs Bennett wanted to go out; she won't be back until after tea.'

'I came to see you, Polly. Shall we drive around for a while; there's something I want to discuss with you.'

'A secret?'

'Yes, but a nice one, I think. Do you need to tell someone where you will be?'

'I'll tell Mother but she'll forget—shall we be gone long?'

'No, I want to be gone again before Mary comes home.'

'Two ticks,' said Polly, and raced along to the hut to tell her mother.

Only when she was sitting beside him in the car did she ask. 'Why don't you want to see Mary, Professor van Rakesma?'

He was driving north towards Mill Hill. 'I'll explain…' Which he did, in a few clear, business-like sentences. 'And this is what I would like you to do—I have a cutting of old Mr Bell's advertisement in my pocket. Would you let Mary see it? Say that you saw it and wondered if it would be more fun than the Bennett children. On no account must you mention me…'

'Why not? Are you in love with Mary?'

He answered coolly, 'Not in the least, Polly. But I have seen her twice with those children, and it was obvious on both occasions that they were making her life a misery.'

Polly nodded. 'She won't talk about it; you see, we haven't any money unless she has a job, and Mrs Bennett is starting to make her work longer hours.' She added, 'It's a pity you're not in love with her because then you could have married her and she wouldn't have had to work again.'

He gave her a smiling, sidelong glance. 'Two people have to love each other if they wish to marry—at least, that is the ideal theory. I admire your sister for the way she is tackling your troubles but there is no love lost between us, Polly.'

'Oh, well…that's a pity. You'd have done very nicely; it's not easy for her to find someone that's taller than she is. She's on the big side…'

'Indeed,' he agreed, 'she is!'

They had reached Mill Hill, and he drove on for a short distance until they reached a roadside café where he stopped. 'An ice, perhaps, before we go back?'

Polly polished off the ice, and since he had thoughtfully ordered a plate of cream cakes with the tea-tray she ate most of those as well.

Back in the car, she said, 'I like your car, and thank you for taking me for a drive and for that lovely tea.

Mary makes fairy cakes at the weekend, but they're not the same, are they?'

'They sound delightful. Tell me about your school, Polly. What do you want to do when you are grown up?'

'I'd like to be a vet, but I don't suppose there will be enough money for me to train; I mean, even if I got trained for free there's still clothes and things... I could be a veterinary nurse, though; that's the next best thing.'

They discussed the future at some length until they were back at her home again, and Polly was delighted when Professor van Rakesma got out of the car and held the gate open for her.

'It was lovely,' she told him and leaned up. 'Bend down so I can kiss you.' She patted her pocket, where the advertisement lay hidden. 'I'll do just as you say and I won't breathe a word. Shall I let you know if she gets the job?'

'I know the gentleman who owns the bookshop; I expect he will tell me, but you can let me know if you wish. Send a letter to the hospital—St Justin's.'

He waited until she had gone indoors and then drove away.

Ten minutes later Mary got home. She had stayed for two hours over her usual time because Mrs Bennett had wanted to visit friends for lunch and spend the afternoon with them. She had come back late, without apologising, paid Mary her sixty pounds and had asked her if she would come an hour earlier on Monday morning.

'I must get my hair done, and that means going into town and you know what the traffic's like at that hour of the morning, so be here punctually, will you?'

'It is difficult for me to come any earlier than ten o'clock,' Mary had said.

'Good gracious, girl, surely you can oblige me this

once? This is an easy job and I pay you well. I'll expect you.'

Mrs Bennett had gone to her room. Mary had fetched the overworked Maggie to sit with the children and had taken herself off home, her temper in shreds.

Which, of course, was ideal from Polly's point of view, although she said nothing about the job at the bookseller's until they had had supper and the pair of them were washing up in the kitchen.

'Was Mrs Bennett beastly?' she asked.

'Yes, rather. And I have to go in earlier on Monday because she's having her hair done. I think she must have guessed that I need the money and don't dare leave...'

Polly flung down her towel. 'That reminds me, Mary, I was looking at the magazines and journals in the library when I went to change my books and I saw this in one of them. No one was looking so I cut it out...'

'Where did you get the scissors?'

'I had my sewing-bag with me—you know I do sewing on Saturday mornings.' She fished in her pocket. 'Here, read that.'

Mary dried her hands and, leaning against the sink, studied the short advertisement. 'It sounds nice—Thursday, Friday and Saturday—I wonder how much I'd earn. It's all day away...'

'Well, you're almost all day away now, aren't you? And you'd have four days at home. Oh, Mary, do write—at least find out about it.' She added, 'You like books too...'

'Perhaps I will,' said her sister slowly. 'I wonder whereabouts it is.'

'Write and find out,' said Polly.

So Mary wrote her letter and posted it without much hope of getting a reply, which made it all the more exciting when she had one asking her to call for an interview at her convenience. The bookshop was open all day except for Sundays, and the owner was always there.

'It's miles away, though—in one of those funny little streets behind Oxford Street. I suppose I could get the underground to Oxford Circus.'

'It's only Tuesday,' said Polly, gobbling her breakfast. 'Go straight there from Mrs Bennett's; he won't shut before five o'clock—you'd have heaps of time.'

'Well, yes, I suppose I could.'

'Of course you could. I'll be home before then; I can start the supper if you're not back. Do go, Mary; it might be the chance of a lifetime.'

So Mary went, rather tired—after hours with Grace and Ben—but with her nose nicely powdered, her pretty mouth lipsticked, her hair smoothed into its chignon and her shoes well polished with one of Mrs Bennett's shoe-brushes.

The shop was where she had thought it would be, hidden away in a narrow street, away from the bustle of the shops in Oxford Street. It was an old house, one of a row of old houses, their small shop windows filled with antiques, old pictures and fine silver. There was a stamp collector's paradise too, next door to the bookshop. She opened the door and an old-fashioned bell tinkled somewhere at the back.

There were several people inside and she stood for a moment, wondering which one was the proprietor, until an elderly man touched her arm. 'You will be Miss Pagett?'

'Yes, yes, I am. You are Mr Bell? You don't mind me coming like this without phoning first?'

'Not at all. Come this way, young lady.'

He led her to a tiny cubby-hole at the back of the second room. 'Sit down, my dear, and tell me why you want to work for me.' He added, 'I know of your father—a brilliant man of letters.'

'Yes, he is, isn't he? He's almost finished his book.'

'Which will bring him fame if not fortune! Now, if you will tell me something of yourself—your education and present employer, if you are employed.'

He listened without interrupting. When she had finished he observed, 'I think that you may suit me very well. Shall we agree on a month's trial? Three full days; that is from nine o'clock in the morning until five o'clock each evening, and on Saturdays until six o'clock. Half an hour for lunch—I have an arrangement with a nearby café who will send in coffee and sandwiches. You will not pay for these, of course. Mid-morning coffee and mid-afternoon tea when we can fit it in. I will pay you eighty-five pounds a week if you are agreeable to that?'

Mary did some rapid and not very accurate mental arithmetic. Even with fares she would be better off. 'Thank you; that suits me very well. I do have to give a week's notice… If I do that tomorrow morning I should be able to start here on Thursday week. Will that do?'

'Admirably.'

They parted, well-pleased with each other, and Mary, oblivious to the crowded underground, did hopeful sums in her head. She would have two lots of wages next week, she reflected happily. She smiled at the thought, and the sour-faced woman strap-hanging within inches of her gave her an outraged look. There was no call for smiles going home in a packed underground train after a long day.

Mr Bell waited until he had shut his shop for the day before telephoning Professor van Rakesma. 'A very pleasant young lady,' he observed in his dry old voice. 'She will suit me very well; I am most indebted to you for recommending her.'

'I'm glad you are satisfied. I would regard it as a favour if you would not tell her that it was I who recommended her.' He didn't enlarge on this, and Mr Bell didn't ask for an explanation.

Home again, Mary went straight to the kitchen, where Polly was doing her homework at the table and keeping an eye on the macaroni cheese in the oven. She looked up as Mary went in. 'Well—have you got the job?'

'Yes, starting next week—on Thursday. Oh, Polly, it's twenty-five pounds more and a free lunch. I'd better tell Father and Mother, and I'll have to fix things so that you can all manage the supper if I'm not home...'

'Oh, don't fuss, Mary; if you leave everything ready I'll manage. I can cook.'

'Yes, love, I know, but you have your homework. I'll prepare things and put them in the freezer. After all, I've four days at home to do it.' She hugged Polly. 'Oh, love, it's such a relief.'

'You'll have to give notice.'

'Tomorrow morning. I must write a letter and give it to Mrs Bennett.'

'She'll be mad...'

'I think so too, but she'll have a week to find someone else, and anyway she could look after Ben and Grace herself.'

She went to look at the macaroni cheese. 'Supper's almost ready. Shall I keep it warm while you finish your homework?'

'Let's have it now; I'll fetch Mother from the hut if you will tell Father.'

Over supper Mary told them that she had a better job. 'Someone who knows of you, Father. A Mr Bell; he has an antiquarian bookshop behind Oxford Street.'

'Old Bell! Well, I never did! He has some splendid books; you'll enjoy working there, my dear.'

'A nice quiet job for you, darling,' said her mother. 'And how convenient that will be; you can take the cards up to my agent. Think of the time I shall save, and I hate the journey up to Bloomsbury.'

Mary agreed cheerfully, and wondered when she would find the time to go there—something she could worry about later, she decided. And presently she sat down to compose a letter of resignation.

Mrs Bennett read it the next morning, a look of unbelieving rage on her face. 'Why, you ungrateful girl. After all I've done for you, leaving at a moment's notice—where am I to get another girl in a week, I'd like to know?'

'An agency?' suggested Mary helpfully. 'There must be any number of girls wanting a job.'

'Don't be ridiculous, Mary. Anyone from an agency would want more money...' She shot Mary a quick glance. 'That is, I doubt if there's anyone around here, and they would want money for fares. Anyway, I consider it very deceitful of you.'

'Deceitful? I've given you a week's notice, Mrs Bennett, as soon as I was offered this other job.'

Mrs Bennett sneered. 'A likely tale. Well, work your week out, and don't come here wanting your job back when you don't find this new one to your liking.' She stared at Mary, her good looks marred by ill temper.

'That's the worst of you half-educated girls—can't settle down in a decent job when you've got it. No wonder you haven't got a husband,' she added spitefully.

Mary, with a great effort, held her tongue.

Leaving the house for the last time a week later, Mary heaved a great sigh of relief. Mrs Bennett had made life as unpleasant as possible—going out of the house the moment Mary got there each morning and on her return finding fault with anything and everything. The children were dirty, she said, and too noisy; they hadn't had their proper meals, they had been made to walk too far... Her complaints had been endless. Mary, with a tremendous effort, had still held her tongue.

She had no time to get nervous about her new job since it was to start the next morning. She did some important shopping on the way home and, while the supper cooked, prepared meals for the following day and then went in search of her mother.

She found that lady with her paints. 'There you are, dear—I don't seem to see much of you these days. Do you suppose cherubs and Christmas roses would go nicely together? Red, white and green, I thought—pink cherubs, of course...'

Mary peered over her shoulder. 'They are sweet, Mother; they'll be a huge success. Look, dear, I shall be away all day tomorrow, Friday and Saturday. The new job, you know. I'll put all the food in the freezer and you'll find everything for lunch in the fridge. Polly will be home around five o'clock, and I should be back by six o'clock.'

'Your father says Mr Bell is a scholar of the first order; you'll enjoy yourself, Mary, I'm sure. We'll manage, your father and I.' She smiled up at her daughter. 'We are so used to having you to see to everything—we've been selfish, I think. When I've finished this batch of cards I'll look around for a husband for you—invite some young people to the house. We might even have a party...!'

Mary gave her a hug. 'Sounds fun, but there's time enough to get me married. I'm sure when your agent sees these he'll come up with another order.'

The shop door had a 'Closed' sign on it when she got there the next morning but as she tried the door it opened and she went in. Mr Bell's reedy old voice, bidding her good morning, came from the back of the second room, and she walked through to find him in his little office, unpacking a box of books.

'Sit down, Miss Pagett, and catalogue these as I unpack them. It is too early for customers, and I cannot put them on the shelves until they have been entered.'

He pushed a massive book towards her. 'I have started...'

So she sat down without preamble and did as he bade her, and all the while he talked between reading out the authors and titles. 'Some first editions,' he told her happily. 'Not well-known authors, but I have regular customers who collect early nineteenth-century writers.'

They worked together for half an hour or more, and when a customer came into the shop he left her to finish entering the last few books. After that he took her round the shelves so that she had some idea of how the books were classified. 'Don't worry if you are unable to help a customer; just fetch me, Miss Pagett.'

She nodded her head. 'Mr Bell, would you call me

Mary? No one ever calls me Miss Pagett—well, the butcher does!'

'I shall be glad to do so, Mary—such a pretty, old-fashioned name. Now, go and make the coffee for us both. There's a small pantry through the door there.'

By the end of the day she knew that she was going to like her work. The shop was dusty and rather dark but it had atmosphere, and the people who came to it were unhurried, with time to browse, and would sometimes go away again without buying anything.

She had taken the money and wrapped books for three customers without mishap, putting the money in a drawer behind the small counter. It would have been the easiest thing in the world, she reflected, to lean over and take the money and run, but she reassured herself with the thought that the customers who came to the shop didn't look the type to rob the till.

The next day was going equally well and then, as she minded the shop while Mr Bell had his lunch, Professor van Rakesma walked in.

She was on her knees, rearranging a shelf of books so near to the ground that no one seemed to have noticed them for a long time, judging by the thick layer of dust on them, but when the doorbell tinkled she looked up.

The professor stood in the doorway, his vast person blocking what light there was. He stood without moving for a few moments, watching her as she scrambled to her feet. At length, he said, 'Miss Pagett? Working here?' His surprise was exactly right—careless, amused, not very interested. 'You have difficulty in finding a job to suit you, perhaps?'

Mary stared at him. How was it possible to love a man who was so tiresome? He hadn't even bothered to wish her good day. She said coldly, 'Good afternoon, Professor van Rakesma. Yes, I am working here. Do you wish to see Mr Bell, or have you come to browse?'

'Both. I'll browse until Mr Bell is free. There are some first editions, are there not? Came this week. Any idea what they are?'

She had taken the trouble to look at them all carefully; she might not know much about the authors but she had remembered their names and some of the titles. 'They are early nineteenth-century, from the library of a house in Shropshire.' She recited some of the authors and he raised his brows.

'You've been doing your homework.'

'I work here,' she told him, still cold. 'They are over there—the second shelf on the left. Mr Bell won't be long.'

He nodded and went to the shelves, and she turned her back. The dusty shelf would have to be finished now that she had started on it. Thank heaven there were no customers to show up her ignorance. She glanced at her watch; Mr Bell would soon be finished, leaving her free to take his place in the office and eat her own lunch, and by the time she had finished Professor van Rakesma would be gone.

Mr Bell came presently and saw him at once. 'Ah, one of my most valued customers. Mary, go and have your lunch while I show him my latest find.' He peered round the shop until he saw her on her knees by the obscure shelf. 'There you are. Run along now.'

She felt about twelve years old when he spoke like that. She rose to her not inconsiderable height and went meekly without a word. He was a nice old man, but could he not see that she was a grown woman of Junoesque proportions, unlikely to run along when bidden? She felt a fool, and probably the professor was laughing.

Her half-hour wasn't quite up when Mr Bell poked his head round the door. 'If you could come. I know your half-hour isn't up, but there are several customers.'

No professor, however. He had gone just like that, she thought pettishly; he could have called goodbye, or said something kind about her job, or asked after Polly. I shall stop loving him, she reflected, knowing that that wasn't going to be possible.

She'd had no idea that an antiquarian bookshop could be so busy; she received money, handed over change and parcelled up books for most of the afternoon. She wasn't of much use selling, but at least she allowed Mr Bell the freedom to talk to his customers and show them his treasures. Hopefully in a few weeks she would be of more use to him.

She was managing quite nicely, he had told her, but she knew that if she wanted to keep the job she would have to learn a great deal as quickly as possible. She closed the door on the last customer and went to fetch her jacket.

Mr Bell was pottering about, putting back books taken off the shelves. 'A good day, Mary, and we shall be busy tomorrow—Saturday. A different kind of customer, though. I'll see you in the morning. Goodnight.'

She wished him goodnight too, and he locked the door as she went out. It had been a warm day and the late afternoon was still pleasant, but the streets were crowded with people going home and the traffic was a steady roar.

She took a breath of moderately fresh air and almost choked on it as Professor van Rakesma, appearing apparently from the ground at her feet, said briskly, 'The car's round the corner. I'm going to Hampstead; I'll give you a lift.'

She found her voice. 'Oh, you startled me. That's kind of you, but I can get home easily on the underground.'

'Don't talk nonsense—it's the rush hour. Come along.'

She went with him, telling herself that she was a weak fool and at the same time happy to see him again. For the last time, she reminded herself sternly as he ushered her into the comforting depths of the Rolls's front seat, shut her in and went round the bonnet to get in beside her.

He drove off without fuss and without speaking, and she watched the people hurrying along home and tried to think of something to talk about. Perhaps it would be better to stay silent until they were clear of the worst of the traffic. She was still making up her mind when Professor van Rakesma spoke.

Chapter 5

'I must find the time to take your sister for that drive I promised,' said Professor van Rakesma. 'Will she be at home on Sunday—some time in the morning? Your parents wouldn't object to her coming with me? We might have lunch somewhere.'

Lucky Polly, thought Mary. 'I'm sure they wouldn't mind, and Polly will be over the moon. It's very kind of you; I don't suppose you have a great deal of leisure.'

'Not a great deal, no. How long have you been working for Mr Bell? You left the lady with the two children?'

'This is my second day.' She added defiantly, 'And I like it; I hope I shall be able to stay and get to know a great deal about books. Yes, I left Mrs Bennett; the children were a bit difficult. Perhaps I'm not cut out to look after them.'

'My dear girl, the sternest of matrons would have found those two a handful. Did the dentist subdue them?'

She smiled. 'For the rest of the day, yes. I hope they get a nice, kind mother's help whom they'll like.'

'They sound like orphans...'

'They need someone to love them.'

His gentle grunt was soothing.

When they reached her home he got out to open the door and then the gate to the drive. 'Thank you for the lift. Shall I ask Polly to come out and you can tell her yourself? She'd like that.' She went pink. 'That's awfully rude; I didn't mean it like that. Please come in and see her.'

The problem was solved by Polly, running down the drive. Mary turned thankfully to her. 'Polly, Professor van Rakesma has invited you to go for a drive...' She held out a hand and had it engulfed in his large cool one. 'Thank you again; I'll leave you to arrange things.'

When she had gone into the house Polly said breathlessly, 'Mary doesn't know that I've already been out with you?'

He smiled and shook his head. 'I've given myself a day off on Sunday; I thought we might go a little further afield this time. Do you suppose you could persuade her to come too? I think a day in the country might do her good.'

'Oh, she'd love it.' Her face clouded. 'But I'm not sure that she'd come; she's always there on Sundays, to see to the dinner and get tea for Mother and Father.'

'Well, do your best; perhaps we can persuade her between us.'

Polly swung on the gate. 'Well, will you bring Richard?'

'Most certainly—he likes the country.'

He said goodbye then, and drove away, and Polly went

indoors. She was a wise child; she said nothing about Mary's going with them on Sunday.

Professor van Rakesma drove himself back home, wondering what had possessed him to suggest spending a Sunday with a teenager and her stand-offish sister. He could, he reflected, have spent it in the company of friends, or driven himself to the little cottage in Gloucestershire, to potter in its small and beautiful garden with Richard for company. He shrugged his shoulders, turned the car into Cheyne Walk, and stopped before the handsome Regency house where he had a flat.

His man came into the hall as he went in. He was a young man, with a pleasant but ugly face and a thatch of fair hair. 'Evening, sir. Your mother's been on the phone; she said she'd ring around eight o'clock. Dinner in half an hour?'

The professor was leafing through his post. 'Please, Fred. It's your evening off, isn't it?'

'S'right. Me and Syl are going to see that new film at the cinema.'

'Splendid. Has she named the day yet?'

'Boxing Day—got to wait a bit, haven't I? But you'll be in Holland, sir, and by the time you get back we'll be nicely settled in—looking forward to it, she is. Hope there'll be enough to keep her busy...'

'I've no doubt you'll find something.' He looked up, smiling. 'Something smells good.'

'Beef *en croute*—just about ready. I've put the drinks in the sitting-room. Richard's in the garden.'

Professor van Rakesma opened a door at the back of the square hall and entered his sitting-room, a pleasant place comfortably furnished with deep armchairs, small lamp-tables, placed where they were most needed, and glass-fronted cabinets on either side of the Adam fireplace.

He crossed the room and opened the door leading to a small garden beyond, and Richard came bounding in to sit at his feet while he had a drink and finished reading his letters. The last one he read slowly, and then read again.

It was from someone he had known for a number of years in Holland; Ilsa van Hoeven and her husband had been friends of the family, and when they had divorced she had continued to see the van Rakesmas. She was a charming woman, good-looking and most intelligent, and she made no secret of her warm feelings towards him. He supposed that one day he might marry her. It was time that he settled down and she would be a suitable wife.

The thought crossed his mind that he didn't particularly want a suitable wife, but he dismissed it, finished his drink and crossed the hall to the dining-room, to sit at the oval table with its gleaming silver and elegant china and eat his dinner.

Presently, with Fred gone and the house quiet, he went to his study to work on his book until after midnight. In the morning he would go to the hospital to check on several of his patients and if he wasn't called to an urgent case he would drive down to the coast to dine with friends.

Mr Bell had said that it would be busy on Saturday, but all the same Mary was surprised at the constant flow of customers. They ignored the expensive first editions and rare volumes, asking for books on fishing, sport of all kinds, history and old maps, and there were a few young women looking through turn-of-the-century books on costumes and manners of that period.

Somehow she scrambled through the day, and when the last customer went through the door she said apologetically, 'I'm afraid I wasn't much use, Mr Bell.'

'On the contrary, you were a great help to me; besides, you have the right temperament. This is the one shop where customers refuse to be hurried, and I saw that you realised that.' He handed her an envelope. 'You will suit me well, Mary. I hope that you will stay with me, although I suppose a pretty creature like you will marry and leave me!'

'Well, I have no one in mind at present,' she told him, her fingers crossed because that was a whopping lie if ever there was one. 'I like working here very much, and I'll learn all that I can as quickly as possible.'

'Good, good. I'll see you next Thursday.' He bade her goodnight and locked the door behind her, and she made her way home, tired and rather hungry. Not that that mattered. She had eighty-five pounds in her purse, and money meant security for another week. It wasn't only that which made her feel happy; she had seen Professor van Rakesma the day before.

Perhaps it was the afterglow of that happiness which made her agree almost without hesitation to go with Polly when he called for her on Sunday morning. She had no reason to stay at home, for her mother and father were having lunch with friends and there was nothing to keep her.

Sitting in the car beside him, while Polly shared the back seat with Richard, she wasn't quite sure how she had come to be there. Indeed, she was vague as to which of her two companions had actually invited her to join them, but here she was, prepared to enjoy herself.

It seemed that Professor van Rakesma was prepared to enjoy himself too—answering Polly's excited questions readily, keeping up a relaxed flow of easy talk but never, she noticed, saying a word about himself.

'Where are we going?' asked Polly. She had leaned forward so that her chin was resting on the back of his seat, her safety-belt strained to its limit.

'I thought somewhere by the Thames would be nice. In Oxfordshire.'

'But that's miles away,' said Polly delightedly.

'Not so far, and once we're clear of the suburbs we can use the M4 for a while.' He glanced at Mary. 'Do you know that part of the world?'

'No. Hardly at all. I've been to Oxford—'

'Mary was going to university,' interrupted Polly. 'Only, Mother was ill.'

He asked casually, 'What were you aiming at?'

'English literature and poetry and, if I could manage it, Anglo-Saxon.'

'Well, you are in the right place with Mr Bell.'

'Yes, I'm sure I shall learn a lot with him.'

'What's the use of a lot of stuffy books?' Polly wanted to know. 'You'd be better to get married, Mary.'

'There is always that alternative,' said the professor softly.

She would make some man a good wife, he reflected. Certainly she was an extremely pretty girl, though a bit too stand-offish—perhaps she was shy. He turned his head. 'We turn off here,' he told Polly. 'I do hope you're hungry.'

The Beetle and Wedge was an old ferry inn by the

river. Its garden sloped down to the water and there was a restaurant on the houseboat moored at the end. Professor van Rakesma parked the car, secured Richard on his lead, handed him to Polly and went along to see about a table. He had booked earlier and they were shown on to the houseboat, which was already half filled with people lunching.

Mary thanked heaven that she and Polly had dressed with more care than usual; Polly had even been persuaded to abandon her fashionable heavy boots for sandals. As for Mary, she had eased her feet into a pair of high-heeled sandals that she had bought in the January sales and which pinched, although they were the height of fashion.

They were nipping at her toes now, and she wished she could take them off. But she forgot them soon enough as she studied the menu while they drank their cool drinks—no alcohol, of course, since the professor was driving and Polly was too young, but Mary's tonic water with its slice of lemon and tinkling ice was just what she wanted.

The set lunch cost thirty pounds, she noted with concern; she couldn't allow him to pay more than a hundred pounds for the three of them. After all, he was only taking Polly for a drive because she had asked him to.

Perhaps he would have preferred to spend his Sunday with friends, or *a* friend, she thought darkly, frowning at the thought so that he said casually, 'I don't think we'll have the set lunch—may I order for you both? The Dover sole is excellent, and how about garlic mushrooms first and a salad?'

That's better, thought Mary, and turned the page. Dover sole under à la carte was almost as much as the whole of the set lunch. Perhaps if she just asked for a

salad... She had no chance; he was ordering, asking Polly
if she liked French fries or potato croquettes, and the
salad when it came was made up of every rare salad vegetable she could think of.

The mushrooms were delicious, and since she had
plenty of common sense she ate them with pleasure and
a good appetite. She enjoyed the sole too, with an un-
selfconscious satisfaction which Professor van Rakesma
found charming and a little touching. He hadn't much to
say to her, though he joined in Polly's cheerful chatter,
pretending not to see that she was slipping some titbit
under the table from time to time to a silently waiting
Richard.

Mary, eating ice-cream too delicious to describe in
normal language, said, 'This is a very beautiful place
and the river looks charming. It must be very popular.'

'It is; it's open all the year too, except for Christmas
Day. I've been here in winter on a frosty day; it's worth
a visit then.'

'Did you come with a young lady?' asked the irre-
pressible Polly.

He took no notice of Mary's quick, 'Hush, Polly, you
mustn't—'

'Indeed I did. She had never been here and she found
it very beautiful.'

'Was she beautiful too?' Polly took no notice of Mary's
quick breath.

He didn't seem to mind her questions. 'Yes. She
doesn't know England very well, so it was a surprise,
you see.'

Ah, here she was, thought Mary. The love of his life,
and Dutch with it. She wished suddenly that she hadn't
come, that she would never see him again, would forget

him, meet a man—any man—she thought wildly, who would want to marry her and thus put an end to all this nonsense of loving him.

She concentrated on eating the ice-cream, and when he asked her if she would like coffee replied in a composed voice that she would.

They sat for a while when they had finished their meal, watching the boats on the river, until Mary, on edge that he might want to get back to his home, said that perhaps they should get back. 'Mother and Father will be home by the time we get there,' she added lamely.

It was mortifying to see how readily he agreed, and this time, when Polly asked if she could sit in front, she was only too glad to share the back seat with Richard who, tired out after a short scamper, put his whiskery little head in her lap and went to sleep.

When they reached the house she invited him in in a voice which, while polite, dared him to accept. Professor van Rakesma, being the man he was, accepted. Being shaken off by the ladies of his acquaintance was something he had never experienced before, and it intrigued him.

He sat in the shabby drawing-room, drinking the tea Mary had made and showing no signs of wishing to leave. Filling the kettle for yet more water for the tea, Mary thumped it on to the stove and Bingo, cleaning his whiskers after his supper, gave her an enquiring glance. 'Yes, well, all right,' she said. 'Only I wish he'd go so I never have to see him again.'

She bore the teapot back and Polly handed round second cups and the last of the Maderia cake which Mary had made early that morning. He had two slices. Anyone would think that he hadn't had a good lunch, she reflected; now she would have to make another cake, since everyone else was eating it too.

It was a great pity that he and her father had found something in common—John Donne's poems. The subject lasted them for the best part of an hour until, at length, he said, 'You must forgive me for outstaying my welcome; it is a pleasure to meet someone with the same enthusiasms as oneself.'

Mr Pagett said, 'You must come again; I have one or two rather special books you might like to examine. As for John Donne, we have another enthusiast here— Mary...'

Professor van Rakesma turned to look at her. 'Then we must certainly renew our acquaintance and share our opinions,' he said blandly, and watched her go pink. She muttered something about not having time and he said, still bland, 'Ah, but one can always find the time for something one wishes to do.'

'Well, I can't,' said Mary, goaded into rudeness so that the pink got deeper.

The professor studied her for a moment, and wondered if she knew how lovely she was when she was annoyed. He thought not. Presently he got up to go, making his farewells with easy good manners, bending his height so that Polly could kiss his cheek and giving Mary a smiling nod and a friendly, 'A delightful day, Mary; I do hope you enjoyed it as much as I did.'

Watching him drive away, she thought that that was the sort of remark which he could have made equally well to an aunt or some acquaintance whom he wasn't likely to see again. Well, he wasn't going to see her again, was he? Not if she could help it.

* * *

Professor van Rakesma, driving himself home, considered his day and, since there was no human companion to listen to his musings, addressed Richard, sitting beside him. 'Quite pleasant,' he observed. 'In fact I rather enjoyed myself. Polly is a delightful child; it is a pity that Mary is so poker-backed.

'I wonder why she is so cautious with me. Do I inspire you with fright, Richard? Do I behave like an ogre? It is possible that she just doesn't like me. If I were an unscrupulous man I might be tempted to do something about that…! When we first met I found her attractive; indeed, I went out of my way to get to know her, didn't I? I wonder why. The instinct to meet a pretty girl again? Possibly.

'I must be warned that she does not share my interest.' He frowned. 'Not that I have any intention of becoming interested.'

To all of which Richard merely rolled his eyes at his master and then went to sleep.

It was after the professor had eaten the dinner that Fred had set before him that he picked up the phone by his chair and dialled a number in Holland.

'Ilsa? Thank you for your letter. I should have answered your other letters, but letter-writing is rather a luxury. I missed you last time I was home—Pleane is coming to stay with me shortly; I wondered if you would care to come with her. You would be company for each other during the day. She wants to do some shopping and you might be able to keep her from being too extravagant.'

'Roel, what a lovely idea! I'd love to come. Could you give me some dates? Perhaps Pleane has it all arranged.

I'll go round and see her tomorrow to see if she likes the idea. You're sure I won't be a nuisance?'

He frowned. He had forgotten how sugary-sweet Ilsa's voice was—or perhaps he was comparing it, against his better judgement, with Mary's sensible, unaffected voice. He said quickly, 'Of course not, Ilsa; it will be nice to see you again.' They talked for a few minutes before he rang off with the plea of urgent reports to write.

Not that he did them. He sat in his chair, thinking. It had been a good idea to invite Ilsa. His youngest sister, still in her early twenties, was a darling girl but impulsive; with Ilsa's company she might be induced to get less carried away by whatever caught her fancy at that moment.

As for Ilsa, he had been aware for some time now that he had only to ask her to marry him to be accepted at once. She had made her feelings almost embarrassingly plain on several occasions. And she was, after all, just the wife he needed—socially acceptable and beautifully dressed, charming, anxious to please. He would see how things turned out when she came. They were old friends, after all; they liked each other, and perhaps liking might deepen into love or at least affection.

He went upstairs to his bed and dreamed of Mary.

'The girl's getting tiresome,' he told Richard as the pair of them went for their early morning walk. He turned his thoughts to planning some kind of entertainment for his two guests when they came, and presently went off to his consulting-rooms.

Fred, watching him go from his semi-basement kitchen, wondered out loud what was up. 'Having a lady-friend, is he?' he asked Richard. 'An old friend, he says. Thinking of taking a wife, is he? She'd better be an angel—nothing less is good enough for him. Got his head in his books half the time and she'll catch him unawares.' Fred shook his head. 'I don't like it for an idea, that I don't.'

Ilsa van Hoeven had put the phone down and gone to study her face in the enormous mirror on her bedroom wall. Her reflection smiled back at her and she nodded approvingly, studying her flawless make-up and elegant hairstyle. She didn't look her age, thanks to the time and money she spent on keeping it at bay. She was still strikingly good-looking, as slim as a wand and always faultlessly turned out.

And she had made up her mind to marry Roel van Rakesma. Her first husband had been a mistake; he had bored her, besides which there had never been enough money. Roel was wealthy, highly thought of in his profession, and had good looks; besides, considering the way he indulged his youngest sister, she would have no trouble in having everything she wanted.

She would go and see Pleane and suggest that she went with her to England for a short visit. She wasn't overfond of the girl, but once she was in Roel's house...

They travelled a week later, and the professor drove to Heathrow to meet their plane. He watched them crossing the reception area, unaware of him, and smiled a little at the sight of Pleane. He was fond of his three sisters but Pleane was his favourite—the youngest, and spoilt, but with a sunny nature and given to doing things on the spur of the moment. It was a pity that he was so busy at the hospital, but Ilsa would keep her company.

He went to meet them then, and Pleane flew into his

arms. 'Roel, isn't this fun? There's such a lot I want to do and I must have some new clothes.'

He laughed down at her and turned to Ilsa. 'Nice to see you again, Ilsa.' He sounded friendly but that was all, and although he bent to kiss her too it was merely the social peck—first on one cheek and then the other and then back to the first. It meant nothing and she had to check her irritation; he wasn't a man to demonstrate his feelings in public, and there were ten days ahead of her.

She smiled charmingly at him. 'Nice to see you too, Roel; it seems a long time.'

She hadn't changed, he decided as they went out to the car. She was a woman whom men turned to look at—a woman most men would be delighted to be seen with—so why did he feel no quickening of his pulses? What had he expected? he wondered, and had to admit to himself that he didn't know.

Back at his house, they lunched together before he went back to the hospital. 'I'll be free this evening; if you're not too tired I've tickets for the theatre.'

He forgot all about them once he was sitting in his consulting-room in Outpatients. There were more patients than ever but he worked unhurriedly, giving his attention to each as though he or she were the only one who had come to see him. It was long after five o'clock by the time the last one had gone, and Sister and her nurses began to collect up the papers and forms while he sat on at his desk, making careful notes, phoning and arranging for admissions.

He finished at last and drove himself home; there would be time for him to change, have dinner and get to the theatre.

They were waiting for him, sitting in the drawing-room, and Pleane at least was bubbling over with excitement.

'We thought you'd never get here. I took Richard for a walk to save time.'

'Good girl. Give me fifteen minutes; tell Fred, will you?'

He was as good as his word, joining them in less than that time, immaculate in black tie, looking as though he had had nothing to do all day.

Dinner was enjoyable; Pleane was amusing and happy, and Ilsa took care to be the kind of woman he would like best—serene and pleasant and not drawing attention to herself. A pity, she reflected, that she wasn't young enough to assume an aura of shyness.

They were actually on the point of leaving when Professor van Rakesma was halted by his phone. He took it from his pocket with a glance at his companions and stood listening silently. Presently he said, 'I'll be over in twenty minutes,' and then gave some instructions before he tucked it away again.

'I'll have to go,' he told them. 'But don't worry, I'll get Jim Crosby to go with you. I'll have to take the car but I'll tell him to get a taxi and come here for you. He is my junior registrar and you'll like him.'

He was busy with the phone again as he spoke and then he said, 'He'll be here in ten minutes—he's got rooms five minutes from here.' He looked at them both. 'I'm so sorry.'

'It doesn't matter,' said Pleane at once. 'At least, I'd have liked you to be with us but I'm sure we'll enjoy ourselves.'

'Someone important I expect,' said Ilsa. 'He must be, to call you out at this time of the evening.'

The professor glanced at her. 'An elderly down-and-out found in the park,' he told her evenly. 'And yes, he's important to me as a patient.'

She made a pretty little face. 'Oh, Roel, you're far too important to go out at all hours just for a tramp.' She smiled at him. 'Now, if it had been a member of the royal family... Surely you have registrars and house doctors to see to the hospital patients?'

'Yes, indeed we do. Forgive me if I go. Jim will be here in a few minutes.'

Driving to the hospital, he found himself wondering if Ilsa would be impatient of the interruptions that were bound to occur when they were married. He found that he was thinking of Mary and brushed the thought angrily aside. The girl was becoming a nuisance, popping in and out of his head when he had other and much more important things to think about...

He got home very late and found Fred waiting with hot coffee and sandwiches.

'Can't sleep on an empty stomach,' he said. 'Had a success I hope, sir.'

'I hope so, Fred. Touch and go—he's undernourished and worn out and out of work...'

'Too many of them. He could do with a nice quiet job in the country, I dare say.'

Professor van Rakesma smiled. 'Fred, are you telling me that it would be a good idea if I had a caretaker at the cottage?'

'Well, now you mention it, sir, yes.'

'I'll bear it in mind.' He got up. 'I must be at the hospital by nine o'clock. Breakfast at eight o'clock? I don't know if the ladies will be down.'

'They said they would, but I can take a tray up easy enough.'

* * *

Mary found plenty to do now that she was at home again—meals to arrange and cook, washing and ironing, shopping. She enjoyed that now that she could pay for everything, although she had to be very careful how she spent it.

She had seen her father frowning over his post at breakfast. The gas bill, she surmised; the electricity bill would be due soon too, and a few more tiles had fallen off the roof. Luckily they were at the back of the house, where they didn't show easily, but if it rained then one corner of the kitchen would be damp... One thing at a time, she told herself, and sat down at the kitchen table to plan the meals for the days when she wouldn't be there.

Mrs Blackett, coming into the kitchen looking crosser than ever, banged her broom down and flung a duster after it. 'That bathroom tap's leaking something awful; if you don't get a plumber to deal with it soon it'll cost I don't know what.'

Mary said soothingly, 'Yes, I know Mrs Blackett.' The dear soul throve on bad news. 'I'll see about it when I go to the shops presently. Shall we have a cup of tea before you start in here? I'll take one to Mother.'

'Nice to have you at home, darling,' said Mrs Pagett. 'Have you met any nice men at the bookshop?'

'No, Mother; they are mostly elderly and learned, if you see what I mean. Will Father be home for lunch; he didn't say...?'

'It depends, Mary; he was going to see his publishers about something or other. If it's cold it doesn't matter, does it? What are we eating for supper, dear?'

Mary went back presently and drank her cooling tea while Mrs Blackett grumbled her way through a second

cup and half a packet of digestive biscuits. She listened
with half an ear to her companion's diatribe concerning
the Government and did her anxious sums.

It would work very well, she decided, on her way to
work again on Thursday morning; it was a scramble, and
there would never be quite enough money, but they would
manage until her father's book was finished. Even then
they would have to wait for it to be published—months,
perhaps—but if she could keep the job everything would
come right later on.

She began her day's work under Mr Bell's friendly eye,
looking, outwardly at least, perfectly content with her
life. She thought of Professor van Rakesma constantly, of
course, but since she couldn't help doing that she did her
best to think of him as a passing acquaintance. It didn't
always work but she did her best.

Not far away as the crow flew, Pleane and Ilsa were
spending their days shopping. Neither of them lacked
money and they spent it freely, and when they tired of that
they visited art galleries and strolled around St James's
Park while they decided what to do next.

They had enjoyed the theatre, and Pleane at least had
found Jim Crosby very much to her liking. They were
going out to dinner that evening, not just the three of
them, but with several of Roel's friends at the River Room
at the Savoy, and they would dance afterwards.

Ilsa, listening to Pleane's chatter, wondered if she
would be able to get Roel alone. So far she had seen
very little of him—at breakfast, and that was tiresome,
for at home she always breakfasted in bed, and anyway
Pleane chattered unceasingly, and in the evenings—but
never alone.

She had her chance that evening. The dinner had been most successful; now everyone was dancing, and as they left the table she said, 'Come on, Roel, the exercise will do you good.'

He hadn't wanted to dance; he had had a long day and he would have been content to sit quietly, but good manners prevailed; besides, she was looking particularly handsome in the soft lights, and her dress was exquisite. She gave him a sympathetic little smile. 'You're tired; how selfish I am. Let's sit here and talk.'

She could be very charming when she wanted, and she was charming now. She had him to herself for some time while the others danced. She went to bed that night well satisfied.

There were still five or six days of their stay left, and she began to plan how she could get him to drive her down to his cottage without Pleane. If she hinted to young Jim Crosby that Pleane would like to see more of the London sights... She went to sleep with a satisfied smile on her face.

She wouldn't have smiled if she had known that Roel was thinking of Mary. Not willingly, though, but somehow it seemed impossible for him to drag his thoughts away from her.

Ilsa was secretly furious when he, in the nicest possible way, told her that it was impossible for him to take her to the cottage. 'I have a consultation on Saturday morning which may well last for some time and possibly take up a good part of the afternoon. Unavoidable, I'm afraid.'

'Well, what about Sunday?' she persisted, pouting prettily. 'I've seen almost nothing of you, Roel, and I'm sure we have a great deal to talk about.'

That was a stupid mistake on her part; Professor van

Rakesma, experienced in avoiding various ladies wishing to marry him, said suavely, 'You forget that I promised to take you both to Westminster Abbey on Sunday morning.' He added kindly, for he had known her for a long time, 'We must keep a trip to the cottage for a future date.'

Ilsa, usually so coolly calculating, lost her head. 'We're not going back to Holland till Wednesday. Surely you could spare half a day?'

She contrived to look so wistful that he said with secret reluctance, 'I'll see what I can do; I'm afraid I've been a very poor host.'

She was quick to deny that. 'No, no—we've had a lovely time and I have enjoyed being here in your home. Fred is splendid, isn't he? Although I think you need a woman here as well.' She trilled with laughter. 'It's a real bachelor establishment, isn't it?'

Her hopes were raised quite erroneously when he said, 'At present, yes.' This time she was wise enough to say nothing more.

It was on Saturday morning that Pleane decided that she wanted to explore. 'We've got all the morning,' she observed. 'I don't want to go to the shops, just poke around. I'll tell Fred that we don't want lunch—we can have it out somewhere. Roel won't be back until the early afternoon. Let's go.'

Ilsa had no wish to explore—she was wearing a new outfit not suitable for showery weather—but it was important for Pleane to like her.

'We could take a taxi,' she suggested.

'I'm sick of taxis; I'd like to walk. You'd better wear some sensible shoes.'

Ilsa had no idea where they were going, but Pleane

had. There were people living in cardboard boxes down by the river and she intended to see them for herself. She was impetuous and very extravagant, but she was kind too, always willing to help where help was needed. She had money in her purse and she was bent on giving it away.

It was obvious within a short time that Ilsa wouldn't get far in her high heels; besides, she was sulking. 'We'll take a bus,' said Pleane, oblivious of her companion's ill humour, and boarded one going to Waterloo, standing squashed and happy until they reached the station.

'Down here,' she said breathlessly, and led the way down a dingy side-street.

'Where are you going? You must be mad…'

'I want to see those people I read about who live on the streets—in cardboard boxes, Ilsa, just imagine…'

Ilsa stopped. 'Then if you want to behave like an idiot, go ahead; I'm not coming. I shall go home and have lunch like a decent human being.' She walked away without looking back and Pleane let her go.

Chapter 6

The clocks were striking five as Professor van Rakesma let himself into the flat. He had been on the point of leaving the hospital earlier in the afternoon but there had been a cardiac arrest in the accident room and he had stayed to do what he could for the man. He wasn't tired, but he was concerned that the man had died despite all his efforts.

Now, as he went in to the hall, he shook himself free from the afternoon's happening; he would take his guests out later on—to dine, perhaps, or to a show if he could get tickets. He was crossing the hall to his study with his bag when Fred joined him. 'You're late, sir; I thought you might have Miss Pleane with you.'

'Pleane? No, she isn't with me, Fred. What has happened?'

'Best talk to Mrs van Hoeven, sir. She's in the drawing-room. I'll bring your tea.'

Ilsa was sitting in one of the comfortable chairs, leafing through a magazine. She had heard Roel come in but she gave a realistic start of surprise as he entered. 'Roel, how late you are. Really, you work too hard; you need someone to make you slow down...'

He had crossed the room to stand by her chair while Richard frisked at his feet. 'Ilsa, where is Pleane? How long has she been away?'

'Oh, so silly, Roel; she wanted to explore so we took a bus to some awful station and started to walk. I said I didn't think it was very interesting, and she said something about going to see the people who live in cardboard boxes by the river. She absolutely refused to come back with me.' She shrugged prettily. 'I didn't know what to do—I mean, what is there to do for such people? And they are bound to be dirty and diseased.'

'So you came back here?' His voice was quiet.

'Yes. I quite thought she'd come to her senses and be back by now.' She gave him a sweet smile. 'I'm sure it's horrid, wherever it is she's gone to—it began to rain and I had on the wrong shoes...'

'What was the name of the station?'

'Oh, Waterloo. It's not a nice part of London, is it?'

'No, and yet you left Pleane alone there. You'll forgive me if I go out again.'

'To find her? But you never will—you'll get lost in all those horrid streets. I'm sure she'll come back when she's seen all she wants to.'

Professor van Rakesma went to the door. 'Fred will give you dinner if we're not back.'

Fred was hovering in the hall. 'Going to find her? You won't want Richard with you, then. I'll have him with me in the kitchen. I'll serve dinner at the usual time, shall I, sir? And do be careful.'

'I will, Fred.'

The car was still outside; he got in and drove through the city until he came to Mr Bell's shop. He went inside and found it half-full of customers, with Mr Bell perched on some short steps, handing books down to Mary.

He wasted no time on polite greetings. 'May I borrow Mary? My sister, Pleane, has taken herself off to some of the shadier streets by the river—she's been gone for some hours—and I must find her. It would be easier if I had someone with me.'

At Mr Bell's nod he looked at Mary. 'You'll come? I need someone sensible and not given to panic.'

It wasn't much of a compliment but she said quietly, 'Yes, of course I'll come, if Mr Bell won't mind.'

'We shall be closing soon, my dear. Run along. Pleane must be found before the evening. Let me know when you find her.'

In the car Professor van Rakesma handed her the phone. 'Perhaps you had better let your family know that you will be late home.'

It was Polly who answered, and he listened with a flash of amusement when Mary said, 'Yes, of course I'm safe; I'm with Professor van Rakesma.' She put the phone back and waited for him to explain.

'Pleane is impulsive—she's a darling girl, wildly extravagant, but she would take the clothes off her back if someone needed them. She has been reading about the homeless who live under the railway arches and along the river—in fact we have talked about it a good deal, but I never realised that she intended to go and see for herself.'

'Is there anyone with her?'

'No. An old friend, Mevrouw van Hoeven, is staying with us, but she returned when they got to Waterloo.' Something in his voice stopped her from asking any more questions.

If the old friend was the woman he intended to marry then of course he wouldn't want her to get involved in what might be, at best, a distressing experience. She said bracingly, 'I've not been in that district, but I should think it would be easy to find her—I mean…' She paused awkwardly. 'Well, she isn't one of them.'

'You're right. She isn't timid, thank heaven. In fact, she's far too friendly—and not always with the right kind of people.'

'She sounds like our Polly. I shan't tell you not to worry, because I expect you're scared stiff, but she hasn't been gone long and we're nearly there. Where will you park the car?'

'Practical Mary. Outside the station—maybe I can find someone to keep an eye on it…' He put his 'Doctor on duty' sign on the windscreen and got out. '*You're* wearing sensible shoes…'

He went away to talk to a traffic warden on the other side of the road, and she was left to wonder at his remark. The emphasis had been on the 'you're'. She felt a faint prick of resentment at the way he had taken it for granted that they would be sensible.

She was glad of them presently, though. They had walked through narrow, damp streets, with blank-faced warehouses on either side and trains thundering over the bridges above them, and she had had a job to keep up with his long strides, but she managed, sensing that he was too anxious to think of her.

Presently they turned into a labyrinth of dreary streets

under more railway arches. Here they found the people
who made these places their homes. They were sitting
around—some were lying asleep, one or two were eating food from paper bags. The newcomers were watched
apathetically until an old woman, surrounded by plastic
bags, called out, 'Hi, Doc. You're early and it ain't yer
night. There ain't no one ill, either.'

He walked over to her. 'Anne, I am glad to see you
on your feet again. I'm looking for my young sister; she
came this way earlier today.'

'I see'd 'er. Pretty young miss too. Gorn further down,
she 'as. Gave me a few bob too.' She waved an arm in its
dirty old coat. 'Yer'll find her.'

He thanked her and walked on, with a silent Mary beside him. So he came here, did he? She knew that teams
of doctors and nurses and helpers came each night to do
what they could, and her loving heart was filled with
pride for him. She didn't speak—this was no time to
talk; besides, he was stopping every few yards, asking
for his sister.

They had gone quite a long way, passing one or two
quarrelsome groups of young men and boys, when Mary
said quietly, 'There she is—sitting with those four girls
and the boys...'

She couldn't be mistaken; Pleane stuck out like a sore
thumb, surrounded by those less fortunate than herself.
She had no jacket—it was wrapped around a thin girl
sitting beside her—and she was emptying her handbag
on to her lap and handing out its contents.

Mary felt Professor van Rakesma's hand grip her arm.
'Yes.' He sounded grim, but as they reached the little
group he spoke in a matter-of-fact voice.

'Pleane, I knew we'd find you here.' He sat down beside her and Mary sat on her other side. He glanced round him, smiling. 'Why, it's Elsie, isn't it? How's that sore throat?'

'Doc—didn't recognise you in yer posh clothes.' Elsie looked around at the staring faces. 'Hey, this is Doc; he's all right. Comes 'ere with food and stuff and doesn't preach. Who's the lady, then?'

'This is Mary, a friend of mine.'

There was a general laugh. 'Need a bit of company, did you, Doc?'

They stared at Mary then, and so did Pleane. 'Roel didn't tell me…' she began, and decided not to go on. 'It's been lovely meeting you all,' she said in her fluent, accented English. 'I didn't know Roel came here, but I'm glad I came. If I lived here I'd come with him.' She handed her empty handbag to the nearest girl. 'You have it. I wish I'd brought more money with me; I'd given it all away by the time I got here.'

The professor produced a handful of coins. 'Get some chips or hot drinks. I'll see you next week. Anyone got a job yet?'

There was a chorus of noes.

'Well, don't lose hope—and keep out of mischief!'

Pleane was shaking hands with everyone, and the girl she had given the handbag to kissed her. Amid a chorus of goodbyes they started on their way back, Pleane walking between them. 'You're not angry, Roel? Only, I just had to see for myself—and I was quite safe, you see, and I'm so glad that you come here.' She looked sideways at Mary. 'It was kind of you to come with Roel,' she said shyly.

'Well, I didn't know I was coming,' Mary explained.

'But Professor van Rakesma asked me if I would—it's easier to find someone if there are two of you.'

Pleane gave her a startled look. 'Oh, I thought you were friends...'

'We know each other,' said Mary primly, and didn't see his grin.

'I asked Mary to come with me because she is the only sensible female I know, guaranteed not to lose her head. Sometimes things can be a little tricky down here.'

Indignation swelled Mary's splendid bosom. So that was all she was good for, was it? She had a mind to throw a fit of hysterics there and then, only she wasn't sure how to set about it.

They walked back in silence and got into the car. Professor van Rakesma had taken a quick look at his sister as they reached it and had said mildly, 'Get in the back with Mary, *liefje*.' He looked at his watch. 'I'll take you home first, Mary—Mr Bell will be closed.'

'Thank you. Shouldn't I ring him, though?'

'I'll do that presently.'

The evening traffic was quiet and he drove almost unhindered to Hampstead; Pleane, who had been chattering almost without stopping to draw breath, became silent. As he stopped at Mary's front door she said urgently, 'I'm going to be sick.'

Mary and Professor van Rakesma got out of the car fast and hauled the unfortunate Pleane on to the grass verge—only just in time. 'I feel awful,' said Pleane and fainted.

'Bring her indoors,' said Mary, and ran up the path to fling the door wide. 'Upstairs, the first door on the left.' She went up after him and tossed the quilt aside so that he could lay his sister down. 'You'd better go and lock your car,' she said matter-of-factly. 'I'll get Pleane comfortable.'

Pleane's pretty face was a nasty greenish-white. She opened her eyes as Mary took off her shoes and undid her thin top. 'I feel so awful,' she said, and was sick again just as Professor van Rakesma returned.

Despite his concern for his sister he couldn't help but admire Mary's calm as she bent over Pleane, holding her head and mopping her up in a matter-of-fact way, murmuring soothingly as she did it.

'Did you have anything to eat, Pleane?'

She nodded. 'One of the girls gave me a sandwich. I think it was fish or chicken; it tasted a bit like tin but I was hungry.'

They were speaking in Dutch and he turned to Mary. 'Something she's eaten. The more she vomits the better.' He had brought his bag with him. 'She will be needing fluids...'

'I'll find a nightie for her and get her into bed. I expect you want to look her over. Is there anything you need?'

'No. If I can get her a little better I can drive her home.'

'Nonsense,' said Mary roundly. 'Whatever next? And you a doctor. She can stay here tonight, and if she's better in the morning you can fetch her then. I'll look after her. If I'm worried I shall phone you.'

She turned her head as Polly poked her head round the door. 'What's up? Anything I can do?'

'Yes, love, fetch one of your nighties; Professor van Rakesma's sister isn't feeling very well and is staying here for the night.' She proffered the bowl just at the right moment. 'And please bring a bowl of water and a towel and sponge, will you, and a jug of water?'

'OK.' Polly's head disappeared.

'Your parents will have no objection?' The professor was bending over Pleane, peering down her throat.

'No. They would be upset if you were to take her home while she's feeling so wretched.'

'You're very kind.' He spoke absently. His gentle hands were prodding Pleane's stomach, and he was asking her questions in a quiet voice.

Mary, standing there with a bowl at the ready, reflected that the Dutch language sounded like nonsense. All the same, she wished she could understand what he was saying.

He was saying to his sister that she would be quite safe with Mary—a most sensible girl, not given to panicking. He added, 'I wouldn't leave you here if I wasn't quite sure that I can depend on her.'

Polly came back presently. 'Mother's still in the shed,' she informed Mary, 'and Father's in his study.'

'Good. Be an angel and make some coffee, please, and I expect Professor van Rakesma would like to wash his hands while I get Pleane undressed.'

He went meekly, hiding amusement at Mary's practical manner. Ushered to the bathroom and offered a towel by Polly, he observed, 'Your sister would make a splendid ward sister.'

'Bossy, you mean?' Polly hadn't taken offence. 'You see, she has to look after us and run our house and make a living; she is used to getting things done, otherwise they wouldn't—get done, I mean. She'd really like to be cosseted and cherished and have some time to do what she likes. I'd like her to get married...'

'I'm sure she will marry, Polly; she's very pretty.' He glanced around him and saw the damp patch in the corner, with the bucket underneath it. It would have to be a man with plenty of money, he decided silently. He smiled at Polly and said, 'Shall we go and have another look at the invalid?'

'Is she very ill?'

'I think not. She ate something this afternoon; once she's got rid of it she'll feel better.'

Mary was sitting on the bed, an arm round Pleane, holding the bowl once more, but Pleane looked a little better now. There was a faint colour in her cheeks and Mary had washed her face and hands. When she saw her brother she broke into a torrent of Dutch and he listened gravely.

'Pleane is sorry to cause such a disturbance,' he told Mary. 'You are sure you don't mind her staying here for the night?'

'Of course we don't mind, and she's no trouble at all. I'm going to stay awhile and talk to her while Polly gives you a cup of coffee. Are you hungry?'

He smiled then and she looked away quickly, afraid that he might see how she felt about him. 'Indeed I am—you must be too.'

'That's easy,' said Polly, hovering in the doorway. 'While you have your coffee I'll get some supper. There's heaps left over—bacon and egg pie and there's the rest of the apple tart.' She beamed at him. 'While you and Mary are eating it I'll sit with Pleane, then I can tell you if she's not feeling so good.'

'Splendid, Polly—if Mary doesn't mind.'

'I think it's a very good idea; by the time we've had supper you'll be able to see that your sister's feeling better.'

It was a pity that Pleane chose to be sick again just

then; Mary hardly noticed as they went away while she
urged her to drink a glass of water.

They came back presently, and Professor van Rakesma
pronounced himself satisfied with Pleane's condition. She
looked like a wet hen but the worst, he assured her, was
over, which left him free to accompany Mary down to
the kitchen where she found that Polly had laid a cloth
on the kitchen table and set out plates, knives and forks.

'Do sit down,' she urged him. 'It's not very exciting,
I'm afraid, but if you're hungry...'

Professor van Rakesma, however, had been taught
his manners when a small boy; he didn't sit down until
she had served them both, and when they had polished
off the bacon and egg pie he gathered up the plates and
fetched the apple tart.

'More coffee?' asked Mary, sorry that the meal was
over, for surprisingly they had found plenty to talk about.

'That would be nice. Should I perhaps see your father
before I go?'

'He'd like that; I'll fetch Mother too. I expect you want
to take another look at Pleane.'

'Yes. I think she'll be all right now, but if I may I'll
phone about eleven o'clock—that's not too late?'

'No, I'll still be up—and I get up quite early in the
morning if you want to phone then.'

'You're very kind.' He sounded formal. 'I'll do that.
If you think she is fit I'll fetch her at some time convenient to you.'

She nodded. 'Any time in the morning.' She poured
their coffee. 'If you want to ring your home the phone is
in the hall. Do use it if you would like to.'

He shook his head and said slowly, 'I have a car phone.'

She said quickly, 'I'll go and tell Father you are here.'

She fetched her mother too and the professor stayed for a short time, saying all the right things in his pleasant voice and presently bidding them goodnight and going upstairs once more to check on Pleane. She was feeling better, but weary from the sickness and spasms of pain. He examined her carefully once more, left tablets for the night, gave Mary a few instructions, bade them all goodnight once again, and went out to his car. Polly went with him.

'You must have had a nasty fright,' she observed.

'Very nasty. Luckily it didn't turn out as badly as it might have done.'

'I like your sister. Is your lady-friend nice too?'

'I don't think I could describe her as that.' He smiled a little but he didn't answer her question. 'I'll be back in the morning. I'm most grateful to Mary.'

'She's super. Such a pity you don't like each other.' She leaned up and gave him a kiss. 'At least, she probably likes you only she pretends she doesn't.'

'Why should she do that?' he asked with interest.

'You can always ask her,' said Polly.

He didn't answer that, but drove himself back home and let himself into the flat. As usual Fred came to meet him in the hall. 'Found Miss Pleane, sir? I was getting a bit worried.'

'Yes, thank you, Fred. She's quite safe, spending the night with someone I know. We found her down by the river...'

'Your pitch?'

'That's right. She appeared to have had a splendid time. Unfortunately she ate some food there and has had a bad tummy upset. I'll fetch her in the morning.'

'You'll be wanting a meal, sir?'

'No, thanks; I had supper at Miss Pagett's home.'

'Very good, sir. Mrs van Hoeven's in the drawing-room.'

'Ah, yes. Thank you, Fred. You gave her some dinner?'

'Yes, sir. I've got Richard in the kitchen with me...'

Professor van Rakesma paused on his way across the hall. 'He can come up now, Fred. I'll take him out presently.'

He opened the drawing-room door and went in.

Ilsa almost ran across the room to him. 'Roel, is she safe? You have no idea how awful I feel—I never thought she would go off like that—she knew that I didn't want to go through those filthy little streets.'

He didn't sit down but went to the French window leading to the small garden behind the flats, opened it and let Richard out. 'Yes, I found her, Ilsa. She's spending the night with some people I know.'

He didn't say any more and Ilsa, sensing that he wasn't going to tell her anything further, wisely said nothing for a while. Presently she said, 'You do forgive me, Roel? It was stupid of me; I should have remembered that Pleane is so impulsive.'

When he didn't answer she asked, 'These people that she's with—they'll take good care of her? Could you not have brought her here? She's not ill?' She gave a little shudder. 'Not caught something frightful from those people she met?'

'She is very tired. She walked a long way; she will be quite herself after a good night's sleep. I shall fetch her tomorrow morning.'

'I'll come with you; it's the least I can do...' She smiled at him, unable to read the expression on his face. Amusement? Amazement?

She was a conceited woman; she had no idea that it was well-concealed contempt.

Mary, pottering around in her dressing-gown, wishful to go to bed but waiting for the professor's phone call, had ample time to reflect upon the evening's happenings.

She was still smarting from the knowledge that he considered her a sensible female. On the other hand she was agreeably surprised to discover that he went out at night to help the hapless men and women who were homeless; what was more, she doubted if anyone knew about it.

Under his impersonal courtesy there must be a rather nice man lurking. He had sat down with that grubby, ill-cared for group of young people as though he made a habit of it. Perhaps he did. He had been nice about his sister going off like that too...

The phone rang and she hurried to answer it, fearful of waking everyone up, which was perhaps why she sounded brisk and a little impatient.

'Got you out of bed, Mary? My apologies. Is Pleane asleep?'

'Yes, I've just been in to see her. She hasn't been sick again and she feels quite cool. I'm in the room next door. I'll hear her if she wakes up.'

'Good. If she wants breakfast in the morning she can have it, but will you take her temperature first? I'll be with you about eleven o'clock, if that's convenient.'

'Quite convenient, Professor van Rakesma. I'll look after her. Goodnight.'

She hung up quickly, suddenly not wanting to talk to him, and went to bed—to wake several times during the night and peer at the sleeping Pleane.

In the morning she had just escorted her to the bathroom, where she had run a steaming hot bath for her—which meant that the water would be lukewarm for the rest of the day—when Polly came racing upstairs.

'He's here and there's someone with him. A lady—ever so smart and all smiles. I don't like her. She looked at me as though I was wearing all the wrong clothes.'

Mary eyed her sister. 'Well, love, I know you're wearing what everyone else your age is wearing at the moment, but perhaps she finds it a bit strange. Go down and get the coffee, will you? It's all ready in the kitchen. And make sure that Mother or Father—both, if you can find them—are there. I'll tell Pleane; she'll be so pleased.'

Pleane wasn't pleased. 'Ilsa's there? But I do not wish to be with her. She is not what you call a sport; she ran away yesterday because she wears high heels and is afraid to get dirty. I can see that she wants very much to marry Roel, and that will not do.'

She got out of the bath and wrapped herself in the towel Mary offered her. 'Now, you would do very well for him, but I think you might not agree; you are not friends, you said yesterday, and I find that strange since you came with him to find me.'

Mary reflected on the perversity of people. Polly had seen her as a suitable wife for Professor van Rakesma, and now here was his sister of like mind, while he thought of her—if he did think at all—as sensible, with her head screwed on straight. She gave a delicate shudder and offered to dry Pleane's back.

'I've done the best I could with that stain on your dress,' she observed. 'I'm not sure what it was, and I don't think I want to know, but I expect if you take it to a good cleaner's they'll get it out.'

'Oh, I'll throw it away. Roel will buy me another one.' Pleane was dressing quickly. 'We were to have gone to church this morning. We are going home on Wednesday and I did want to go to Westminster Abbey.'

'You could go to evensong.'

'Yes? You go to this evensong?'

'Sometimes, but usually we all go in the morning.'

'And you couldn't go this morning because I am here. I'm so sorry.'

'Don't worry; we were going this evening anyway.'

'I wish I could come with you.'

'We'd love to have you, but I expect your brother has other plans.'

Pleane said nothing more, and presently they went downstairs to the drawing-room to find Ilsa talking to her parents. There was no sign of the professor.

Pleane shook hands with Mr and Mrs Pagett, said hello to Ilsa and introduced her to Mary. 'Ilsa's a friend of my mother's,' she explained, and Mary hid a smile at the indignation on Ilsa's face. After all, she wasn't all that old.

She exchanged various civilities and, saying that she would fetch the coffee, went to the kitchen. Polly was there, carefully pouring the coffee while Professor van Rakesma leaned against the table, eating one of the cakes that Mary had made that morning.

His good morning was genial. 'I must apologise for spoiling your Sunday morning and bringing Ilsa with me; she was so anxious to see that Pleane was quite well again.' Something in his voice made her look sharply at him, and he met her eyes with a guileless stare. 'You have all been so kind.'

He carried the tray in and Polly took the cakes; Mary stayed behind in the kitchen for a few minutes, mumbling an excuse about more coffee, but really it was because she didn't want to see him with this Ilsa woman. Who had disliked her on sight. Mary took several heartening breaths and went to join everyone else.

Ilsa was sitting on the edge of the little Victorian balloon-backed chair which needed a new cover so badly; she gave the impression of being uncomfortable while behaving with impeccable good manners. She refused a cake with a sweetly rueful smile. 'I have to be so careful of sweet food,' she explained.

Mary, biting into her own cake, murmured with false sympathy. 'There's so much of me that it doesn't matter what I eat,' she said cheerfully, and Professor van Rakesma, listening to her mother explaining about her greetings cards, turned a laugh into a cough and agreed pleasantly that robins at Christmas-time were always popular.

Ilsa was on edge to go, but neither he nor Pleane were to be hurried. Richard had come with them and was sitting by his master, gobbling any oddments of cake which came his way, and providing a topic of conversation.

Mrs Pagett, free from her daughter's inhibitions, plied her guest with questions—was he married? No? Then he ought to be. Had he a family in Holland? Yes? And where did they live, and were any of them married? How many were there and how often did he go back to his home there? Did he intend to live in England forever?

Mary, making polite small talk with an impatient Ilsa, listened to his answers and stored them away for future reflection.

The two men went away presently, to look at some manuscripts of her father's, and they didn't return for half an hour or more, by which time Ilsa was white with bottled-up annoyance. Her goodbyes, when at last Professor van Rakesma observed that they really should be going, were uttered in a voice cold enough to cause even gentle, whimsical Mrs Pagett some astonishment, but nothing could have been warmer than Pleane's thanks and her brother's firm handshake.

He didn't shake Mary's hand, though; he thanked her formally for her help and made no reference to their meeting again.

'Oh, well,' said Mary, shutting the door firmly as he drove away. 'That's that.'

The rest of the day stretched tamely ahead of her now that he had gone. She banged about in the kitchen, preparing the Sunday joint, and wished that he wasn't so tiresome, turning up just when she was schooling herself to think no more of him.

She and Polly went for a walk that afternoon, and after tea accompanied their parents to church. Evensong was Mary's favourite service; she sang the hymns with pleasure in her clear voice and felt better—until she turned her head cautiously to see who was singing with equal enthusiasm only in a deep, rumbling voice. Professor van Rakesma, no less, with Pleane on one side of him and Ilsa on the other.

Mary turned her head quickly, but not quickly enough, so that she had time to note that Ilsa was wearing a striking outfit and a most becoming hat. She sat through the sermon, not hearing a word of it, wondering why he and his companions should be there, but it wasn't until they were leaving the church that her father observed, 'Ah, I see that our guests have come.' And when Mary looked at him enquiringly, he added, 'I'm sure that you will give them one of your delicious meals, my dear.'

'Delicious meal—when, Father?'

'Why, presently, Mary; I invited them for supper. Professor van Rakesma and I have a mutual interest in the
history of mid-Europe; it will be a splendid opportunity
for him to examine several books that I have...'

Mary reminded herself that she loved her father
deeply, thrust aside any unfilial thoughts which crowded
into her head and concentrated on supper as they moved
slowly towards the church porch.

Professor van Rakesma, Ilsa and Pleane were there,
talking to the vicar and her mother and Polly, and they
joined them, exchanged a few words with the vicar and
began to walk slowly out of the churchyard.

Mary had greeted everyone politely, avoided Polly's
eloquent eye and engaged Ilsa in conversation. Her remarks received short shrift and it was a relief when her
mother and father were invited to get into the car with
Pleane and Ilsa and be driven the short distance home,
which left Mary and Polly free to tear through several
shortcuts and get there at the same time.

Everyone went into the drawing-room, where Mr Pagett offered sherry, and afterwards Mary slid away to the
kitchen to poke her head into the fridge and the larder and
look at the remains of the joint, a wedge of cheese and,
thankfully, bacon and eggs. They would have to wait at
least half an hour, she thought, rapidly gathering what
she would need for a bacon and cheese quiche.

While the oven heated she made the pastry. 'And if
it turns out like lead they'll just have to eat it,' she told
Bingo, who was watching her from his chair. The bacon
fried and the eggs beaten, she almost flung them into the
pastry case and banged the oven door on it.

'They'll have to eat a salad,' she informed him. 'Thank heaven there are some lettuces in the garden.' She thumped her gleanings from the vegetable rack on to the table and turned round to see Professor van Rakesma standing just behind her. 'Now what do you want?' she asked him crossly. 'Of all the tiresome men...'

He said gravely, his lids lowered over amused eyes, 'I fear we have put you out. I will make some excuse and we can go in a few minutes.'

'Oh, no, you don't! I've just put a quiche in the oven; you'll jolly well stay and eat it.'

'If you say so. Shall I fetch some lettuce from the garden?'

She was chopping tomatoes, grating carrots and slicing beetroot. 'Yes—no, you'd better not. You'll get your hands dirty.'

'It wouldn't be the first time.' He wandered out of the kitchen door and presently returned with two lettuces which he put in the sink. 'Mary, I'm sorry about this; I had no idea that you knew nothing about it. Your father invited us and I took it for granted that you would know. Pleane very much wanted to go to evensong and he knew that.'

'Yes, well... I was very rude to you just now; I apologise, but you see we don't entertain any more and there's not much in the fridge.'

'I'm sure we shall enjoy our supper, whatever it is. Shall I lay the table?'

'Lay the table? You? But I don't suppose you know how—I mean...' She frowned. 'You know very well what I mean.'

'Try me and see. Here or in the dining-room?'

'Oh, not here, not with—' She stopped just in time. 'In the dining-room, and thank you. Everything you'll need is in the dresser over there.'

Chapter 7

Professor van Rakesma, put on his mettle, laid the table with a precision and nicety which would have earned Fred's praise, and, that done, he wandered back into the kitchen, where Mary was setting out the biscuits and cheese.

'Don't you want to go to the drawing-room? Father said there were some books...'

'Presently, I fancy. I left him enjoying a talk with Ilsa.'

The silence went on rather too long. 'She's very handsome,' said Mary, 'and that was a lovely hat. I hope she doesn't find us too dull.'

He didn't answer, which was annoying of him; she cast around for something else to talk about, since he obviously had no intention of going. 'I expect your sister is enjoying herself—' that was rather a silly remark

to make after yesterday's adventure '——shopping and so
on,' she went on lamely.

'Don't try so hard, Mary,' he said. 'We may not be
friends, but we know each other well enough by now to
be able to cut out the small talk.' He glanced at her. 'And
now I have annoyed you.'

'Anything you say is of complete indifference to me,'
said Mary grandly, and tightened her hand on the wooden
spoon that she was holding.

He laughed then, and threw up his hands. 'I cry *pax*;
shall we bury the hatchet until we meet again?'

'Certainly, but we aren't likely to meet any more.'

'Don't tempt fate.'

'Pooh,' said Mary, and took the quiche out of the oven.

To her surprise supper was a success. The conversation never flagged, composed as it was largely of Christmas robins, first editions, and, on a more serious note,
the homeless Pleane had met, and although Professor
van Rakesma spoke with some authority on the subject
he didn't mention that he went down regularly to the riv-
erside shelters.

Only Ilsa was silent for most of the time, pushing her
supper round her plate in a well-bred fashion, brighten-
ing up when the professor spoke to her, smiling at him
in a sweetly understanding manner which set Mary's
splendid teeth on edge.

Once the meal was finished, her father bore his guest
away to his study and her mother led Ilsa back to the
drawing-room to listen in her vague, kind way to her
view on a number of subjects.

'Of course,' she declared, 'I shall dismiss Fred; I don't
approve of manservants. A good housekeeper and daily

help is quite enough at Roel's flat. It's large, but it is easily run.' She gave Mrs Pagett a wistful smile. 'Of course, I'm quite hopeless at anything to do with housework.'

'Oh, so am I,' agreed Mrs Pagett cheerfully. 'Such a waste of time, I always think, and Mary is such a splendid manager; I'm sure I don't know what we would do without her. You intend to marry?'

Ilsa turned an earnest face to her. 'Oh, most certainly, Mrs Pagett.'

Mrs Pagett, who wasn't always as vague as she appeared to be, thought of the look she had surprised on her elder daughter's face when she had glanced at the professor and felt a pang of grief for her. They would have made a splendid pair; if only he had fallen in love with Mary instead of this hard-faced woman sitting opposite her. She said conventionally, 'I'm sure you will be very happy.' And, since she was a kind woman, added, 'It must have been sad to lose your husband.'

'Oh, I divorced him. He didn't understand me and he bored me. He was so serious, and I believe that one should enjoy life. I like theatres and dancing and lovely clothes.' She gave a little trill of laughter. 'And lots of money. But we all do, don't we?'

Mrs Pagett agreed quietly, reflecting that from what she had seen of Professor van Rakesma he didn't appear to be any less serious than Ilsa's former husband. Perhaps being in love would alter him.

He came into the room with her own husband then, and she could see that Ilsa was sadly mistaken in her wish to change him. Here was a man who might fulfil his social obligations with charm and good manners, but they had no chance against his work as a doctor. She watched Ilsa turn to him with a charming smile.

'Roel, I've had such a lovely evening, but perhaps we should take our leave.' She glanced at her watch and gave a start of surprise. 'It's almost ten o'clock.'

He made no demur, and when Mary and Polly came into the room goodbyes were said and Pleane, who had been in the kitchen with them, declared that she would see them before she went back to Holland. 'I wish you lived nearer,' she said, 'but next time I come you must come and stay with us. There's heaps of room in Roel's flat.'

If her brother heard this invitation he gave no sign, but Mary saw Ilsa's angry glance. She said loudly, 'We would like that very much,' and was kissed three times, continental-fashion, by Pleane. Ilsa shook hands and Professor van Rakesma gave her a cool nod.

'What a very nice man,' observed Mrs Pagett as they went back to the drawing-room. 'And so is his sister—but I don't much care for his friend; she didn't much care for us, did she?'

'No, Mother, but I expect she leads rather a different life from ours. You know, clothes and hairdressers and beauty parlours and a busy social life.'

With a sudden flash of waspishness her mother said, 'She must be looking forty in the face. Perfect make-up of course, but I could see the wrinkles.'

Mary gave her mother a hug. 'Mother, how unkind,' she said, and laughed. 'Why didn't you like her?'

'She said that painting greetings cards was childish.' Mrs Pagett frowned. 'She said several things that made me want to shake her.'

'Well, it's a good thing that we shan't see her again. Are you going to bed? Or shall we make a list of shopping for tomorrow?'

* * *

Breakfast was just finished when an enormous floral arrangement was delivered to Mrs Pagett. She opened the little envelope tucked in among the roses and lilies and read it out loud. '"Thanking you for your kind hospitality"—' She looked up. 'I can't read the signature; it's dreadful writing...'

'"R van R",' said Mary. 'How kind of him. Where do you want them, Mother?'

'Where we can all see them; I'll find a place while you are shopping.'

On Tuesday morning, just as Mary and Mrs Blackett were sitting down for their mid-morning cup of tea, Pleane and Ilsa arrived. Mrs Blackett had gone to answer the doorbell—not because she felt it her duty to do so but because she wanted to see who it was. She came back into the kitchen and sat down again. 'Two ladies. Want to see you, Miss Mary. Very posh.'

'Someone collecting for the church?' hazarded Mary. 'Where is my purse?'

Pleane and Ilsa stood in the hall and she was instantly vexed that she was in an elderly cotton dress with the sleeves rolled up, and, worse, her hair lay in a thick plait over one shoulder.

Pleane didn't appear to notice; she went to meet her with a wide grin. 'I know we're a nuisance, but I did want to say goodbye once more. We're off early tomorrow— everything's packed...' She looked down at her elegant person. 'That's why we are all dressed up.'

'Will you have a cup of coffee?' asked Mary, and Ilsa answered before Pleane could speak.

'How kind, but we wouldn't dream of interrupting your housework—the taxi is outside waiting. We have to go to Fortnum & Mason for my mother's special brand of tea; we can have coffee there.'

Mary spent a moment wondering if Ilsa's mother was as unpleasant as her daughter. 'A long way just to get some tea…'

'Ah, but we usually have it sent, you know. But since I am here it seemed a good idea to get it and take it back with me. Pleane, are you coming?'

Pleane had an expression on her face which reminded Mary of her brother—a bland look which gave nothing away. 'I am just going to see Mrs Pagett—I didn't say goodbye to her properly.' She smiled at Mary. 'Is she in the shed?'

'Yes, but I'm sure she'd love to see you again. Would you like to go too, Ilsa?'

'No, no. I'll wait in the taxi.' She watched Pleane go through the drawing-room doors into the garden and then turned to look at Mary; the look started at her bare feet in their shabby sandals and moved slowly up to her face. She smiled then, but her eyes were like blue glass. 'Walk down to the gate with me if you can spare the time; I'm sure Pleane won't be long.'

So they walked down the short, neglected drive, Ilsa stepping carefully in her high-heeled shoes. Mary choked back a wish for her to trip up and fall flat on her face, dislodging the elegant hat and dirtying the deceptively simple outfit she was wearing, but of course she didn't.

It wasn't until they reached the open gate that she spoke. 'We must come and see you again,' she said. 'I shall be back very shortly; there is so much to do—the flat needs new covers and curtains and I shall change the colour scheme. I must persuade Roel to get rid of Fred too; I was telling your mother—a good housekeeper and a daily woman must take over.' She laughed a little. 'Men are so useless at that kind of thing, aren't they? Or perhaps you wouldn't know.'

Mary was leaning on the gate; her plait had fallen over her shoulder and half hid her face. She said, 'No, I wouldn't know. You're going to make rather drastic changes, are you not?'

'Very drastic—and not just in the flat. I shall see to it that Roel's life is changed too. A social life is so important.'

'You're going to be married?' Mary managed to ask the question lightly.

'My dear girl, isn't it obvious?'

'No...'

'Well, of course, if one is influenced by one's feelings, even when they are mistaken...'

Mary turned her lovely brown eyes on Ilsa's smiling face. 'I'm glad we shan't meet again,' she said clearly. 'Here's Pleane.' She turned her back on Ilsa and went to meet the other girl.

'Your mother is a darling—almost as nice as mine, Mary. Ilsa, you look as though you're sucking a lemon; it makes you look quite old.'

She kissed Mary and went out to the taxi and Ilsa, without speaking again, followed her.

Back in the kitchen Mary added boiling water to the teapot and sat down at the table.

'Well?' said Mrs Blackett, all agog. 'Oo was it, then?'

'The doctor who looked after Great Aunt Thirza—it was his sister. And the lady with her says she is going to marry him.'

'Oh, yes? There's many a slip, I always say. That was

the tall one with the made-up face? Can't say I took a liking for 'er.'

'Neither did I. She was going to Fortnum & Mason to order a special brand of tea for her mother.'

Mrs Blackett gave a guffaw. 'Very la-di-da, and what's wrong with teabags, I'd like to know?' She took her mug to the sink. 'I'll go and give that dining-room table a bit of a polish before I clean up 'ere.'

Mary drank her tea, made a cup of coffee for her mother and went down to the shed.

'That nice girl came to see me,' observed the older woman happily. 'Such a chatterbox too…'

'Mother,' said Mary, 'did Ilsa tell you that she was going to marry Professor van Rakesma?'

'Ah, she was here too, was she? As a matter of fact, not in so many words but as good as, if you see what I mean. All that talk about changing his home and getting rid of someone called Fred—his manservant, presumably. She'll make him a bad wife; the man must be out of his mind.'

Mary said tartly, 'Presumably at his age he knows his own mind well enough.'

'Yes, that's why I'm rather surprised. He didn't behave as though he loved her, did he? His manners are so good it was hard to tell. He's not one to wear his heart on his sleeve, is he?'

'I have no idea, Mother.'

'You sound as though you don't like him, love.'

'I don't know him well enough to say one way or the other. I hope he'll be happy with Ilsa.'

Two fibs in one breath.

Mrs Pagett murmured, 'Of course, dear. What a delicious cup of coffee.'

* * *

Professor van Rakesma had rearranged his visits and consultations so that he could see his sister and Ilsa on to their early morning plane. He was going out of his door with Richard for their morning walk when Pleane came racing downstairs. 'I'm coming with you,' she told him, and slipped a hand under his arm. 'I want to talk.'

He looked down at her with affection. 'Do you ever want to do anything else? What have you done now? Fallen in love again?'

'No, no, it's not me this time—it's you. You and Ilsa.'

'And what about us? Something I should know?'

He was half laughing and she said quickly, 'No, don't laugh. Do you like her very much, Roel?' And at his quick frown she said, 'No, don't be cross—and I'm serious. Don't tell me it's none of my business.'

'Very well, I won't. Have you quarrelled with her, *liefje*?'

'No. I never liked her very much, you know, but she comes to see us a lot and says she's our oldest friend—that kind of thing—and she bosses me around. But it's not that. She's going to marry you—did you know?'

'I have sometimes wondered if she had that in mind.'

'Don't, will you? She's all wrong for you, Roel. You need a wife like Mary Pagett, who'll stand up to you and not waste your money, and will have hordes of children for you.'

He squeezed her hand and said kindly, 'Pleane, Mary and I are almost always at daggers drawn...'

'Except when you want someone to help you—like when you came looking for me.'

'That was the exception which proves the rule. No, my dear, I'm afraid that wouldn't be a very good idea.

But if it will relieve your mind I promise you that I don't intend to marry Ilsa; indeed I have no plans to marry at the moment.'

With that Pleane had to be content; if Roel said he wasn't going to marry Ilsa then everything was all right; he was a man of his word.

She would have been relieved if she had known that he had been shocked at Ilsa's light-hearted attitude to Pleane's escapade. Until then he hadn't realised how self-ish she was, and how uncaring of things which touched on her comfort or peace of mind. Any ideas of marry-ing her which he had been harbouring at the back of his mind had been swept away.

He stayed with them until it was time for them to board their plane, bade them goodbye, gave Pleane a final hug, and then drove himself back to his home.

'Got half an hour?' asked Fred, coming into the hall, duster in hand. 'I've a pot of coffee all ready for you.'

'Splendid, Fred. I'd like it now—I'll be in the study.'

Fred came in presently, poured the coffee and stood waiting by the desk.

Professor van Rakesma looked up from the notes he was studying. 'Fred?'

'It's like this, sir. Mrs van Hoeven told me that she won't want me no more when she comes; so what's me and Syl going to do?'

The professor sat back in his chair. 'As far as I know, Fred, Mrs van Hoeven won't be coming here again; per-haps there has been some misunderstanding, for we are certainly not going to marry.' He smiled suddenly. 'And, when I do marry, I can promise you that you and Syl will stay with us for as long as you wish to—and I hope that will be for a very long time.'

'Thank you, sir. It had us a bit worried.'

It had the professor a bit worried too; he had never, to the best of his knowledge, led Ilsa to believe that he intended to marry her, although he knew that if he had done so she would have accepted at once. He would have to make it plain to her next time they met. If he could find someone whom he would want for his wife it would make things so much easier...

Mary's face flashed beneath his lids and he dismissed it at once; they struck sparks off each other whenever they met and she made no bones about her indifference to him. But then, of course, he reminded himself, he was indifferent to her too.

He returned to his case-notes and forgot about her, for the time being at least.

He didn't get home again until the early evening. He had had several private patients to see at his rooms in Harley Street, and from there he had gone straight to the hospital to do a ward round. The man he had been called to see on the day of Pleane and Ilsa's arrival was getting on well, and he pondered the idea of offering him the job of caretaker at his cottage at Adlescombe.

The man had no family and no friends and, being homeless, had been unable to get a job for lack of references and an address. He could take him on for a month and see if he was suitable. He was a quiet man, who had seen better days and would never be fit for heavy work again, but there was little to do at the cottage.

He was still thinking about it when Pleane phoned to say that they were home again and to thank him for her holiday. 'And all those lovely clothes.' She added, 'Ilsa went home; she said she'd phone you from there.'

Ilsa did ring later that evening, but it was Fred who

answered her, to tell her with well-concealed satisfaction that Professor van Rakesma had been called back to the hospital to an emergency and he had no idea when he would be back.

She hung up without leaving a message and Fred went back to the kitchen to tell Richard that she wasn't half put out. 'You didn't like her, neither,' said Fred. 'Doesn't like dogs nor cats. I don't call that natural.' Richard, an intelligent beast, didn't call it natural either.

Mary attacked the housework with even more vigour than usual after her conversation with Ilsa; she refused to admit, even to herself, that the idea of never seeing the professor again made her feel quite ill, and as for his marrying Ilsa... Her mind boggled at the very idea.

'A pity I shall not be seeing him again,' she told Bingo—a sentiment, if she had but known it, which was shared by Professor van Rakesma, albeit reluctantly.

She welcomed her return to the bookshop on Thursday. A change of scene, she told herself, would soon put things in their proper perspective. And certainly she was busy enough to preclude any sitting about being sorry for herself.

It was going on for six o'clock on Saturday afternoon when he came into the shop. It was already crowded, and his bulk meant that everyone was standing almost shoulder to shoulder. Mary, wreathing her substantial person through the throng, intent on brown paper and string, ran full tilt into him.

He put an arm round her to steady her, but only for a moment. 'Doing good business, I see. Any chance of seeing Mr Bell?'

'He's in his office.'

He nodded. 'I'll drive you home.'

'There's no need, thank you all the same; the underground is very quick.'

'Don't be childish, Mary. You know as well as I do that it's much more comfortable for you if I drive you there. And no sneaking out of the back door...' He had gone before the peevish words on her tongue could be uttered.

There was no sign of him when she ushered the last customer out of the door, and there was no sound of voices coming from Mr Bell's office. Perhaps he had had second thoughts. Despite her resolve not to go with him she felt disappointed; she would have enjoyed re-iterating her refusal, she told herself firmly, and put her head round the office door.

Mr Bell was there, deep in a book, and, sitting on the other side of his desk, was Professor van Rakesma, his commanding nose buried in a little leather-bound book, which she recognised as one of Mr Bell's choicest first editions.

She said quickly, 'Goodnight, Mr Bell,' nodded in the professor's general direction and closed the door gently.

Not smartly enough. She had reached the shop door when his hand came down on hers, about to turn the knob. 'I'm not coming with you,' she said as he swept her across the pavement, round the corner and into the car before she could draw breath.

Richard was asleep on the back seat, but he got up to greet her as she settled in her seat with what dignity she had left. 'I cannot think,' she began, 'why you persist in annoying me, Professor van Rakesma.'

'I am not sure myself,' he told her mildly. 'You are a perpetual thorn in my otherwise disciplined life.' He turned to look at her. 'To mix my metaphors, you are like a sore tooth that I'm unable to leave alone.'

Her brown eyes flashed with temper. 'Well, a thorn, indeed, a sore tooth—whatever next, I should like to know?'

'I've been wondering that myself. Do you suppose we might cry quits and become friends?'

Friends, thought Mary wildly. Who wants to be friends? And he's almost a married man. 'Certainly not.'

'You don't like me?'

He had begun to drive towards Hampstead.

'I didn't say that.'

'Good. In that case let us at least assume an armed neutrality. I need your help.'

'Mine? Whatever for?'

'Well, if I may tell you… I have a cottage in Gloucestershire at Adlescombe near Stow-on-the-Wold. I go there for weekends occasionally, and when I can manage a few days off. I have decided to have a caretaker there but I think there are one or two improvements which should be made—the kitchen and so forth—before he takes up his residence. It needs a woman's eye, though. If Pleane had been staying longer I would have got her to go with me. I'm free tomorrow if you would be kind enough to give me the benefit of your advice.'

'What sort of improvements?' asked Mary cautiously.

'I'm not sure; that's why I'm asking you to come and see for yourself and tell me.' He gave her a sideways glance. 'That is all I'm asking, Mary.'

She didn't allow her thoughts to dwell on the enchanting prospect of spending a whole day with him; she would remember to be friendly in a detached way, bearing in mind all the time that he was going to marry the hateful Ilsa and taking care not to ask questions. Of course, if she were Ilsa she would never allow him to spend the whole day with another girl, however business-like the intentions were. She must feel very sure of him…

'Yes, I'd like to come, thank you! Is your cottage quite empty? I mean, does someone go in now and then and dust around and make sure everything's safe?'

'Yes, Mrs Goodbody from the village "pops in"—those are her words—now and then. I've no idea what she does; there doesn't seem much point in dusting if there is no one there. It all looks perfectly all right when I go.'

Of course, when he was married to Ilsa it would be a good idea to have someone there to keep the place in a state of readiness. She couldn't imagine Ilsa putting on an apron and peeling the potatoes.

'I'll call for you around half-past nine—if that's not too early for you?'

'I'll be ready. Do you want me to bring some food—sandwiches and so on?'

'Fred will see to that. I shall bring Richard with me.'

'Oh, good. I expect he likes the country.'

He drew up outside the house and got out to open her door.

'Would you like to come in and have some coffee?'

She hoped that he would say no while at the same time not wanting him to drive away. All the same, when he refused politely she felt let down.

'Thank you for the lift,' she said then, anxious not to keep him—perhaps he was going out that evening. 'I'll be ready in the morning. Goodnight.'

He smiled, and got into the car and drove away and she stood on the doorstep and watched him go.

Spending the day with him would mean some re-organisation of Sunday.

Polly, when told the news, volunteered at once to see to lunch. 'As long as you leave everything ready to put in the oven. You'll be home for supper, won't you?'

'Gracious, yes. By teatime, I should think. I'd better make a few of those little cakes. I'll go and talk to Mother. Is she in the hut?'

'Yes. Father's over at the vicarage.'

Mary was up early to find the sky overcast, which was in a way a good thing because she could wear the green cotton jersey dress—which was about the nicest one she had—without looking too warmly clad.

Breakfast was over and everything left in apple-pie order by the time Professor van Rakesma thumped the doorknocker. He was admitted and then spent ten minutes or so chatting to her mother and father.

He looked calmly self-assured, utterly to be trusted and pleasantly detached in his manner—all of which pleased Mrs Pagett, which was what he had intended.

Polly, running round the garden with Richard, thought once again that it was a pity that Mary and he couldn't get married. He'd be a splendid brother-in-law.

He took the M40 out of London. Traffic was light and the Rolls ate up the miles in a well-bred silence while they talked in a desultory fashion about nothing much, bypassing High Wycombe and then Oxford and finally stopping in Burford at the Lamb Inn for coffee and to allow Richard to stretch his legs. The village was charming and very peaceful, and they walked for ten minutes or so, content to be silent in each other's company.

They turned on to the road to Stow-on-the-Wold presently and then to Adlescombe, a village of no great size with houses built of yellow Cotswold stone—most of them cottages around the church. Professor van Rakesma drove down the narrow main street and into a short, gateless drive.

The cottage was bigger than its neighbours, with small, latticed windows, a solid front door with a little porch, and dormer windows in a slate roof which was old and moss-covered in places. There was a nice arrangement of shrubs and flowers all around.

A delightful little house, thought Mary, very much aware of his great arm flung around her shoulders as he helped her out of the car.

'You must want to come here very often.'

'Yes. It's delightful, isn't it? Come inside.'

He unlocked the door and she went past him into a small lobby and then into the room beyond, which was low-ceilinged and beamed, with an inglenook and windows at both ends of the room. The furniture was exactly right—oak and simple, with comfortable easy chairs and two vast sofas on either side of the fireplace. The floor was wooden, worn by the years and covered with several lovely, slightly shabby rugs. There was dust on the gateleg table by the far window, although everything was tidy and clean.

'A good polish,' said Mary, and Professor van Rakesma gave a shout of laughter.

'But you like it?'

'It's exactly right.'

She looked questioningly at him and he said easily, 'I spent a long time getting exactly what I wanted to furnish the cottage. Some of the furniture I brought back from Holland.' He opened a latched door. 'Come and look at the kitchen.'

It was small and rather bleak. There was an Aga against one wall, and cupboards and shelves, an old porcelain sink and a solid table with Windsor chairs. There was everything there but no colour.

'Pale yellow walls, rush matting, a picture or two, and another shade on the light.'

There was an old-fashioned dresser opposite the Aga. There were plates and cups and saucers on it, obviously bought without any thought of a colour scheme. 'Orange and blue,' said Mary. 'Glasses and jugs—and flowers, of course.'

'Of course,' agreed Professor van Rakesma gravely. 'Come and see the dining-room.'

It was a small room, with exactly the right wallpaper, a round mahogany table with four chairs round it, and a Georgian sideboard with nothing on it. The curtains were chintz, the same as those in the sitting-room, and there were cushions piled on the window-seat. There were a few paintings on the walls—gentle landscapes, nicely framed.

'Perfect,' sighed Mary, and followed him through the narrow door in one wall, behind which were narrow stairs. They led to a roomy landing with several doors. He opened them all and invited her to look around.

Three bedrooms, charmingly furnished, two bathrooms, and a small room which she could see would be very handy for a number of purposes—a sewing-room, somewhere to do the ironing or write letters, even put an unexpected guest or house a baby's cradle.

She joined him on the landing. 'It's all quite perfect. Just the kitchen needs something done to it.'

'Yes—come back downstairs; there's one more room to see.'

Just outside the kitchen door was another, opening on to a large, pleasant room, quite empty. 'I thought this might be turned into a bed-sitting-room for the caretaker...' He leaned his vast person against one wall and waited for Mary to speak.

'It's big enough to divide up. A shower-room at one end; no need for a kitchen but he'd need an electric kettle. A divan bed, chairs and a table, warm curtains and some sort of a fire. A nice russet-red, so that it looks welcoming.' She paused. 'That's only what I think,' she said apologetically. 'I dare say you have your own ideas.'

'I asked you to give me some advice, Mary. I'm grateful. I'll get the whole thing started as soon as possible.'

'Will you? But perhaps whoever comes here might not like it—the colours and so on.'

'I don't imagine that the caretaker will mind what colour his curtains are as long as the kitchen functions; he won't bother his head with colour schemes.'

She gave him a candid look. 'I wasn't thinking of the caretaker. Supposing you marry?'

'Ah, yes. Well, we can cross that bridge when we come to it.' He added slowly, 'Probably she will change her mind and I shall have it redecorated—that will be no problem.'

I must be mad, thought Mary, offering ideas about the place when it should be Ilsa doing so. Why didn't he bring her down here while she was staying with him?

'Did Ilsa come here?' The question popped out before she could stop it.

He seemed to find nothing strange in her question. 'No, not this time.' He closed the door and they went back into the kitchen. 'Shall we have our picnic? We could go into the garden.'

It wasn't just sandwiches; there were little rolls, butter in a covered dish, several cheeses, chicken drumsticks, miniature sausage rolls and a pork pie, as well as custards in little glasses, strawberries and clotted cream. There were china plates, cutlery, linen napkins and bottles of tonic water and lemonade. They sat on a wooden bench at the end of the garden, and even though it was still rather a dull day it was full of colour.

'You must have a very good gardener,' said Mary, her mouth full of chicken.

'He comes in each week, and I enjoy pottering around when I'm down here.'

He made no demur when she suggested that they might go back. 'If you don't mind,' she added, 'but Mother expects us for tea.'

Richard, happily tired after a day nosing around the garden, flopped on to the back seat and went to sleep, and Mary, nicely full, envied him. It would never do to fall asleep, though; she racked her brains for small talk and was affronted when Professor van Rakesma said, 'Don't bother to make conversation. Have a nap if you like.'

Which caused her to be wide awake on the instant. 'I am not in the least tired,' she told him frostily. All the same, she kept quiet, sensing that he was busy with his thoughts. It must be because I love him, she decided silently, that I can guess his moods. I do hope Ilsa loves him too.

She mustn't think about that. For lack of anything better, she began to recite silently 'The Lay of the Last Minstrel' which, while boring her, kept her mind off him.

Polly came running out as he drew up outside the house. 'Good, just in time; I've put the kettle on...'

He had got out to open Mary's door and free Richard. 'I must drive straight back, Polly. I am so sorry; I would have enjoyed having tea with you all, but I have an appointment and I'm going away very early in the morning.'

To Holland, thought Mary miserably, and said brightly, 'Then we mustn't keep you. Thank you for a lovely day; I enjoyed it.'

'I too, Mary. Please make my apologies to your parents.' He whistled to Richard, dropped a kiss on Polly's cheek, got into his car and drove away.

'Did you have a lovely day?' asked Polly.

'Quite perfect.' There would never be another day like it.

Chapter 8

It was on the following Saturday, shortly before Mr Bell closed his shop, that Professor van Rakesma came into it. Mary, parcelling up books for a peppery old retired colonel, faltered at the sight of him, so that the brown paper came loose and she had to begin all over again while the colonel muttered. Her heart was thumping so loudly that she felt sure that everyone there could hear it, and no amount of self-control could prevent the colour in her cheeks.

Professor van Rakesma, pausing in the doorway, studied her from under lowered lids, wishing that he could forget her and get on with his hitherto satisfactory life. But somehow she had disrupted it woefully. He bade her a cool good day and went in search of Mr Bell, collected the books put aside for him and went to the door where, much against his will, he turned round and went to the shelves that she was tidying before going home.

'I should like some more of your advice, Mary.'

He sounded faintly annoyed so she answered coolly, 'I'm going home in a few minutes, Professor van Rakesma. Perhaps another time?'

'Now, I'm afraid. A question of crockery for the kitchen at the cottage. I'm going there tomorrow and the decorator will be there. Would you come back with me to my flat now and tell me which to have? It won't delay you for more than an hour; you can phone your mother from my car.'

'He who hesitates...' Mary hesitated, and was lost. 'Very well, just as long as it doesn't take more than an hour.'

He nodded. 'I'll be outside.'

She had had no idea where he lived. The graceful house in Cheyne Walk enchanted her; she stood on the step before the door and looked over her shoulder at the river across the road; to live there would be very satisfying. The door opened and Fred, his face composed into no expression, held it wide.

'Ah, Fred. Miss Pagett has come to advise me on the china. It's in the kitchen? Mary, this is Fred, my manservant and right hand.'

Mary put out a hand and shook Fred's.

'A pleasure, miss,' he said, and meant it. Here was a fine-looking young lady, with lovely brown eyes and an enchanting smile, worth a hundred of that Mrs van Hoeven. Fred, a staunch Methodist, sent up a brief and urgent prayer on behalf of his master.

He led the way to the kitchen, so that this delightful lady could look around her, and offered her a chair. The crockery was spread all over the solid kitchen table. There were several samples of various patterns and colours and she studied them carefully.

'They are all pretty; I like that one there, the biscuit-coloured background with the yellow crocuses and the green handles.'

'Good,' said Professor van Rakesma. 'Fred, where did we put the patterns of materials?'

Fred opened a drawer. 'Here we are, miss.' Mary sat down again and fingered the samples. They were all lovely, but she made her choice finally and the professor said, 'While you are here what about the curtains for the bed-sitter?'

She chose those too, and then got up to go with a murmur about getting home.

'A cup of tea first; Fred, we'll be in the sitting-room.'

'Really—' began Mary.

'Yes, yes, I know. Tea will only take ten minutes, though, and you'll be home at the time you told your mother. Come in here.'

'Oh,' breathed Mary, rotating slowly in the middle of the room. 'How beautiful and—lived in, if you see what I mean. You must be very happy living here.'

'I'm glad you like it. Come and sit down. You're still enjoying your work at Mr Bell's shop?'

'Yes, very much—and he is so kind; I know so little about the book world, but I'm learning.'

Fred came in then with the tea-tray; silver teapot, china cups so thin that one could almost see through them, a plate of little cakes and another of tiny cucumber sandwiches. These he placed on a small table beside Mary. It was the best he could do at such short notice; if she came again he would make sure that he had one of his chocolate cakes ready for her...

She thanked him with a smile and the professor, watching, admired the way her tip-tilted nose wrinkled when she smiled. A charming nose, he conceded, and accepted a cup of tea while he talked easily about this and that. She answered him readily enough, but he sensed her reserve behind the pleasant manner and wondered why it was there. He had to admit that he found her interesting; he would like to know more about her...

He was secretly amused when she said briskly, 'Thank you for my tea. I must go home now.' He wasn't a conceited man, but he was well aware that he was sought after by the younger ladies of his acquaintance—not one of whom would have wished to leave him so promptly.

He said, 'Of course,' so readily that she wondered if she had stayed too long, and made no bones about going then and there.

Fred, on the look out, was there to open the door for them. He beamed his thanks at her appreciation of her tea and stood watching them drive away. Now that, he reflected, was the right kind of young lady for his master to wed—not that he had shown any special interest in her, more was the pity. He went back to the kitchen and phoned his Syl, who listened patiently and finally said, 'Well, we have to leave it to fate, don't we?'

'If fate needs a hand I'm more than willing,' said Fred.

Invited to come indoors with rather a lack of enthusiasm, Professor van Rakesma made himself agreeable to Mrs Pagett, allowed himself to be led away by Mr Pagett to look at some old document in Anglo-Saxon, spent ten minutes with Polly and Richard in the garden, declined

coffee or a drink and then went back home, his goodbyes
affable and, in Mary's case, cool.

'The girl is taking up too much of my time,' he told
Richard. 'What is more, I find her unsettling.'

Mary finished getting the supper which Polly had
started to cook. He was going to his cottage but he hadn't
invited her to go again. There was no reason why he
should. She knew quite well that she wasn't at her best
in his company; her efforts to behave as though she considered him a mere acquaintance were inhibiting. All the
same...perhaps Ilsa would be coming soon, to see the
place for herself and approve the alterations. She wouldn't
approve, of course, if she discovered that Mary had chosen the curtains and china.

'Well,' said Mary reasonably, 'neither would I!' Bingo,
eating his supper, raised his head for a moment and stared
at her; his feline ears had caught the unhappiness in her
voice.

The professor didn't go alone; his new caretaker went
with him. Nathaniel Potts had made a good recovery. He
was a small man but wiry, with a round face and a fringe
of grey hair. His eyes were blue and guileless and Fred,
having met him, had pronounced him just the job. 'Nice
old codger,' he'd observed. 'Just the thing for the cottage,
sir. He'll settle in a treat.'

It was apparent immediately he followed Professor
van Rakesma into the place that he was just right there.
'I can live here?' he wanted to know. 'Why, sir, it's beyond my wildest dreams.'

'Good. We'll go into your duties presently; I suggest
that we go along to the pub and have a sandwich, then we

can come back here and make sure that you have everything you need. I'll be down some time next weekend. Sometimes I come on the spur of the moment, so keep a stock of basic food in the fridge. See that you eat properly and look after yourself. The doctor here is a good man; I know him slightly. Go to him if you are worried. You have my phone number; Fred will always be able to get hold of me if I'm needed.'

The professor drove back to Cheyne Walk that evening. Nathaniel Potts had settled in quickly, a look on his face as though he had just won the pools. 'I can't believe it,' he had said to him. 'I'd just about given up... You won't regret it, sir...'

Mary had little opportunity to brood over her own worries; her father had told her that he still owed the bank money. 'I shall have to repay it from my capital,' he explained, 'which leaves our circumstances still more strained. I shall be unable to give you any money this week, my dear, as what I have must pay the gas bill.'

'Don't worry, Father, I can manage the housekeeping—although there's not much over for paying any bills. How is the book going?'

'Another month or so.' He looked anxious. 'Of course it will need to be typed before I can take it to my publishers. An expense...' He sighed. 'There is talk of a publishing date for Christmas.'

'Oh, good,' said Mary, and managed a smile. Christmas was months away—Polly would need a winter coat before then, and she wanted a new hockey stick for her birthday. Perhaps Mr Bell would suggest that she worked an extra day. She went away to do the ironing, thinking of all the dreadful things she would do to the man who had swindled her father. A waste of time, she told herself, but it would be nice if there was someone she could moan to—Professor van Rakesma, for instance.

There were fewer customers in the bookshop that week; it was high summer now, and people had gone on holiday. It gave her the opportunity to do some much needed sorting out and rearranging while Mr Bell shut himself in his office and browsed happily. It also gave her the opportunity to think about the professor. Her imagination ran riot, picturing him in his fine flat, entertaining friends, driving to their houses in his splendid car—and perhaps Ilsa was there too. She had said that she would be returning...

Professor van Rakesma was certainly driving his splendid car—to and from the hospital or to his consulting-rooms, or speeding up one or other of the motorways, lending his skill for the benefit of some patient. Certainly he had no leisure to entertain his friends or to visit them; it seemed to him that there was a positive epidemic of people with heart conditions requiring his aid, and his leisure was so sparse that when he did get a quiet hour or so all he wanted to do was to sit quietly at his desk and get on with his book.

Fred served him tempting meals, tut-tutting to himself when his employer didn't come home until all hours or left the flat at some unearthly time in the morning. A wife was what he needed, observed Fred to his Syl, but not that nasty woman who never said thank you and looked at him as though he ought not to have been there. 'In my own kitchen too,' said Fred.

By the end of another week things had quietened down a little; the professor had his meals at almost normal times and left the flat at a reasonable hour each morning. Life was back to normal again, allowing him time to think about Mary. It was some time since he had last seen her. He promised himself that on the following Saturday he would go along to Mr Bell's shop and see how she was getting on. They might go to the cottage on Sunday. Perhaps it would be a good idea to take Polly with them...

He didn't have to wait until Saturday, however.

Mary was tidying the kitchen after lunch on Monday when the phone rang and a voice announced that it was Polly's form mistress speaking and would Mary come and collect her sister, who had become ill.

'Have you sent for the doctor?' asked Mary. 'Is she sick or has she had an accident?'

'Very sick, feverish, and she doesn't seem at all herself. I suggest that you fetch her home and get her own doctor.'

Not a very satisfactory answer. Mary ran to give her mother a watered-down version of the lady's report and drove over to the school. Polly was lying down on a couch in the gym, her usually rosy cheeks waxen, her skin hot.

'Probably some sort of flu,' said the form mistress. 'I dare say a few days in bed will set her back on her feet.' She added, 'I'm sure she's looking better.'

Mary thought that she looked awful, but she didn't say so. 'I'll take her home and let you know what the doctor says.'

They helped Polly to the car between them and Mary, usually a cautious driver, was for once not cautious at all.

Getting Polly up to her room was no easy matter; she seemed half-conscious and unsteady on her feet and, once put to bed, lay there shivering despite her fever. Mary took her temperature and went to the phone.

Dr Hooper had just finished his morning rounds and

was sitting down to a late lunch, but he promised to be there within the next fifteen minutes, which gave her time to go and tell her mother.

Mrs Pagett was devoted to her children, but the sight of any of them ill upset her badly. She went with Mary to see Polly and said in her wispy voice, 'Oh, Polly, darling, whatever is the matter?' She turned to Mary. 'She's had measles and chicken pox and mumps.'

'Yes, Mother. Dr Hooper will be here presently, and he will know what to do. Would you be a dear and get a tray of tea? I've interrupted his lunch and he might be glad of it.'

'Yes, yes, of course. You stay here, Mary; I'll let him in when he gets here.'

Doctor Hooper had known them all for a long time. He peered at Polly over his old-fashioned spectacles, took her pulse, looked at her tongue and took her temperature. Then he sat down on the bed.

'A nasty virus infection,' he said. 'There is a lot of it about. It hasn't got a name but it's very unpleasant. Antibiotics, I think, and stay in bed until you've finished the pills you'll be taking. Plenty to drink, and eat when you want to and whatever you fancy. You may be sick, but try and take no notice of that.'

He stood up. 'I'll leave you in Mary's capable hands.' He glanced at Mary's anxious face. 'Come downstairs with me, my dear, and I'll write that prescription and give you a few directions.'

Downstairs he warned, 'Even with the antibiotics Polly will probably get worse before she gets better. You can manage? You may have a few disturbed nights.'

He was right; Polly tossed and turned that night and most of the next day, peevishly refusing to eat or drink, wanting Mary to stay with her. Doctor Hooper came on the following day, said that he was satisfied that she was no worse, told Mary to get as much rest as she could and went away again. A busy GP, he still found time to sit with Mrs Pagett for a few minutes and reassure her that Polly would soon be better.

'You're sure? I can't settle to anything…'

Dr Hooper, who knew her well, said, 'My dear Mrs Pagett, the best thing you can do is go to that little studio of yours and return to your painting. She is in good hands; Mary is a level-headed girl—a born nurse, if you ask me. Can't think why she hasn't married before now.'

Although Polly was a little better on Thursday Mary saw that it would be impossible to go to Mr Bell's. Very reluctantly she phoned him, and was told by the kind old man to stay at home until her sister was fit and well again. 'I shall miss you,' said Mr Bell.

By some quirk of fate Professor van Rakesma, with half an hour to spare that morning, decided that he had time to call at Mr Bell's and collect a book he had wanted. They passed the time of day briefly and he was on the point of leaving when Mr Bell observed, 'I am missing my helper at the moment…'

'Oh, why is that?' The professor had stopped on his way out and turned round.

'Her sister—Polly, I believe her name is—is ill and Mary must stay home and nurse her. A virus infection, I understand. She is quite poorly.'

He was surprised at the look on his companion's face. 'Mary is a most efficient girl; I imagine she is managing very well.'

'Yes, yes, I'm sure she is. Let us hope she will be back soon.'

An hour later, between appointments, the professor left his consulting-rooms and sought out his receptionist, who was elderly and devoted and never at a loss.

'Mrs Rigley—' she had always been and would always be Mrs Rigley, although they were the best of friends '—I need to speak to a doctor somewhere in Hampstead. Probably on the Golders Green side. The name of the patient I want to ask about is a Polly Pagett.' He smiled. 'Am I asking the impossible?'

'Give me a little time,' Mrs Rigley told him calmly. 'It is by no means impossible, but probably a lengthy business.'

It was five o'clock and he was on the point of leaving the hospital when she telephoned him. 'Doctor Hooper, Professor; I have his address and phone number here.'

'Mrs Rigley, you're an angel.' He made a note of them. 'Has it hindered you too much? Don't stay late…'

'No, Professor. You have only one patient here tomorrow morning, at noon. You are to lunch at the hospital before the meeting there.' She added briskly, 'I've booked Mrs Morley for six o'clock tomorrow evening. She can't get here any sooner.'

'Thank you.' He wished her goodbye and rang off and dialed Dr Hooper's number.

Half an hour later he let himself into his flat, and as usual Fred came into the hall to meet him.

'I must go out again Fred; can you hold dinner back for a while?'

'No problem, sir!'

'While I'm gone go through the food in the house and see if there's anything suitable for a young girl who feels pretty rough. I'll take it with me in the morning. I'll need to leave here around half-past seven.'

'I'll see to it, sir.' Fred, dying of curiosity, kept his face expressionless and the professor took pity on him. 'The young sister of Miss Pagett has been taken ill; I've spoken to her doctor, who has no objection to my paying a call on her. I'll take Richard with me.'

He stopped on the way to buy flowers. For Polly, of course.

Mary opened the door in answer to his knock. She was tired, and her hair had escaped from its usual neat French pleat, her nose needed powdering and she longed to put her feet up. She stood and stared at him.

'Oh, I'm so glad...' she said, and caught her tongue between her teeth just in time. 'Polly's ill.' For a moment she thought she might burst into tears. She swallowed them back and added, 'You know?'

'Mr Bell told me. Dr Hooper has no objection to my seeing her if you would like that.'

'Oh, I would—and so would she. Do come in. Do you know Dr Hooper?'

'Er—no, a telephone acquaintance, shall we say? You need a night's sleep, Mary.'

'I'm quite all right. Polly gets restless during the night—'

'You sit with her?'

'Until she settles down again. Would you like to come upstairs? Mother is painting and Father is not back yet.'

'There is no one to relieve you?'

'There's no need. Mother gets upset if any of us is ill, but she sits with Polly...'

She opened Polly's door and he followed her in. Polly

was lying staring at the ceiling but she turned her head as they went in. 'Professor van Rakesma—how did you know that I was ill? Mary, did you tell him?'

He had come to stand by the bed and picked up one of her hands. 'No, Mary didn't tell me. You feel quite wretched, don't you? But a few more days in bed and you'll begin to feel your old self again. Dr Hooper gave me a good report of you.'

He sat himself down on the side of the bed. 'These are to make you feel better,' he said, and laid the flowers on the quilt.

'Thank you, they're lovely. Are you going to stay for a little while?'

He turned to look at Mary. 'Half an hour, if I may? While you do whatever you want to downstairs.'

He wasn't only the man she loved but he was kind and thoughtful too, and someone to lean on, albeit metaphorically. She nipped smartly back to the kitchen, saw to the supper, fed Bingo and went to tell her mother that they had a visitor.

'Bless the man,' said Mrs Pagett. 'Just when he's most needed. Is he staying to supper?'

'No, he has to go very shortly; he's sitting with Polly while I get the supper.'

Mrs Pagett looked conscience-stricken. 'Oh, dear, I could have done that—or sat with Polly; I did mean to…'

Mary bent to kiss her parent. 'Darling, don't worry! There's almost nothing to do. Can you spare a moment to see Professor van Rakesma?'

'Yes, of course; I'll come now. Is your father back yet?'

'No. He should be here at any minute, though.'

They went into the house together—Mary to the kitchen, Mrs Pagett to her younger daughter's bedroom.

Mary heard her come downstairs presently with the professor. They both came into the kitchen and she paused in puréeing the potatoes to ask what he thought of Polly.

'Doubtless a virulent virus—luckily Polly is very fit and healthy. She should begin to feel better within another forty-eight hours. She will be off-colour for a week or two, though.'

He declined her offer of coffee, bade her a friendly goodnight and went out to his car with Mrs Pagett, who then wandered back into the kitchen. 'Such an agreeable man. I wonder how he found out which doctor we have?' She added vaguely, 'Well, I suppose they all know each other.'

Polly had brightened up considerably at his visit, but her sleep that night was fitful. She was too hot, too cold, thirsty, her legs ached...

Mary gave up her bed presently, and sat in a chair near her in her nightie and dressing-gown; she dozed fitfully too. Some time after six o'clock she slept deeply, and was roused by the doorbell. Polly still slept, and the house was quiet, but a glance at the clock told her that it was half-past eight. She flew downstairs and unbolted the door; it would be Mrs Blackett, she thought, forgetting it was Friday...

The professor, with Richard beside him, and bearing a large hamper, stood in the porch. Mary stood gaping at him, still not quite awake, then she said in a wobbly voice, 'I overslept,' and burst into tears.

Professor van Rakesma, never a man to hesitate, bore her gently back into the hall, closed the door behind the three of them, put the hamper on the nearest chair and took her in his arms. He didn't speak until her sobs dwindled into sniffs and watery gasps. 'Another bad night?

This won't do, you know. We'll have you lying in bed beside Polly…'

He mopped her face and thought how beautiful she was—hair in a glorious tangle, a pink nose and puffy eyes, and swathed in a shapeless dressing-gown only fit for the dustbin. The thought struck him with some force that he had fallen in love at last—that, indeed, he had been in love for some time. But first things first.

'Come into the kitchen and put the kettle on and I'll unpack this. Bingo won't object to Richard?'

'No, he's the mildest of cats.' Mary gave a great sniff. 'I'm sorry to be such a fool.'

'Think nothing of it. Are your mother and father still in their room?'

'Yes. I usually take them a cup of tea about eight o'clock.'

'Shall we have a cup first? I'll get breakfast while you dress.'

'Get breakfast? But can you cook?'

'Of course I can cook. A limited menu, mind, but would scrambled eggs do?'

'Oh,' said Mary. 'I'm so glad you're here.'

She was suddenly shy, and put a hand up to her tousled hair. 'Oh, dear, I'm sorry to be so—so—'

He didn't let her finish. 'Shall we have that cup of tea?'

'Yes—yes, of course.'

He put the hamper on the kitchen table and started to unpack it while the kettle boiled: a cold roasted chicken, an egg custard in a pretty little dish, tiny fairy-like cakes, a bottle of champagne, a milk jelly in a delicate shade of pink, a box of brown eggs, and a nicely arranged pile of small crisp biscuits on a patterned plate.

Mary, coming to look, said, 'My goodness, how tempting it all looks. Polly will love everything.'

'Fred did his best. He's a good cook!'

'He made all these? But how kind—and kinder still of you to have thought of it.'

He said quietly, 'I like Polly.'

They drank their tea quickly and Mary carried a tray up to her parents, went to peep at Polly and then to dress. She groaned aloud when she caught sight of herself in the looking-glass. What must he have thought? she wondered.

The professor kept his thoughts to himself and concentrated on getting breakfast. He laid the table, broke the eggs, cut bread and set to work on arranging a tray for Polly. He had finished when Mary came downstairs again, this time very neat and tidy, not a hair out of place, although she hadn't had time to do her face. Looking at her, he decided that she looked even better in her old dressing-gown, especially with her hair all over the place.

Mr and Mrs Pagett came down next, greeting the professor as though it were quite normal to come down to breakfast and find him there. 'I looked in on Polly,' said Mrs Pagett. 'She's still asleep. How delicious these eggs are, Mary.'

'Professor van Rakesma got breakfast, Mother.'

Mrs Pagett took this in her stride. 'Then you are to be congratulated, Professor.' She caught sight of the delicacies set out on the dresser. 'And just look at these—for Polly? How very kind. She *is* getting better?'

His answer was quietly reassuring. They had reached the toast and marmalade when Polly's voice, rather querulous, reached them.

'May I go up and see her?' asked the professor. 'Perhaps another face…'

He sat down on the bed and smiled at Polly's rather white face. She put out a sweaty hand and took his. 'I did hope you'd come,' she told him. 'And you did. How did you know?'

'I have spies everywhere.' He took her pulse and noted that it was slower; she looked less feverish too. 'You're on the turn,' he observed. 'Dr Hooper is going to be pleased with you. Now, to oblige both your doctors, you must start to eat a little. I brought some food with me— Fred, my manservant, got up early and filled a hamper, so don't hurt his feelings by not eating everything in it.'

'I'll try, I promise you, and do please thank him. Does he look after you? Is that the man Ilsa wanted to sack? She said he wasn't suitable…'

'I find him entirely suitable, and I hope he will stay with me until we are both very old men. He's going to be married at Christmas to a rather nice girl called Syl.'

'Will she work for you too?'

'Oh, yes; we shall need extra help.'

'Are you going to get married?' Polly had heaved herself up against her pillows and he leaned forward and shook them up.

'Yes.'

'Not to Ilsa?'

'No.' He smiled slowly as she stared up at him.

'Who to?' She smiled too, a wide grin of expectancy. 'Tell me.'

He told her and she leaned forward and flung her arms round his neck. 'It's a secret between us,' he pointed out.

'Of course. I'll not breathe a word. You're sure?' She glanced at his face. 'Yes, you are! That was a silly question. Do you suppose you would mind if I called you Roel?'

'I should be delighted; I am quite weary of being addressed as Professor van Rakesma; it makes me feel excessively middle-aged.' He stood up. 'I must go. I'll come and see you again, but not tomorrow—the day after. I shall expect to see you plump and rosy-cheeked and at least sitting in a chair.'

He went presently, taking Mr Pagett, who wanted to go to the British Museum Library, with him, and Mrs Pagett, after helping Mary clear away the breakfast and putting everything away in the wrong places, drifted down to the shed.

Mary whisked upstairs, washed Polly's face and hands, brushed her hair and straightened her bed. 'Breakfast,' she said. 'You should see what Professor van Rakesma has brought for you. There are some dear little savoury biscuits that his man Fred made specially for you and a box of brown eggs. I'm going to scramble one for you with some of those biscuits and you're going to eat the lot.'

Rather to her surprise Polly said quite cheerfully that she would.

Dr Hooper, when he came, pronounced her better. 'Another day in bed and then she may get up for a while. I don't need to come for a day or two, but if you are worried you know where I am.'

So when Professor van Rakesma came again two days later, just as Mary was putting the kettle on for tea, he found Polly sitting at the kitchen table, gobbling a milk jelly and the last of the little cakes. This time he had brought sponge fingers, a pot of salmon pâté and some more of the little savoury biscuits, and it seemed quite natural that he should sit down too and have his tea with her and Mary. Mrs Pagett was in her shed and Mary took her tea down to her.

'He's here again? Oh, good. I'll be up presently; I must just paint in these cherubs' faces.'

She joined them, ate several sponge fingers and expressed her relief that Polly had recovered.

'Ah, yes, Mrs Pagett. I was wondering if you would allow Polly to spend a few days at a cottage I have in Gloucestershire? There is a caretaker there and I'm sure you'd agree to Mary's going with her. It would be just the thing to set her on her feet again. It's very quiet but I'm sure they would find enough to do together.'

'You wouldn't be there?'

'No. I would, of course, drive them both down and bring them back.'

Polly's eyes were shining. 'Oh, may I, Mother, please…?'

Mary said nothing at all, but her heart galloped along at a great pace at the mere thought of it. Her mother might say no; she schooled her features into serenity.

'That would be good for Polly, wouldn't it? I thank you, Professor, most sincerely. I'm sure it will do her good, and we can manage for a few days without Mary; I'm quite sure she needs a rest too. Their father won't object, I know. When do you want them to go?'

'Saturday afternoon? And if you can manage for a week I could bring them back on the following Saturday morning.'

'Of course. Mary will fill the freezer with meals so that all I have to do is warm them up, won't you, dear? And Mrs Blackett will clean the house as usual.'

'That's settled, then.' He glanced at Mary. 'May Richard stay with you? He loves the cottage and Nathaniel will look after him.'

He went presently and Mary wandered upstairs in a delightful dream, to peer in cupboards and drawers and decide what to take with them.

She rang Mr Bell that evening; Polly was well enough to leave alone now, and she needed the money. He was delighted to have her back, even when she explained that she would be away again the following week. She heaved a sigh of relief and sat down to think out suitable meals for her mother while she was away.

She enjoyed being back at Mr Bell's; she was still tired from worry and lack of sleep but she had a week of doing nothing much to look forward to. She put everything ready before she left home on Saturday morning and, since Mr Bell allowed her to go home at three o'clock and the professor had said that he would come for her then, she allowed herself to feel the excitement which had been bubbling up inside her. The face she showed him as she got into the car was serene enough, however.

Polly, still pale, but excited, was waiting for them and, waved on their way by their parents, they got into the car with an equally excited Richard and a calm professor who drove away.

There was no need for Mary to talk on the journey; Polly hardly paused for breath, and when they reached the cottage and got out she stood staring at it. 'I don't believe it,' she cried. 'It's just like a dream, Roel; how can you bear to leave it?'

Chapter 9

The cottage looked at its best—Nathaniel had seen to it. The furniture glowed, there were flowers in all the rooms and the evening sun cast a soft light over everything; Mary paused in the hall and shook his hand and looked around her. 'It's quite perfect,' she said, and he beamed at her.

'I'm happy that you think so, miss.' He looked at the professor then, and was rewarded with an approving nod. 'The bedrooms are ready, sir, and there's supper laid in the dining-room.'

'Good, you've done excellently, Nathaniel. We'll bring in the cases and have supper at once for I must get back to town.' The professor looked at Mary. 'Would you go upstairs through that small door in the dining-room? Your rooms are at the front. We'll bring up your bags.'

Their rooms were charming, with sloping ceilings and

sprigged wallpaper and satinwood beds and dressing-tables. There was a bathroom between them and Polly ran from one to the other, for once speechless with delight.

The men came up with their luggage and the professor said, 'Nathaniel will take you round the place later; I'm afraid I haven't the time; I'll have to go when we've had supper.'

Nathaniel, it seemed, could cook; there was a steak and kidney pie with a light-as-air crust, new potatoes and puréed spinach and after that he served up strawberries and clotted cream with macaroon biscuits. Since the professor was undoubtedly anxious to be off they didn't linger over the meal.

'Use the phone whenever you want to,' he told them. 'If you run short of money Nathaniel will let you have whatever you need. I'll be down next Saturday morning. Enjoy yourselves, and please take care of Richard for me.'

They went out to the car with him and he bent to kiss Polly's cheek. 'I shall expect to see you looking your usual self,' he told her. He didn't say anything to Mary but kissed her—a gentle, unhurried kiss which left her pink and breathless.

It was easy to slip into the peace of their days. They slept soundly, despite Mary's certainty that she would lie awake every night and think about Professor van Rakesma. His kiss had meant something—something he hadn't been able to put into words in front of Polly and Nathaniel. However, she told herself that she might be thinking it meant more than he had intended.

Strangely, the thought didn't worry her; she slept soundly every night and got up to eat a splendid breakfast and walk to the village with Polly and a happy little dog to do the shopping for Nathaniel. Her other offers of help he gently refused.

'It's a real pleasure to have you young ladies here, miss, and I've time enough to see to everything. The professor has been down once or twice to see about the alterations you suggested. Very satisfactory they are too; the kitchen's a fair treat to work in—and if you would care to see my bed-sitting-room?'

It had been furnished exactly as she had suggested too, and was as cosy as she had envisaged. 'You're happy here.' It was a statement not a question.

'Indeed I am, miss. I don't suppose the professor told you about me? I was down and out, you see; they found me in the park and brought me to St Justin's and he examined me. A heart attack, it was. He saved my life and then bless me if he doesn't offer me this job.' His nice, elderly face was very earnest. 'Cut my right hand off for him, I would.'

'I know,' said Mary. 'I know exactly how you feel.' They smiled at each other before she said briskly, 'Shall we go to the village and get those chops for you? He's a splendid butcher, isn't he?'

Polly was in her element; she had made friends in the village almost at once, besides which there was Richard to take for walks and the lovely garden in which to sit and do nothing. Every now and then she would say, 'I wonder what Roel's doing now?' Mary never answered, although she wondered too.

He was making careful plans which involved a good deal of telephoning on Mrs Rigley's part and several sessions with his senior registrar, as well as a number of phone calls to his home in Holland. It also meant a visit to Mr and Mrs Pagett...

The week was too quickly over; one day had slipped into the next and each one had been more delightful than the last. All the same, Mary longed for the weekend and Professor van Rakesma's arrival. 'And for heaven's sake call him Roel,' begged Polly, her own exuberant self once more. 'I do.'

He came on Saturday morning just as Nathaniel was getting the coffee. It was a lovely morning and he came straight through the house and out into the garden to find them sitting on the wooden bench at the far end.

Richard saw him first and rushed round in circles, barking his pleasure, while Polly raced across the lawn to fling herself at him.

'I'm well again—see? I'm getting fat; Nathaniel's such a marvellous cook. Mary's getting fat too!'

He dropped a kiss on her cheek and stared across her head at Mary, on her feet now and coming towards them. 'Not fat,' he said, 'just nicely curved in all the right places.'

The remark made her blush. All the same, she said, 'Hello, you're just in time for coffee. Would you like it out here? I'll go and tell Nathaniel...'

'I'll go,' said Polly, leaving Mary staring at him. After a moment she said, 'We've had a lovely week; Polly's quite well again and I feel fit enough to spring-clean the house and dust every one of Mr Bell's books.'

'Good. I've been talking to your parents; another week off won't hurt, Polly—but not here. I'm going over to Holland on Monday—will you both come with me?'

When she opened her mouth to speak he said, 'No,

don't say anything until I've finished. Pleane is longing to see you both again and my mother will be delighted to meet you.'

He had spoken in a matter-of-fact way and she did her best to answer him in the same vein. 'It sounds very tempting, and how kind of you to think of it, but we haven't got passports…'

'Visitors'—obtainable at any post office.'

'Yes, well—but I've been away from home for a week; I really ought to stay—and—and…'

'Do the washing and the dusting and cook the meals? I know. Will you leave that side of it to me? Maisie—remember her?—would love to spend a week with your parents; she likes a change from nursing now and then.'

'But she is NHS. They'd never allow her to come.'

'NHS? I don't remember saying that she worked for the NHS. She works for me and several other consultants who may need a private nurse from time to time.'

She thought about that. 'Were you paying her, then? When she came to Great Aunt Thirza's house? Because if you were I owe you money for her fees.'

'By all means pay me back, but later. We're discussing a brief trip to Holland at the moment. Will you come?' And as she hesitated and Polly came dancing out he said, 'Polly, would you like to come to Holland with me? Just to round off your convalescence?'

'Me? And Mary? Roel, you darling, of course I would. When are we going?'

'You can't disappoint Polly,' said the professor unfairly.

'Well, if you think she needs a little more time before she goes back to school… You're sure your mother won't mind? I mean, she doesn't know anything about us.'

'I imagine Pleane has told her a very great deal.'

'Where do you live?' she asked, aware that she stood no chance against the two of them, and not much caring.

'In the north—Friesland. A small village near Leeuwarden.' He didn't offer more than that and she didn't like to ask.

'Mary, say you'll come,' said Polly. 'You must, just think—just lovely to see another country; Mary, you must, you must!'

The Professor added quietly, 'Yes, Mary, you must.'

She nodded slowly. 'Very well, it would be most— most interesting. Just for a few days.'

'A week.'

'Will you be there?' She couldn't resist asking that, not seeing the gleam in his eyes.

'Yes, most of the time. I shall have to go to Leeuwarden, and down to Amsterdam and The Hague, but I shall have some time to show you something of Friesland.' He added, 'Besides, Pleane will be there.'

They drank their coffee then, and presently Polly took him away to look for water voles living by the little stream which bordered the end of the garden, and Richard went with them, leaving Mary alone with her thoughts.

She was mad to agree to go, she knew that; she would probably meet Ilsa, who would demonstrate the fact of her impending marriage to him in no uncertain way. She would put up with that just for the delight of being with him for a little longer. I'll come back home, she reflected, and go back to Mr Bell and make myself indispensable to him. And in a few months, when Father's book is published and everything's all right again, I'll take the librarian's exams and make a career for myself.

Even as she thought about it she knew that it was

highly unlikely; there would never be enough money to make it possible. She choked back self-pity and went to find Nathaniel. They had become firm friends during the past week and she wanted to be sure that he would look after himself properly when there was no one at the cottage.

They drove back to Hampstead after lunch. Nathaniel had given her a bunch of flowers from the garden and wrung her hand. 'I hope I'll see you again, miss, that I do—and the young lady too. It's been a pleasure looking after you.'

She thanked him, told him to take care of himself, and got into the car beside the professor, and, with Polly chattering away from the back of the car and Richard expressing his pleasure at being with his master again, they drove back through the fading summer countryside.

'It must be beautiful here in the autumn,' said Mary, making conversation.

'Yes, indeed.' He wickedly allowed her to wring the subject of the autumn—indeed, of all the seasons—dry.

'Can you be ready by Monday, early afternoon?'

'I expect so, if I start as soon as we get home.' She sounded a bit tart. 'It isn't very long. And I must phone Mr Bell…'

'Ah—well, I was there during the week and mentioned that you might be going with me; he thought it a splendid idea.'

'Did he? Did he really?' She hoped that she wouldn't get the sack after so much time away from the shop. It was as well for her peace of mind that she didn't know that Mr Bell had already engaged a suitable applicant in her place. 'For,' Professor van Rakesma had told him, 'I intend to marry Mary.'

Mr Bell, a romantic at heart, had been delighted.

Her mother and father were delighted too to see her back, but enthusiastic about their trip to Holland. 'Maisie came to see us today,' said her mother. 'Such a very nice person; she will do the housekeeping while you're away, dear, so we shall be quite comfortable.' She turned to Roel. 'You'll stay for tea, Roel?'

He shook his head. 'There are some patients I must see this evening. I'll be here on Monday afternoon—we'll catch the night ferry from Harwich.'

Presently he took his leave and Mary, who hadn't forgotten his kiss, received his casual nod with a cool one of her own. He hadn't meant it, she thought bitterly. Then, since she was a fair-minded girl, she thought, why should he? He was going to marry Ilsa. He had probably been amusing himself. She didn't quite believe that, though.

The weekend was a frenzy of activity; the washing machine laboured non-stop, Mary ironed and pressed and packed once again, and put the house to rights after Mrs Blackett's half-hearted onslaughts with the furniture polish. She made neat lists for Maisie's guidance too, and on Monday morning hurried to the shops with the last of the housekeeping money to buy groceries.

She had forgotten that she would need money in Holland so it was an agreeable surprise when her father called her into his study. 'You'll need pocket money,' he told her. 'My publishers have advanced me something on royalties; take this, my dear, and don't worry. I have sufficient to keep us going nicely for some time.'

'Father, how splendid. I'm so glad. You won't need to give Maisie much; I've stocked up with quite a lot of food. You're sure that you and Mother will be all right?'

'Quite sure, my dear. You've earned this holiday; enjoy yourself.'

The professor arrived punctually, this time without Richard, and this time Mary said firmly that she would sit in the back. He made no demur, and as they drove to Harwich he and Polly chatted almost without pause. Mary, replying to the odd remark thrown at her from over a shoulder, told herself that she didn't mind.

She wasn't sophisticated enough to ignore the delights of the ferry. She and Polly shared a cabin which they considered the acme of comfort, and then joined the professor at dinner. Neither of them had any fears about seasickness; they enjoyed every morsel put before them, drank the glass of wine he chose for them and went to their beds, to sleep soundly until the stewardess wakened them early the next morning with tea and toast.

They were among the first away, and the Rolls, once on the motorway, travelled fast. They were approaching Delft when he suggested coffee and parked the car in the great square in the centre of the lovely little town, and took them to a small café overlooking it. As well as coffee, he ordered *krentenbollen*, a rich version of the currant bun, and they sat for a while, eating them and watching the cars going to and fro, while he told them of the Nieuwe Kerk, towering over one end of the market square.

They drove on presently, going north, bypassing Leiden and then Amsterdam, making for the *Afsluitdijk* motorway which would bring them to Friesland.

The countryside was different here, with wide open fields separated from each other by narrow, water-filled ditches; the farms, with their great barns built on to them at the back, looked prosperous, and there were cows everywhere. Every now and then there was a glimpse of water too.

'The lakes,' said the professor. 'We live beside one.'

He turned away from the main road presently, along a narrow brick road, which led away into the distance to a cluster of trees. When they were reached they were found to surround a village built beside a large stretch of water.

'Is this your home?' asked Polly.

'Yes, just a little further.' He drove through the village street, lined with small houses with shining windows and spotless white curtains, and, when the road rounded a bend, drove between stone pillars, along a short drive and stopped before a gabled house. Its flat front was pierced by several rows of large windows, the front door was massive and solid, and there was a wrought-iron balcony above it.

Mary's heart sank; it was all so grand. They hadn't got the right clothes for a start; his mother wouldn't approve of them...

The front door was flung open and Pleane came running out to fling her arms around her brother's neck. 'Roel, you're here at last. Polly, come on—come with me. Mary, it's lovely to see you.'

She went ahead with Polly, and Roel turned to Mary. 'This is my home, Mary,' he told her. 'Welcome to it.'

After that everything was all right. True, his mother at first glance looked rather formidable, for she was tall and stout and her blue eyes had the same direct look as her son's, but her welcome was warm; they were led away to tidy themselves, up a grand curving staircase, along a wide landing and into two rooms overlooking the grounds at the back of the house.

Left alone, Polly came dancing into Mary's room.

'Isn't this just too gorgeous for words? He never said, did he? Perhaps he's so used to it that he doesn't notice how grand it is. He's going to be here all day tomorrow as well as today; he said he'd show us everything.'

Mary, making sure that her hair was securely pinned, observed, 'It's certainly very beautiful; he must miss it.'

'Yes, but when he marries he'll come here more often; he said so.' She went to peer at herself in the triple mirror. 'His mother doesn't live here, you know. There's a house in Leeuwarden.'

'How do you know all this?'

'I asked, of course. We're friends, Roel and me.'

'I,' said Mary. 'We'd better go down.'

The house might have been grand but the atmosphere was homely. In the vast drawing-room, where they had drinks before lunch, there was knitting on a chair, books and magazines scattered on a side-table, a tabby cat perched on the window-seat and two dogs lolling by the open French window.

They were big shaggy beasts, with little yellow eyes and a great many teeth. 'Bouviers,' said the professor. 'William and Mary; they look fierce but they're your friends for life once you belong.'

Mary put out a balled fist, and had it sniffed and then gently licked. 'They're splendid creatures. I don't suppose Richard has ever seen them?'

'No, I'm not sure if they would like each other.'

Any doubts Mary had had about their welcome were dispelled by the time lunch was over. His mother might have looked severe but her smile was gentle and kind and she laughed a lot. 'Come and sit by me and tell me about yourself,' she invited Mary as they drank their coffee.

'Pleane is going to show Polly the garden and Roel has some business to attend to.'

A pleasant hour passed while Mevrouw van Rakesma chatted and asked questions in the nicest possible manner, and since there was no sense in not being honest Mary answered truthfully.

'What do you intend to do with your future, my dear?' asked her hostess kindly.

Mary told her. 'If I can pass the exams I can make quite a career out of it. Not necessarily in a library—museums and large country houses sometimes have good jobs going.'

'You don't wish to marry?'

'I'd like to marry, but I'm not going to,' Mary said calmly.

They had a splendid day after that—touring the house, listening to its history, hearing about the village and the people who lived in it.

The next morning they walked there with the professor, who seemed to know everyone who lived there by name. They went into the little whitewashed church and looked at the names of long-dead van Rakesmas, carved into its stone floor, and they walked by the lake, watching the yachts, of which there were any number.

'People come for the weekend and their holidays—it's possible to sail from one lake to another.'

'Have you got a yacht?' Polly wanted to know.

'Yes. Perhaps I'll have the time to take you out on it.'

'But not tomorrow?'

'Tomorrow I have to work, and the next day, but I'll only be away for two days.'

He had gone by the time they got down for breakfast the next day and that morning Ilsa came.

Polly and Pleane had taken the dogs for a walk down by the lake and Mary was sitting with Mevrouw van Rakesma when Ton, who looked after the house with his wife, opened the door to announce that Mevrouw van Hoeven had called.

He was pushed aside by Ilsa, and Mevrouw van Rakesma frowned. Her greeting was pleasant enough, though. 'This is unexpected, Ilsa; I thought you were in The Hague.'

'I met the director of the Leeuwarden Children's Hospital yesterday; he told me that Roel was in Holland.' She turned to Mary. 'What are you doing here?'

Mary said, 'Hello, Ilsa. We're paying a visit. We came over with Roel.'

Ilsa's eyes narrowed. 'Really?' She turned back to Mevrouw van Rakesma. 'I wanted to see Roel; he's here of course?'

'He's away—will be for a few days. Do sit down; Ton will bring coffee.'

'Where is he? I've got the car...'

'He didn't say; I know he's visiting several hospitals and will be away for several days. Would you like to leave a message, Ilsa? He'll be sorry he's missed you.'

Ilsa had recovered her charm. 'No—no message. I'm quite sure he'll ring me as soon as he is free. After all, it's to see me that he has come.' She glanced at Mary as she spoke. 'We have a number of decisions to make.'

Her hostess said nothing to that and Ilsa went on, 'We saw so little of each other when Pleane and I were staying with him. I believe I must go back with him, so that we can get everything settled.'

'That would perhaps be best. Ah, here is the coffee.'

Ilsa was wearing gloves with her elegant outfit, so unsuitable for her surroundings. She slipped them off, but neither of her companions saw the ring on her engagement finger. She put the glove back on again, drank her coffee, talking amusingly while she did so, and then declared that she must go. 'I'm lunching in Dokkum,' she explained. 'Such a dull little town, I always think.'

She made her graceful goodbyes to Mevrouw van Rakesma and turned to Mary. 'Do walk to the car with me and tell me what you think of Friesland—so different from Hampstead, is it not? And this is such a pleasant house.' She was leading the way out of the lofty wide hall. 'I have always loved it; it will be delightful to live here.'

They reached the car but she made no attempt to get into it. 'I must say I admire you for trying, Mary. Did you really think that you stood a chance against me? Roel and I have had an understanding for years, and we shall marry shortly.'

'There was no reason why he should tell me, Ilsa,' Mary said quietly.

'Oh, yes, there was. You may think you're concealing your feelings very well, my dear, but he saw through you weeks ago. He's too kind to say anything to you, but surely you have the wit to see that he brought you here so that you would understand once and for all that he is merely a friend, helping someone who needs a job and money; he's always helping people… You don't have to believe me, but I'm going to see him now, for I know where he is.'

'I don't believe you,' said Mary in a proud little voice. When Ilsa took off her glove once more and held out her hand, and she saw the diamond sparkling there, though, she knew.

'We shall announce our engagement and marry very

shortly.' She smiled at Mary. 'But of course you won't be at the wedding.'

She got into the car, waved gaily and drove away. Mary watched her go; she had thought during the last few days that Roel was growing fond of her, and she couldn't forget his kiss but, despite disliking Ilsa, she could see that she might be speaking the truth. She had spoken with such certainty. It all made sense too. Roel had never mentioned his future plans, but then why should he since he knew that she wasn't included in them? His kindness had been just that and nothing more.

She was walking slowly back to the house when Pleane and Polly joined her. 'Did we see Ilsa driving through the village? Did she come here?' Pleane wanted to know. 'She hasn't been near us for ages, not since we came back from London.'

'She called to see your mother; she's on her way to have lunch in Dokkum.'

'I bet she was surprised to see you,' said Polly.

'Well, yes, I think she was.'

'Was she friendly? What did she talk about?'

'Oh, nothing much. Did you have a good walk?'

She's upset, thought Polly, and began a long description of where they had been, and when they joined Mevrouw van Rakesma she was careful not to mention Ilsa, although Pleane said something softly in Dutch to her mother.

A good cry, that's what I want, thought Mary, joining in the talk, smiling and nodding and not taking in a word. If only they hadn't come; if only they had stayed at home and got on with a life which had nothing to do with Roel. There was no help for it, though; they would have to stay until he drove them home again and she could concentrate on forgetting him. Polly must forget him too, and she would be hurt, for the pair of them had become firm friends.

He was coming home in the evening—in time for dinner, he had said; Mary got into her one festive dress and took a good look at herself in the pier glass. It was a sober garment, meant to last several years—dateless and simple and mousy brown. Not a colour she would have chosen from choice, but it had been cheap in the sales and was the kind of dress which would pass muster almost anywhere. If she hadn't been so pretty it would have been a disaster; as it was it did nothing for her. Not that it matters, she told herself.

They sat in the drawing-room waiting for him; the dinner hour passed, and his mother had just wondered out loud what had happened to him when Ton came to tell her that the professor had phoned to say that he would be unable to return home until the next day and expressed his regrets.

'An unexpected meeting,' said Mevrouw van Rakesma, translating for Mary and Polly's benefit. 'We will dine at once, Ton,' she said, and then in English, 'One can never be sure of anything with a doctor in the family, can one?'

They played Monopoly and Trivial Pursuit after dinner until bedtime, and Mary was thankful when her hostess declared that she was going to bed.

'Let William and Mary into the garden before you come up,' she told Pleane. 'Mary, you look tired…'

So Mary went to her room too, undressed slowly and lay in the bath for a long time, making unlikely plans for her future which involved a great deal of hard work ending in success and a splendid career. She didn't believe any of it but it prevented her from crying. Only when she was in bed she gave up her ideas of being a career girl and thought about Roel, and cried into her pillow very quietly, so that Polly wouldn't hear.

Roel was there when they went down to breakfast, out in the garden with the dogs, and she was glad that there was time only to wish him good morning before his mother and Pleane joined them.

'A successful trip?' asked his mother, pouring the coffee.

'Yes. I must come over again in a couple of months—there's a seminar—and I may have to go to Brussels later on.'

'But you'll be at Cheyne Walk for the rest of the time?'

'Yes, although I intend to take a few weeks' holiday fairly soon.'

He caught Polly's eye and smiled a little. 'What have you been doing with yourselves?'

'Being lazy,' said Polly.

Pleane added, 'Ilsa came yesterday.'

'Yes.' He looked at Mary, who had her eyes on her plate. 'I know.'

So Ilsa had been truthful after all—that was why he hadn't come home. Mary crumbled toast and composed her face to a state of cheerfulness; to anyone not knowing her well it looked genuine, but Polly and Roel, knowing her well each in their own way, knew better.

'I'll take the dogs for a walk,' said Roel as they finished breakfast. 'Mary, a walk would do you good; come with me.'

It was hard to think up an excuse in front of everyone else there and she hesitated too long. 'You won't need a jacket—' he glanced at her feet in their neat shoes '—and you're wearing sensible shoes. Come along.'

He swept her out of the house and down the drive, into the lane, and turned away from the village towards the lake.

After a few minutes he asked, 'What's the matter, Mary?'

'Nothing—nothing at all. It's lovely here; you have no idea how much we're enjoying ourselves, and your mother is so kind.'

'Don't waste time waffling. I asked you what was the matter.'

'If you don't mind I don't want to talk about it.'

'I do mind. What did Ilsa say to upset you?'

'Nothing—nothing at all…'

'Very well, and now tell me what she said.'

'Don't you bully me,' said Mary crossly. 'You've been very kind to us, and I'm grateful, but I wish we'd never come. You've helped us enough.' Her voice rose to a wail. 'I want to go home.'

'If you won't tell me I'll have to guess. Ilsa told you that she was going to marry, probably gave you some proof of it, perhaps told you that she was going to meet me. Am I right?'

Mary nodded, not looking at him.

'She may even have hinted delicately that I was aware of your feelings towards me and was concerned about them.'

'She told you…?'

'I haven't seen her, but I've known her for some years. You're a goose. My dearest girl. Don't you know when a man's in love with you?'

She said sharply. 'How could I possibly? I'm a thorn in your—'

He stopped walking and swung her round to face him.

'Did I say that? I must have been mad. But I'll say this, and you had better believe me. I love you, Mary; I want you for my wife. I think I have been in love with you for weeks.'

'Oh, have you? Have you really? But you're going to marry Ilsa. She said so; she said you were going to be married quite soon and she showed me her engagement ring.'

'Exactly what did she say? Can you remember?'

'Oh, yes. She said that you and she are going to be married shortly; she said she knew where you were. She said... The rest doesn't matter.'

'She was quite right in a way. She is going to be married shortly, but not to me. The ring she showed you wasn't mine, my darling; she's to marry a middle-aged tycoon with a great deal of money who lives in Florida.' He tightened his arms around her. 'So that takes care of Ilsa.'

'Yes, well,' said Mary, wriggling in his arms.

He held her fast. 'Shall we discuss us? Our future— our glorious future together. But you haven't told me that you will marry me yet, my darling.'

'Oh, I will, I will. Isn't it funny that we didn't like each other very much to start with? Well, I thought you looked nice...'

'And I thought you were the most beautiful girl in the world.'

'Really?'

'Really. Now stand still; I'm going to kiss you.'

Mary, a sensible girl, knew when to do what she was told!

* * * * *

"Gracie, will you look at me?"

Stifling a sigh, she turned her head to face him. Those melty brown eyes were full of self-recrimination and regret.

"I'm sorry," he said. "I never should have touched you. I'm too old for you, and I'm not any kind of relationship material, anyway. I don't know what got into me, but I swear to you it's never going to happen again."

Hmm. How to respond?

Too bad there wasn't a large blunt object nearby. The guy deserved a hard bop on the head. What was wrong with him? No wonder it hadn't worked out with Marjorie. The man didn't have a clue.

But never mind. Gracie held it together as he apologized some more. She watched that beautiful mouth move and pondered the mystery of how such a great guy could have his head so far up his own ass.

Maybe if she yanked him close and kissed him, he'd get over himself and admit that last night had been amazing, the two of them had off-the-charts chemistry and he didn't want to walk away from all that goodness, after all.

Yeah, kissing him might shut him up and get him back on track for more hot sexy times. It had worked more than once already.

But come on. She couldn't go jumping on him and smashing her mouth on his every time he started beating himself up for having a good time with her.

No. A girl had to have a little pride.

He thought last night was a mistake?

Fair enough. She'd actually let herself believe for a minute or two there that they had something good going on, that her long dry spell manwise might be over.

But never mind about that. Let him have it his way. She would agree with him.

And then she would show him exactly what he was missing. And then, when he couldn't take it anymore and begged her for another chance, she would say that they couldn't, that he was too old for her and it wouldn't be right.

Don't miss
Their Secret Summer Family *by Christine Rimmer,*
available May 2020 wherever
Harlequin Special Edition books and ebooks are sold.

Harlequin.com

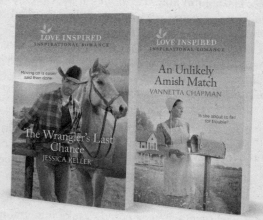

Ruthie Eicher awoke with a start. She blinked in the
darkness and touched the opposite side of the double
bed, where her husband had slept. Two months since the
tragic accident and she was not yet used to his absence.

Finding the far side of the bed empty and the sheets
cold, she dropped her feet to the floor and hurried into
the children's room. Even without lighting the oil lamp,
she knew from the steady draw of their breaths that nine-
year-old Simon and six-year-old Andrew were sound
asleep.

Movement near the outbuildings caught her eye. She
held her breath and stared for a long moment.

Narrowing her gaze, she leaned forward, and her heart
raced as a flame licked the air.

She shook Simon. "The woodpile. On fire. I need
help."

He rubbed his eyes.

"Hurry, Simon."

Leaving him to crawl from bed, she raced downstairs, almost tripping, her heart pounding as she knew all too well how quickly the fire could spread. She ran through the kitchen, grabbed the back doorknob and groaned as her fingers struggled with the lock.

"No!" she moaned, and coaxed her fumbling hands to work. The lock disengaged. She threw open the door and ran across the porch and down the steps.

A noise sounded behind her. She glanced over her shoulder, expecting Simon. Instead she saw a large, darkly dressed figure. Something struck the side of her head. She gasped with pain, dropped the bucket and stumbled toward the house.

He grabbed her shoulder and threw her to the ground. She cried out, struggled to her knees and started to crawl away. He kicked her side. She groaned and tried to stand. He tangled his fingers through her hair and pulled her to her feet.

The man's lips touched her ear. "Didn't you read my notes? You don't belong here." His rancid breath soured the air. "Leave before something happens to you and your children."

Don't miss
Dangerous Amish Inheritance *by Debby Giusti,*
available April 2020 wherever
Love Inspired Suspense books and ebooks are sold.

LoveInspired.com

LISEXP0420